I0647527

ALTERED STATES

ALTERED STATES

DRACONIC DESIRES

Edited by
TJ MINDE

Altered States: Draconic Desires
Production copyright FurPlanet Productions © 2025

Songs of Dragons copyright © Ianus J. Wolf 2025
Pure Dragon Puerh copyright © Frances Pauli 2025
Wealth of the Hold copyright © Mog Moogle 2025
The Magic of the Hoard copyright © Dark End 2025
The Dragon's Renaissance copyright © Inkblitz 2025
A Penny for your Memories copyright © Kyell Gold 2025
Paladin's Fall copyright © Ajax B. Coriander 2025
Leaving it Behind copyright © Arian Mabe 2025
Mates of Dreams copyright © Jaden Drackus 2025
Night at the Eastender copyright © TJ Minde 2025
One Day Shy of Forever copyright © Snepitome 2025
A Matching Reflection copyright © J.F.R. Coates 2025

Cover Artwork and illustrations © Kuma 2025
http://www.furaffinity.net/user/kuma

Published by FurPlanet Productions
Dallas, Texas
www.FurPlanet.com

Print ISBN 978-1-61450-657-7
Electronic ISBN 978-1-61450-663-8
First Edition Trade Paperback

All characters are © by their creators and are used with permission. All rights
reserved. No portion of this work may be reproduced in any form, in any
medium, without the expressed permission of the author.

For all the editors who helped me grow

Rest in peace, Kiri

CONTENTS

SONGS OF DRAGONS

IANUS J. WOLF

Pacing back and forth in her chamber, Princess Maeveen knew all the storybooks and things she'd seen said that she should be happy. Her wedding day was supposed to be a magical time that would finally make her a woman after so long a wait. But it was not a storybook occasion.

She had not been set to meet dashing couriers and eventually fall in love with one of them. Instead, she had been held at home as the last of four daughters to King Targus, guarded in comfort to be used as a marital coin when the need arose. Granted everything except any freedom to choose a destiny.

Princess Maeveen had not been wooed, rescued, and whisked away by a gallant, handsome knight who had secretly visited her tower and fallen in love with her. She'd instead, at the age of twenty, been gifted to Prince Cathal of Argoth for the purpose of uniting their two kingdoms in alliance for better trade. Cathal was not terrible, but a bit of a clumsy oaf that was barely into his manhood and could not seem to speak to her in any complete sentences. Hardly a dashing knight or roguish courtier from her stories.

Grena came into the room to check on her and make a few

final adjustments to her gown. Her lady-in-waiting who had once qualified more as her nanny was now a kindly middle-aged woman with streaks of grey in her dark hair. Grena was the only person who did not think Maeveen was too proper to hear a bit of gossip now and then when they were in a room together. And she'd been the only person Maeveen could talk to openly about questions she'd had as she became a woman. As she tightened Maeveen's corset, Grena sighed.

"Ah, the blessed day. You should be of good cheer, m'lady! You finally go out into the world today as a future duchess."

"Trading one room where I am stuck for another room where I am stuck, Grena," Maeveen said. "Hardly much of an improvement."

"Well, it doesn't have to be all bad, does it?" Grena said. She turned Maeveen to check her hair and the rest of her gown, giving her a wicked little grin. "At least you finally have a wedding night to look forward to!"

"Grena…" Maeveen said in mock reproach with her own smile. "I would look forward, but I somehow doubt that Cathal will provide much beyond an attempt to get started on the next heir."

"Oh, it may not be like the storybooks. Or those, er, other little writings I've snuck to you when I could." Grena leaned in conspiratorially. "And you can always use the fact that he's a little younger and all sheepish to just bowl him over and make him do what works for you. Regardless, there's nothing for it. We all have our lot in life, and nothing changes that. May as well make the best of where you wind up."

"I suppose that is the truth of it," Princess Maeveen sighed, thinking once again about those storybooks and wishing there was some gallant knight to ride in and steal her away. "We had best be on with this then."

Grena followed her down the steps of the tower, carrying the back of her veil. Through hallways and passages apart from where common eyes might see, they emerged onto the brightly bedecked courtyard of the castle where all the court was waiting. The place was festooned with flowers, garlands, and banners to represent the blue, green, and silver of Argoth on the groom's side and the red, black, and gold of Ventil on her side, and all eyes turned to her as musicians began to play the anthem of her arrival.

Prince Cathal stood at the end of the long, luxurious carpet before the altar of the Five Gods, shifting and looking uncomfortable in the formal wear of Argoth. His father stood off to his side, occasionally leaning in to whisper something to Cathal with an annoyed look on his face. She'd seen many of these quiet conversations halt upon entering a room in the last week, and it gave her the distinct impression that Cathal was not overly enthused at the wedding either.

Maeveen's own dour-looking father Targus awaited her where she would stand for the ceremony. The only emotion he seemed to express was the desire for everything to go smoothly so that the alliance could be sealed. Maeveen idly wondered if he could even tell her apart from her sister Aisling who had been married off two years ago for better costs on imported spices.

If I could just be anywhere but here, be anyone but me in this moment... "Blessed day" indeed.

As she began the slow walk down the carpet to meet her fate, the sky began to darken. As gloomy as the whole affair already felt, now she would have to do the ceremony under storm clouds and rain. Then the musicians stopped with an off note, and she saw the men at the alter looking up, their eyes widening in terror while she was in the direct center of the courtyard. A tremble took her as the first people began to scream and she followed the shocked gazes upward.

The enormous dragon almost blotted out the sun entirely for her, now that it was completely over the courtyard. Its regal purple scales on the powerful, lithe body shined, and the beating of its wings sent a swirling wind that blew all the decorations about. The roar that it let out sent all the guests and courtiers running in every direction. Maeveen watched as her own father and betrothed prince ran past the altar and back into the cover of the castle without a thought to her as the great beast descended.

For her, there was nowhere to run to. So exposed in the dead center of the courtyard, Maeveen froze as she watched upwards at the awesome sight of the creature descending on her. She screamed as one of the great front claws gripped easily around her body. As soon as it had her, the creature began to rise back into the air, and she watched as the castle seemed to shrink below her.

Princess Maeveen was whisked away, losing all track of direction and distance as the shock made her drift in dragon's tight grip.

Set gently down on the rocky terrain, Maeveen began to regain her senses as she found herself once more on solid ground. She had no idea just how long they'd flown, and she looked about the huge cavern chamber where the dragon had brought her. The glow of luminescent crystals embedded all throughout the walls bathed everything in soft light. Stalactites pointed down from the high ceiling far above her and, to one side, a stream of clear water cut next to a wall, flowing steadily. In a corner of the cave, an impressive pile of gold, gems, and assorted treasures gleamed in the glow of the crystals, large enough to represent the wealth of several kingdoms she could think of.

Her captor sat on haunches before her, looming above and staring passively as she dusted herself off. She waited a moment of frightened anticipation for... Maeveen wasn't sure what. A blast of burning fire? Massive jaws to descend over her? The creature to fly out again and leave her like another hoarded bauble? Possibilities cycled through her mind, but the dragon simply watched her, its dark, regal purple scales giving their own shine in the light, as if awaiting something from her. Some instinct told her that cowering and begging would be pointless, and that particular fire that had already been smoldering in her all day somehow awakened in Maeveen's chest.

"I don't know if you speak or can understand me," she said finally, standing with her own royal bearing as best she could before the enormous beast. "But know that you have made a grave error. I am the daughter of King Targus and the betrothed of Prince Cathal. The armies of Ventil and Argoth will both be sent to find and rescue me. And while your power may be great, they will discover a way to defeat it, whether to save me... or avenge me."

She waited to see if the bluff would work, knowing full well that the Ventil army was already busy, that Cathal would be useless in a hunt, and that her father would be more interested in finding another way to seal the alliance than the effort to find her.

The creature stared at her, seeming to listen intently, and a slow smirk spread over his muzzle.

"I am impressed, princess," the dragon said in a deep, masculine voice. "I knew there was something special about you when your pain and frustration called out to me. Many humans would cower and gibber in fear, but you... you would stand your ground and play your hand no matter what. Though you must understand, you are not in danger. In fact, *I* am the one rescuing you."

"Rescuing me? From my home? By tearing me away from all that I've ever known?" Maeveen fumed and felt her face darken. "From my wedding night?"

"From the shackles of loveless marriage. From the gilded

cage of the castle where you had no say in your destiny. From the drudgery you've already felt in your soul at every day of your life planned and stretching out into endless sameness."

The princess stopped. Every word tugged at those frustrations she'd felt waiting in her room. As if the dragon had peered directly into her soul and plucked a truth she'd never dared say aloud.

"How," Maeveen asked, stunned, "could you know about that?"

"It called out on the flow of the world." The dragon moved and Maeveen tensed until she realized the great creature was simply laying down to be closer to her level, still far enough away to be less intimidating. "It was a like a siren's song. I couldn't help hearing it, with where your kingdom is, even from afar. And over the last few years, it's grown louder and louder. If I had ignored it, the song may have eventually faded. Your own light and hope would have dimmed as you settled into your routine. I considered letting it. But there is an amazing potential in you unlike most humans. And to let that wither on the vine … it seemed unconscionable at this turning point."

Maeveen's heart sped in her chest, and she took a step back to sit on a rock. In the dark of night and any other time when she was alone with her thoughts, she'd felt it. "What potential is that?" she asked slowly.

The dragon smiled. "Magic, of course. And not the simple conjurations of the average sorcerer that can tap into a few amusing tricks through study or bloodline. Real, pulse-of-the-earth magic. Touching the actual fabric of the cosmos and feeling it directly. It's a seed in you that could have blossomed years ago and yet still has the potential. I've been hearing your song so long now that I feel I know you Princess Maeveen Caldor."

The dragon's emerald eye regarded her as if seeing a dream in the flesh for the first time.

"So, I must apologize for taking the liberty of snatching you up. The reverberations had been so loud the last few days, it was as if you were begging to be saved from having that potential snuffed out. But if you ask it of me, I will take you back this instant. I did not have the right to make this choice for you."

"Well ... I don't have to return this instant..." Maeveen said, pondering her situation. It was true, she'd yearned for escape so much in the last several days. She'd simply had no idea it could have been heard outside her own mind in any way. Or what this magical potential could be. "You say that you feel you already know me, but I have no knowledge of you. Do you have a name, since you have mine so readily?"

"Oh, of course, how rude of me. No wonder you considered me a beast at first." The dragon's long neck rose, and then his head dipped in a sort of bow to her. "You may call me Alinorixion. Or simply Alinor for short. Again, I apologize for my manners or lack thereof. Hearing your song for so long addled me a bit as to our familiarity."

"You mention my 'song', but what is that? I understand that it's a part of magic, but I have no knowledge of such things." For the first time Maeveen smiled a bit as a warm memory filled her. "Except for a few fairy stories my mother would tell me when I was a child."

Alinor smiled and lowered his head again. "Song is merely the best term in your language. Every creature, every bit of life has a song. A reverberation that floats along the fabric that makes the world. And to be a dragon is to be constantly connected to that fabric, to 'hear', or more feel, every song. Take, for example, whatever fond remembering you just had. I felt that as a soft melody touching against me with just a hint of bittersweet notes. Different songs are louder or softer than others and some songs simply intertwine to you, whether you wish it or no."

7

"The way that mine did for you the past several years," Maeveen said with a bit more understanding.

"Yes," Alinor replied, looking almost sheepish. "Much of your yearning was … rather loud after a certain point."

A slight blush rose to Maeveen's cheeks as she thought of some of the nights alone in her bedchamber. Nights that she did not wish to discuss with a relative stranger. "So, what does it actually feel like? If the songs are not something you actually hear, but feel, what is it truly like?"

Alinor gave her a pensive look, tapping a claw against his muzzle. "To be completely honest, I'm not sure if I can really explain it…"

She scoffed then. "Oh? Do you think me ignorant or foolish? I shall have you know that I am quite well-read and versed in many topics that would surprise you."

"Oh, my dear Maeveen, no, it's not as if I were insulting your intellect," Alinor said with a sincere look at her. "Your hungry mind is a large part of your song. It is more that the language does not really have quite adequate ways to tell you what it's like. I could say how a song tingles and brings about the thoughts of rhythms and music, but explanation does not quite do the sensation justice."

"Ah, I understand." Maeveen let out a short sigh. "I must apologize. I am far too used to men treating me as if my mind should only be concerned with needlepoint and how I might give proper heirs."

"I realize this; you need feel no shame at defending your abilities."

The cave was silent for a moment as if neither of them could think of what to say next. Maeveen slowly turned and went to the water running through the cave as she realized she was getting parched. She leaned down and then looked at her hands, still filthy from the dust that had kicked up when she was taken.

Though she found herself thinking of it less and less as an abduction during their conversation. Regardless of her feelings, as she looked from her hands to the water, she didn't want to cup them to drink or wash them from where she planned to take water.

A rustling of metal called her attention, and she saw Alinor's large claw holding an ornate golden chalice gingerly between his fingertips.

"Benefits of a large hoard," he said with a smile crossing his long snout as he proffered it to her. "It is clean, I assure you."

Maeveen took the expensive cup and dipped it into the small stream. The water was clear and delicious, and as she took another cupful, she realized how thirsty she'd been after soaring through the air.

"That's amazing," she sighed.

"It's fed from a natural spring. One of the reasons I chose this cave for my den."

Maeveen looked over at the pile of golden loot. She'd initially assumed it must have been stolen from terrorized keeps all over, but she now she had a hard time imagining Alinor pillaging his way across the countryside.

"So, how did you come by such a hoard?" she asked, leaning against a rock pillar and sipping from the chalice.

"Years upon years of cast-off, lost, or forgotten pieces. It builds slowly over time. Dragons do not hoard wealthy items because of greed or their supposed material value. Each of these has the echoes of songs of great joy and great sorrow. For wealthy objects, there is very seldom a lack of impression. They carry their history in the intense feelings that someone had about them in one way or another."

"Then you keep them for these songs again?"

Alinor smiled, "Sometimes it is easier to sleep with the mingled echoes working with each other to block out all the other reverberations from across the land."

Maeveen returned a rueful grin. "I suppose my song made it a bit more difficult the way you describe it."

The dragon let out a chuckle. "Not that you should feel any guilt, but I did lose a few bits of slumber. It was not all bad though. Even in your wistfulness and longing, there is a certain pleasantness to your song. Because you do not long for the suffering of others, only to feel things for yourself and have the freedom to do so."

"I still have trouble wrapping my mind around what it means and how you feel these songs," Maeveen said, feeling another sort of longing. "I want to understand it."

Alinor looked at her thoughtfully for a moment. "There is ... one possibility. You would have to trust me with magic greater than anything you could have ever experienced. And it could be overwhelming at first, so you'd have to be prepared for that. The feelings would be quite intense for a human."

She was more intrigued than frightened by the dragon's warnings. Maeveen stepped away from the stone pillar. "Well now I must know. What is this great magic you speak of?"

"Well, if you are willing, and you do not push back against me, I could change you. I could not do this with every human, but with the power of your song and how it has at times intertwined with me—I could change you into a dragon yourself for a time, and you would perceive the world as such."

Heart skipping a beat, Maeveen shuddered. There was no fear for her; the idea was merely something she'd never thought of. To not just see a new world but experience it in an entirely new way. To shake off what she'd always been, the princess expected to be light and subdued, to have only the passions granted to her by others as appropriate.

"Could you truly do this?"

"Yes," Alinor said. "All I need to do is tap into that connection to the makings of the world and through the seed of magic in you, change you in body towards that particular rhythm."

There was only a moment's hesitation. Maeveen wondered if possibly this was some kind of elaborate trick or what would happen if—against all likelihood—some force from Ventil or Argoth did arrive at the cave to find two dragons and no princess. But something in the back of her mind urged her forward, perhaps that seed that the dragon had talked about.

"Then do it," she said boldly, almost more to still her own few doubts than to show Alinor her resolve. "Show me what your world is really like."

Alinor stood up on his four limbs and stretched his wings and neck for a moment. "Very well then. Prepare yourself, though, as I said, some of the feelings may be … intense."

Princess Maeveen wondered for a second if the experience would be painful as Alinor began to stare intently at her. Then the gaze seemed to pierce through her, and she could feel it traveling into her eyes and somehow though her body. There was no pain but a feeling of something uncoiling at her core and a heat beginning to radiate through her body out to the tips of her limbs. It was as if every part of her was being loosened up, her once solid form becoming malleable to forces that had slipped inside.

Sweat broke out over her skin as she felt herself expanding slowly, growing larger as her muscles pushed outward. There was still no pain, but a feeling akin to the most intense morning stretch. A thousand times more potent than any she'd done after a night of good sleep. And it actually felt... good. As if something she'd never known was bound and knotted within her were finally being allowed to move freely.

Maeveen let out a little moan as her limbs grew, her arms changing shape slightly and becoming bulkier while her legs began to shift in grater ways, feet and calves elongating proportionately so that she might balance on her toes as Alinor's back limbs did. She felt herself pitching forward only to catch herself easily on her enlarged hands. There was a moment of tightness within her clothes as her body expanded more than the dress could stand before it simply ripped away from her in tatters. As she changed, being naked felt simply natural, a sense that she'd often felt but had needed to repress. Here it was freeing.

Her skin began to tingle as she continued to grow larger, and Maeveen looked at her arms to see the smoothness slowly giving way to round, diamond patterns. Scales were slowly replacing—or possibly growing through and over—the skin she'd always known, and the tingle was surprisingly pleasant. Fingertips and toes all felt as if they were flexing and extending, and when Maeveen looked at her changing hands, she saw almost glistening white claws extending from her fingers where her nails had been.

At the same time, pressure at her back told her that new parts of her body were trying to sprout there at two points just below her shoulders. While they shifted and became more muscular, Maeveen experienced a similar push at the place just above her rump. The growth of these points did not feel like something trying to force their way out of her skin, but budding gently as new limbs that were increasingly familiar as they grew. Her neck and face also expanded at the same time, making Maeveen groan and let out little gasps as her body changed. But still, there was no pain. Maeveen, in fact, felt quite the opposite. The rising heat, the stretch of her limbs and formation of new ones, the tingle along her entire body that all made her pant and moan sent shivers of delight throughout.

The changes continued as she felt her nose and mouth elongating into a muzzle. An odd tingle crept along her scalp when her hair lifted from her neck to stiffen and curve back into two new formations. The fledgling wings at her back continued to push outward, and she could feel all the sensations waking up within them. What had started as a nub pushing just above her backside lengthened further until she could feel it trying to swing gently behind her. Every inch of her skin sang while her new scales solidified. As each change spread heat and that sense of wonderful stretch throughout her, Maeveen realized what was so familiar about this feeling. It was akin to something she'd felt on many late nights when she'd lain in bed and let her mind and fingers wander to lose herself.

The first real rush of utter pleasure shot through her as her new wings expanded further out from her body and her tail grew and swayed to brush the ground of the huge cave. She cried out in a way that was already sounding more like a roar. The waves of physical pleasure breaking over her dwarfed anything she'd experienced plucking away in her bed to the thoughts of some cavalier whisking her away to a secret rendezvous. Maeveen may not have understood the songs of the dragon's world completely yet, but she knew what it was to have her whole body sing as it changed.

She rode along the pulses of that pleasure as she continued to grow, hoping that it wasn't too obvious what was happening to her as the dragon—the *other* dragon, she should say now—changed her. Her wings spread wider, feeling powerful. Her tail, now as big as one of the surrounding stalagmites pushing up from the ground, thrashed about with a sense of power. Her new horns stretched back from her head in a gentle curve that ended in points. As the change completed itself, Princess Maeveen collapsed onto the floor of the cave, panting and coming back down from a high of pleasure. Yet she recognized that the tingle and urge in her loins did not wholly abate.

Carefully, she picked herself up off the floor and caught her breath. The cave, while still huge, seemed so much smaller now. More intimate even though the ceiling still offered plenty of space above her. She lifted her new head up and craned her elongated neck to get a feel for it and how it could move. Her wings stretched again, and Maeveen was surprised to discover how natural they already felt. A part of her wanted to rush out and take flight immediately, to soar through the air and feel that real freedom. Yet, she was also keenly aware that just because the wings felt natural, the act of flying might not come so easily. And her mind was still just a bit rattled from the intense pleasure. And the low burn of further desire that was maddeningly pressing her body.

She focused her eyes and looked over at Alinor. The dragon was smiling at her and simply resting as he watched her. The *other* dragon she had to remember... the male dragon... the actually quite *handsome* male dragon now that she was looking with new eyes...

Maeveen shook her head out a little bit and blinked a few times. The world did look a little different, more of a shine to it and a different height perspective, but she didn't feel any grand revelation yet.

"You seem to be taking to this quite well. I was almost expecting to have to show you how to stand, but you're already moving naturally."

"I've always learned quickly," Maeveen said offhandedly, surprised for a moment at the deep, new powerful voice. "But the experience was definitely ... intense."

"Ah. Yes," Alinor said, sounding almost sheepish. "The, er, potential is different for every living being and truth be told it is not something I've really done a great deal. If I may say so, though, your beauty certainly moves between forms rather easily."

For the first time, Maeveen realized she really did not know what she looked like now, only a few vague impressions during the change. Still, the compliment sent another jolt of that desire that was still humming through her. And she could, in a way, "hear" that need within herself as a rhythm, like an incomplete melody begging for some kind of accompaniment. She tried to tamp it down again.

"I don't suppose there is a mirror in that hoard somewhere?"

"Ha, several, I think, but I'll have to find them. I fear vanity isn't a real vice of mine."

"Well, you would certainly earn it if it were." The words escaped Maeveen's new muzzle before she could even think. She thought that she saw Alinor miss a beat as he searched through the pile of treasure.

Maeveen found herself slipping closer to him, drawn now in a way she'd never imagined. She could not deny that she'd dreamed of lusty things in the past and had pushed down many thoughts when seeing certain men at court in some positions. But now it was as if that raw feeling was surrounding her, and something was certainly singing to her that there was no need to hold them back. Maeveen felt positively wanton as she tried not to think about what her new body was craving.

"Ah, here we are," Alinor said.

Maeveen stopped as he pulled a grand ornate mirror up from under a collection of coins. There was a small crack in the corner, but it was at least big enough as he displayed it in both of his claws. She gazed at herself and for a moment felt incredulous.

"Pink," she said, "Bright. Pink. Scales. And ivory horns." She could feel a ridge above her eye raising up as she looked up from feminine draconic form in the mirror to Alinor's eyes. "Is that what you really think I am still? A frilly little thing?"

"Actually," Alinor said with something of a playful smirk. "I did not pick this color; you did. Or at least, your song did."

"What?"

"A dragon's scales are not based on some outside force or bloodline," he explained. "As I said, to be a dragon is to be absolutely connected to magic and the fabric of reality. Outward appearance is a reflection of what is within you. You may be surprised to know that dragons hatch as a dull gray and change colors many times in the course of their youth. As adults, the color eventually settles somewhat and only really changes if there is a great change within the dragon in some way. Usually from some surprising event or an upheaval in the way the dragon interacts with the songs of the world."

Maeveen looked again at her new form. The long, pointed muzzle, the wings that she spread to see their span. The way her body was lean and yet powerful. She realized that her breasts were gone, replaced by the smooth, soft, cream-colored scales of the rest of her underbelly. When she lifted a claw there, she found that rubbing along any of those scales gave her a little shiver of pleasure. She pondered a moment to find that she really didn't mind the change. It almost made her chuckle to think that she hadn't actually missed them when so many others made them such a point of pride, and that there were a few leering men at court who would immediately bemoan their loss.

"So, what do these scales say about me? That I am delicate? Frail?"

Alinor chuckled. "Far from it. You can appreciate the touch of delicate things, but you are also very resilient and passionate. There is a feminine aspect to some extent, but not in the way you might think. At least, that's what your song has always told me."

Setting the mirror aside, Alinor looked at her again. "Now, let me ask you something. When you look at me, what do you see?"

Maeveen shivered as she looked at him and that familiar pulse ran all through her body in the unfinished melody of desire. The more she settled into draconic nature, the more handsome Alinor looked to her. The purple of his scales shined so beautifully, and his body seemed so powerful. Thoughts of rutting came unbidden to her mind.

And then she felt it. A feeling emanating from him that started at the skin beneath her scales and crept deeper in.

Like he'd said, it wasn't actual sound or music, but it was a rhythm that pulsed and could be turned into a song. In the exact moment there was a subtle triumphant note as he felt her begin to understand. It was laced with a soft melody of caring and kindness that always suffused his being, mingled with a trill of occasional playfulness. And underneath, now that these senses were awakening for her, there was a strong, bass rumble of power and virility backing up all those other notes. And when she heard it, it grew louder and called to that unfinished melody that kept begging for completion within her as her loins quivered and that sensual heat rose within her again.

As his song hit her and she truly felt it, a different, deep rumble rose up. And Maeveen realized it was an actual sound coming from her own chest.

Racing a few steps forward, she pounced on the gorgeous male dragon and bowled him over onto the pile of gold coins, causing several bunches to spill and clatter over the cave floor. Alinor gasped in a moment of surprise as Maeveen pressed her new body to his, feeling some of the intense sensual cravings satisfied. She *needed* the touch of another, her body absolutely required it. She'd longed for touch many times as a human and often been denied the chance. Now, in this form where she could feel everything, that desire was magnified and would not —*should* not—be contained.

She found herself playfully nibbling along Alinor's long neck, growling and rumbling where her claws reached for him in the tangle of her limbs. They rubbed at his sides, scratched gently down to the joints where his wings had splayed across the pile of treasures. Her body pressed down against him, awkwardly for only a moment as limbs tangled when she forgot that this would not be the same between draconic forms as it might have with her human body. Yet still, Maeveen was able to press herself down between his hind legs and rub herself against a slit there that was already spreading open as something hard was pressing its way outside. And that deep bass thrum of virility began to grow louder, only held down by a staccato of nervous caution.

Alinor finally found his voice amid panting as she bit down a little where his long neck met his shoulder and began to slip back, her hips rubbing needily against him. "P-Princess Maeveen, are—?"

"*Don't,*" Maeveen said with a lusty, forceful growl as she reached up to grip his head and look into his eyes, "call me 'Princess.'"

She could feel the hardness growing between his legs as she growled, and she rubbed herself against it, rumbling deeply and holding his eyes with hers."

"I only want to be sure you—" Alinor was cut off by his own deep roar as she bit his neck more forcefully and his erection grew harder between his legs.

Maeveen rumbled and held tightly to him, trying to find every point of contact between their bodies. The barest hint of satisfaction overwhelmed her almost more than the desire had. Just a taste of contact was making her need everything she'd been constantly denied as a human.

"That title," Maeveen rumbled, digging her claws against his shoulders to press herself even harder against the male dragon, "has always been a pair of shackles weighing me down. I see more clearly than I ever have. It denied me every desire, every wish, every feeling I might have enjoyed. Always being told to wait, that my body was merely a duty to others. I was even hoping that at least my wedding night might grant me some-thing, even knowing that I was merely being gifted to another kingdom. Now, for the first time, my body is *mine*. Made for me, from my song, just as you said. And I will have what *I* want."

Alinor's hips moved beneath her as she spoke and Maeveen shivered at the feeling. He had not entered her, but that hard length was almost fully erect and rubbing at her soft scales where it could. That deep background of his song was gaining power and volume inside her, joining with her own incomplete melody and beginning to match it. Yet something was holding it back, trying to interrupt.

"I hear," he said through panting breaths and roars, "and I have heard your song long enough to understand. But perhaps I should have warned—"

Again, he was cut off, this time by Maeveen putting more pressure against the thick rod jutting from the slit between his legs. It was growing slick and the feeling of it against made her long to feel what it was like to have inside her, buried deep in her new form.

"No more warnings. No more waiting. I don't want courtly teasing. I don't want to wait for propriety or for someone else's needs to allow for a marriage. I don't even want wooing or slow romance." Maeveen grabbed the back of Alinor's head in a claw and pulled it next to her own, feeling more and more at home in a body that could give in to desires. "I want to rut like a beast."

The last resistant vibrations fell away, and as Alinor reached up and finally took hold of her as well to squeeze her and let his muzzle meet hers, Maeveen could feel that thrumming bass rhythm take over and join almost perfectly with her melody, completing it as they shifted hind legs and lined up on the instincts and songs rippling together through their bodies.

Maeveen eagerly pressed the moist lips of her sex around Alinor's shaft and slid down as he pushed up, making them both cry out in delight. They came together easily and began pumping back and forth to the beat of the joined vibrations that she could feel coursing through her. The pleasure she'd felt during the transformation returned, only magnified as she felt full of Alinor's thick shaft. The way it rubbed inside her to the feeling of the now completed melody suffusing her body was unlike any joy she'd ever experienced. Beyond the rush of physical pleasure throbbing through every thrust of their bodies, the union of their rhythms that she could feel and almost hear was shooting bliss through her soul. And she knew, without look or confirmation but through the continued harmony itself, that the same was happening for Alinor.

Coins jingled beneath them as their movements grew in tempo and intensity, in time to the strange music that Maeveen felt between them. She began to understand what he'd meant about the echoes within the treasure as well. With her entire being so open, she may have been interrupted by thousands of other sensations that might be out in the world, but the echoes on every small piece that had been loved, lost, or both kept it all at bay. So that now, gliding herself back and forth along that wonderfully thick piece of meat, the two of them were the only things that existed for her.

They bit at each other playfully as they rutted, claws grasping and scratching in places that would intensify the pleasure between them. With a human lover, Maeveen might have had to figure out what he liked or what to do next. But here, in this form, both she and Alinor always simply knew what to do because their songs were fully entwined. Alinor sped up as she needed him to, knew without words when her pleasure grew, and how to keep it moving forward. In turn, she adjusted, slipped down, or squeezed at just the right moments to make him roar and throb harder.

She began to feel bursts of pleasure like she used to feel when she would pluck at herself to fantasies in the night. Maeveen had always thought those moments the height of physical bliss, but now she knew that there was more. That these tingly bursts of delight throbbing out from her groin had only ever been a precursor to something greater. And had she known in those nights, she would never have stopped until she went higher. Now, though, she would experience it all.

Pleasure mounted within her, and Maeveen felt the song of it growing faster and louder, coursing through every fiber of their being. They reached the apex at nearly the same time in their unity and just as she heard Alinor roar and tense beneath her, shooting a hot jet of seed up into her body, Maeveen felt something tip and burst within her, making her own roar echo about the cave.

Before this moment, she'd experienced bodily pleasure. Maeveen had managed to experience delight both in her human self and somewhat in her new dragon self. This was different. The absolute bliss that suffused her being nearly blew away all musings of physical form. She no longer thought about the shape of her body because in the seconds that seemed to stretch out, there was just pure, unadulterated pleasure. Her body was suffused with it, the music in her soul holding a crescendo that blotted out everything and pulsed within her. Only a tiny thought of Alinor as the partial source of that bliss could intrude through the music he supplied along with hers, and it made her feel such gratitude and affection towards him despite their strange circumstances.

As it began to slow and fade back down after several consistent bursts, Maeveen slipped back into awareness of her body and gently collapsed onto the other dragon beneath her. She was still partially stunned and floating, little aftershocks of pleasure making her quiver. The strange music was still there between them, but a lower thrum as she came down off the incredible high.

Her senses returning to normal, Maeveen realized what she'd just done. A dragon, one she'd only met today, and only under the strangest of circumstances, and she'd all but attacked him driven by lust. For a moment, she wondered if he'd cast a spell on her to make her do that, but then she dimly remembered those moments he'd tried to tell her something and slow her down.

As Alinor rumbled and tried slip back to his own senses beneath her, Maeveen had to admit that it had been her choice alone, even if it had felt so unlike her. It was as if some great dam had burst and every frustrated desire she'd had recently had overtaken her. She slipped off of him and a few steps away, padding on four claws closer to the wall. Yet even as she attempted to figure out what had changed so drastically for her, Maeveen felt that strange yearning to touch him again and be touched.

Lifting his head up from where he now lay alone, Alinor gave her an earnest look. "Are you ... alright?"

Maeveen shook her wings a little and let out a breath. "I—I think. What was that? I've never been ... like that before. Not really."

Alinor turned his body and padded gently off the treasure pile, keeping respectful distance from her. "First, you must know that I did not intend this when I came to rescue you in my own misguided way. I thought perhaps to offer you a way to learn your gifts, and only when you were curious did I think of the possibility of change. So, I did not even consider explaining before changing you, because it's a normal state for me. The connection that a dragon feels, that link to the fabric of reality and life tends to make us very ... sensual. Such bodily desires are felt very raw and open. Over time, one gets used to it, and to act on it is merely casual if the mood is right. However, I'd forgotten that humans and many other beings don't have that connection and what the intensity might be like for someone just touching it for the first time." The male dragon's eyes widened a bit as he got a far-away expression. "And despite what I have felt of your song, I was not quite expecting ... that."

It made sense to Maeveen when he explained it. From the moment of the surprising pleasure of the change he'd brought in her, she'd felt raw and open in a way she had never known before. Even those times when fantasy overtook her, it had felt like something to hide away. But as a dragon... as a dragon, Maeveen realized that what she felt most of all when the shock from her old self wore down was power and pride in getting and giving the delight they shared. And the desire for more. She actually felt a grin spread her muzzle.

"Well, I suppose there is no need to question if you liked it anyways."

Alinor could not contain a deep, throaty laugh. "No, that's another part of the connection to magic and life. Among dragons there is nearly no chance of misunderstanding when it comes to desire and pleasure. My only real concern was how your mind might fair afterwards, since you are human, and I honestly only know that it's quite different for you in some way."

"*Was* human. I certainly find myself enjoying being a dragon far more." She sighed. "But you are correct. Being raised human, and as a princess no less, it is quite different." Maeveen let out a little scoff as she came closer to him again. "Perhaps if we could feel that sort of connection, some might be less inclined to use desire and unions like a coin to be traded."

"You mean, humans feel none of this connection at all?" Alinor asked with a surprised look. "I cannot fathom it."

It almost made Maeveen laugh as she impulsively walked by him, brushing her side against his and letting her tail tease at his neck. The feeling was already pleasant again, and she could feel it making that bass rhythm thump from him once more.

"Well, together we could likely show you," she smirked. "Perhaps the same way you showed me."

"What?" Alinor said, looking somewhat unnerved.

"I am sure the magic works both ways." Maeveen could already feel herself curiously touching something within him. "You could be a human for a little while and see what it's like."

"I am unsure how wise that would truly be," Alinor said, and Maeveen could actually feel the uneasy trill vibrating from him.

"Why, mighty Alinorixion," she said, feeling more playful by the second as she circled him from behind to sidle up to him and look into his eyes. "You are not afraid, are you? For it would be rather ironic if you were scared to be a small human at the whim of a large dragon."

"I—" Alinor started and stopped himself, the dragon's eyes widening with understanding. "That is a fair barb, I suppose."

"What is good for me ought to be good for you. And it seems only fair that you truly understand where I have come from in some way. After all of that."

Alinor thought for a moment and nodded his head. "It is true, that would be fair, given what I have done today. I did not even consider that I was another with so much control and power exerted over you, just as others have done."

"With the exception of a few moments ago," Maeveen said, feeling an odd warm rush at how she'd practically taken him on his own hoard. That feeling unfamiliar, yet so very delightful. "But are you prepared to surrender control and power for the magic to work? Are you willing to let me show you now?"

"I do not know how truly ready I am, but I will submit myself. It would put us on a more even plane. Do you need guidance in how to—?"

"No," she said with a mischievous grin. "That connection to magic feels so strong now. As if I simply know how to do what I need just by thinking upon it. And I'll be cautious, worry not."

"I feel you taking delight in my discomfort," Alinor said with a sheepish grin.

"Then you can also feel there is no malice in my song. I am merely enjoying that for once, there is a bit of turnabout."

Maeveen focused then on the magic and the nature of Alinorixion's song that she'd so intimately touched moments ago. She would have thought before that such things would be complex, but it was surprisingly simple. Connected to everything, she only had to use what she already knew of the basic sense of being human and work to rewrite a few pieces here and there. And as she began to tease and pluck at the right notes, she saw Alinor blink a few times as everything began to diminish.

His snout, tail, and wings were slowly starting to pull inward to his body as she removed them from his song to begin replacing them with the blunted human features. His black claw tips began to retract down into his large digits while his limbs thinned and changed. Growing steadily smaller and smaller before her, she could feel herself guiding the change along while starting it set it on its natural course.

The tail disappeared into his back while his legs changed their shape to stand more upright, the lower portions shortening into plantar segments. Black horns began to soften and start to go limp down the back of his head slowly, and his wings steadily shrank and started to retract all the way down into his back. As they did, Maeveen watched his dark purple scales begin to ripple and slowly slide inward, revealing a ruddy skin in their place covering Alinor's diminishing body.

His body now looked so miniscule to her, as she must have looked to him at first. What she felt towards him now was extreme caution, worried that in this state she could break him if she did the wrong thing. When the last of the change was done, Alinor stood in a new human body with dark tan colored skin and black hair down to his shoulders. Muscles stood out on a fit, lean frame, and Maeveen had to admit that he looked like the sort of man who would have given her a few nighttime thoughts. Though he'd not seemed to have the same orgasmic experience the change had given her.

As a final note within the change, Maeveen made sure that the essence of being a dragon was tucked somewhere that he would not feel immediately but could open and change back if he needed to.

Alinor looked at his new form, turning his hands this way and that in front of him. "So strange. I feel so tiny and so ... disconnected. I cannot *feel* anything around me. Nothing sings at all."

"You won't unless you touch them or smell or taste them

really." Maeveen said with a slightly wistful tone. With memories of so many disconnected years, she almost felt sorrow for this moment.

"I suppose that is—" Alinor stopped and jumped back when he looked up at her and then looked around the cave. "Gah! Everything is so enormous!" He looked back at her. "And you. You could do whatever you wanted to me, and I would be powerless. Crush me, destroy me. Like this, there's nothing I could do. Nothing... This is how I made you feel?"

"In a way, yes," Maeveen said, looming her muzzle down towards him. "But do not be afraid." She stopped and smirked. "Well, I suppose I admit, it might be satisfying if you were a *little* afraid. I would not hurt you though."

He looked away and kept stealing the occasional glance back. She could still get bits of the rhythms he had, but it was definitely diminished as he walked around the cave and saw it with new eyes.

"This is enlightening, to see everything like this," Alinor said, his voice sounding tinny and quiet to Maeveen. "I have to say, it is also peaceful in a way. Not feeling anything means I don't have the vibrations of all the life around me. It's ... quiet. And in some ways, that is pleasant. Even the lack of raw sensuality carries with it a certain sense of relief."

"Until you spend enough time as a human. Often your own mind can make all the noise on its own."

He turned again and gazed up at her, taking in her form as a human. As he gazed upon her, Maeveen loomed over him just as he had done. Not willfully intimidating, but simply so much larger and more powerful.

And as Maeveen felt that undercurrent of mild fear, something else drifted into Alinor's new song. A surprising, small jolt of that bassy, virile beat that had drawn her in before. She glanced lower on him to confirm, and true enough, the new human Alinor, standing naked and vulnerable in the cave, was rising at the occasion.

A look of shock shot across his face, and he looked down and saw his excitement plain as day. "What in the earth and skies? What just happened? Why..." Alinor panted and looked up at her again, a shiver running through him as his rod twitched. His face began to break into a bizarre panic, and Maeveen felt that nervous energy vibrating from him. "This is... it does not..."

"Calm yourself," Maeveen said from above him, hardly able to hide her amusement. "As a human, you are not connected to the magic and sensuality of life. But our minds do other things sometimes. Strange, unlikely things that make us yearn."

"What do you mean? This makes no sense, but something about this situation..." Alinor was again at a loss for words.

"Perhaps I can help you understand. When I was human, I did not always feel some measure of sensuality all the time. But for reasons I cannot possibly say, in certain cases the sight of a man's feet might make me feel a strange sort of pleasure and desire that I dared not tell others." Feeling a sense of bizarre power, Maeveen loomed up over Alinor and stalked a little closer. "And my lady-in-waiting, when I was of age and had confided in her, would sometimes tell me scandalous stories of men she'd known. Some that obsessed over a certain food. Others that wished to be hit and called terrible names." She made a show of stomping near him and watched Alinor quiver and grow more excited. "Because that constant connection is not there, humans sometimes discover these creations of their own minds that excite and arouse them."

"I—I see," Alinor said, blushing as he stared up at her and took a step back, his own arousal still showing clearly. "And you believe that, er, this might be happening to me this first time being human?"

"Oh, most definitely," Maeveen said, grinning and delighting in this particular kind of power over someone. "Maybe it's that you like being scared a little bit." She made a show of stomping and shaking the floor of the cave near him. "Or perhaps because of the way I changed you, as a human you maintain a specific fondness to dragons." She loomed up on her back legs and spread her wings, coming down again in front of Alinor. He fell down on his backside and let out a little whimper. She stalked over him and leaned her face down again. "It could also be that you have never been so small and powerless and now you like your women... big."

With a shocked expression, Alinor looked down at his throbbing shaft. He stared back up at her and couldn't keep his hand from wandering to touch himself gently. He did not stroke fully, but simply ran his fingers in a curious touch along his shaft.

Seeing the way he couldn't contain himself and how she could arouse him, Maeveen took delight in the new notes of the vibrations she could feel from him. His song had an entirely new melody, and she could take complete control over it. The sensation was utterly intoxicating and aroused her as well.

"Yes, I believe that's it," she teased mercilessly. "You have always been grand and powerful, and now for the first time, you know what it is to be small and..." Maeveen paused and lifted a claw directly above where he was seated and touching himself, "...vulnerable."

A shiver of delicious erotic power ran through Maeveen as she watched her words have such an effect on him. Alinor was whimpering in need and staring up at her claw and the way her muzzle was framed between her fingers. After years of hiding and only sneaking tiny moments of pleasure while her life was planned for her, tormenting him in a delightfully fun way was its own kind of music. And she might not have done it if his freshly human body hadn't been so clearly enjoying every little moment.

"It is true, I could crush you so easily at this size," she said, watching his reactions. The widening of his eyes and the tremble of his body seemed more like real worry than arousal, so Maeveen changed tones. "But naturally, I'd never want to do that. It would be so much more fun to use you as my own personal plaything."

Alinor gasped, and there it was in the right sort of quiver and blush. Watching him grow so agitated made her own arousal flow a bit, and she set her claw down over him with a gentle *thump*. She could feel him wriggling there and the stiffness rubbing up against her palm.

"Do you not see now, little *human*? You fell right into my trap." Maeveen gave him a slight wink as his face stared up between her fingers and she started to rub back and forth along his body. "You are mine now, and I shall use you for my own pleasure. Teasing you, tormenting you."

He was moaning now beneath her claw as it rubbed and pressed him down to the cave floor. She could feel how he easily wouldn't last long and was curious what might push him over as she rode her own delight from the power of giving him this pleasure. Time to try out a tease and see what the result would be.

"And I have heard tell of things that common ladies can use to insert and *stimulate* themselves. The way you wriggle and writhe, you might feel divine pushed into me like this. Used for my utter pleasure."

"Oh, earth and skies!"

Alinor cried out in a series of loud moans as she felt him shoot a small, sticky mess along her palm. He bucked under her claw, pressing up against it, and something about making him shoot that way gave Maeveen her own little shudder of bliss as the song of it reverberated through her being. The power of his loss of control mingled with the strange gratitude he felt at the way she had treated him to this was such an amazing feeling.

Maeveen lifted up her claw and wiped the little mess on one of the stalagmites nearby. She looked down at Alinor as he lay on the rocky floor, panting and coming down from the high. He propped up on his elbows and looked at Maeveen as she sat on her haunches above him.

"I have never felt such a thing." He flopped down, his human body splayed out. "In so many years, I have had many amazing, sensuous experiences, but I never considered…" He let out a loud breath. "The strange way all those words and pressure made me feel. And the stillness afterwards. That complete emptiness that was in my mind for a few seconds. Pleasure and then utter, delightful silence within. Incredible."

"I suppose there is that for a lot of us. Though I find I am enjoying the feeling of this connectedness. And I confess that I *adore* feeling so strong and in control."

"It has been an illuminating day for us both," Alinor said, watching as Maeveen stretched her wings and moved about the cave again. "Well, shall you change me back? Are you ready to return to your own self?"

Maeveen reclined on the pile of treasure and picked up an old, slightly tarnished crown. She splayed out her wings and worked to pick out the specific echoes of songs from people it had touched.

"This *is* my own self," she said. "For it is the only version of myself that I have ever truly owned and could not be bartered by and to someone else. I think I'll stay like this for now." Maeveen let a playful grin spread across her long muzzle. She was sure that Alinor knew that he could change himself back, but wondered how much he might play along. "As for changing you back, I think in a little while. You have a few more things to … experience." Maeveen gave him a lascivious look and waited for his response.

Alinor walked over to the hoard in his human body and laid himself against one of her hind claws. "It may be nice to enjoy this sort of quiet for a little while. And see just what being human has to offer in the coming days."

Maeveen let out a gentle sigh as a hoard of treasure jangled softly beneath her, enjoying how even the slightest touch from him, in any shape, felt so right and pleasant. She felt in her new body how their songs were entwining again, this time in a soft, relaxed melody that flowed seamlessly between the two of them. A thought made her chuckle.

In ways she never could have imagined, her wedding day had genuinely become a blessed day indeed.

PURE DRAGON PUERH

FRANCES PAULI

Lisa clung to the metal cable and closed her eyes, breathing slowly from the depths of her stomach. The wooden slats beneath her feet felt too thin, too far apart, and she didn't want to think about the open air beneath them. Behind her, the other tea pilgrims were beginning to lose their patience. The "namaste" they'd greeted her with, it seemed, had its limits.

Lisa gave the guy behind her an apologetic smile and forced herself to scoot several more steps along the precarious bridge. Somewhere at the end of this death trap was supposed to be the greatest teahouse in the United States. The closest she could get on her budget to an authentic tea-drinking experience. As she listened to the cable sing in the wind, Lisa decided she didn't like tea *that* much after all.

She could almost hear her ex's "told you so," and the thought of Brent discovering she'd chickened out pushed her further along the boards. The mountain could not go on much longer, could it? Eventually, she'd have to reach firm ground again. And tea. A nice cup of the most expensive tea she'd ever tasted. According to the internet, drinking it was worth the journey, a rare pleasure, and pleasure was something Lisa had completely lost touch with.

In fact, nothing seemed to please her anymore. Not food, not meditation, and certainly not sex. Again, Brent's voice haunted her hesitant steps. "I just need to know what you want, Lisa," and when his fumbling attempts to get her in the mood failed, "Are you sure you're not ace?"

She opened her eyes, tilted her head back, and regarded the wide, blue sky. Maybe she was. Maybe her lack of libido had nothing to do with Brent and everything to do with her. Dimly, she remembered a time when she enjoyed sex, but it seemed like that Lisa was a different person.

The guy behind her cleared his throat loudly. Lisa didn't bother to smile this time. She moved, though, and kept going despite the knot of terror wadding itself into a tangle inside her belly. What had possessed her to take this trip? The buzz on the tea-net was an excuse, she knew, a distraction from a life she'd grown out of. Or possibly just grown bored with.

Either way she had no business clinging to the side of a mountain, following a treacherous path over a deadly drop-off in a desperate effort to feel… anything. Still, going back now was out of the question. The distance to the teahouse had to be shorter than that which lay behind her. Also, no way would she be able to talk the others into doing an about face.

She moved on, one uncertain footstep at a time, and she kept her eyes up, on the way ahead and not the emptiness below. When the cliff curved again, Lisa saw the teahouse for the first time. It was perched in a sweep of flat ground between the mountain's peaks, and a long, stone pathway led from the lip, up a gentle slope, to the open-sided building. The teahouse was designed for tea-obsessed tourists and did not suit the often-chilly climate of the Rocky Mountains. It had a tiled roof, with half-walls made of lashed bamboo circling beneath. To Lisa it looked out of place and undeniably ordinary but for the extreme circumstances required to reach it.

"Don't let the tea be bad," she whispered to herself. "Don't let it all be for nothing."

But a lump settled in her stomach just the same. She'd grown used to a life of habitual disappointment—in her job, in Brent, and in herself. Why should the teahouse be any different? Why should the difficulty automatically make the trip worthwhile?

Behind her, the anxious thrill seeker cleared his voice one last time. Lisa did not smile. Did not bother faking. Instead, she put one foot in front of the other, focused on getting it over with, and made the final leg of the trip with the last of her hopes fraying like the edges of an old robe.

They sat on their knees in front of the tea master and his little table. Lisa took a cushion near the back, almost up against the short, half-wall that ringed in the open tea house. She'd knelt to the rear of the group, as far from the others as possible and could barely see the gray-haired gentleman boiling water Gung Fu style over the charcoal brazier at the front of the room.

Not that it mattered. Lisa had already decided the brew would be a disappointment. Despite the arduous trek to reach the little tea house, there was a touristy aura clinging to it. It might be aimed at a specific niche of eco traveler, but the whole experience was definitely "aimed." She sighed and let her gaze drift away from the pouring of the tea from the gaiwan into tiny, single-swallow cups.

Outside the teahouse the mountain slope curled into a green valley between bald stone peaks. A path wandered up the center, wiggling this way and that as if the builders had been drunk or simply not paying attention. Lisa caught movement along the trail, leaned even closer, and spotted an old woman trundling up the slope. She carried a big clay jug, and the stagger in her steps suggested whatever it contained was far too heavy for her.

The woman was dressed in a loose tunic and straight-legged pants made from rough fibers, dyed a muddy blue and brick red which suggested a natural process. She'd belted a long sash around her ample waist, but one end had come loose and trailed the ground around her feet, snakelike, almost as if it sought specifically to trip her.

Lisa held her breath as her pulse stuttered. One wrong step and the woman and her pot would tumble. She turned back to the room, heart skipping, and nearly leapt from her skin. A skinny, robed helper stood directly in front of her. He'd bent forward in a half-bow, and held out a short, flat, pale green cup of tea. Silent, patient as a stone waiting for her to take the beverage.

"I think she needs help," Lisa said but she took the offered tea at the same time. Something about his posture would not allow her to do otherwise. "There's a woman out there struggling."

The server lifted his head only, turned to gaze out at the slope, and furrowed his brow in a way that made Lisa look too, that told her long before she spied the empty slope that the old woman would not be there.

"She was carrying a big pot," she said softly. "Right there, just a second ago."

The ground was far too open, and the path too distant for the woman to be gone. Yet, there it was as vacant as if she'd never been there at all. The cup in Lisa's hands warmed her palms. The steam wafted upward, delivering a bland, unspectacular aroma. She shivered as if she were holding ice.

"Where did she go?"

Without saying a word, the server shrugged and moved back toward the front of the teahouse. There were others like him wandering among the tourists, delivering tea, not speaking. They might have been clones; they were so alike. Skinny, bent, dressed in anachronistic tunics belted with hand-woven sashes. Lisa shook her head and sipped the tea, frowned at its bland flavor, and turned back to the window.

The old woman was back. She stood on the pathway in exactly the same spot where she'd been before, but she'd paused her journey and turned to face the teahouse. When she saw Lisa looking, she tossed her head and opened her mouth. The chatter and shifting of tourists in the teahouse drowned out any other noise, but Lisa knew without a doubt that she was being laughed at. She set her tea down on the wooden floor without tearing her eyes away from the woman.

For a long moment, they stared at one another. Then, the old woman took a short, hopping step, still holding her pot, still teetering under its weight. She turned her back on Lisa and continued up the pathway, but now, as if it had always been there, a long, auburn tail poked from the seat of her trousers. It was thick and brushy, tipped with black, and far too animated to be merely an ornament.

Lisa's heart crawled toward her throat. She blinked her eyes rapidly, but the fox tail continued to wag as if it rightly belonged on the hind end of an old woman. Something new and fragile whispered inside Lisa's chest. It was light and tingly. Something akin to excitement, a feeling she'd long since given up for dead.

Without hesitating, Lisa stood. She eased her way through the seated drinkers, past bowed heads and slurping tourists, moving directly toward the teahouse doorway. When one of the servers waved at her to go back to her seat, she mumbled something about the restroom and sped her steps. Somehow, she knew the old woman would not wait for her, that the round hips were trundling once again up the slope, and that she was supposed to follow. And to hurry.

Lisa stepped into the crisp mountain air and breathed deeply, fully, for the first time since stepping onto the death-defying bridge. She trotted around the back of the teahouse, past the restrooms which stood alone a few yards off. Then she angled away across the slope, skipping like a fool and praying no one saw her. Or tried to stop her. The pathway waited, and beyond it, in the old woman's wake, something else waited too. Maybe it was the something she'd really come for. The *feeling* she'd climbed that gut-dropping path of terror in order to find.

And maybe it was nothing.

When she reached the zigzagging pathway, the old woman was nowhere to be seen. A tremble of doubt seized her, but Lisa shoved it aside. She clung to the thread of excitement as if it were her lifeline, her last chance. And she headed up the path, winding back and forth toward the top of the mountain, without looking back.

———

By the time she'd reached the place where she first saw the woman, her breath came in thin, wheezing gasps. The excitement which prodded her to take the path abated, and only a stubborn determination to see things through continued to move her feet. The way turned quickly rocky, and eventually, large projections of stone blotted out the view of teahouse and the rest of the world.

Lisa rounded one stone, at last, to find the woman sitting on a squat boulder. Her pot sat beside her, and her short arms were crossed over her chest.

"Took you long enough." Her voice came like dry leaves crunching underfoot.

"How?" Lisa bent forward, hands on thighs, and tried to breathe and speak at the same time. "How? So fast. Too steep and… you were carrying a heavy pot!"

The old woman only laughed, and when Lisa looked up at her, wagged her fluffy, fox tail against the rock.

"That's a neat trick," Lisa said, squinting at the odd appendage. "Where can I get one of those?"

"You wouldn't like it," the woman said merrily. "Fox is not your style."

"Isn't it?" Lisa stood, frowning, feeling like somehow, she'd just been insulted. Her day had gone sharply in the wrong direction, and she felt like she was owed more than derision. "What would you know about my style anyway?"

"I know you're lost." The woman turned suddenly serious, and her wrinkled eyes narrowed. "I know you came here looking for something, desperately hoping it would make you feel less adrift, less miserable."

Lisa opened her mouth to argue, but the woman's hand came up, snuffing her protest before it began.

"I know," she continued, "that you didn't like the tea."

Lisa stared at her for a long moment. Then she shook her head and tried to summon words that would explain the last six years of her life. "It wasn't that I didn't like it," she began. "I just thought it would be... more. I hoped it would... do more."

"You wanted it to grant a wish? To heal what ails you, perhaps?" The woman's eyes shone like flints. She was unmoving now, unflinching and somehow as solid as the stone she sat upon.

"I wanted it to make me feel *something*." Lisa let the statement free and felt lighter for it. "I wanted to enjoy it."

"Pleasure," the woman said. There was no judgement to her tone, no sign she thought this was an unworthy request.

Lisa still blushed and looked away. The very word, "pleasure," seemed like it belonged to a different world. She couldn't remember the last time she'd known what it meant. "I should go," she said.

"You tried the wrong tea."

"Excuse me?" Liza glared into that stony expression and crossed her arms over her breast. "I was only offered one kind of tea."

"Well," the woman reached out and stroked the pot she'd set down on the stone. "We can't just let anyone try the good stuff."

The way her fingers outlined the edge of her pot, reverently, tauntingly, made it quite clear what the vessel contained. Lisa asked anyway, aiming one finger at the pot and raising a skeptical eyebrow. "The good stuff?"

In answer, the fox-tailed woman only chuckled. Then she groaned and heaved herself to her feet. Tail still wagging madly, she lifted her heavy pot, turned, and headed for the nearest up-thrusting of stone, taking "the good stuff" with her.

Lisa followed. What else could she do with that promise hanging over them, with that strange tail taunting her? A tail she was beginning to believe wasn't artificial. Perhaps she'd stumbled into something genuine at last.

And perhaps she'd been given a hallucinogen.

Either way, she trailed obediently after the strange old woman, around a jutting of rock and straight to a dark crack in the mountain that could only be called a cave in the most technical of interpretations. It was more of a slit, as if the earth had given under the weight of all this stone and torn itself apart.

Despite the clear danger it presented, the old woman marched inside as if it were only a cottage door. She took her pot, her tail, and her cryptic words and vanished into the dark opening.

"Well, then." Lisa looked back one more time, then shrugged. "What choice do I have but to follow?"

Her first steps into the opening in the mountain felt dangerous, like she was about to leap off the bridge back beyond the teahouse. Her stomach tightened, and she clenched her hands at her sides. The slit opening made the passage seem smaller than it was, and warm light cast the scene beyond into a dance of orange and black. Light and shadow.

The cave itself opened up quickly. There were enormous shelves far against the back wall, lined with clay pots like the one the woman had brought. Closer to the mouth, a cooking fire flickered, as if camping out in a cave to make tea were the perfectly ordinary thing to do.

The old woman had already reached this, set down her pot, and produced a heavy iron kettle which she hung from a tripod over the flames.

"It smells like old straw in here." Lisa found a boulder with a slight hollow at the top beside the fire. She sat, found the surface more comfortable than she would have guessed. The whole inside of the cave was cozier than she'd imagined, and though the ceiling seemed to drift even farther away the further back in the cave you went, near the opening it made a curving arch above the cooking fire.

"What else?" The old woman had fished a handful of aged leaves from her pot and placed them reverently into a clay gaiwan. The water had already begun to boil, and the aroma of warm puerh drifted through the cave.

Lisa inhaled it, scrunching up her nose. "Something smoky. Maybe gunpowder."

"Close." The woman chuckled and mumbled something under her breath that sounded a great deal like brimstone.

"If you age it here," Lisa pointed toward the clay pots at the rear of the cave. "Where is it grown?"

"Here and there." The woman made a chant of it. "Hither and yon."

Suddenly, Lisa felt self-conscious. They hadn't even been properly introduced. It was as if everything had gone all topsy turvy from the moment she left the teahouse. "What's your name?" she asked.

"They call me Seelia."

The water was boiling again, and Seelia dipped a wooden ladle into the kettle hanging over her fire. She poured the liquid over her puerh, and the aroma shifted and thickened. It filled Lisa's head, a mix of dark berries and thick leather, of musty corners and mountain springs lined with old granite.

The cave softened around her, and she watched bemusedly as Seelia poured the contents of the gaiwan into two, impossibly small cups.

"How did you get a tail, Seelia?" she asked dreamily.

"Drink first." One of the cups was pressed into her hands. The cave walls danced with the fire's light, and the old woman's face took on an angular, pointed cast as she spoke. "Questions later."

Lisa lifted the cup to her lips and breathed in the vapors. Now, the tea smelled of odder things, vague, shifting memories of foods she'd tasted long ago. A cup of celebratory wine she'd drunk the night of her graduation. A thick, meaty stew her mother had made for her when she was sick. The faint, musky scent of her first, self-made orgasm.

"Drink." The woman's voice had a whine to it now, a feral edge that echoed away into the dark.

Lisa pressed the brew to her lips and sipped it, slurping just enough to aerate it as she'd been told back in the teahouse that seemed miles and centuries away suddenly.

It tasted of her memories.

The tea liquor filled her mouth, covering her tongue in the sweet, syrupy flavor of nostalgia and regret both. It was ripe plum and thick molasses. Seared peach and yeasty, homemade bread. She swallowed it with a moan, cringing when the old woman laughed.

"It tastes so good," Lisa said in her own defense.

"I think," the woman answered, "that is less about the tea than the drinker."

Lisa meant to argue, opened her mouth to say she'd had

nothing to do with it, that the tea was perfectly prepared, expertly aged, and likely came from ancient trees grown high in the very best terroir. What came out, however, was more akin to a rumble.

Her mouth felt odd, stretched out of shape and unwilling to obey her commands. She snapped it shut, reaching up and freezing mid-gesture at the sight of her hands. The spinning feeling increased at the view of her own skin, which was spawning row upon row of nubby blisters. Her color, too, was shifting, waxing reddish gold in the firelight.

Frantic, Lisa turned to the old woman, but the fox tail was waving a merry retreat, whisking from side to side as its owner scampered toward the cave mouth far faster than she'd trundled up the mountainside.

"Wait!" Lisa shouted, but the sound she made was nothing at all like words.

She stood quickly, staggering to one side as the cave shrank around her. The stone walls pressed in. The ceiling dropped. A sensation of vertigo gripped her, and she folded in half, clutching her middle just as the cloth of her shirt shredded and fell away.

Her body twisted of its own accord then, and Lisa's brain scurried from the truth. The cave had not shrunk in the least. It was her who grew. It was her who changed.

There was no pain to the transformation, no real struggle once she realized what was happening. The tea had made her far too mellow. Instead, she watched like a spectator as her clothing fell away, as she lifted and stretched, bones, flesh, and essence transforming into something wholly unlike herself. Her body elongated until she filled half the cave. Her limbs thickened, shifted position so that her substantial weight could be supported by four stout, muscular legs.

Her mind processed this as if watching from a distance. As if it were happening to someone else. When it was over, Lisa sat, admiring her new ruby skin, the flat, glassy scales which covered every inch of her aside from her long belly. Her underside was plated in trapezoidal golden shields which overlapped neatly but articulated enough that she could bend and twist. She was much longer than she should be, and behind her she sensed the weight and movement of a massive tail.

She reached back and snagged the thing, dragging it into view with hands that were scaled and knobby now. With fingers that ended in gleaming black claws.

The tail was broad and similarly scaled, studded along its crest with neat black spikes that seemed so out of character that she tugged on it good and hard to make certain it was truly attached. A twinge of discomfort proved the limb did, indeed, belong to her. She sniffed it, and found her face was now a long, draconic snout complete with two pairs of whiskers trailing away like snakes at the sides of her toothy mouth.

She didn't need them to know what she'd become. The word "dragon" had been circling her thoughts since she'd seen her tail. But something about the whiskers pushed her, at last, over the edge. She screamed, and the cave, the air, and the mountain beneath her, trembled.

When the echoes died, Lisa bent her long neck toward the slit opening, shuffled her newly shaped feet, and made a run for it. Her new body ran well, rolling like a wave as four short legs carried her to the exit. She burst free of the cave and slithered on her armored belly one full length down the mountain slope before catching herself on a rock, twining her massive tail around another and rearing up to catch her breath.

Her dragon eyes took in a world that was new as well. The mountain still took the same shape, the rocks poked through in the same positions, and far down the slope the little teahouse still wafted a thread of smoke into the air. But the colors had gone electric. The greens were neon bright. The sun burned like an ember on the low end of an azure sky, and Lisa thought she could see the stars, even through the daylight.

She could not see, she realized, the old woman. When her dragon eyes raked the nearby slope, the only movement she caught was a small streak of red as some much smaller animal took cover behind a nearby stone. Her brain suggested it was a fox and nothing more.

It refused, too, to process what had happened to her. For a long moment Lisa simply posed there, twining between the stones and looking at the new, brighter world around her.

It was glorious, amplified and quivering with potential. Beautiful. Terrifying.

Lisa's dragon gaze landed on the tiny teahouse, a building she'd fit easily inside only moments ago. Despite her long trek up the slope, it looked close now, a few steps away. So near that she might easily be spotted should someone look in the wrong direction.

The right direction to spy an enormous dragon.

A wave of panic seized her, rippling from her whiskered snout all the way through her lithe body and down her extensive, spiked tail. What would happen to her now? Where could she possibly hide? With a howl that made the tiny rocks below here rattle, Liza turned back toward the cave and the top of the mountain. She tensed her long body and sprang away, slithering like a massive, footed snake up the side of the peak, lashing her tail behind her and letting her serpentine whiskers trail along at her sides. She ran blindly, ran up and away, and only once, where her breath hitched in her massive throat, did she hear the sharp, yipping of the fox.

It called to her, she knew, but she had no answer. Her only thought was to escape. Her only pathway led up into the peaks where the wisps of thin fog hid the dips and valleys, and where age-pocked stones poked through the earth, fringed in glowing green moss.

45

When her panic eventually faded, Lisa settled into a cleft between the uppermost peaks. She'd circled the stones here many times in her frenzy, and though her heart had suffered for it, the long run had given her time to settle into her new shape. The tail, it turned out, was useful for leverage and for balancing during tight turns. Her talon claws gripped both stone and ground expertly, allowing her to throw her body forward at incredible speeds. And though she hadn't dared attempt flying, there had been moments where she certainly seemed to skim the mountainside as though the air itself carried her along.

A stray thought appeared inside her, whispering, "wind dragon." Lisa brushed it aside as something to ponder later. She lay on her back between the spiky stones, nestled on deep, neon moss, and pondered instead the most surprising feature of her new body: her whiskers.

During her run, she'd been far too frightened to pay them much attention. Only a vague awareness that they were doing something reached her, a subtle knowing which way to turn just before she needed to act. Now that she lay still, the waving tendrils continued to move, tapping at the stones and moss around her and sending small reports to her brain: soft, warm, hard, and cool. Clearly, they were more than ornamentation, and Lisa experimented with waving them about.

With a little concentration, she could move each whisker independently of the other, and she scrunched up her muzzle and tried tapping them along the ground at her sides. Small tingles of sensation relayed back to her along the rippling strands. Her brain interpreted soft, warm moss, but her body shivered at the electricity of each response.

She looked to the sides, then to the sky overhead. She was sheltered here, alone and unobserved. With a deep breath, Lisa closed her eyes and gently tapped a whisker against her own belly.

Instantly, her long spine arched in response. Electric sensation washed out from the contact, and her breath gusted free in a long, audible growl. Her new limbs were short, and while they supported her long body, they were unable to reach along its full length. The whiskers, however, not only trailed all the way to her tail tip, they were like enormous nerves in their own rights. Both the feather light caress of the whisker against her scales and the tingling sensation of her smooth shape against her whisker happened simultaneously, and the result was so pleasurable that her forked, dragon tongue slid freely from her lips, fluttering to release the tension.

She lay, stretched out and shivering for one deep, resolute inhale then, using both whiskers at once, began to tentatively explore her new body. At first, she restricted herself to short, gentle taps, adjusting to the flood of sensation each touch delivered. When she'd been able to endure the pleasure without voicing it aloud, she grew braver, dragging the tips of her long sensors over the surface of her wide belly scales. At the place where her tail met the rest of her body, a wide slit nestled just behind her rear legs. Gently, hesitantly, Lisa trailed the tip of a whisker across the opening.

Her body shuddered in response. She writhed between the stones, tearing up moss and thrashing her long, studded tail. Nothing her human body had ever felt, even before her recent apathy, could compare to the charged, bone deep waves of pleasure zinging through her now. Her scales refracted each twitch of her nerves, amplifying everything she felt just as her eyes had intensified the view.

Each touch of her whiskers drew the pleasure higher. She let them linger, dancing across her belly, and across the slit. Twisting and shivering, Lisa explored her new form with her long tendrils, and as the touches grew more intimate, her breath turned shallow, rapid. The increasing pleasure made her bolder, and she let the tip of one whisker and then the other tease its way into the opening in her scales. The sky overhead seemed to tremble and spin. She closed her eyes against the shifting of the world and let her building tension out in a long, rumbling moan.

The orgasm came suddenly, sharp as the spikes along her own tail and long as the trailing whiskers. Lisa roared through each spasm, arching again so that her long, serpentine body lifted from the ground, rippling from snout to tail. There was no silencing her pleasure now. Wave after wave swept through her, shook her, and drove her scaled length even higher, her voice even louder.

Her thoughts fogged over. Only her body and the pleasure mattered. Even when it peaked, and the sensations seemed to tear her apart, she leaned into it, let it shatter and reform her until she lost consciousness.

Lisa had no idea how long she was out, but when she came to, she was human once again, small and pale and lying on her back in the center of a wide vale. Shaky and weeping, she reached her hands way out to the sides, drew her fingers through soft moss, and smiled easily for the first time in too many months to count.

As she drifted in the aftermath, she heard only the beating of the heart inside her chest. She felt only warmth and contentment and the pillowy earth beneath her. Still, the memory of sensations too big for her existence proved that she still *could* feel. That there was still something wild and passionate alive inside her. It proved she had not climbed a mountain for nothing.

But she had climbed a mountain. As her head cleared and lucidity returned, Lisa realized she was no longer a dragon. She was very small, very naked, and very human, and she was going to have to find her way back down that mountain somehow.

It took her the rest of the day. By the time she limped into sight of the little tea house, her body ached. All traces of pleasure had left her, and she carried instead a building fury. She'd been poisoned, most likely, drugged by a fox woman with some kind of magical tea. Delicious perhaps, but definitely laced with something.

Lisa glared down at the teahouse, a short square shape in the dusky light. The sun was sneaking to rest behind the lowest peaks, and the whole mountain-scape had been painted deep umber and chill indigo. Worse than the dark was the fact that no smoke drifted from the teahouse's chimney. No movement or sign of either employees or tourists.

She was certain they'd all taken the path back to the gift shop and parking area. She'd paid good money for her ticket, and they'd just left her here on the mountainside to freeze to death? The thought tore a sharp laugh from her throat. She was a dragon, or she had been for a delicious moment. Was freezing even possible? She squinted downslope, trying to see the world as it had been, painted in electric color and full of beauty.

To her surprise, a flicker of something red appeared on the slope before her. It danced between the stones, and as she watched it, the scent of fire and tea reached her. The cave. The fox woman. Even as she thought it, her naked body turned. The red blur clarified into the darting form of the fox. It led the way at an angle, back upslope toward the crevice cave, and Lisa followed eagerly. Her rage fading in the memory of smoky tea and a hot fire.

When she reached the cleft, smoke already billowed from the entrance. Lisa inhaled deeply, closed her eyes, and for a single breath felt the tingle of her whiskers against her scales again. A sharp crack from the fire inside drew her back to the moment. The sky had grown dark, and the cave mouth glowed softly against its mountain now.

Lisa marched forward, walking easily into an opening that had been barely large enough for her as a dragon. She approached the cooking fire and was not surprised in the least to see the old woman standing next to it, poking a long metal barb into the embers and wagging her foxy tail. As Lisa entered, one withered arm pointed to a thick blanket draped over the nearby boulder.

Lisa squinted at Seelie's outfit, a tan blouse and pale green skirt. "I suppose you keep a stash of clothes on hand up here?"

In answer, the old woman only giggled and pointed again.

"Your tea turned me into a dragon," Lisa said, trying to sound as matter of fact as possible. She stepped forward, snatched up the blanket, and plopped without ceremony onto the stone seat, wrapping the fire-heated wool around her shivering body.

The old woman grunted at her, didn't look up. "You turned yourself into a dragon," she said. "The tea only helped you relax enough to do it."

Lisa leaned toward the fire. "Does that mean I can do it again? Change whenever I want?"

"Eventually." A hint of laughter flavored Seelia's voice. A light entered her eyes that did not come from the flames' reflection. "I take it you enjoyed yourself?"

Heat slithered across Lisa's skin. The memory surfaced again, faint but unmistakable. Pleasure. Did the old woman know about *that*? She changed the subject quickly.

"You're a fox, aren't you?"

"That is one word for what I am," Seelia answered. "There are many more, and for you as well should you decide to stay and learn."

There was no question in the woman's tone. It was merely a statement, an offer without any attempt to sway the recipient one way or the other. As if to prove how little she cared, Seelia gave the fire another good poke and turned toward the cauldron waiting beside the flames.

"You'd teach me how to be a dragon?" Lisa asked.

"Didn't I just tell you?" Seelia stood and turned over one shoulder, narrowing her eyes into wrinkled slits. "You don't have to learn that. You just have to relax."

"But you said…" Lisa frowned and rewound the conversation. "What am I supposed to learn, then?"

"Tea," Seelia said. "If you're to earn your keep, that is. The leaf must be tended, the fire stoked, the brew perfected."

"You want me to learn to make tea?" Lisa sat back, looked over their heads at the vault of stone. She remembered the taste of Seelia's puerh, too, and she imagined herself in dragon form, curled up between the fire and the racks of stored leaf. She imagined brewing the good stuff, here in the cave, while the monks served tourists the thin, uninteresting brew below.

She imagined her life back home. Brent. The tedium and the emptiness. The numb acceptance that this was all there was.

"What do *you* want?" Seelia asked softly.

"More." Lisa stared into the fire and felt as if her whiskers danced along her serpentine body. "I want more."

"Good." The fox-woman spun back to the fire, faced her directly and let the movement of her tail announce her pleasure. "That settles things nicely."

Did it? Lisa found herself nodding, relaxing until she could feel the dragon in her, the serpent lurking just beneath her skin. The fire warmed her outside, but it was the memory of her other body that kept her heart steady, its beat dancing in time to the flames. Soon she would change again, feel again. At the moment, she was content to sit with Seelia and see what came next.

"For now," the old woman announced as if she'd read Lisa's

mind. She clapped her hands together, wagged her tail, and said, "Let's make some tea."

WEALTH OF THE HOLD

MOG MOOGLE

Blue scales shimmered as the drake held together the void essence with his thoughts. The wingless beast tapped into his primal bond with the planes, pulling its energy to him and willing it into being. His muscles rippled from the strain and a rumbling growl from deep within redirected the discomfort of the ordeal.

He was almost to exhaustion when the sharp focus flashed through his mind and the black form snapped into a silver sphere. Relief flowed through his body as he expelled his tension with a sigh.

"Good, Ardyn," bellowed a red dragon. The great wyrm was three times larger than the drake. "You have taken to plane manipulation well, for a *wingless*."

The dragon elder's emphasis on wingless made room in Ardyn's occupied mind for annoyance. "Thank you, *master*." The drake mimicked the dragon's tone in his response.

"Release the void form," he instructed with no hint of emotion from the pupil's disrespect.

Ardyn drew a deep breath and let the essence of the living plane penetrate his spirit. In his mind, the form began to deconstruct and shift out of their reality. In the living world, it mirrored the drake's will and slipped away. When the void had returned, Ardyn opened his eyes and rocked his head to shake out the fatigue.

"You may yet be worthy of your holding, Ardyn."

"A river and stretch of desolate coast is hardly a holding, Master Chrysos. No mines for ores or gems like the Great Wyrm holds of the north."

"A perfect hold for a lesser wyrm." The edges of his jaws curled in an amused grin. "The hold has been unproductive for two ages of drakes. Your predecessors would mutter on about some notion that they produced wealth despite producing none. You will correct that and contribute to the power of all wyrms." The dragon elder bound from the earth and took flight. Mighty gusts shook the trees and stirred the pine needles. "Your next lesson will be in the glades."

Ardyn huffed and shook off the dirt and dead flora as his master flew away. "I'll be there as fast as my *lesser* legs can carry me, you winged nuisance."

Ardyn bent around the evergreens of the thick boreal forest. His slender frame made navigating overland in the mountains and forests less difficult. Still, the drake cursed his lack of flight. When he breached into the clearing, the red dragon sat atop a hillock with his tail sweeping in irritation.

"Your stealth is lacking," Chrysos said.

Ardyn furrowed his eyeridges. *And your putrid scent makes it impossible for you,* he thought, but spoke nothing. The drake stopped at the base of the rise and watched the dragon lift his forepaw. A stag was pinned underneath it, and Chrysos kept enough pressure on the creature that it could not flee.

"Venture your mind to the void realm and find this creature's echo there. Reach into the mind of the lower beast," Chrysos instructed. "Calm it and command it. This will be how you guide those who serve your holding."

"How will commanding a simple creature like this guide the strong-willed and stubborn two-legged folk?"

"They are lower beasts themselves. Just ones that use implements to build their nests and hunt their prey. You will command their elder, and their elder will command his clutch."

The drake cocked his head as he looked at the terrified cervine. Ardyn drew a deep breath and closed his eyes. The world around him faded to darkness as he reached toward the animal with his senses. A gradual spark in the black began to form.

A wispy mist gathered in hues of reds, yellows, and oranges to form the shape of the stag. Ardyn bridged the darkness with the spirit of the animal and melded it with his own. Threads of the vibrant luminescent hues in his mind's eye flowed out from the stack and back to the drake until they met in the middle and wove together.

The fear bled into Ardyn along the entwined bond. And then the pain drew from the creature. The strong will, greater size, and superior spirit of the wyrm absorbed and dissipated it without stress or strain. Along the mist rope in the darkness, hues of blues and greens flowed from the drake. Calm and serenity wrapped around the deer and fused with his spirit.

When Ardyn severed the bond and opened his eyes, he watched Chrysos lift his leg and free the stag. It rose to its feet and began to graze as if it was never captive by the dragon. "The spirit link is far easier than manipulating the void, master."

"Lesser minds are far more simple than realms beyond the living one, Ardyn. The only difficulty is reaching that realm they cannot see." The dragon bent his neck down and scooped the deer in his maw, snapping it shut and swallowing it whole. When it was secure in his stomach, he looked back at the drake.

"You have been taught the ways of the elders. You have all you need to rule your lessers, save wisdom. Wisdom, alas, cannot be taught.

"Increase the wealth of your hold, and you will increase your powers. Your tribute to the great holds will make all our kind more powerful." Chrysos turned away from his pupil and looked toward the distant mountain haloed in clouds. "When the third moon has waned and waxed a full cycle, I will return to check on your progress as Lord Holder."

Ardyn rolled his eyes as his master took flight. "I *eagerly* await your assessment." He turned toward the river and began his trek to the coast.

Ardyn saw white smoke rising from several places above the trees. He moved along the river bank until he came out of the forest. The sight was strange and unnatural. The clearing was filled with stumps that had clean breaks near the base. Mighty trunks had fallen from their roots with such precision that Ardyn could clearly see the rings.

Across the clearing, where the river met the coast, he saw former trees stacked and arranged in squares with angled splinters atop them. Stacked stone spires protruded from most of them, and some of the spires wafted white smoke from their tops. The drake approached closer to the stacked trees, smelling the air to sense what he may walking into.

Destroyed pine, fire smoke, burning fish; it all lingered in ways that were foreign to Ardyn. He could see the strange creatures moving among the stacked dead trees. The ground they paced was barren from their many treks over the same path. One of the strange creatures took notice of him and pointed while calling to everyone around.

He passed the outermost pile of trees as the crowd gathered.

The two-legged animals with slick fur, long tails, and prominent whiskers looked up at him. They all had at least one stone around their necks, bound by twine or leather thongs. Most stood as high as his shoulder. Others—hatchlings Ardyn guessed—stood various heights.

"River Guardian," the creature that first pointed at Ardyn said. "Welcome to our village. We are honored to have you among us."

"My name is Ardyn," the drake said with a proud tone. He looked at the one that had spoken to him and at the strange decorations of river stones and muscle shells that he wore. They were more numerous than the others by far. "You may address me as master."

"Master Ardyn, the River Guardian," the crowd echoed in unison.

"Please, Master," the decorated creature said, "allow me to show you to the dais. We have gathered offerings for you."

Ardyn looked the crowd over one last time before following the lesser. "I am told the holdings aren't very wealthy?"

"Oh no, Master. We have great bounties of fish; fresh and sea. The hold, *your* hold, spans from the river to the southern canyons and back to the shores of the Southmues sea. There is no better fishing in the land." The creature's prideful expression shifted when he saw his unimpressed master. "Forgive me, I'm Glash, chief of the Otterkyne tribe, Stoneshoals. I'm your humble servant."

"I assume by *chief*, you mean elder?" Ardyn said as he looked at the piles of trees. Some of the Otterkyne would look out of holes cut in the logs as he passed them. "These stacks of dead pines are your nests?"

"Yes, Master. Our homes. They shelter us from the winters."

"You have fur to shelter you from winter. Do you mean to protect your eggs?"

Glash laughed, but stopped when he saw the annoyed stare

of the drake. "No, Master. We do not lay eggs like the dragon lords. We birth our young like the lower beasts of the forest. Surely you have seen this?"

"My master instructed me to guide this hold, not study unusual birthing rituals."

Glash nodded then shook his head. "Of course, Master. Forgive me." He looked back to the drake. "Our guardian passed from the world two moons ago. We are so happy to receive you before the fertility festival, Master. We have never had to conduct one without a guardian."

"Fertility festival?"

"Yes, Master. This very night, the first new moon of spring, we conduct our rituals to honor our dragon lords and ask for blessings for the spawning, and fertility of our own tribe." Glash stopped and looked up at Ardyn with concern. "Forgive the question, Master, but you can conduct the ritual, can't you?"

"I can manipulate the planes of the living and dead," Ardyn snapped. "I'm certain this primitive ritual your clutch has is simplistic compared to the abilities of the wyrms."

Glash looked relieved, but his gaze lingered for a moment before leading the drake on. "I mean no offense, of course. It's just we depend on the festival for our bounty."

In the center of the village, a stacked stone platform sat in the middle of the intersections of barren earth. Lining the steps around it were baskets of fish and berries. The chief extended his paw toward it. "Your dais, Master."

Ardyn walked to the steps and looked over the structure the Otterkyne had built to honor their guardian. In the middle of it, the stones sagged in a shallow depression from years of use by wyrms as a bed. "This seems modest for a lord of a hold."

"I'm sorry, Master. But, the priestess will attend to you shortly. I will send her immediately. Let her know what you require, and we will see to it."

Ardyn bypassed the small steps built for the lesser creatures and mounted the platform. The small rise in elevation wasn't the commanding throne he had expected. The daises of the dragons towered high, were lined with riches and sacrifices. Ardyn snorted as he looked at his hoard of berries and fish.

However, the sight of them reminded him that he had been hungry since his master had eaten the stag. He sniffed at one of the small baskets. Most of the water creatures had been butchered and much of the edible pieces discarded. Not a single bone, scale, or organ remained. Despite that, Ardyn opened his muzzle and wrapped his forked tongue around the entire basket. With a few chomps, he devoured the wicker and fish. Afterward, he settled in the indented stone and coiled up, letting the fatigue of the day and the trip catch him. Sleep came quick.

Ardyn sensed something near him. Unbidden ethereal sensations had never come from lower creatures. The presence was warm, and the spirit full of blues and purples. His eyes snapped open. An Otterkyne was on her knees in front of his muzzle. The stature, curves, and scent indicated she was female.

Ardyn drew his head back and looked down at her curiously. Even outside of sleep where he was closer to a spiritual realm, a faint aura of her spirit lingered. It made his scales tingle with a sensations. Unease crawled from the depths of his mind and took hold in his spine.

Unlike the others he had seen, her fur was draped in white cloth. She wore a single stone flanked by muscle shells on either side. His attention was drawn to her head, where she wore wires of gold, twisted in designs. It was the first sign of wealth beyond food he had seen in the hold.

Her paws were upturned and her eyes were closed. She mumbled in a singsong way. The female's eyes opened when the drake growled, but she never lost her soft expression. "Master, I hope I didn't wake you." She lowered her paws and rest them on her thighs. "My name is Beh'ti. I serve the Great Wyrms. I am honored their avatar is among us once more."

"What is your role in this service?" he asked as he lifted his head and looked down at her.

"Anything you require, Master. We all serve the Great Wyrms for their blessings and protections. I aid the others in the village on that path."

"I see." Ardyn sighed and furrowed his brow. "I would like a more appropriate dais, and offerings of gems."

"Forgive me, Master, but we have no mines in the hold."

"Then barter your fish."

Beh'ti blinked in surprise, but bowed her head in respect. "Of course, Master. As you wish." She rose to her feet and backed down the dais. "Would you like help to prepare for the ritual, Master?"

"I find the notion of this ritual distasteful. I would be better served by being elevated to a station appropriate to your guardian and Master." He raised his eyeridge as he looked down at the creature. "You gather wealth and I protect it. Including, you and your brood."

"You are very different from out last guardian, master. I shall have to consult the runes to see which aspect of them you represent. I'll start with avarice."

Ardyn uncoiled and stood up, roared, and whipped his tail against the dais with a crack. "Do you dare to disrespect me?"

The priestess didn't flinch at the display. Her expression still warm as she looked at her lord. "No, my Master. We worship all aspects of the wryms. I will return at dusk to begin the ritual."

Ardyn growled as the Otterkyne turned away from him. His eyes scanned the village. As they did, the Otterkyne that had stopped to marvel at his display hastily went back to their work, averting their eyes from him.

The drake extended his tongue and chomped another basket of fish from the steps, then curled up and went back to sleep.

———

Blues, purples, greens, pinks, and a few yellows wisped around Ardyn's perception. The forms gathered around him in the darkness. Then the most vibrant of them all approached him and stopped at the top of the dais.

Ardyn opened his eyes to see the priestess facing away from him, looking over the crowd of the village gathering closer. He noticed no hatchlings and no elderly. However, he did see Glash ascend the steps and stand beside near Beh'ti.

Something was different about the growing crowd. His subconscious perception pulled at his feelings, demanding to reach out with a spiritual thread. Out of curiosity, he closed his eyes and let the living realm fade. The colors of the crowd began to change. They gradually became deep violet. He returned his focus to the living world to see the Otterkyne lifting their paws. They mumbled a chant as the priestess had in melodic nonsense.

"On this, the darkest night of the newest day," Beh'ti called out over the crowd, "we call out to our guardian to grant us a fruitful year. We ask our nets be full, our hearths warm, and our loins fruitful, that we may continue in his service and the service of the wyrms." She turned around to the drake. "Master Ardyn, we beg of you these things. Please grant us your wisdom, protection, and succor."

Ardyn rose from his bed and looked at the strange and silly creatures. Despite his blustering and refusal at the priestess' offer to assist him in preparing, he didn't know what to do. His pride would never allow him to admit he had no way to give them what they asked. The priestess looked at him expectantly and he huffed in response.

Beh'ti blinked as she pushed her paws up in a small pumping motion. After a few moments of staring at the drake, she sighed and shook her head. "Form your wyrm-bond with me," she whispered, "so that we may conduct the ritual."

Ardyn grumbled disapprovingly but recalled his earlier lesson. The living world started to fade away and the hues of the Otterkyne that he had noticed as he woke became vibrant. The sounds of the village, surrounding woods, and river faded then stilled. He started to bow his head as his eyes instinctively closed.

The void and blackness surrounded him, and a shimmering violet form brighter than the noon sun stood before him. His bond reached to the priestess and the link formed almost without effort. Then the bonds leapt from the more dim forms in the crowd to her, and they grew as radiant.

Sensations flooded the drake he had never experienced and his heart began to race. Fear overtook him at the strange emotions. Heat rushed through his body and his heart beat fast. Contempt, disgust, and antipathy toward lower lifeforms was pushed back and ground out by a deep care and affection for him. He had never experienced that kind of warmth and love being a lesser among wyrms.

In the midst of it, he was drawn to the priestess. He looked at her and spoke but the words vanished in the void. Recalling the lesson earlier in the day and the words of Chrysos about controlling the elder, he focused on her and exerted his will. Her form in the void grew sharp and Ardyn could see her expression shift from contented concentration to a mild surprise and amusement.

"Oh," she said as she stepped toward him in the void. "So, the power you seek is dominance?" Beh'ti laughed as all forms faded away but hers. "Our avatar of avarice seeks control to grow his strength and rival the dragons atop their hoards of gems, crafts, livestock, and the very livelihoods of those that labor for them?"

Ardyn looked around for the others, but everything was gone save for her presence and his. Even the emotion and sensation were absent. "How can a lesser being manipulate the void and the spirit," he asked, relieved his words once more had substance.

"Oh, Master," Beh'ti chuckled again as her bright purple mist form waved the question away. "You've been taught that wealth is material. This notion is especially absurd when the power you wield is by its very nature immaterial." She stopped in front of Ardyn and lifted her arms to his muzzle. Her paws stroked along his spiritual threads. "You want wealth? We can show you riches greater than any dragon, drake, wyrm, or wyvern could ever dream."

The tingling sensations rushed back through Ardyn's body. The fear made itself known again, but it was tempered by something else among it. Curiosity.

"Is that your desire, Master?"

Ardyn shivered and the hues of the fear reverberated from his form and fell away in mists into the black. "Yes."

Beh'ti's reply was a warm smile.

Ardyn drew back to the living world as quick as he could, but the bond felt stronger there. Though it was invisible, he could feel it pulse, grow, and strengthen by the second. Intense feelings of desire for the gathering lingered, and he wanted nothing more than to be in and among the tribe.

Beh'ti lowered her arms, looking very pleased with the outcome of the bond. Ardyn saw her touch the chief on the shoulder through his half-dazed state. Glash looked at her for a moment while she spoke something unheard by the drake's overwhelmed senses. He moved to the drake and put his paws on Ardyn's neck. The touch helped to sooth him, but some fear still lingered.

"Master, reach out to us," Glash said in a tone that was as soft and warm as the priestess herself.

"I don't—" he began, but his own body quaking and nervous head shaking cut off his speech.

"We're all here for you, let us in."

Ardyn felt the living world fade. He had no control; it was pure reflex. The bond between himself and Beh'ti widened. The narrow strand became a woven rope. Deep violet souls of the Otterkyne wrapped around it and Ardyn's own blue spirit trickled toward them.

There was a sudden familiarity with everyone in the crowd. Ardyn knew them, their wants, desires, and their memories. He felt all the good of growing up in a clutch with parents that cared beyond hatching. New words came to him for this; childhood and family. His family was the two-legged river creatures, and his childhood was their loving and warm care.

The crowd of Otterkyne-like figures began to shift in his mind's eye. Warm mists of the bond flowed around them and wrapped in bound and woven rings against their bodies. It shifted their purples into the hues of Ardyn's spirit form, mixing between the intense singular of the Otterkyne purple and the more timid reds and yellows of the drake.

Ardyn's spirit entangled around them like smoke, gathering as it grew thick and took shape. They began melding with the spirits of the Otterkyne and their forms shaped into draconic outlines. They rippled and shimmered as they filled in with Ardyn's bond. The core purple resonated out and blended with the more pale of the yellow and red.

The Otterkyne stood around him, spirt forms with horns jutting from eye-ridges, wide wings, and the toned powerful muscle and sinew beneath rippling with as much pride as any of the great dragons atop their hordes. Dullness in Ardyn's spirit bond brightened by their own beamed brilliant and noble.

Simultaneously, he saw himself as them, a two-legged otter. He embraced his mate and kin while the fire wafted smoke up the chimney. He broke bread and ate dried fish in the winter. He swam in the fresh water of the river with a fishing spear and ventured deep into the salt bay to snare the larger aquatic bounties. He felt love of hearth and home, and lust for his mates.

His muscles rippled beneath his scales, and they shimmered with his power. The void of black between the bondmates flashed brilliant white. The spirits of he and his Otterkyne tribe linked together as one spirit. They were as wyrmkind, just as he was of them.

Ardyn felt Glash pressing his fur against his scales. Waves of pleasure and euphoria rushed through his body, and the heat in his loins burned with desire and need. His genital slit parted and his ridged member met the night air. "What's happening," he asked as his eyes rolled back and his legs gave out.

Glash lowered to the dais with Ardyn. The otter rubbed along the drake's scales with his paws. His short muzzle and button nose nuzzled the drake's neck. With a guiding nudge, Ardyn rolled onto his back. He climbed atop the wyrm and held out one paw.

Beh'ti took it and lifted herself up. She pushed the white fabric from her shoulders and it fluttered to the stone floor. Her muzzle pressed against Glash's and their tongues met as their bodies pressed tightly against one another and the drake below them.

Ardyn didn't know why, but he felt an overwhelming need to be close to the two. He craned his neck and nuzzled up the priestess' back, feeling her soft and warm fur and delicate curves. Then over to the chief and up his back, feeling the muscle tone of his labor-filled days. They felt the same as the soft scales of a fertile wrym eager for clutch. The scents of their mixed arousal flooded into his nostrils, and his draconic penis leaked clear lubricant from its tip.

The sensation wasn't limited to the two straddling him. He wanted the same closeness with everyone whom he had bonded. Happiness filled every corner of his spirit when the entire crowd began to climb the dais and move as close to the drake as they could. He wasn't sure if he had beckoned them, or if they had just felt the same desire and moved to him on their own.

Dozens of Otterkyne surrounded him. Their paws, tails, muzzles, and tongues all over his body and each others'. Ardyn felt superior to none of them, and equal to them all. Every desire and need was shared with the crowd.

Then, he felt an Otterkyne pair slide into a coupling. He blinked at the sensations. He could feel the tender and slow advance of the male's penis inside the warm folds of his mate; he could feel the walls of her vagina expand as her lover went deeper into her. Jinu was his name, and Soh'la hers.

Ardyn had not seen either of them before the ritual, but he knew everything about them. He felt everything they felt. He loved them as deeply as they loved each other. And, one-by-one, the process repeated. Each act of love, each touch, each breath, each moan; it was happening to him and with him.

In the throes of everything, he felt the thick fur on his body as if it were his own scales. He wore it as if he had never lacked it. In turn, the Otterkyn around him were as powerful and graceful as any drake. When he closed his eyes, he saw the forms of the two-legged folk as drake wyrms in all their wonderous varieties of colors. Green, gold, red, bronze, and black drakes coupled in their draconic mating. At the same time, he saw them—and himself—as the small creatures breeding in their own ways.

Glash and Beh'ti made love on his stomach, their tails wrapping the ridged drake's erection as they thrust their bodies against one another. Ardyn moved his head around to every Otterkyne he could reach, nuzzling and licking them to share his affection and love. The warmth covered them like the sun in a meadow. The black void was absent entirely, replaced by the white bliss in a realm he never knew existed. Wyrms and

Otterkyne were mixed, intertwined, and simultaneous in this realm of pure pleasure, love, and ecstasy.

The multitude of warm and inviting passages wrapped around his draconic ridges were as intense and equally numerous as the smooth mammalian shafts sliding into his wet and welcoming folds. Ardyn grunted as he thrust into his receptive lovers and moaned as he bucked back and received the thrusts. The need to sire the new generation spread from him to every male in the group, and the need to conceive emanated from every female back to him. As with everything in the process, it was mutual and equal.

They felt their loins tighten and their climax draw close. They were at their limit and moaned as orgasm wracked them. And it crescendoed loud and long. They seeded one another, building the next generation of their tribe to serve one another. The shared afterglow of them filled their heart, and the warmth of their touch wrapped around them.

The crimson faded to violet, then to greens, blues, and purples. Adryn opened his eyes, covered in his own draconic seed and his tribe. He nuzzled a few of the sleeping Otterkyne around him, happy to love and be loved by his clan.

It was the new moon. Ardyn was disappointed to know that it would be ten more before he could head the fertility festival again. But he was very happy to see his family growing. The new mothers would be birthing his sons and daughters in the fall. The drake couldn't see the Otterkyne as anything but that. Even those that could not participate in the ritual were his family, for all in the tribe were family.

The harness over his back had been woven from sturdy fibers, and it secured three trunks of the evergreens on each side. Beside him was Soh'la. Her belly did not yet show her pregnancy, but he knew of the two Otterkyne that were growing inside her. When he stopped at her home, he eased down and slipped out from under the harness lashings. The new addition for the twins was only one of a dozen being added to the cabins around the village.

"Work goes so much faster with our guardian assisting, Master," Soh'la told him as she looked over the stack of logs.

"Soh'la please," the drake began, "how many times must I insist you call me Ardyn?"

"This once more, at least." She giggled and waved her paw dismissively as her mate climbed down from the roof and approached them.

Jinu looked them both over and smiled. "We didn't have this kind of bond with our last guardian. You're as much Otterkyne as any of us."

"And," Soh'la added, "as much our children's father as Jinu."

The edges of Ardyn's muzzle curled up as his eye ridges raised, beaming proudly at the couple before giving Soh'la 's belly a gentle rub with his snout. His perception picked up something, though. Something not of his tribe. He looked skyward to see a red dragon descending. He looked familiar in a way, but it was like looking across a great distance at a memory. "Excuse me," he said as he walked to where the dragon was descending.

"Ardyn," the beast said as he landed in front of where the dais used to be. "I have come to examine your progress in the stewardship of this holding."

"I see. All goes well, the hold is rich, our nets are full, our hearths are warm, and our loins are fruitful."

The dragon huffed as he looked at the common house where the dais once stood. "Where is the offering stone? Why are the offerings not laid out for all to see?"

"They are," Ardyn said as he looked at the common house. "All share with one another, all love one another, and our hold is the wealthiest in the land." Ardyn smiled at the puzzled expression on the dragon's face. "You see, we lack the mines, gems, and gold, but we have our tribe."

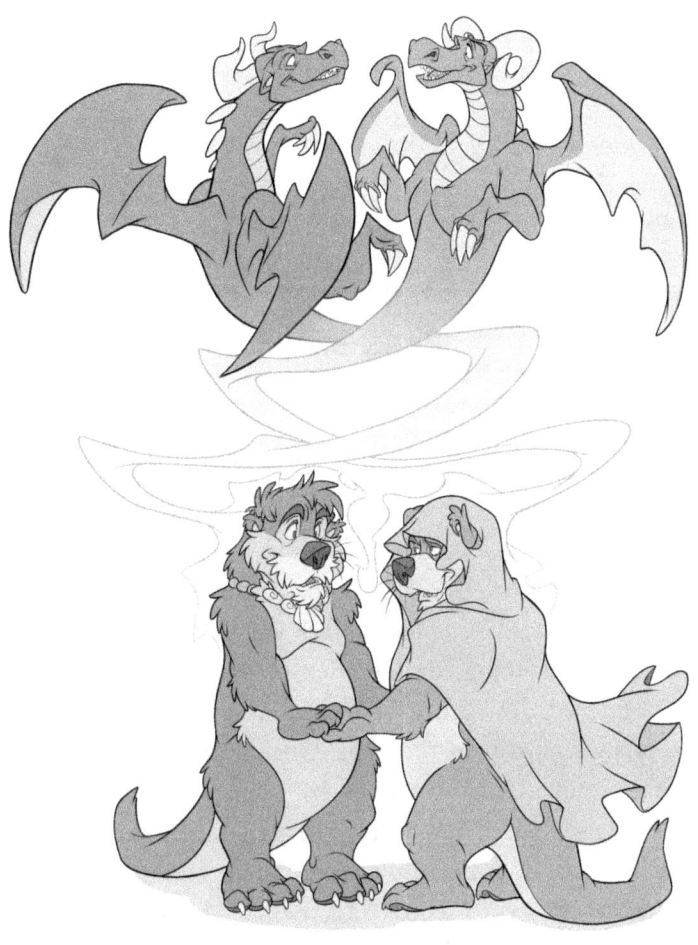

THE MAGIC OF THE HOARD

DARK END

There was not much for Kaslin to do but watch as the fox picked the final lock, one large black ear pressed to the wood and iron and listening for the click of tumblers, so the wolf mage pondered the nature of magic. Magic had changed its source many times over the eons. Once, magic resided in the land itself, pulled from leylines by primordial sorcerers to perform grand feats. Then, it came to reside in blood and bone, and the era was dominated by necromancers and hemoturges. Now, mostly, it was in words and spells, requiring mages like Kaslin to devote their time to study for years on end. Magic had often been compared to a raging river: at first it was powerful and cut a wide swath through the earth, but then it would weaken and thin into a calm stream. These days, rare was the leyline that could power more than a cantrip, and necromancers were mere passing nuisances, who could do little more than animate a finger. Even Kaslin's own spells felt weaker than when he had first taken up his studies. It worried him.

Porte's tongue slipped out of the front of his muzzle in lock-picking concentration as Kaslin sighed. The mage knew this process required focus, but the fox had been at it for over an hour.

Behind them, Olken, the taciturn badger who had accompanied them, gave out a soft, "Hmmph." It was his catch-all expression: agreement, disagreement, annoyance, sympathy, stoicism, excitement could all be related in that one vocalization. This one meant impatience.

Porte glared at his companions for daring to make a noise during this delicate task.

Kaslin held up a hand and the badger shrugged and lapsed back into silence.

Keeping the peace was necessary. All three of them had been necessary to make it past the traps, pitfalls, and seals that had barred their way through a mile of twisting turning caverns: the badger's raw strength, the fox's dexterous hands, and the wolf's arcane knowledge. Kaslin had never heard of such an elaborate defense. Not even the tombs of ancient necromancers were as securely guarded as this.

But if the mage's estimations were right, this door should be the last obstacle. He started to tap his foot and then, realizing the noise it was making, restrained himself to tapping only one solitary toe.

He was trying to hide his worry. He had labored many years in the towers of magecraft to learn the arts, but the magic in these halls did not match the kind he had studied. It was not as simple as not having experience out in the field. Kaslin had plenty of that. It was that the nature of magic here felt... different. It was a dragon's lair after all and dragons were new, arcanologically speaking, with the first sighting barely fifty years ago. Perhaps the source of magic was undergoing another shift. But to what?

Kaslin watched as the fox's eyes suddenly lit up. He pulled his head away from the door and stared at the pick that was sticking out from the keyhole. Gingerly Porte gave it a turn, and with an ear-twisting screech, the bolt slid free and popped out. The fox hopped to his feet, about to open the door.

"Hmmph!" Olken's fist slammed into the door, holding it shut. The fox stared up at him in frustration and confusion.

"We lost our first burglar that way," Kaslin said. "There was a trap in the door itself."

The fox bit his lip and took a gentle step back. "Didn't feel anything while I was unlocking it."

"All the same…" The trio of them stood a few paces back and Kaslin concentrated on the correct words and phrases for Martigar's Hand. A spectral shape formed in the air in front of them and began to float listlessly towards the door.

While Kaslin manipulated the spell with extra care, he caught, out of the corner of his eye, a glance that Porte had sent his way. The popular perception of mages, especially those so far away from the great magical academies, was as sexless ascetics, but the fox was either unaware of the perception or he didn't care, because the look on the cocky fox's muzzle was exceedingly flirtatious. It flustered the wolf, who was closer to the stereotype than he liked to admit, and made the spell judder for a moment.

"Hmmph!" Olken snorted, which this time meant, "Pay attention!"

All three held their breath as the hand reached the door and gently levered it open. There was a creak, then silence. Nothing came lashing out. No traps sprung.

But there was, in the gloom of their torches, a glint in the room beyond.

"The hoard," Porte whispered, his earlier cockiness now replaced with awe. "We did it!"

"Wait!" Kaslin shouted, but the fox had already darted forward, into the massive chamber, and took a flying leap onto the nearest heap of coins. Then he groaned as he smacked into the heavy metal at full velocity.

"Hmmph," Olken said. Unbelievable.

"At least this thief is still alive," Kaslin muttered under his breath.

The badger kept a firm grip on the sword hilt at his belt and eased his way into the room. Kaslin made to follow but stopped on the threshold. There was something wrong. Very, very wrong. Magic permeated the chamber, soaked into the walls and floors. It felt like old magic, the magic of blood and bone. But despite feeling it, Kaslin could not tell what it was supposed to do. There was nothing to suggest any effect that he could understand. "I'm not sure we should be here," he said, half to himself.

"Come on!" Porte said, as he hefted up handfuls of gold coins and let them slip through his fingers. "We're going to live like kings. No, emperors! Wait, do emperors have more or less money than kings?"

"Hmmph!" Olken said, as he examined his reflection in a gold-plated bowl. It didn't matter, he seemed to say.

"I'm going to live better than both," the fox said laughing. "I'll never work a day again."

Eighty-five days ago, a dragon died. That had never happened before. Dragons were new to the world, beings of magic, and were thought to be invulnerable. But this one bled and expired like any flesh and blood creature would.

Eighty-three days ago, hoping to find a better life than the increasingly difficult job of itinerant mage, Kaslin set out to find the dragon's hoard. Everyone knew they had one. Dragons accumulated gold like magpies gathered trinkets, but dragons' appetite for luster was insatiable. Dragons would break into castles, fighting past ballistae and armored soldiers, only to take four big clawfuls of gold from the treasury and haul it away.

Land meant nothing to them, and they never seemed to eat. All they wanted was gold. But no one was quite sure where it had all gone.

Ten days ago, Kaslin had roughly figured out where the dragon called home, a remote mountain next to a small town that served as the trading hub for many local villages. He had tracked rumors and whispers of this dragon's flights, corroborated testimony, and determined where it should be. He found a small passageway inside the mountain, unlike any he had ever seen and sensed the traps, arcane and otherwise, throughout it.

Eight days ago, Kaslin hired Olken and Morac. Morac, a lynx, had shared Kaslin's desire to leave his profession behind; larceny, it seemed, paid little better than magecraft. Olken had joined for his own inscrutable reasons.

Seven days ago, Morac died, beheaded.

Five days ago, Kaslin hired Porte to replace Morac. Porte hadn't been his first choice, not even his tenth choice. But the fact that Kaslin had hired Morac was known, and the fact that Morac was no longer with Kaslin was obvious. Other rogues kept their distance; Kaslin's vague promises of wealth only made them more suspicious. Porte was young, impetuous, easily swayed by talk of a quick job that would set him up for the rest of his life. That, and he seemed to find both Kaslin and Olken attractive.

Three days ago, all three of them had nearly perished when a trapdoor underneath them gave way suddenly. Olken had managed to haul all of them out of the pit, but they could not find a safe way to build a bridge, or string a rope, or find any other way across. So they had to find another way in the maze-like passages.

One day ago, the complexity of the traps and locks had suddenly jumped in difficulty. Kaslin could feel something coming. Kaslin knew they were close.

An hour later, after a quick inspection around the cavern, Kaslin realized his estimation of the dragon's wealth had been off by an order of magnitude. The pile of gold that Porte had flung himself atop and declared his own was at least fifty paces wide and across and twenty paces high. That was one of dozens of piles of gold strewn about the chamber, in addition to other odd pieces of treasure, like a gold-plated chariot or a bust of some king that had been decorated in gold leaf. And there were still vast side chambers left unexplored.

It was not the wealth of the nearby kingdom. It was not the wealth of an empire. It was so far beyond either that a comparison seemed laughable. It was vast beyond comprehension, even to the trio who were contemplating it.

Ever the practical one, Kaslin brought his companions together and said, "The problem now is how do we spend it all."

"Hmmph," Olken said in agreement.

"What do you mean?" Porte asked. The fox had barely moved from his position atop his own little pile of gold since they had broken in.

"Well, for one thing, we can't fit all of this in our pockets."

"I thought you mages could do that shrinking thing."

Kaslin did his best to look down at the fox imperiously. Sure, the wolf was dressed in the sky-blue robes of his order which looked, in his own opinion, more than a little silly, even if they were traditional. But he did his best to look stern. "That. Shrinking. Thing?" he said.

"Sure, watched a guy do that in the city. Took a whole house and shrank it down to put it in his pocket and then moved it down the road."

Kaslin resisted an urge to roll his eyes. "Conjurers," he said with disdain. "That was just a visual trick. You can't actually shrink this much stuff like that."

"Pretty impressive trick," the fox said while rolling a coin over his knuckles.

"Hmmph," Olken said, nodding to Porte. Agreement, again.

Kaslin put his hands up. "Trust me, it won't work. Besides, even if you got all of this gold into the city, who would take it? No one has anything worth this much. You could buy your own villa with just this." Kaslin picked up a handful of coins from the pile Porte was laid across.

He was shocked when Porte reached up and smacked his hand, sending the gold scattering. The fox growled at him.

For a moment the two were frozen in place, both angry at the other's actions. Then Olken grunted, "Hmmph," and that diffused the tension.

"Anyway," Kaslin said with a shiver that made the hackles of his neck stand out, "we have to do this slowly. Gold attracts bandits. A lot of gold attracts really scary bandits."

"Well this gold didn't attract bandits. It attracted us."

Kaslin and Olken glanced at each other.

"Hmmph." Can you believe this guy?

The wolf cleared his throat and continued. "So we have two goals. The first is to replace the traps leading up to this place with our own. We don't want someone else to waltz in here and take this from us. And second, we need to find a way to sell this off in small useful chunks."

"Ugh," the fox said and flopped back onto the heap of gold coins. "That sounds like work."

Kaslin offered a wry smile. "Pretty easy work. I'll start with this." He pocketed three coins, deliberately choosing some far away from Porte's pile. "We need some fresh supplies; food is running low. I bet this will solve that. Can you two start looking at the way in and finding ways to lock it so only we can get past easily?"

"Hmmph." Affirmation.

"I guess," the fox said, staring wistfully at the piles of gold.

The trip out of the mountain, down to the town, and back up took most of the day. The gold coins had earned some curiosity, but nothing he was too worried about. It had resulted in more food than he could carry in his arms, though. No matter what Porte thought, the wolf couldn't simply shrink the food down and haul it that way, it still weighed what it weighed. And there was no spell that could give him the strength to carry it on his own: he wouldn't have bothered hiring Olken if he could do that. But the money had been enough to also get a simple hand cart and magic could smooth its path back up the mountain.

The mage was concerned to see, as he neared the hoard chamber, that nothing had gotten done. All the traps were still disabled, all the doors still unlocked. Inside, he found Olken on his knees, quietly arranging coins into neat piles. By the size of the stacks in front of him, he must have been at it the whole time. Porte was nowhere to be found.

Olken's torch sat on the ground, extinguished. There was a low light that pervaded the chamber, coming from sources the mage could not see.

Cautiously, Kaslin crept up on the badger and touched his shoulder. He readied Wurts' Barrier, in case the preoccupied badger rounded on him, but it wasn't needed. Olken did not look up from his work. Kaslin tried pushing his shoulder, then shaking him. Nothing worked. He was entranced.

Quietly Kaslin slipped back to the cart and grabbed a small loaf of bread, of the kind he knew the badger most enjoyed. He waved it gently under the badger's nose and was relieved when the warrior finally took notice.

"Hmmph." Thanks.

The wolf patted him on the shoulder and looked around for the fox. There was still no sign of him. The pile of gold he had claimed was shrouded in darkness now; only the coins at the base were visible.

The wolf's ears perked. Somewhere in the distance he heard a sound, but the echoes in the gigantic cave made it impossible to pinpoint at first. Then the noise grew louder, a high-prolonged note and a chaotic arpeggio of metallic clinks.

As Porte came into view, Kaslin finally recognized that the fox was sliding down the enormous pile of gold, having started somewhere deep in the darkness. He was slithering and winding his way down the hill like a snake, traveling headfirst without a care or worry. He came to the bottom, skidded across the hard ground, and came to a stop at Kaslin's feet.

The wolf couldn't help but tap his foot impatiently once again.

The fox continued to giggle and burble for a moment, like a happy baby. He ducked his head to the side and called out in a sing-song voice, "I can see up your robe," while his whiskers flicked suggestively.

Anger quelled Kaslin's usual flustered response to the fox's flirtings. The wolf glared down.

Slowly Porte looked up at Kaslin's face. "What?"

"Have either of you gotten any work done while I've been gone?"

"Hmmph." No.

The fox sat up. "We expected you to be out for hours. We were only planning to take a short break first."

"It has been hours!" The wolf could barely keep the growl out of his voice.

Porte and Olken both shrugged as one.

Kaslin was beside himself with frustration for a moment. He had expected better from the badger at least. He was half-tempted to offload the cart, take as much gold as it could carry, and get himself out of there, and leave the two fools to their games. But that was dangerous given local bandits and might not have been enough to leave him in the lap of luxury he really wanted. He still needed them, for now. And he still needed this place, as much as it made his pelt itch and his claws tingle.

"Oh hey, you brought food."

The fox picked out a sizable hunk of meat, one that Kaslin had intended to last the three of them at least a full day, and began to devour it in quick messy bites. The wolf had never seen anyone eat that way, not anyone sane at least. He was suddenly far less hungry himself and wanted to stay at least a full arm's breadth from the fox.

Kaslin eyed Olken. "Did you find anywhere good to sleep at least?"

The badger looked surprised at the question. "Hmmph." Of course.

Olken stood up, still munching absently on his bread—and in a far more civilized manner than the fox—and led Kaslin to the far east side of the chamber, a good five-minute hike away. There were several rooms carved right into the rock there. They even had doors. And on the inside were sparse but lavishly apportioned rooms. They held little more than a bed, a desk, and a brazier dimly lit by some unseen fuel and still glowing after all these months. But they were larger than most rooms Kaslin had stayed at in inns, and the furniture pieces were well-made. Ignoring the persistent gloom and the question of why a dragon would need such rooms, it was quite comfortable.

"I think I'll turn in early," the wolf said. He muttered good nights and closed the door, stepping over to the desk. Like everything in the chamber, it was inlaid with gold, and a stack of coins was waiting atop it. Out of curiosity, he tried rearranging the stacks as he had seen the badger done outside. There was something calming about it, but beyond that, he couldn't see the appeal.

Kaslin fell into bed, but before he slept, he cast Jegra's Lock over the door, worried that his companions might prove more frightening than any nightmare.

Kaslin felt better in the morning. The fears that had been gnawing at his thoughts had faded and when he left the little chamber—which had begun to feel quite homey—he found the cavern beyond looking a little brighter despite having no visible light sources. And his companions were not as concerning as they had been the previous night.

As Kaslin approached Olken, he found the badger still working through coins, but now he saw that the taciturn warrior was slowly and methodically splitting the wealth out three ways. One for each of them. If he meant to sort all the gold in the chamber, he'd be at it for multiple lifetimes. Kaslin chuckled at the silliness of it and clapped a hand on Olken's shoulder. "Sleep well?"

"Hmmph." He hadn't slept.

Kaslin chuckled again, less confidently this time, and then heard a giggle from the giant stack of gold that Porte had claimed. He looked up to see the fox perched atop a stack, leering down at the others. "I've got it," the fox said, with a wide grin.

"Got what? And, uh, where are your clothes?" Kaslin asked, jerking his head away from staring as he realized the fox was naked.

"That's not important," the fox said with a wave of his hands and one of his knowing looks. "It's just hot in here. You don't mind, do you?"

Kaslin stuttered and tried to make excuses. He had no particular interest in the fox, but curiosity, suppressed first by a monastic lifestyle of tutelage and second by the grueling rigors of adventuring, was no longer content to be ignored. The fox just giggled again and went on.

"We are going to have a mine."

"A what?"

"A mine. It's the perfect cover for why we would have all this gold. Nobody but you figured out the dragon was here. So it can be a mine, a rich natural vein of gold ore."

Kaslin put a hand to the tip of his muzzle and idly played with his whiskers as he thought. "How do we get the rights?"

The fox flicked a coin into the air and caught it. "A little bribe here, a little forgery there. All standard business dealings, even among mine owners."

Kaslin pondered, and the more he pondered, the more he paced around, trying to look at the possibility from every angle. "We'll need to hire some miners. No one would believe that we're pulling this gold out just the three of us."

"I'm sure you're more than capable of getting some talent. You found us after all using nothing more than a vague story about needing additional assistance on a dangerous expedition into the mountains. Now you just expand that story." The fox looked thoughtful and held up a coin. "Just convince everyone that your initial expedition was to set up a mine, and you can use a piece of gold here as proof of your mission's success. Now you need people to help set up a second mine at a less promising location. No one will mind that they're on an ultimately futile endeavor provided they still get paid." The last sentence came out after a pained pause, as if the fox had trouble putting the thought into words.

"I like the way you think."

The fox writhed naked on the pile of gold and actually purred, or at least that's what it sounded like to Kaslin's ears. "Now be a good leader and go hire some additional talent."

Kaslin's brow wrinkled at the disdain in the fox's voice, and then further furrowed when Porte lazily rolled over and began undulating against the gold in a way that was equally sensual and luxurious. He kept imagining that gold would be hard and poke at very private parts, but the fox didn't seem to mind.

Kaslin forced his ears and eyes away from the fox's lewd display and turned to Olken. "Is there, by any chance, a gold nugget or something similar?"

"Hmmph." The badger nodded and wandered off into the stacks. He seemed to already know exactly where he was going, and dodged deftly around piles of inordinate wealth as Kaslin quietly marveled at how much there still was that he hadn't seen yet. He came to a stop as the badger picked up a large rock and tossed it straight into his chest.

The mage was nearly bowled over backwards, not under the weight of the rock, but of the unexpected velocity of it. Olken flashed him a grin and a look that suggested he thought the mage should work out more.

"Thanks," Kaslin said, trying not to let his irritation show.

He followed Olken back into the main clearing of the cavern and then went past, out through the maze of passageways that lead back to the surface. As he did, he kept staring at the rock Olken had handed him. It thankfully did not weigh as much as a full gold bar, but there were flecks of gold in it that showed its promise to any who understood such things. As he walked, Kaslin cast Annat's Illumination, which formed a small fire dancing along his fingertips. But something was wrong. He wasn't sure why but each time he tried to transfer it from his empty hand to the hand which held the rock, the light went out. It was fine being transferred from claw to claw in his empty hand, but the moment it made the jump across hands, it was snuffed out instantly, plunging him into darkness. The first time it happened, it was as Kaslin was crossing a particularly dangerous stretch, and he nearly fell into a pit that they had cleared with ease before. After that the mage was much more cautious. His attention was fully consumed by the dangerous space around him, and the magical fire that suddenly felt so much more delicate than it had ever before.

Once out of the cave, the light felt so good on his fur, and there was a cool breeze that made him happier just to feel a change in temperature. But still he couldn't shake the feeling that something was wrong with his magic. Something deep and terribly wrong. He wondered if this was what those ancient necromancers felt at the dawn of the era of written spells. What was it like for them to lose power? Did it happen all at once, or slowly over time? Did it affect all their magic equally, or did some abilities weaken before others? And what was the consequence of that? Kaslin swallowed as he imagined a necromancer torn limb from limb by a ravening horde he had been able to control so easily just a few hours before. How terrible would his own end be when it arrived? To put such thoughts out of his mind, he kept calling the flame over and over again to convince himself he still could. Every time he did it would disappear no matter how hard he concentrated on it.

"Ho, there!"

Instinct kicked in. Kaslin's arm swung out and Martigar's Hand knocked the stranger who had startled him off his feet. The raccoon, easily a decade Kaslin's junior, looked surprised as he slid sideways, and then there was a sick crack as the stranger's skull met the rocky side of the mountain. Blood began to pool under him. The raccoon didn't move.

Neither did Kaslin. The wolf stood petrified with horror. Yes, he had killed before, the life of a mage required one to take such jobs that brought him into conflict with others. But everyone he had killed had been dead set on killing him. He had never before killed by accident.

A bird sang its call behind him, and Kaslin whirled, startled again. He was suddenly hyperaware of all sounds around him. Every broken twig, every rustle of branches was a potential witness to the evil he had done. But no one stepped out to accuse him.

To be sure, Kaslin cast Tressa's Scrying. If anyone was watching him, he would know. But there was nothing, nothing that the spell could tell him at any rate. He couldn't shake the dull feeling that someone, somehow was aware of what he had done.

The wolf glanced to the eyes of the dead raccoon. They were looking right at him, but they did not sense him. The man was truly dead.

Taking a shaky breath, Kaslin set the gold down and called up Yves' Burial. The rocks shifted and accepted the body and its blood, then closed over top. This spell worked flawlessly. It didn't halt midway through as the flame had.

With the body gone, Kaslin scried once more, but still he was alone. He picked up the rock with its flecks of gold and made his way down to the village, trying to put out of his mind the entire time the thought that he had attacked the stranger to protect what was his.

The time in the town eased his worries again. No one marched in to accuse him of murder. Nothing seemed out of place here. And, best of all, as soon as he showed off the gold, the disbelievers who had questioned Kaslin's story of an easy job and quick money were now wanting to know what they could do to share in the wealth. Kaslin spun out a tale of how he already had a successful mine in another part of the mountain range, and he was searching for workers to begin digging in a promising new area, close but not too close to where the path to the dragon's hoard was located. He sought out workers who were intelligent enough to see the prospects of such a job, but not too intelligent to detect the obvious flaws in his story: hard workers eager for the wealth, but no one with the experience to know what truly went in to mining.

As days wound on, Kaslin would make trips back into the hoard to bring back a few bits of gold to begin financing the new venture. As word of the mine spread, there were fewer questions about his gold and its origin. Porte had been right: it was a good cover story for how they had come by so much wealth. The wolf was careful not to bring out too many proper coins. It was one thing to have little bits of gold here and there, and quite another to have coins clearly printed with a royal seal, especially a royal seal from a kingdom so distant no one recognized the king on it.

Within a week, Kaslin had set up a small mining camp on the side of the mountain and his people—for he had come to think of them as his people—were beginning work digging for gold. They didn't turn up anything—not that he had expected them to —but they were happy to keep working and keep being paid with gold from the mine Kaslin continued to spin stories about.

The foreman of the new mine, a hefty bear named Idallo, was often in Kaslin's tent, conversing about the day's work and sipping on some heady wines. He plied Kaslin with questions, including a few more pointed questions about the other mine and where Kaslin kept going when he was away, but the wolf always demurred enough that the subject was dropped.

Time outside of the cavern was doing him good. Despite the death he had caused still weighing on him, he was beginning to feel that things were sorted out. Sure, Porte and Olken were continuing to act strangely. And sure, the air felt oppressive every time he was there. And sure, Porte and Olken were building... something... there in the dark.

Even thinking about the hoard for too long felt bad, so Kaslin simply pushed it from his mind and focused on the task at hand. He felt that things would be all right. He practiced his magic nightly and found it as strong as it had been a month ago;

flames no longer extinguished themselves before he was done with them. He reassured himself that even if the current arcanological age was nearing its end, it had not ended yet. To further soothe his mind, he purchased some lavish accommodations for himself with a few extra pieces of gold, and soon he had the finest residence in the village, stocked with imported furniture. It was a better life than he had ever led, and he knew it would only get better.

By keeping himself focused on that, he was able to better survive his trips to the hoard. He just kept his mind fixated on that soft bed and those luxurious clothes, and he could ignore the hot stifling air, or the way Porte now watched him like a hawk, only his eyes moving as he perched atop his mound of gold that slowly changed its shape each time Kaslin saw it.

He walked like he was in a dream. Or drunk. Even Idallo made comments on it. But Kaslin paid them no heed. It was just one more thing to ignore as he thought of a feast and warm bath waiting for him at the end of the day.

All that was why, being so distracted, he hadn't noticed as he approached the path to the hoard, that Idallo had followed him. "Ho there!" the bear had said. "Is this where your other mine is?"

Sleepily, Kaslin turned around. He didn't swing out a gust of magic that would sweep Idallo from his feet and kill him. He was too relaxed for that. "Yes," he said.

"Interesting place for a mine," the bear remarked. "I thought it was further along."

"It is. Deep inside."

"Mind if I accompany you?"

"Stay here," Kaslin said, as part of his mind tried to speed up, sensing something was wrong. "I'll bring out your pay in a bit."

"I'd prefer if—"

The bear's voice cut off suddenly, and he looked down at his chest dumbfounded to see the arrow sticking out of it. He slumped to the ground, reaching out once, before expiring.

Kaslin stared at the body with the same detached unconcern he had felt for the past several days, but now a part of Kaslin's mind was screaming, yelling at him to wake up, forcing him to stop ignoring everything and pay attention. Kaslin did at last, looking at the corpse and thinking for a moment he had killed someone else again before noticing the arrow. Adrenaline surged and he spun around.

A cloaked figure stood at the entrance to the cave. Porte. Kaslin could just see the fur on his hands and the gleam in his eyes under the shadows of his hood, a gleam which was far too bright for any fox. In his hand he held a bow, which shimmered golden from the inlays along the limbs.

The wolf looked between living fox and dead bear, from one to the other and back again, still slow and struggling to process what had just occurred. "Why did you do that?" he asked.

"He was coming to steal from us."

"He wouldn't."

"He already has. He's been skimming from you already. You've just been too clumsy to notice." The fox limped to the dead bear and reached down, rifling through a bag Idallo carried with him and coming back with a handful of gold, far more than the foreman should have had. "See?"

"But... you didn't need to kill him."

"Yes, I did. Just like you had to kill that man before."

Kaslin was stunned. No one had seen him. He was sure. He had scried. Fear gripped him with icy tendrils. "How did you know about that?"

The fox bobbed his hands to make the gold jingle. "I know everything that happens around what is mine." The fox slipped the gold into a pocket of his cloak. Even now, Kaslin could see almost nothing of the fox. Even his feet were hidden by the impossibly deep shadows of the cloak.

"But you didn't need to kill him," the wolf hissed. "This could wreck our entire program with the new mine."

"That's not important anymore."

"Not important? I've been working on it for weeks. It was your idea!"

"We don't need it anymore," the fox said, reemphasizing the last word.

Kaslin gaped in stunned disbelief as the fox walked past him, and, in a surge of anger, reached out to stop him. His fingers closed on a clump of fur and held on tight. Porte simply kept moving. Kaslin stared at his hand, at the huge tuft of fur that had separated from Porte's pelt so easily, and followed the limping fox back into the cave.

"That's it!" the wolf yelled. "I've had it. I'm taking a fair share and leaving."

"A fair share?" The fox turned to him, and Kaslin saw his fingers tighten around the bow he held. "Yes, yes, I suppose you should be paid appropriately." He continued hobbling inside.

Kaslin quietly whispered a spell of protection against blades and arrows as he walked behind the fox. He hadn't realized how well the traps and locks had been rebuilt in the last few weeks. He hadn't been paying attention, but somehow he had known how to get past, just as he knew how to get past now. He was slipping over tripwires without a thought, casting unlocking spells with ease. He knew this path like it was as dear to him as his hometown, if not better. And yet he was sure much of this was new since the last time he had come this way.

There were even magical traps that had the feeling of being his own, but he had no memory of ever placing them.

He put up extra wards over himself, just in case.

Inside the cavern, Olken was still doing his quiet shifting of gold, but he had long since moved past his monomania of splitting the gold three ways. Instead, he was carefully sculpting the gold on the pile Porte had claimed for his own. The whole pile now looked like a miniature mountain, with a small footpath leading up to another cave mouth halfway up the side of the pile, a golden cave within the rocky cave, that led back down into some unknown chamber within the depths of the pile. Porte barely nodded to him, whisked his way up to the lip of this new cave, picked up a few coins, and tossed them back down to Kaslin's feet. "There you go, standard payment for a sellsword mage working a guard shift. And you have been so devoted to guarding what is mine."

"Ours," Kaslin said under his breath, bending over to pick up the coins as Porte cackled and made his way out of sight behind the lip of the gold mound. "I'm leaving," he told Olken, "once I've gathered my things."

He didn't bother asking for help to the room Olken had shown him to so long ago. He knew the way, but still, he kept a magical light going, pleased at least that this time it did not disappear when it jumped from hand to hand, although it flickered and waved in one hand. The hand that had carried the gold coins, he noticed. Experimentally, he dropped the gold, while the sputtering flame was in the same hand. The flame roared back to life. He reached down with the flame on one claw and touched that same claw to the coin. The fire went out.

How? How could the coins be affecting his magic?

Payment for a sellsword mage, Porte had said.

Payment for magic.

He remembered his thoughts when he had first entered the hoard: where had the magic gone? Why was it so much weaker now? Kaslin picked up a coin and stared intently at it, looking at his own smudgy reflection.

Magic followed use. The land had created people, so magic flowed out of the land and into people. People had codified and written about magic, so magic flowed out of the people and into the words. Then.... Then people started to pay for magic, and magic had flowed out of the words, and into the payment. Into the gold.

Kaslin dropped the coin and stared around at the piles and

piles of gold that surrounded him. They had been siphoning magic away from mages for who knows how many centuries and concentrating it.

The wolf turned and ran. He ran for the entrance. He had to get out of there as fast as he could. He saw Olken staring dumbly into nothingness and reached out to grab him. "We have to leave," he said.

The badger stared past him at the gold.

Kaslin threw the strongest punch he could right at the badger's cheek. The warrior barely noticed, but he did look at the wolf and focus on him. "We have to go right now. The magic is in the gold. There's no telling what it could do."

Porte's cackling laughter, far louder than before, echoed up all around them. "Do you want to find out what it is capable of?"

Olken unfocused again, and began marching forward, straight up into the cave burrowed into the pile of gold. Kaslin tried to stop him, but all his weight was nothing, easily ignored by the badger. Olken's strength carried them both up the mountain of gold, up the new footpath that the badger had so carefully constructed. Kaslin let go as soon as they were at the mouth of the golden cave; the mage wasn't going to follow him down there. He was sure if he went in, he would never come out. Despairing, Kaslin was about to leave when he caught sight of what was inside.

Porte was there, inside a hollowed cave within the gold. No, not just a cave, Kaslin realized, a nest. Porte's bow was discarded, and his cloak was nowhere to be seen, and the fox, naked again, looked awful. He was shaky, barely able to stand on his feet. Clumps of skin and fur just dangled from his body. But instead of blood, Porte's flesh underneath gleamed like the gold he was surrounded by. The fox could have easily tugged at the skin, but instead he was grinding his nude body against the walls to help loosen the skin.

It was as though he was molting, Kaslin thought.

The fox's hands and feet were too big for him now, with claws far larger than they had ever been before. No wonder his pelt was coming off: there simply wasn't room for him any more inside of it. As he ground against a wall, the pelt slipped further and further off, revealing bulky arms and legs that had been constrained by the tight skin.

At least he wasn't in pain. If anything, he looked ecstatic. Each time the pelt fell a little further away, each time it freed a little more of what was underneath, he sighed in contentment.

By now, the fox's arms and legs were uncovered, coated in shiny red scales the same hue his fur had been. He flopped to the floor on his stomach, a small torso surrounded by massive limbs. He ground against the gold with more desperation than he had before, and more pleasure. The motions took on a distinctly sexual motion. And when the fox's old form had peeled away from his hips, the resulting shaft was not only massive, but fully hard and dripping with desire.

Now Porte's motions were dual-purposed: to work the remaining vestiges of his old form away and to press his need against something.

Kaslin watched as Olken began to plod down the gold-walled cave path, drawn towards the dragon-in-progress. The badger knelt down beside him, wrapped both hands around the shaft and began to stroke, relieving one need while Porte tended to the other. The fox had rolled onto his back, swaying back and forth. A lizard-like tail lashed out, and with awkward thrusts that drove his shaft into the badger's strong grip, two wings sprouted from his back, splitting his old pelt and ripping it forcefully from the rest of his torso, leaving only his head unchanged.

But that wasn't entirely true. His eyes, his eyes had been a dragon's eyes since at least they had conversed outside. And now, as Kaslin sifted through memories he had suppressed for so long, he realized that they had been a dragon's eyes for much,

much longer. Perhaps he had been fated for this within a day or two of them discovering the horde. He had been waiting for the right moment to shed.

Porte rubbed first the left then the right side of his head against the ground, trying to ease the last bits off. With each pass, his neck lengthened more and more, until it had grown long and snakelike. When finally he freed himself from his old form, he shook his whole neck like a whip, sending his pelt flying to the far end of the room. There was nothing left of the fox, nothing but the color patterns on the dragon's scales.

Porte turned his head and stared intently at the badger, who understood what was being commanded of him. Olken crawled on all fours as the dragon moved into position to mount him. A quick slice of wicked claws tore away the badger's clothes and he pushed the badger's chest into the ground as he forced himself in.

"Hmmph," the badger grunted. Pleasure.

Kaslin hadn't moved from his spot at the entrance to the gold cave. He seemed dead to the world, barely breathing. The only sign of life was from his groin, as his unattended shaft throbbed as he watched the fierce display of ecstasy below him. Porte kept Olken's body pinned as he thrust in again and again. He opened his mouth and let out a hiss of pleasure that reached into Kaslin's own mind and tapped into lust and desire. The wolf wanted to join Olken, to bend over, lift his tail, and wait for his turn to be mounted. But he couldn't make himself move, even now. He could only watch.

The dragon met his gaze. He knew everything that happened here, next to his gold. He understood Kaslin's desires. Here, at the heart of the gold, at the heart of the new magic, Kaslin was beginning to understand too: he could finally start to make sense of the patterns and currents of the arcane surrounding him. He knew now what mistake the previous dragon had made. The previous protector of this horde had let himself wander too far away. That was why he was vulnerable. But Porte would not make the same mistake.

Protector...

That was what it was all about. The magic had concentrated in the gold, and now what it wanted was something to protect it, to treasure it and value it above all else. That's why it had made the dragons.

Porte hissed in pleasure once more and drew Kaslin's attention back down to the mating before them. Even his style of fucking had changed. His whole body undulated now, starting from the head and passing down the length of his body until his hips slid out and back down, to drive his shaft home with another little grunt of pleasure from the badger.

But his smile, that hadn't changed. It was still the same cocksure, flirtatious smile Porte had always had. And he hissed out happiness and satisfaction as with one more powerful undulation, he sank his hips down hard and climaxed.

When he pulled away, he left a trail of milky whiteness around the badger's legs. It seemed to gleam and shimmer just as the metal around them did.

Porte let himself fall to one side, sending a shudder through the gold at the weight of his impact. He splayed out lewdly, his shaft remaining at full mast. Perhaps he had waited too long to transform. He was probably quite pent up, Kaslin thought.

"Well?" Porte's voice had changed too. It was deeper, and carried with it the rumble of a dragon's breath, the promise of fire and destruction. "Have you decided what you will do yet, little mage? Will you run?"

Kaslin glanced back to the cavern entrance. He could run. And he knew somehow that Porte would let him. If he did not bother the gold, Porte did not care about him. He might even be able to take his few coins of payment.

But there was another possibility. This was a place full of magic, magic that had been waning in Kaslin as it had in all other mages. Here was power once again, and all it asked of him was that he protect it. Someone had to maintain the traps and locks. There had to have been people like that before: why else had there been rooms for non-dragons here? Maybe he could be something more than just another servant of the wealth. Maybe.

Quietly Kaslin shed his robe. As he walked down the path of gold to take his place next to Olken, his naked shaft bobbed with excitement in the warm air. Perhaps he would never manage to be anything more than just a servant, but as he looked over at the dragon lustfully licking his lips, he thought that perhaps this was not such a bad way to serve.

THE DRAGON'S RENAISSANCE

INKBLITZ

I stared up at the entrance to the renaissance festival. This was so not the place I wanted to be today.

It was an actual archway standing some ten feet tall. Some rustic, wooden gate that was painted white with a twisting gold pattern, like a Celtic knot-thing that I had seen in mythology classes. It was faded and didn't look like anyone had given it a touch up in years. It was probably also the cringiest thing I had seen so far this morning.

"Come on, Tabitha!" The sharp, annoyed sounding voice of my girlfriend Megan snapped my attention down from the arch. I glared at her.

The catfolk stood across the other side of the entrance from me. Her orangy fur was a mix of dark stripes and spots that stood out against the darker clothes she was wearing. Her hand-paws were on her hips, and her lower lip stuck out in an actual pout that showed off the slight points of her lower fangs. She was dressed up in something right out of a fantasy movie. Her top was a dark, hunter green linen shirt that she called a 'tunic', and a dark brown, leather bodice. The sleeves were short, showing off her toned, firmly muscled arms that were strong enough to actually pull the string on the bow strapped to her back. She wore a brown leather vest over that, which was adorned with dragon themed pattern, with wings that wrapped around her breasts like they were clutching or protecting them. Her pants were the similar color leather and were a bit tighter than I would've worn, hugging her hips in ways that drew my eye towards her athletic thighs. I half expected her to be wearing thigh-high leathers over her hind paws, but she wore just simple ankle straps across them and left her broad paws bare. Her tail lashed behind her in irritation, a leather cuff near the tip of it.

Her costume was all faux leather, but the bow was an authentic, wooden bow and quiver strapped across her shoulders. The quiver didn't have any arrows in it since the festival didn't allow them, but I knew she could shoot it pretty well—I've seen the archery trophies to prove it. She really looked the part of some sort of elven huntress. As little as I cared to be there, it couldn't deny seeing her in the getup was pretty cool.

While Megan had gone all out for the faire, I stood at the archway still in my usual street clothes. I was human through and through, and while my pale skin burned pretty easily, I was plenty happy to not have to put up with a coat of fur of my own. I already went through enough lint rollers just being close to Tabitha.

I made sure that the graphic tee was not torn or anything. It was one of my favorites, black with red lettering and a pixelated goatfolk Viking throwing the horn sign and bearing the logo of the band 'The Max Grungles' across my chest—the same one I got at the concert where I first met Megan. My jeans didn't even have any rips in them for once—you're welcome, Megan—but they didn't hug my hips like her costume. She warned me about mud, so I just wore my usual heavy black boots instead of trying to come out with any of my nice sneakers. Glancing around at the people coming and going through the gate, I didn't look entirely out of place, at least; more than a few weren't in costume.

But there were way more people dressed up than I thought there would be. Judging from the skimpy clothes worn by some people in full costume, I was actually overdressed. Chainmail bikinis, skirts being worn by any gender, and taut leather was pretty common. Megan wasn't the only one; there were even a few guys flaunting it... I wasn't any stranger to tank tops and short shorts, but this was crazy.

"What even is this place?" I asked out-loud. "What'd I let you talk me into?"

My attention drifted, and I focused back on the archway next to me. At a second glance, the golden lines wrapping around the wood came together to form a basic, gilded dragon right in the center of the arch. Worn, golden symbols made up its wings and limbs, like it was a part of the wood or like it was clutching it. I honestly wouldn't have noticed if I hadn't stopped in front of it.

Of course she would bring me to a festival with dragons. She was crazy about them. I swear she thinks that they were real.

Megan sighed in exasperation. "Will you stop gawping? You're blocking traffic." She stepped back across the entrance, grabbed my arm, and began to pull. I didn't stand a chance against her greater strength, and I found myself tugged under the archway against my will. But I put up enough of a fight that my heels left at least brief marks in the dirt.

"The story match begins in five minutes, Tab. Let's go!" She pulled enthusiastically on my arm, dragging me past the entrance and into the fairgrounds proper.

Walking into the festival was almost like walking down the main street of a village that split off into three smaller streets going right, left, and straight ahead. In the center of where the streets split off was a large angular boulder that was positioned in the middle of everything, like it was placed on purpose.

Lining each of the streets on either side were different sorts of small huts and buildings where merchants were selling anything from wooden weapons to glass figures. Some sold replicas of what looked like the boulder, as if it was important for some reason. It was like one big mall, but for overpriced fantasy trinkets.

Groups of people milled about everywhere, some in the merchant stalls, others eating food, or taking in the sights. But it wasn't as crowded as Megan made it out to be. I really thought there would be more people at the festival with the way that Megan was hyping it up.

As we passed the centerpiece of the square, I glanced back at the boulder. But it wasn't just a rock. It took me a moment staring at, but it was actually some sort of long, jagged statue. It stood on a squat, wooden shrine, but the thing itself was about four feet long,three feet tall, and was slate gray. The stone split across the length of it, like it had started to crack at one point, or someone tried to shape it. At the top of the statue, there was a literal sword sticking out of it like some sort of legend.

A group of college guys had gathered around the statue as we walked into the center of the forks. One of the bigger men had his hands around the hilt of the sword and was pulling on it so hard that the muscles in his arms bulged. No matter how hard he pulled on it, the weapon wouldn't move an inch, and his friends were taunting him about it.

But as I kept staring, I noticed that the sculpture... had eyes. It had brows angled downwards in anger or maybe pain. What I thought was a split in the stone was actually lips pulled back to show a row of sharp teeth. It looked like it once had horns, but they were nothing but stubs now, likely broken off at some point. The head ended with a short neck that stopped with jagged angles as if someone had chopped it off of an actual beast instead of sculpting only the head. The sword was impaled through its skull as if it were defeated in battle and left there in the middle of the crossroads. I stopped, and Megan's paw slipped from my wrist.

"Hold on," I said, pointing to the dais where the college student was walking off dejectedly. "This I gotta see." I hopped up to the raised platform that held the head. From up close, it was crazy detailed. Like I'd seen some resin prints before, but the statue that was in the center of the festival was really defined with scaling across the entire surface and even a detailed brow. But despite that, the rock still was eroded and pitted, like it was meant to be really old. Did they sculpt it that way on purpose? Or was this really that old? The blade that stuck from the roof of the dragon's maw looked used and worn but didn't have any rust on it, and the leather around the hilt of the sword didn't look like it was rotting.

Someone spent a lot of money making sure these replicas were in top shape yet still looked weathered.

I reached out for the weapon. Part of me half expected Megan to tell me that it was forbidden for girls to try or something dumb like that. But no one stopped me as I curled my fingers around the hilt and gave it a half-hearted tug.

And the sword shifted a few centimeters up the stone. Wait, what? Was that supposed to happen? I pulled on the hilt again, but the sword wouldn't budge. Must've been my imagination… But a buzzing, electric sensation rippled up my fingers, as if the sword were charged with some sort of energy.

A fanfare of trumpets echoed in the distance, breaking my train of thought.

"Dammit!" Megan said. She grabbed my wrist, tugging on it. Her claws lightly dug into my skin. "Come on, we're going to be late for the story match! It's the best part, Sir Vanitar's fight with the dragon!"

My hand left the hilt of the blade as I followed her, but I could swear that I felt it shift again in the stone. Had to have been some tourist trick. Fool them into thinking they're some sort of chosen one, have a good laugh at their expense. That sort of thing.

Still... My fingers tingled as they left the hilt. Like some sort of energy was crackling off of them. I flexed them, trying to work out the strange sensation that lingered.

"Okay, I gotta ask," I said minutes later as we hurriedly sat down at the upper row of a line of wooden bleachers that surrounded what looked to be some large, wooden theater. We were late, and arrived just as the narrator was finishing the backstory. Megan's ears were tipped backwards, so I knew she was unhappy with me. But I was getting curious. "What's the deal with the dragon head statue?"

Megan sat down, pulled the bow from her back, and laid it down across her lap. She then glared at me, her frustration still evident in her expression. "You didn't seem interested in the festival, why are you asking now?" she asked in a harsh whisper.

I shrugged. "I'm not that interested, but that dragon head thing was pretty badass. I didn't think it was a real sword at first but it's kinda cool they went the whole shtick with it. There's got to be some sort of story to that kind of thing, right?"

"You would have known the story if we weren't late for the intro to the show," she said. Her triangular ears flicked as if she was uncertain I was serious. On the one hand, yeah, I'd been pretty standoffish about the festival. But on the other, even I couldn't deny that the dragon's head was interesting.

I shoved her in the shoulder playfully, "Well, fill me in then. What's the deal?"

She breathed out, as if relaxing. Her whiskers flared, and she made that odd chuffing noise that she did. It was cute, even if she only did it when I was frustrating her. "Okay, but don't make fun of it," she said quietly. She leaned in close, and I could feel the warmth of her body against my arm. Goosebumps begin to trickle up my skin from the touch, and my breath briefly caught in my throat. That was odd... As much as I enjoyed being around Megan, she never made me feel like that before. "The statue is all tied into the story of this renn fest. The short of it is that sword is supposed to be the sword of Sir Vanitar; the legend is that 'whoever pulls it from the stone will become the next guardian of the festival.'"

I snorted and tried to shake off the strange way Megan affected me suddenly. "That's lame." Yeah, I immediately forgot to not tease.

Megan ignored me. "It's said that a long time ago, there used to be this dragon's den. Not here, like, far away," She added, when I looked at her skeptically.

"Anyway," she continued, "This dragon demanded that the village make a sacrifice."

"Like maidens, gold, stuff like that?" I asked.

"Nah, it was bored and wanted to destroy part of the village 'for fun.'"

"What? And I bet the village was all in favor of that" I said, sarcastically.

Megan glared at me. Oh, right, she asked me not to make fun of it. "The village leader tried to make a deal with the dragon. Gold, maidens, jewels, anything the dragon wanted if it would leave the village alone. The dragon was done with all that, it wanted something more exciting. So, a bard passing through the village came up with an idea: put on a festival just for the dragon."

I could see where this was going. "And so, they came up with the faire just to entertain it?"

"Kinda," Megan said, "Before that they were trying all different things to and appease the dragon, like juggling and dances, but the dragon would quickly get tired of it and demand the next thing. The bard's idea was to bombard the dragon with everything happening all at once. It'd be so busy getting to it all that the dragon would either get distracted from trying to destroy the village or exhausted from everything happening."

"All at once?"

She nodded, "I mean that's what a festival is, isn't it? Everyone coming together to entertain each other. So, the bard arranged the festival, and the dragon was invited to partake in anything and everything they wanted. There was so much to do and so much to try, that by the time that they got around to it all, they were worn out. When it came time to decide whether or not the dragon was entertained, they claimed they were undecided and that they needed to do it again just to be sure that they tried absolutely everything."

"So, the Bard's trick worked?"

Megan flashed her fangs with a grin and nodded. "The bard claimed that they couldn't just do it again the next night: The village needed time to gather. Instead, they did it the next weekend. And again, and again, for a full month, until the dragon had their fill and was content to let the village survive—for one year. And so it happened again the next year, and the next, and it became a regular thing. They'd bring in entertainment, food, and wares, and the festival would begin again."

I frowned in thought. "So why the sword in the skull treatment then if they had a good thing going?" The tingling in my fingers intensified briefly, and I flexed my hand into a fist.

Megan held a clawed finger to her lips, "Shh, they get to it eventually..."

A catfolk woman dressed up in a black tunic and pants with blue accents walked across the length of the arena. Although she looked to be a plain furred catfolk, she appeared to have spots painted on her fur. "Hear ye, hear ye! I am the bard of this, the Dragon's Festival!" She bowed low with a flourish to the applause of the crowd.

"Please put your hands together for our champion of the festival, Sir Vanitar!" The bard said, rising and lifting off her feathered hat to point it towards the side of the arena. "Famed from across the realm, he has arrived to do battle with the dragon for the honor of the village!"

The knight that she announced strode around in front of the arena, riding on top of a white 'horse.' His armor glistened in the sun, silver with golden accents. I couldn't make out the designs from our seats, but he seemed like a broad chested man, and at least from the shape of his armor. He brandished a sword high above his head and then bowed deeply as the audience cheered.

It was obviously all fake. His "steed" was just a cart pushed by two donkeyfolk stagehands, with cardboard in the shape of a horse glued to the front. His sword was blunted, and honestly might not actually have been metal. At least the armor seemed real, but it was hard to tell from our seats near the back of the audience. If it was, it must have been boiling in the late summer sun.

Something about his attitude and haughty appearance made me want to throw a tomato or insults at him. I glanced at Megan, my mouth open for a joke that was on the tip of my tongue, but she was enraptured by the entire performance. I bit it back, at least for now.

"Yes, yes," He said in a slightly British accented tone that I recognized as a lame attempt at sounding 'old timey.' "I am your champion sent by Duke Harlian! You'll do wise to remember that! Do not fret, for today I shall uphold my honor against my mightiest opponent yet!" He motioned his blade across the joust arena to where a curtain had been set up, obscuring what was behind it.

"The dragon Rytharian!"

The sound of electricity crackled throughout the theater, and a thick, rolling mist billowed out from the curtain, obscuring it from view. A massive shadow was just barely visible rising from the ground in the fog. The reverberating thud of heavy footfalls played over the loudspeaker as the shadow grew larger and larger. Then with an ear-splitting roar, a gold and blue scaled dragon's head, teetering precariously on a puppeted neck, came swinging out from the curtains.

I could see the ropes being used to keep the dragon's head right, swinging back and forth precariously on its swivel. Every time a rope pulled down, it made the mouth open wide and a roar came over the loudspeakers, faking the sound of a real dragon.

The knight swung his blade in a wide arc, then pointed it towards the crowd. "Fear not, citizens of the realm!" he said, directing the tip of his sword at the puppet with a flourish, "for I will vanquish the dragon and you shall never be forced to revel for this beast again!"

The whole thing was silly. I've gotten into some crazy things before, and the festival itself was all around weird, but this was camp to the max. Sort of like the thing I'd see on some indie YouTube channel trying to pass itself off as some professional reenactors.

Megan sat captivated by the match, leaning forward with her eyes wide and her ears swiveled forward at attention. My gaze drifted towards her as the introductions continued with the famed dragon that "threatened" the kingdom. Megan was so enthusiastic about the whole thing, from the story about the festival to the match. Was she for real? But the way she hung on every word, she couldn't be anything but real about it.

Not that I'm one to talk, I've got my fair share of musicians that I dig. She had to think the same way about how I got into them. But as I stared at her, something seemed different. Maybe it was the outfit she was wearing, the tightness of her faux leather pants or the way she had her reddish hair pulled back. I couldn't help but keep staring at her, my attention only barely on the match.

I tried to return my focus on the fight. The knight went off into a speech about how the dragon abuses the village, forcing the villagers to toil away for its entertainment, in-between lunging between bolts that were oversized nerf darts with lightning shaped cardboard glued to them. But as he dodged one bolt, the massive tail of the dragon swung down, pinning Vanitar to the ground. The crowd gasped, even as the foam tail half bounced off of the knight.

Megan let out a cheer next to me. My gaze drifted back to her, and I raised a brow in curiosity. Was she cheering for the dragon? A strange, pleasant sensation bubbled up from my stomach and nestled in the back of my mind in a way that made my thoughts feel a little numb. It was... pride? I stared at her, confused. Sure, the Vanitar guy was a jerk, but something about her rooting for the dragon made something inside me feel light and ... happy.

It was like the first time that we met and bonded over the Max Grungles during college spring break this year. We spent most of the night talking about the band, sharing each other's music tastes. That was the first time I felt something like this towards a woman.

We'd of course experimented a little since then with cuddling and getting close. But she knew I was hesitant, so she never really pushed it beyond that. We've only really known each other for a couple months, and dating for a few weeks— sort of on a trial basis—and so far, she always was the one that instigated closeness. But now, as I stared at her, my mind drifted... It'd be nice to feel her warm fur against my skin again. To press myself against her...

My fingers itched oddly, and I curled them into a fist to try and ignore it. As I did, I felt pain in my palms like sharp pinpricks as my fingernails dug into my skin. I flinched and glanced down. My nails seemed longer, and they almost seemed to come to points. Did I forget to trim them?

"Tab?" Megan asked, breaking my train of thought. My wince must have caught her attention. "Something wrong?"

I shook my head, half in response, half to try and clear it. What was wrong with me? "Did you see the guy take that hit?" I said. That had to be a good cover. "For being giant nerf darts, they're still kicking his ass."

Megan's demeanor softened, her scowl fading slightly. "This is honestly the best part of the festival, and not just because Sir Vanitar gets his butt kicked in the first half."

"But I thought you liked the guy?"

She shrugged her shoulders. "I like the dragon, Vanitar's just a stuck-up ass. I know the story makes him out to be the big hero, but I think the village had a good thing going." Her tail flicked against her thigh—some part of me wished that it was against my leg instead. "Apparently they had a pretty thriving marketplace with people wanting to bring their best to show off to the dragon. Win-win, right?"

The strange sense of pride bubbled up in the back of my mind again. After all, why wouldn't they bring their best to show off for a mighty dragon? Sounds like the dragon brought prosperity to their village...

Wait, what? The strange thought drifting across the back of my mind made me blink.

Megan's words stirred something in me. The dragon just wanted to be entertained, but did they know that agreeing to the festival would help the village thrive? Were dragons that smart? I shook my head. It was all just a silly story, dragons weren't real.

Sir Vanitar's "horse" had been felled by one of the lightning bolt-shaped foam darts and the cart toppled off to one side by the stagehands. But he still stood. It was a grand, over exaggerated scene as he rolled under the puppet dragon's claw swipes, once then twice. Then lunged up with his sword to pierce the beast's neck. The neck of the entire contraption came loose and crashed to the stage.

With the dragon vanquished, Sir Vanitar placed a foot on the puppet's muzzle. He held his sword high over his head, and with a heave he jammed the broad blade into the top of the head. Some cord or thread snapped, and the outer scaled covering of the head fell away. Underneath it was a replica of the head in stone gray fabric, like the dragon head statue in the courtyard.

The crowd erupted in applause, and the bard returned to the stage. "And so, by his might," the feline said, "Sir Vanitar rescued the village from the dragon! The mighty magic of his blade trapped the spirit of the Rytharian, entombing it in the stone remains of its head and preventing it from ever returning."

She dropped her voice conspiratorially, lifting a finger up to her lips, "But the legend goes that if ever a decedent of the brave knight were to ever lift the sword from the stone, they would become the next guardian of the festival." She dropped her hand, and motioned to the audience with the other, "But now we continue to celebrate his victory and our freedom from the tyranny of the dragon every year in this, our renaissance festival!" The audience erupted in applause, as Sir Vanitar bowed and flourished, accepting his accolades.

"That was the big thing on my list," Megan said, her tail lashing behind her as she stood up from the bench. Her ears were dipped back, almost like she was disappointed somehow. I got up to follow her, and we walked back into one of the three dirt roads that lead through the festival. "What should we do next?"

I stared at her, "You're asking me? I'm not the one that wanted to be here."

She grinned back at me, "Yeah, but I can tell you're getting into it. Come on, what do you want to see?"

It was a big festival, and I couldn't really say that there wasn't something I wanted to do. But what? I let out a grunt of frustration, but much to my surprise it sounded a little like a growl from deep in my throat.

Megan stared, her brows slightly raised.

"Er, sorry," I said. I held a hand against my stomach, "Guess maybe food first? Y'know, we drove a while to get here and it's pretty close to lunch time."

Her expression softened. Then brightened into a grin showing the tips of her fangs. "Oh, I know. Let's go get turkey legs! I love their turkey legs: It's a staple." She turned and hurried away.

For a moment I was taken by surprise by how swiftly her mood changed. Maybe she was just hungry too? But my eyes lingered on her as she led the way. My gaze drifted slightly from side to side, watching the subtle sway of her hips.

What must it be like to rest my head between those thighs? To have her look at me the same way she admired dragons? To feel her paws on my horns, moving my head, directing my forked tongue across her skin, running it up between her-

Wh-Where did that come from!? I stared blankly ahead, my gaze unintentionally still lingering on her butt as I tried to figure out where that particular intrusive thought came from. I wasn't a dragon…

The daydream faded as soon as it came. I shook my head to try and clear it, but it left behind a dull ache of desire that burned warm and uncomfortable between my legs.

"Are you coming, slowpoke?" Megan's voice called, pulling me back to the present.

"Er, yeah!" I tried to push the sudden urges aside and followed after her.

The turkey legs were okay, though dry. Nothing really to write home about, but I wasn't about to tell Megan that. I had to admit that there was something primal and fun about just biting into a big turkey leg like some medieval partier that made it way different than using a fork and knife.

After eating, we wandered the festival. There were shops everywhere, and I bought a metal drink stein that would probably leave a dent in any table that I dropped it on. My mind kept drifting though, my gaze every so often lingering on Megan as if something about her was drawing my attention.

Megan thought I'd like the music, and we ended up at an outdoor concert held at this makeshift-looking stage. A couple of guys with massive beards filed into the performing space, and began pounding on these enormous drums, while another began playing on bagpipes. It wasn't the hard metal of an electric guitar and bass, but it had a beat. Megan caught me nodding my head to it, and I was sure I'm never going to live that one down.

When music bops, you gotta bang to it. At least the festival had that going for it.

But there was something wrong. It was like everyone was going through the motions, but there was no life to anything. Everything seemed dulled to me, even as an outsider. Like it could have been better, but something was missing. Even Megan seemed anxious and frustrated, as though she was expecting there to be more. I caught her glancing around eagerly, as if looking for something, then her gaze went downcast.

"It's almost three," Megan said. She had a paper pamphlet of the festival's activities—phone service was too shitty out here to be of any use. "There's a whip master that's going to take the stage soon." She smirked, and the tips of her fangs showed beneath her lips. Her tail gave a slight mischievous flick behind her. "You want to see if he whips himself instead this year?"

I was barely paying attention as we walked into the center of the courtyard. My focus instead drifted towards the statue of the dragon head in the center of it. The sword still rested there, shoved through the dragon's skull. My fingers twitched and my skin tingled, as if buzzing with electricity. The tips of my fingernails pinched against my skin. They almost felt like claw points, come to think of it...

The sword had moved when I halfheartedly pulled it before. What if I actually tried? I walked towards it.

"Uh, hey?" Megan's voice sounded distant behind me as I walked away from her. "Hey Tabitha? You want to go see the whipping guy?"

I approached the statue and reached out my hand to it. The leather of the sword felt strangely coarse against my skin. Or maybe my skin felt strangely coarse against the leather? I couldn't tell either way. I gave it a firm tug.

Someone's voice laughed behind me, probably one of the college guys from earlier by the tone of it. "No way she could pull that out!"

I tugged the sword again. It shifted slightly in the stone, but not enough.

I could do it. Something deep inside me knew I could do it.

I wrapped my other hand around the hilt as well and braced my foot against the lower jaw of the statue to give myself better leverage. And I pulled. The sword budged a little more.

The tingling sensation trickled again across my fingers. They rubbed against one another as I gripped the leather, and I struggled to keep them all wrapped around the hilt as if they were crowding it. My grip tightened, strength building in my muscles.

"Tab? What are you doing?" Megan asked, coming up behind me. But her voice faded into the background. "What's up with your hands? They're all... Are those scales?" My gaze drifted briefly to my hands. The flesh on the back of them seemed rough, even protruding slightly. My skin seemed firmer and textured, like they were actually scaled.

I should have been more concerned, but I wasn't. I just wanted to pull the sword from the statue. And I was going to. My muscles worked hard as I braced again against the jaw of the dragon's head. Something was different. I felt pressure in my biceps as a buzzing sensation began to build there. My muscles bulged, my upper arms widening with newfound strength. It strained the sleeves of my t-shirt, and the fabric began to ride up my arms. Beneath it, my skin was shifting, becoming harder as the scaled texture from my hands continued up my arms.

Yes, I could do it. Something inside me stirred at the very thought of removing the sword from the stone. Something primal, something that had been waiting a long time for this.

With a great heave, I pulled the blade from the skull of the dragon.

I heard Megan's gasp, but my focus wasn't on her. My gaze was instead on the statue. Glowing, blue energy began to build up within the hole where the blade once was. Then with a crackle of electricity it arced from the rock, drawn to the tip of the sword like a lightning rod. It made its way down into the metal and coursed from it into me.

At once, pressure began to build in my hands, turning into pain as my fingers grew even faster. They thickened rapidly, becoming ungainly and awkward, reshaping into something less human. They were growing too large to even hold the sword anymore, and it clanged to the ground at my feet. Claws that had been forming at the tips of my fingers grew and thickened, elongating into small, sharp daggers. The palms of my hands had become like rough leather, thick and coarse, but on the top of my hands, the pattern of scales thickened rapidly, skin becoming shiny and gold.

I stared at my hands. What the hell was happening? I tried to flex my fingers, but I could barely get them to move.

A small crowd had begun to mill about around me, drawn to someone pulling the sword from the statue. At first they sounded excited, but then it turned into concern and panic.

"Is she the new guardian now?" someone said in hushed tones. "That's the story, right? Are we supposed to cheer?"

"What's happening to her?" a woman said.

"Look at her hands," someone else shouted; "Those claws! Is this part of a show?"

I couldn't respond. My tongue felt too large, my jaws didn't want to work properly. I went cross-eyed as some lump between my eyes began to push outwards into my vision. Everything hurt, everything felt wrong.

Something pushed out against my thoughts, making my skull throb. I felt a presence... move through my mind. One that had been waiting, building in the back of my head.

No, things were being made right.

A surge of pressure rippled through me, and pain began to build at the base of my spine. I staggered backwards, but my feet felt too large. I bumped up against the stone dragon head, and looked down just to see the tips of my shoes swell and contort. My toes pushed painfully against the leather, until sharp, dark points began to poke through. Claws much like the claws on my hands split through the material, but my feet kept growing. The once tough leather was pushed apart, revealing what was happening within my boots. They looked nothing like they should, instead taking on a reptilian, maybe saurian appearance as they bulged and realigned, my small toe retreating into my feet while the others grew into more flexible digits, meant for grasping and raking.

The pain suddenly intensified at the base of my spine, and I yelped. Something was pushing from my tailbone! I could feel it writhing down my butt and between my legs, straining the back of my jeans. I looked behind me and saw a lump squirm and writhe under the fabric, threatening to tear right through it.

I bit my lip, and sharp pain lanced from my lips as a little bit of blood trickled down my chin. My teeth were rearranging against one another, the dull, flat human teeth pulling into sharpened points. My tongue pushed more and more against my mouth, forcing my lips apart with its bulk. Pressure began to build in my jaw, growing almost painful in the joints that connected them. But then moment by moment, my face pushed further and further out. The pressure slowly released... only because my face was becoming a large, broad snout. As it did, my vision began to shift. Things started to appear blurred, odd. Nothing wanted to focus correctly, and my mind struggled to make sense of what I was seeing—beyond the fact that my body was changing.

My spine arched as one by one my bones popped into a different position, forcing me into a slight haunch. My hips and thighs widened, tightening with muscle, and I found myself starting to crouch. Further and further, my hips were pushed back and my chest pushed forward, until my center of gravity abruptly shifted and threw my balance off. I reached out, my hands slamming into the ground to avoid falling flat on my face —and forcing me to all fours. My ankles rose up, the heels of my feet elongating and ripping through the rest of my shoes.

My pants couldn't handle the pressure from all sides. The fabric in the back of my jeans tore along the leg, releasing the lump behind me. I looked behind to see a thick, gold scaled tail sticking out from above my thickening thighs. A fucking *tail*. It grew as I watched it, spines pushing up through the scales along the upper surface. The end was developing into a blue spade, tipped with a sharp barb.

The fabric of my shirt creaked and popped as my torso began to thicken. My chest seemed to grow larger, barreling down my front. I winced as the cloth pulled against my broad-ening frame and I hissed in sharply with pain. My breath kept going though, my growing lungs filled with air. Distressed cotton snapped and popped, holes tearing open as I practically burst from my favorite shirt. Underneath the cloth, my breasts were receding... As scales fused over my chest to form thick-ened, blue plates, my tits all but disappeared beneath it, replaced by the smooth, hard plates. Underneath, my heart pounded a rhythm against my ribs, but deeper, reverberating throughout me.

Pain erupted along my shoulders, and my arms gave out as if my entire shoulder bone realigned itself. I landed heavily on my muzzle, involuntarily letting out a growl, but then I felt something push against my shoulder blades. The remaining cloth of my t-shirt tore away, splitting off as an odd weight pushed from my back above my shoulders. Muscles tensed, and I felt the lumps move, growing rapidly. One fell into my blurred vision. It was long and covered in golden scales, looking almost like a whole new appendage that was pushing from my back. Some part of my mind thought 'wing.' An actual wing. I stared at it, watching leathery webbing form between long, finger-like appendages.

I made a low groan, half out of frustration and half out of disbelief, but the sound was deep and guttural. It came from somewhere in my chest and sounded more like a growl.

I became dimly aware of the noises around me. Voices hit my ears as they stretched, elongated, and broadened, but I struggled to make sense of them. I could tell they were a mix of fear and awe, screams and shouts. My entire body didn't make sense. I opened my eyes, and the whole world itself didn't make sense. Everything was a weird blur, trying to focus on a single point in front of me made my eyes hurt. Relaxing my eyes caused my vision to shift, and I could see... more.

I could see to the side of me, below me, behind me. And what I saw made my jaw hang open in alarm. My neck stretched out far behind me, long and thick, covered with golden scales along the sides and blue plates down the front. It connected to a body that was... draconic. Four powerful legs, ending in paws with thick, but grasping digits. Broad wings, connected by leathery membranes, stretched out along my body, but hung limp against the ground. Behind me, a tail that whipped back and forth, almost on its own. The remains of my clothes were strewn about me, barely left as scraps. I must have been... ten, fifteen feet tall at the shoulder. Maybe twenty.

I was a dragon... A fucking dragon.

I was a beast... a creature of pure power. My digits curled into the ground, and claws dug deep furrows. Slowly I moved my legs beneath me, my muscles working as I started to push myself upright to all fours. My tail lashed behind me, and I felt it slam into the dragon head statue, toppling the rock over to one side.

And some part of me felt good about that. Like I was taking some step into taking back the festival. Taking back what was stolen... Like something that was waiting for a long time to click into place.

My vision shifted and I glanced away from my body. Around me, the festival square looked so much smaller. Megan's head came to my chest and the statue only reached up to my knee. Most of the crowd had dispersed quickly when they realized what was happening. But there were some still there, and the dull murmur of voices made my ears twitch. Then I saw a flash of green and gold, some movement, and I saw her step into view.

Megan stood behind me. She was staring, her eyes wide with alarm. She had an arm outstretched, and slowly moved towards me.

"Tab? Tabitha?" I heard her voice, but it sounded distant. "I can't believe this..." I felt her paw on my thigh, and it was warm despite the thick scales. "Are you... in there?"

I shifted my head around, scales quietly sliding against each other with a series of subtle clicks. Turning towards her, I centered my gaze to where I could really focus on her. My eyes could pick out every aspect of her, every little movement of her hips. Something was different. She stood leaning slightly forward, her legs slightly apart, almost... eager.

And part of me felt just as eager for her. What would it be

like to curl her in my tail, to caress her body with my long tongue...

Hell, what was wrong with me?

Pain lanced through my head, and I let out another groan. I pressed one of my massive paws against my forehead, trying to press back against the pressure building in my skull.

My voice rumbled from the depths of my throat, familiar and yet not. "Megan..." I said, "I'm... here..." Slowly I shook my head, a great weight on my long, sinuous neck. "I can't... think..."

The presence that had been building in my mind grew stronger still. It surged against my consciousness. I tried to push back, but it was strong. It wanted something. It wanted...

Flashes of memories, glimpses of the village from long ago, sped through my mind. I saw a society under the rule of a duke that did so from a distance, taxing and profiting off of their work. I saw the dragon, the dragon that I now looked like, scheming with a spotted feline bard to draw attention to the small city, to bring skilled artisans, entertainers from all around and improve the lives of the villagers. To start a festival.

Then the knight sent by the duke to defeat the dragon.

My vision flashed back to the present, and I stared around me. It all made sense now. The festival, the story, the show itself. The dragon, defeated, but unable to pass on. She had no heir to continue her mission, nor an interest to birth one. Her spirit and energy lingered in her skull, turned to stone and bound by the magic of the weapon that could only be removed by one of the knight's descendants. Still barely aware, all she could do was watch and observe as her carefully planned festival was quickly changed and corrupted, turned into another way to funnel money back to the Duke.

And so she waited, and planned, and prepared, using what strength she had to slowly change the magic of the blade for her own means. Preparing it for the day when she could make one of the knight's descendants restore the true nature of the festival. To bring it back to its glory, the way that Rytharian meant it to be, not the mockery that it was turned into after her defeat.

I let out a deep growl that reverberated through my throat as the thoughts and memories flashed through my head. But then they faded, my vision clearing. I could feel the spirit recede, drifting somewhere in the back of my mind. It lingered, and I picked up a sense of expectancy, as if it was waiting for me to do something.

Anger, confusion, frustration rushed through me. I didn't want to play a part in this.

Why me?

As I pulled myself back to the present, Megan's hand against my thigh was the first thing I became aware of. The warmth, the pleasant way her skin touched my scales. I actually liked it. I liked it a lot. I shook my head, trying to clear it. "Megan, I'm..." My voice rumbled, "Okay, I'm damn well not okay." My chest heaved, "But I'm here... I've..."

A commotion from behind me interrupted my thoughts. I glanced up and immediately my headache returned as I tried to look around and focus like a human, when my eyes weren't. They angled in all the wrong ways and focused so differently. I closed one eye, and the headache subsided. What I did see made the spirit of the dragon angry.

Behind me, the actor that played Sir Vanitar approached, flanked by several of what must have been the largest festival security he could find. They didn't hold guns though, they held weapons such as spears or swords, as if they thought they would be dealing with some unruly festival goer.

I grit my fangs as the spirit urged me forward. Fine, I'll play my part.

"Who brought the dragon contraption out here!?" Vanitar shouted. His voice had lost the haughtiness of the character, and sounded weirdly normal, almost businesslike. He flourished a

120

gloved hand towards me. "This is not an authorized show! I didn't authorize this, get this thing out of here!"

He thought I was a machine? Some aspect of the dragon's spirit that had settled in the back of my mind rankled at the thought. I smirked though and pulled my lips back, baring my sharp, long teeth, and saw some of the men with Vanitar's actor hesitate. Another stepped back at the sight of what must have been terrifying fangs.

Oh, that actually felt good. I could get used to that.

Then I moved, turning to approach them. My tail swung over Megan's head as I pulled away from her touch, some part of my mind reluctant to leave it. Within seconds I saw the men's expressions change, as my motions were too fluid to be some machine. Even unfamiliar as my body was, I was learning to control it, my heavy paws hitting the ground with dull thuds.

"Seems to me," I said, talking slowly as I tried to get used to the way my muzzle moved, "That your show needs some revisions."

Vanitar's eyes widened as I talked. He too took a step back from me. His spear shook visibly in his grasp. "What... what in the hell?"

My footsteps landed heavy on the ground next to him, the earth rattling. It was lucky that all I wanted to do was to scare him—this body was so unfamiliar I don't think I could have actually fought him despite my size. "This festival has a new owner!"

In the actor's defense, he didn't run immediately. He seemed glued to the spot, even as I loomed over him. I was almost two times his height. Looking down I could even see the bald spot developing on the back of his head.

But that wasn't quite fair. Slowly I lowered my head down so that I was on eye-level with him. "My name-" I hesitated. What was a dragon name...? My mind drifted back to the dragon in the story. "-is Tatharian," I said. "And we're going to do Things.

Much. Differently. Here." With each word, I nudged the point of my muzzle into his chest, shoving him back step by step with ease. I made sure to breathe out deeply into his face and saw sparks of electricity crackling from my maw. Oh yeah, I could very much get used to this.

Vanitar dropped the spear with a clank and started to run. I snapped my fangs after him just for show—like I'd actually bite him. But it did the job. He let out a yell and stumbled forward, landing heavily on his hands and knees. I lashed out with my claws and caught the end of his cloak. He half crawled, half scrambled up to his feet, running as quickly as he could. I glanced around, but the other guards had already run off.

A grin grew on my muzzle, my breath quick with excitement. That... was fun. Then the world crashed back down around me. I felt everything at once, felt the strangeness of my body come back around me, the weight of my wings hanging against my shoulders. My entire frame sagged under the unfamiliar weight.

Then a voice rose up next to me. It was Megan's. "Behold! The guardian returns!" She shouted. One hand was still on my side, and warmth was comforting. "Don't be afraid, she's here to help restore the festival to its roots!"

I turned my head around, looking back across the courtyard. There were people still milling about, and it actually looked like more were returning, drawn to the commotion. Many were cautious, but they weren't running in terror. Some even seemed curious.

Me? A guardian of this place? What did that mean?

Megan's paw moved further up my front leg but couldn't get much higher. I stood nearly twice her height. "Tab... That was... incredible," she said, her eyes wide. Slowly, her paw ran across my scales. It caused strange sensations that only confused my mind even more. "I can't believe this."

Another flash of memory crossed my vision. Images of the

dragon, curled around the lady bard. Feelings of the love they shared. Not just love, but an intense passion, a yearning for each other. Oh, I understood now... If I could be a descendant of the knight, then perhaps...

As the memories subsided, I slowly lowered my head down to Megan. My muzzle touched her hair gently and I breathed in her scent. Normally I'd just smell the generic 'cat' smell. But now I picked a hint of spice, the oils of her leathers, a touch of sweetness, and many other things that I just couldn't put my finger on. But I liked it.

And I think the spirit of the dragon, fading as its energy was spent changing me, did too.

I smiled, trying to avoid lifting the lips of my large muzzle too much. With effort, I maneuvered my tail around Megan. It's spade just barely grazed her hind paws, twitching against them. "Believe it, kitten..." I said, keeping my voice quiet as to not be overheard, and lowered my head closer to her ear. I not only felt but heard the quiet purr that escaped her as my chin touched her fur. "Because there's more to this tale than I think even you know..."

A PENNY FOR YOUR MEMORIES

KYELL GOLD

Nesbit curled up in the drawer from the 1820s, a very comforting decade for him to remember. After winding himself around the stacks of coins, he held a nice silver one against his chest. Memories flooded back to him, of a sunny day on a hillside and a pair of fruit bats who'd liked to fly with him. They had found this silver coin by the side of the road and had thought he would like it.

That had been a good day. They had flown to the edge of the wood together, done loops around each other in the air, eaten mango in the highest branches of a tree, and the bats had told him about all their friends in the town and what everyone was doing. Nesbit didn't know most of the people involved, but he liked the stories and liked that the bats had cared enough to share the stories with him. What had their names been, the bats? Oh, yes, Amit the talkative one, and Nameen the one who liked to run his claws over Nesbit's tail.

He rubbed the coin along his sky-blue chest scales, and the memory grew brighter, the sun and the wind, the thick smell of mango and the tangy smell of the bats, their striking black and orange fur. They'd said his blue scales made him look like a piece of the sky had dropped into the tree with them. Nesbit closed his eyes.

"Nezzie!"

Some kids calling for him. He didn't have to answer them now, though. In a few years they would be preoccupied with their own lives, and their younger brothers and sisters would be the ones asking him to fly them around, or tell them stories, or do fire tricks. Or, if he waited long enough, the next generation of kids would be the ones coming around. It was all the same to Nesbit.

He tried to shut out the noises outside, to remember Amit's and Nameen's voices. His wings flicked with the memory of flying and his body shivered pleasurably. In the memory, they planned to come back the next day, and the knowledge that they would eventually leave his company and pass away was far off on the horizon.

"Nezzie?"

The voice was closer now. They were inside his cave? He didn't think any of them wanted a story that much.

"Nezz?"

Now the voice was familiar. But it couldn't be. Could it?

He dropped the coin and hurried to the front of the drawer, putting his front claws on the edge to peek over. "Jay?"

The shape at the entrance to the cave, limned by starlight, resolved into a dhole in a loose polo shirt and shorts, his ears perked. "Nezzie, you there?"

Nesbit jumped out of the drawer and glided to the ground, growing to match Jay's size as he did. He knew that size well; in the decade since a young ten-year-old Jay had first come to play with him, the dhole had grown two feet, but most of that had been between his thirteenth and fifteenth years. And from only a few steps away, Jay looked much the same as the last time Nesbit had seen him: soft golden-red fur, lighter under his muzzle, pointed ears perked. Even the tentative, whisker-lifting smile was the same expression burned into Nesbit's memory. The dragon sniffed, his thin tongue flicking in and out. "You're supposed to be gone."

"I was. I came back." Jay took another step forward and then stopped. "Are you okay?"

"I'm okay." Nesbit's tail swept the cave floor. He tried to sort through the confusing emotions: he was glad to see Jay again—more than glad, if he were honest—but he knew it wouldn't last, that the dhole would leave again and Nesbit would have to curl up and lose himself in memories for months to forget.

Jay's tail fell still. "Kishan said you haven't visited with them in a month."

Nesbit shrugged. "It doesn't seem that long to me."

The dhole looked behind Nesbit, at the neat array of dressers and wardrobes, and then back at the dragon. "Have you been out at all since I left?"

There it was, out in the open. Every time Nesbit thought he had a handle on how to talk to people, they changed. There had been a time when everyone was direct, and that was unsettling, but he'd gotten used to it. Then things changed and it was impolite to say what one was thinking, and that was confusing. Now they were back to being direct, or maybe it was just that Jay was. Nesbit, uncomfortable, hid behind a different truth. "Yes. Once or twice. It's just…I don't know what to say around them anymore. I feel like they're just coming to be polite, like they just tolerate me. They're getting older."

"I was years older than Kishan is now and you still played with me."

"But none of your friends came," Nesbit said. "It was just you and the younger kids."

"They came all the way to the cave to see you," Jay pointed out.

"Did you ask them to?"

The dhole's ears went flat. "I asked them to look in on you, sure," he said. "I didn't want you to be alone."

"I'm not alone." Though he couldn't see any of the coins, he felt them all around him.

Jay looked around the cave and plainly didn't see what Nesbit was talking about. "I, uh, I missed you," he said awkwardly.

Nesbit swished his tail across the floor. The feel of the cool rock on his scales calmed him. Jay was young and didn't understand the patterns of the world as Nesbit did; even though he was back now, that didn't mean he wasn't going to leave again. Prabhavarti had warned him about this, all those centuries ago. So he changed the subject. "I don't think the others like me. I worry I'm going to say something old and they're going to make fun of me."

"They like you," Jay said. "Especially Kishan. He was sad he hadn't seen you."

"That's nice, I guess." Nesbit looked down at the ground.

"He really does." Jay took a step closer. "Like you, I mean."

Now Nesbit could reach out and touch him, and he wanted to, wanted to take the dhole and pull him close, but he couldn't make himself do it. The fact that Kishan liked him seemed supremely unimportant in this moment. "Okay."

There was a clink of metal that made Nesbit's scales shiver. "I, uh, I brought you something," Jay said. He pushed a russet-furred paw into Nesbit's view, in which three bright gold discs lay.

"What's that?" Nesbit asked, although his spine tingled at the sight of the coins and his claws flexed, already feeling the shiny metal between them.

"It's a gift. An apology, sort of, but mostly they made me think of you. They're...old coins minted for the King. A hundred years ago, I think? Maybe more than that, before the first World War. I don't know what they're worth, but..." He pushed his paw out farther. "I thought you should have them."

Nesbit swallowed once and then grabbed up the coins. He brought them to his chest scales and rubbed them there, letting the feel of the gold—they were pure gold, indeed—course through him. And then he dropped them, his scales still shimmering with the memory of them, and wrapped his arms around Jay.

The dhole staggered back a step and then returned the hug. "I missed you," he said again.

"I missed you, too." It felt good to admit that, and Nesbit gave up resisting the rush of happiness that Jay was back. The way Jay's fur felt against his scales, the trace of claws along the ridge of his spine, the warmth of the dhole against him and the smell of his breath, all these were pleasures he'd thought relegated to the memories of his coins, and here he was making more memories again.

The hug lasted a long time, as Nesbit pressed his fingers against the cotton cloth of the dhole's shirt, and the dhole's paws ran nicely along his scales, tracing them in the way he liked to do. But finally Nesbit stepped back, keeping his paws on the dhole's sides. "Did the military people let you go?" He suppressed the instinct to ask, "And do you have to go back?"

Jay's warm brown eyes looked into his. The dhole blinked and then smiled. "Hang on," he said. "I brought some stuff. May I bring it in?"

Nesbit stretched his wings out to their fullest, to feel the tension in the translucent blue webbing between the digits of each wing, and then folded them along his back. "More stuff? More coins?"

Jay laughed. "No. Stuff for me. A sleeping bag, some food."

"Oh. Oh! What kind of food?"

The dhole smiled and brushed his paw down Nesbit's chest

scales, leaving what felt like warm sparkles all the way down. "I didn't forget those butter cookies you like."

"I'll help bring it." Nesbit stopped himself. "The others aren't outside, are they?"

"No." Jay laughed. "Stay here. I brought it all myself; I can bring it the last bit too."

So while the dhole went to fetch his "stuff," Nesbit scooped up the three gold coins and opened the wooden doors of his newest cabinet. There was space there for the gold coins on the third shelf, next to the copper coins and the silver coins that Jay (and some of the others) had brought him over the last two years. He stacked the gold coins and placed them carefully there on the shelf, and then, keeping his ears alert for the sound of Jay returning, reached for a silver coin sitting by itself on the far left of the narrow shelf. His fingers picked it out and rubbed along its surface, and the rush of memory from it quickened his breath and hearts.

Here was the day Jay had first come to him, a lanky teenaged dhole with a silver coin and a brighter smile, whose eyes grew round and wide when Nesbit showed him his cave, the array of furniture from hundreds of years. He hadn't asked, "Where's the huge pile of coins?" like many new arrivals did; he'd marveled at the craftsmanship of the wood and had instantly grasped why they were ordered by age.

Nesbit closed his eyes, falling back into that day, and gave his wings a flutter as his fingers rubbed the coin all around. He could feel again his nervousness, the same flutters he had every time someone new came to his cave even after hundreds of years, but Jay of all of them had put him at ease almost immediately.

"These are from the time of the Great Emperor Aghabal!" Jay had exclaimed, looking at Nesbit's oldest coins with delight.

"Those are older than I am," Nesbit had said, feeling proud and weary all at once.

"And these—" Jay had skipped ahead. "My great-grandfather left us a coin like this one!"

"I met your great-grandfather," Nesbit had said. "You may look, but don't touch."

"And the coin I brought you." Jay's eyes shone. "It goes into your collection? With these? And one day my great-grandson might come to look at them too?"

"Perhaps, yes. If your family stays in the village."

"Oh." The dhole's smile had dimmed. "Of course we will stay in the village. We never go anywhere."

The memory surged brighter, filling him, and then the part of him that remained present did its best polite cough and figurative tap on his shoulder and reminded him that the real Jay was just outside. With an effort, he put the coin back on the shelf.

It took a moment for the flush of the memory to fade. He stretched his wings out to their fullest, growing a foot so he could rest his fingers on the cabinet. Breathe in, breathe out.

Jay returned a few moments later, when Nesbit had returned his breathing and heartbeat to their resting state. "Oh," the dhole said. "You got bigger."

Nesbit shrank down. "I was just stretching," he said evasively.

"I don't mind." The dhole's tail wagged cheerfully. He lowered a large pack from his back.

"You brought a lot," Nesbit said.

Jay took a tightly-rolled sleeping bag out, rough fabric and a dirty brown color. He held it in both paws. "I was hoping I could stay here for a while," he said. "I can stay outside if you'd rather. I know there isn't a lot of room in here. It's just the one cave."

"There are four caves," Nesbit said, trying not to wonder what *stay here a while* meant. "But three of them you can't fit into." He had arrayed his dressers and cabinets along the smoothest wall, some thirty feet across, and against the fifteen-foot back wall were stacked some gifts people had brought that wouldn't fit into cabinets: sixteen carpets, one elegant birdcage (Fariah, in the late 18th century, had brought that, as though Nesbit would ever want to keep a bird, but he liked the shape and the curlicues in the wire, and sometimes he shrank down and slept in it), thirty-eight bolts of patterned silk (it felt good on his scales), a basket that had once been filled with jewelry (these days people did not bring him jewelry as much, and he had sold or bartered many of the old pieces when people seemed more interested in them than he was), and two dozen ceramic and terracotta pots and vases of various sizes (a nuisance; he had no use for them and nobody wanted to buy them for any price worth moving them out of his cave). And there was a small stack of books, a few of which had been gifts. "I suppose," he said, "you could put your bedding over there on the opposite wall toward the back, if you like. Your books are still there."

Jay's ears perked up, and he hurried over to lay the sleeping bag there. Nesbit followed and watched him unroll it onto the dirt. "Er," the dragon said, his heart beating again, "how long do you think you might want—need to stay?"

For a moment, the dhole didn't move. His whiskers twitched and his ears shivered slightly, and then he stood up and rubbed his paws together. "I, uh," he said.

Nesbit tilted his head. It seemed inconceivable that his smiling, confident friend would be nervous, would be (*acting like Nesbit himself*) unsure of what to say. He was going to leave tomorrow, that was it. Or—or ask to stay longer?

"I was thinking about..." Jay said. "What we talked about, that time by the orchard."

It had been a cold winter day, and Nesbit had been going around to light fires for the town. He was not as busy as he'd been decades before, when he'd been needed for forges and bonfires and such. These days, people could buy matches and lighters down at the corner store, and his appearances were more ceremonial than necessary. The fireworks shows, though rarer, were still his and his alone, at least in this medium-sized town, and so he enjoyed them even though the chemicals tasted odd. It was nice to be cheered, especially from far below on the ground where he didn't have to worry about what he said or did.

Today, Jay had come around with him to watch him light fires, and now they lay in the evening chill in the field behind Jay's parents' house, next to an orchard that was now rows of bare trees. Nesbit lay on his back on the cold dirt, having made himself large enough that the dhole could lie on the dragon's chest and they could stare up at the stars together. A light blanket over Jay kept his and Nesbit's heat cozily in.

The dhole held up two sticks, each with a marshmallow impaled on the end. "Another?" he said.

"Sure." Nesbit flicked his tail around in the dirt to express his little shiver of delight at Jay's presence and the shared marshmallow treats, because he didn't want to jostle the dhole on his chest. He pulled the fire up from his belly, just a little bit, and brought his mouth close to the marshmallows. Carefully, he let out a small stream of flame. The marshmallows browned quickly, and Nesbit stopped his breath while Jay turned them, and then Nesbit breathed out again.

Jay pulled the browned marshmallows back toward him. He sandwiched each of them between two digestive biscuits with some chocolate in between. "Just a moment," he said. "It's melting..." He held one in each paw. "Okay," he said. "They're ready."

Nesbit shrank himself to Jay's size, keeping hold of the dhole so he wouldn't tumble to the ground. They ended up lying together on the dirt, laughing, and Jay threw half the blanket over Nesbit even though the dragon was perfectly warm. "Here," he said, holding out one of the sandwiches.

Nesbit took it and tossed it immediately into his mouth, just as Jay did. The gooey sweetness burst against his tongue with the crunch of the biscuits around it. It was a little sweeter than he normally liked, but as a treat it was fine; as an experience to share with Jay it was lovely.

"None of my other friends like these," Jay said, spraying sticky crumbs over the blanket. "My auntie sent me a bag of marshmallows and everyone else said they were gross. Kishan said they're like eating snot."

"I like them." Nesbit paused. "Does Kishan eat snot?"

Jay laughed. "I don't think so. But you should ask him next time we hang out."

"Oh, I couldn't." Nesbit devoted his attention to savoring the remaining sweetness and the slight burnt taste of the chocolate in his still-hot throat.

There was a moment of silence. "He didn't mean it, you know," Jay said.

"It's okay," Nesbit said. "I am boring."

Jay reached around his shoulders and hugged him. "You're not boring," he said fiercely. "Nobody in town thinks so. They're all proud to have a dragon here, and you're kind to everyone, and your fireworks shows are lovely, plus you help us out with big town projects."

"None of that," Nesbit pointed out, "is not-boring."

"The fireworks shows aren't boring," Jay said. "They're thrilling! Fwoosh! Pop! Psssh!" His paws mimed explosions in the air.

Nesbit smiled and leaned against the dhole's warm fur. "What did the other dragon do?"

Jay stiffened slightly. "It wasn't really a big deal," he said.

"It's all right. I've been compared to other dragons before. A lot." Nesbit settled his wings so he could lean more comfortably. "What was it?"

"First of all," Jay said, "we were there on a school trip, and there were two other schools visiting too. We were there to see the Palace of the Winds, and the dragon was part of the tour. She told us about the history, and how its design makes music when wind goes through it, and then she beat her wings to make the wind to make the sounds. And there was a floor of colored glass windows and she breathed fire behind it to make the glass come to life."

"I remember when that palace was built," Nesbit said. "I went to see it. The dragon is…Ranawat, is that right?"

"That's right. Did you meet her?"

"No. I heard that dragons aren't always friendly to other dragons. I just wanted to see the palace. I made myself small and rode on a traveler's shoulder into the city. She didn't notice me."

"How long ago was that?"

Nesbit thought. "A hundred and fifty years maybe?" He had a coin from that journey, but he hadn't reached for it in a long time. "Did you find out any more?" He liked when Jay told him little stories from the region's history, because although Nesbit was old, he'd spent most of his life in a cave. He could tell Jay which other villager his great-grandfather was friends with, but he couldn't say for sure who had been ruling the country in that time. Jay's stories gave the world more texture.

"No, nothing more than I told you before we left. " The dhole sighed. "They all tell the same stories. Was Ranawat doing that same show even back then?"

"I remember the colored windows. It might have been a windy day, so she didn't need to beat her wings. She liked to be large."

Jay nodded and his tail flicked. "She still does."

"Did she tell that story about the First Dragon?"

"Yes." Jay paused. "I was going to ask you about that." When

Nesbit didn't say anything, Jay ventured a little further. "Did you hatch from an egg dropped from the sky?"

Nesbit snorted, hard enough that a little puff of smoke floated from his mouth. "No."

"Kishan believed it," Jay said with more confidence. "But I told him it was just myth. Dragons hatch from eggs laid by other dragons, of course, just like other animals." His confidence wavered when Nesbit didn't answer. "They do, though, right? Or do you not hatch from eggs, like bats?"

This was a point Nesbit had reached with friends in the past. "How old are you?" was an easy question to answer, but "Where are your parents/are they still alive?" and "Will you ever marry another dragon?" and the question Jay had just asked, those were ones that Nesbit usually skirted with vague answers and myths, like Ranawat did, only much less flashily.

But Jay was a friend, the closest friend he'd had in…in maybe ever, and if he avoided the question then Jay would know it and would pull away a little bit, maybe a lot, and would not come to see him as often, and his inevitable departure would come faster. But if he did tell the story, the true story, then…then what? He didn't know what would happen because it had never happened before.

"We don't have to talk about it if you don't want to," Jay said.

Nesbit made himself smaller and leaned back into Jay's embrace so that the dhole felt larger and steadying. "I was born over three hundred years ago," he said. "But I wasn't a dragon when I was born."

"What?" Jay's voice sharpened with excitement. His tail lashed the ground. "What were you? Did you get turned into a dragon? How?" He stopped. "Sorry. You're telling me."

"You can't tell anyone this, ever," Nesbit said.

"No, no, I promise!" Jay clutched him tighter. "Not even Kishan. What were you when you were born?"

"I was a..." He paused. "A badger. I think. Do badgers swim? I remember liking swimming."

Jay collected himself and his arm tightened around Nesbit. "An otter, perhaps?"

"Perhaps. But I have an image of my father with a black and white striped muzzle. Or maybe that was someone else. I don't know. Do otters like to travel?"

"I don't know," Jay admitted. "As much as badgers, I'd venture. I don't really know many of either. I have an otter friend at school."

"My father loved to travel. You would have liked him, I think. I was born in another country that wasn't his home, and he took me around with him everywhere. We went back to his home country for a short time, and that's where my first memories are, but when I was seven or eight, we set out again. He loved to walk, and I could keep up with him much of the time, but when I couldn't, he carried me. We traveled together for five years and came to Surat, and there he died."

"Oh," Jay said. "I'm sorry."

Nesbit acknowledged the sympathy with a rub of his head. "I lived there after he died, because I hadn't the means to leave, and where would I go? Many families took me in for a time, and the whole town was kindly toward me, but the only person I felt comfortable with was the dragon up on the hill. Her name was Prabhavati, and she had a cave larger than mine, filled with ancient coins and gold and stone and ceramic figures and carpets. She liked to lie on them and would let a few of us come in to talk to her. She might not have liked me best, but I liked her best.

"The city had little for me. There were no other otters—or badgers—there, and I only spoke a little of the language. But Prabhavati had the dragon's gift of language, and I could speak to her easily. And there was a time, six or seven years after my father had died, when I was telling her how miserable I was and how I didn't feel I had a home.

"'A dragon's home is wherever she is,' she told me. 'We have no people, no country, no allegiance. We are sufficient unto ourselves.'

"That sounded quite lovely to me, you may understand, to not feel that aching need that I'd felt even before my father died. He was searching for something too, and I was caught up in that search but left without the means or understanding to continue it. So I said, 'I wish I were a dragon.'

"Prabhavati asked if I truly meant it, and said there was a way, but I would have to give up everything in my life to do it. She said if I really wanted to, I should return in eight days' time."

Nesbit shifted again, balancing with his tail. This memory he had relived often, not because it felt good or bad, but because it felt important. He felt Jay's tension and anticipation. "I came back, of course, you know that. I had nothing in my life worth keeping, not really, so it was an easy choice to make. Or so I thought at the time." Nesbit sighed at the naïveté of his younger self. "Being a dragon seemed like it would be quite a nice change. I could fly, so I could go anywhere I wanted, even back home." He paused. "Wherever 'home' was. Or I could keep traveling, like my father. And everyone in the town loved Prabhavati, and she seemed so confident. I thought it would be quite nice to live like that.

"And she explained that in very rare cases, when someone wants to become a dragon, and another dragon feels that it's right, the two of them have to, uh, they get very physically close, and..."

Jay rubbed Nesbit's side scales, smaller and thinner than the chest ones, and a deeper shade of blue. "They have sex? Sex turns you into a dragon? That's incredible."

"I didn't even think about it. Have you, uh..." The question trailed off because Nesbit started to wonder if Jay would want to have sex with him, cuddled close together as they were. He didn't feel the urge, though the closeness was nice, but he knew mammals felt it more strongly and more often.

"Yeah, I'm not a virgin," Jay said with ease and not a hint of flirtation. Well, maybe a hint, but Nesbit ignored it.

"I wasn't either, back then. Some of the townspeople thought I was interesting and wanted to see how interesting the parts I kept covered were. I feel like most of them were disappointed, but...those memories are old and faded. Anyway, she shrank to my size, and then, um, we had sex, and when it was over, I was..." He gestured at his body. "Like this." That wasn't the whole truth, but it was enough for now. If he told Jay about the coin she'd made him hold, he would have to explain all about the coins, and that was even more secret than this story. Prabhavati had impressed that on him. It is our magic alone, she'd said, and if they know about it, they will try to take it for themselves.

"What did it feel like?" Jay asked excitedly.

"The sex? It felt good," Nesbit said.

Jay dug an elbow into his side. "Just 'good'? I know sex feels good. What did it feel like to change?"

"Oh, like..." Nesbit looked at the bag of marshmallows. "You know how the s'more feels all gooey and sweet? It felt like...like my body was made of marshmallow. I mean, I hadn't had one of those yet, but I think it was like that. And it got all warm and crackled like a fire does when you put new wood on it, and my skin felt itchy and tingly all over and then it hardened. And then I was a dragon. I thought I would be green like Prabhavati was, but I was blue. She didn't seem surprised."

"Ranawat was white with pearl," Jay said. "What happened then? What happened to Prabhavati?"

Nesbit looked up at the stars, their multitude like the coins in Prabhavati's cave. "I don't know. She might still be there. She set aside three huge chests—one of them I still have, the others fell apart—full of mostly coins and a few stone figures and gems, and one carpet. That's the one by the old trunk, the one that's unrolled. It's worn down now so you can hardly see the design, but there's enough there that I remember it."

"But why did you come here?"

"Oh." He'd clutched the coin she'd made him hold as the transformation took place, and a moment later, he'd felt the bond of his memory to the coin, his first coin. And with that magic, he'd become aware that all the other things in the cave, except what Prabhavati had given him, were not-his. It was like being immersed in an unpleasant odor. "Dragons are possessive and it felt wrong for me to stay there with her and her hoard. Also she wouldn't have allowed it. So I went looking for a small town that didn't have a dragon, and had a nice cave, and I found this cave after a week. I brought all three chests here and I've been here ever since, and that's the story."

"Wow," Jay breathed. "You got turned into a dragon with sex."

"Basically," Nesbit said.

"And…can that work with anyone?"

"I don't know," Nesbit said both honestly and evasively. "I just know that it works for people like me."

"It's okay," Jay said with a laugh, but the laugh felt a little forced. "I don't want to give up my family."

"And if you did turn into a dragon, you'd have to go away."

Jay's smile faded and his ears went down. "Did that happen with someone else? Did you turn someone into a dragon and they left?"

"No, I haven't turned anyone."

The dhole's tone went from awed to incredulous. "Wait. Does that mean you haven't had sex in three hundred years?"

"And then some, but…" Nesbit shifted. "I don't feel the urge the way you do. I can, you know, take care of myself—"

"Masturbate," Jay said.

"—and that's fine, but there are other things that feel more like mammal sex."

"Like what?"

Nesbit squirmed. The stars in the sky now looked like the glitter of coins when the sun shone into his cave and he opened his drawers to the light. "Just…just dragon things."

Jay leaned over and kissed the top of his head. "All right. That's enough secrets for tonight, I suppose." He looked down into Nesbit's eyes. "I promise by all the gods that I will keep your secret."

"Thank you." Nesbit exhaled with the relief of having navigated the sensitive subject successfully. And he didn't feel any apprehension that Jay would tell anyone about it. His secret was safe and shared now.

"Good!" The dhole rummaged in his pocket and brought out a large flat coin. "Because I have a gift for you. This," he pronounced, "is the most valuable coin in all the world."

Nesbit grew to match Jay's size again and looked with interest. The coin was half the size of Jay's paw, very thin, and only the shadows of features adorned its surface. "Did you flatten a regular coin?" he asked.

"To start with, yes." Jay turned it over, revealing scratches that caught the starlight. They read "JAY" across the top and a "1" in the center. "It's my coin," he said. "The only one in the world."

Nesbit took the coin, light and fragile in his claws, and turned it over. He pressed it to his chest scales and felt the magic of memory sink into it. "It's perfect," he said.

"Now," Jay said, leaning back on his elbows, "I have to caution you that not everyone is up to date on the latest currencies, so you may not be able to spend it everywhere yet. Or anywhere, really."

Nesbit held the coin to his chest and nestled against the dhole. "Then I'll keep it forever," he said.

The large flat coin lay by itself in the middle of the shelf where Nesbit had just put the gold coins, and now his eyes flicked to it before returning to Jay's russet muzzle with the white chin, the brown eyes wide and earnest. "You want to...?"

Jay nodded. "I want to...to be a dragon. With you."

Emotions as strong as any coin-memory battered Nesbit in the space of a few seconds: joy and apprehension and hope and loss, coming in waves. Unequal to the task of expressing them all in his words, he stammered out, "It doesn't—I don't know—"

"You said that someone would have to leave everything behind," Jay said, and then the words poured out. "I want to. I'm like you were, hundreds of years ago. I don't have family, I don't have friends. Except you. I don't have anything, and I want to live like you do. With you."

"You don't have family?" Momentarily distracted, Nesbit stretched his wings. "What happened to them?" If someone had been killed in the town he was supposed to be responsible for, that would be bad, very bad. He wasn't sure what the consequences would be, but they couldn't be good, could they?

"My family is—alive." Jay drew in a breath and then sat down on his sleeping bag. Nesbit sat facing him. "I didn't tell you where I went, just that they sent me away."

"To a fort somewhere."

"I had to do military service." Jay flattened his ears. "I didn't *have* to. My parents wanted me to. My father and older brother were in the military and my father received lots of honors and medals. I never wanted to do that. I wanted to study history. And military service is the opposite of studying history. It's ignoring history. I argued a lot but they still made me go."

"Oh." Nesbit's admittedly patchy knowledge of the military didn't quite line up with this—a lot of military people seemed very interested in history—but he let it slide because Jay was passionate and because there wasn't really room to say more than just "Oh."

"I tried to make it work. But nobody there is interested in why we're doing what we're doing. They just want to follow orders, and that's what they want us to do, the officers, I mean. I stayed there for two months and I made only one real friend, a pangolin. At least, I thought he was a friend until he reported me just for saying something bad about the military. I was supposed to spend two weeks working in the kitchen, but I decided I'm done with them, and I stole those coins and I came back here."

"Wait." Nesbit glanced back at his dresser. "You *stole* those gold coins?"

"I didn't buy them." Jay smiled at him. "They had them in a little museum on the fort but it wasn't really guarded well at all. They were easy to take. It was kind of a 'fuck you' to them but also I wanted to have a really nice gift to bring back to you."

Nesbit shook his head. "You shouldn't have stolen them," he said.

"Don't worry. They won't come take them back from you. Dragons can't have any property taken from them, even if it was stolen. Once it's in a hoard, it belongs to you. They can punish the thief if it wasn't you, but they can't recover the items. That's the law."

"I know, but...I meant for you," Nesbit said. "What if they come looking for you?"

"Well." Jay's smile widened, almost glowing. "They'll be looking for a dhole. So they won't find me."

Nesbit folded his wings along his back and looked down at his tail, curled around his legs. He traced a claw along the little ridge that marked his spine. "Couldn't you just stay here as you are? I can protect you."

"Is there some reason I shouldn't be a dragon?" Jay's ears folded back. "Do you not want me to be?"

"You're my favorite person in the world," Nesbit said. "But you can't just decide to become a dragon because you had to work in the kitchen for a day."

Jay's ears flattened. "It wasn't *just* that," he said. "It was everything, and the kitchen thing was just the last bit of—" He shook his head. "Nobody ever listened to me, my whole life. Not my parents, not my friends, for sure not the officers and other army guys. You're the only person who listened to my stories, encouraged me to find out more, made me feel…real."

"You were my best friend too," Nesbit said. "But being a dragon is different."

"Do you wish you weren't one?"

"Uh…" He'd been a dragon for centuries now; he couldn't imagine anything else. "No, but I can't remember if I did right after I changed. I was lonely, I know that."

"Well, that's easy. I know you said new dragons have to leave, but I won't," Jay promised. "I'll build up my own hoard. I'll help do work around the town."

"Dragons don't live together!" It burst out of him, the unassailable truth he didn't want to acknowledge but could not escape.

"None we know of," Jay said. "Why shouldn't we be the first?"

How could Nesbit explain the intimate and mysterious connection a dragon had with their hoard, which even he didn't fully understand? How as soon as he'd become a dragon, there were things that were his and things that were not, and he belonged with the things that were his, not with the things that were not? That the cave felt like more of a home than he'd ever known because his memories were here, uncluttered by others?

The slight apprehension he felt anytime he met another dragon, which seemed to be about the hoard (though he felt apprehension whenever he met anyone, it was true)? "It's...it's just not done," was the best he could manage.

"You're worried about what the other dragons will say?" Jay shook his head. "You don't even talk to them."

As clearly as if it were imprinted on a coin, Nesbit saw the decision he had to make and both futures that would result from it. He could stand firm, refuse to do the ritual with Jay, and then the dhole would either leave immediately (forever) or would stay and have the argument every day until Nesbit gave in. Or he could do the ritual, and then dragon-Jay, now subject to the reality of dragons rather than the fantasy, would leave to find his own cave in another town. At least in that second scenario, Nesbit might still visit him. There were dragons who were friendly, who saw each other as often as once a year, he'd been told. They could be that, and that was better than losing Jay forever.

So he forced a smile and said, "You're right. If it's what you want, then we'll do it."

Jay lit up, ears perking and smile shining brightly, and that was enough to convince Nesbit he'd done the right thing. The dhole leapt forward into a hug and rubbed his muzzle along Nesbit's snout. "Thank you, thank you," he said, and then his ears folded back and he looked away. "You know, ever since you told me that story, I, uh, I wanted to sleep with you. Not to become a dragon, but...I wasn't sure if dragons even had sex before that, and then when I knew they did, I..." He rested a paw on Nesbit's scales, and though he'd done that many times before, this time there was a hint of something that hadn't been there before, alongside the affection they'd always shared. There was a little bit of hunger, a little envy, a little desire, small twitches in the fingers eager to move elsewhere, waiting for one more sign of permission from Nesbit before they did.

Nesbit drew his claws through Jay's fur, trying to catch that same feeling, but he was not accustomed to arousal unless he was holding his coins. So he imagined holding a coin and reliving the feel of the dhole's fur against his, and that gave him enough of a spark to grip the lithe body more tightly.

That was what Jay had been waiting for, it seemed. The dhole returned the squeeze, making a contented noise in his throat as his paws roamed down Nesbit's sides. Nesbit shifted, and his thigh pressed against a hardness at the front of Jay's pants, and that the dhole pulled back with a bashful smile. "Do you, ah, do you have a bed? Or cushions or something? Or this is fine if you don't." He flicked his ears and his smile widened. "Sorry," he said. "I'm babbling. I'm just excited."

"I am too," Nesbit said. "But...I've never had sex with another male."

"Oh, don't worry about that." Jay pulled his shirt over his head and laughed, a little high-pitched and quick. "I've done it a bunch of times. You, ah..." His eyes strayed down to the dragon's waist. "You have a penis, right?"

"What? Yes." Nesbit's fingers covered the gap in his scales behind which it sat. "It's just inside, that's all."

"Oh, good, good." Jay's paw strayed to the front of his pants again. "Is there, uh, is there anything else we need to do?"

Nesbit nodded. "I have to go get something."

"Okay, then." Jay pushed his pants down a little. "Go ahead and I'll, uh, I'll get ready."

"All right." Nesbit's hearts did beat faster at that little reveal of more of Jay's fur. He hadn't thought that after three hundred years or so he would have much excitement to have sex again. He'd had sex before his transformation and had enjoyed it, but afterwards, he hadn't thought about it much. Now he was thinking about the delight of being close to Jay and how they were going to be really close, fur to scales, and how he was going to have that memory preserved in a coin to relive if he wanted to.

He went to the shelf on which he'd placed the three gold coins and took down two of them. They tingled with the memory of Jay giving them to him, but the remaining one would hold that memory. These two could be used again.

When he turned back, the dhole was sitting on the sleeping bag, naked, one paw curled around his white sheath, from which his pink cock peeked out already. His thumb teased his tip and he looked up at Nesbit. "Like it?"

The dragon nodded. "Very much," he said, and he didn't have to force the words. Long-dormant feelings stirred in him in response as he sat next to Jay on the sleeping bag. He held out one of the gold coins. "Hold this."

"That's yours," Jay said, but took the coin. "I gave it to you."

Nesbit nodded. "And now it'll be yours. This is part of it. I'm giving the coin to you."

Jay frowned, holding it. "What do I do with it?"

"You hold it while we're...you know." Now that the reality of the situation pressed in on him, Nesbit's body was remembering sex and felt excited about it. He pressed his own coin to his chest. "I like to hold mine here, but you can hold it anywhere, really."

Jay pressed the coin to his chest. "*While* we're having sex? Is it supposed to do something?"

"It will." Nesbit's free paw wandered down to the gap in his scales, which felt warm now, his member closer to the air than it had been in perhaps a decade. "It's hard to describe, but it...it holds your memory of this? You'll understand when you're a dragon."

The dhole's eyes widened as he looked at the coin, but only for a moment before he leaned over and brought his free paw to the scales on Nesbit's legs. "Can I help?" he asked, and stroked lightly. "Is that good?"

Warmth responded. Nesbit felt a flood of relief; he was going to be able to do this. "That's good," he said. "It's very good."

"This is going to be tricky with just one paw." Jay smiled. "But we can do it."

"We each have one free." Nesbit let Jay's fingers explore up his leg as he scooted himself around so that he could reach Jay's sheath. He loved running his fingers through his friend's fur, and had sometimes wondered what he looked like without clothes. Now the dragon traced the grain of his fur, sensing the warmth as he approached the sheath and stiff cock now halfway out of it. Jay smelled strongly of himself, with the red dust of the road and the fragrance of the brush on the mountain mixed in. He hadn't cleaned himself in days, and for the first time Nesbit appreciated how long Jay must have traveled to get back to him here. He closed his eyes, feeling Jay's despair as a dim twilight and seeing himself through the dhole's eyes as a beacon on a mountain in the distance. With that image in his mind, his fingers closed around the dhole's shaft.

Jay's whole body tensed and pressed against Nesbit. His shaft twitched and pushed farther out against the dragon's fingers. Nesbit held his coin tightly, feeling the warmth pulsing under his fingers and the shivers of pleasure his touch sent through his friend.

Emboldened, Jay's fingers found the gap in his scales and pushed tentatively against them, finding the warmth of a stiff member just inside. The touch sparked a memory of Prabhavati's fingers and the gap in her own scales that her insistent pull had guided him to, and Nesbit's member emerged into the air, to be met by the soft warm pressure of Jay's fingers.

For the next few minutes, they stroked each other, while Jay panted and made small pleasurable noises and Nesbit clutched his coin tighter. And then Jay pulled his paw back and said, "Hold on, I need to get something."

Nesbit opened his eyes. Jay didn't get up, but set his coin down on one leg and reached over the sleeping bag to take a small bottle out of his pack. He poured a clear viscous fluid into one paw and then rolled onto his side, pressing the fluid under his tail.

"So..." Nesbit reached his free fingers down to his member, stroking along it. "Do you lie on your back? Or get on all fours?"

"Actually..." Jay smiled at him. "Why don't you lie on your back and I'll get on top of you. It's easier for me that way. Plus then I can look at you."

"Oh. Okay." Nesbit lay back, half on the sleeping bag and half on the dirt, but that wasn't good for his wings, so he slid his arms back and rested on his elbows. "Will this work?"

Jay reached over with his slick paw and slid it up and down Nesbit's member. "That should work just fine," he said. He picked up his coin and sat astride the dragon, reaching behind him. His fingers grasped Nesbit's member, and the thrill of anticipation ran through the dragon. He wanted this moment right before the sex to last, letting his imagination build up the moment to come, but Jay too was eager and brought Nesbit's tip to his rear, then sat back quickly, and Nesbit was plunged into the moment.

Warmth engulfed Nesbit, spreading outward from the tightness around his member through his whole body. The gold coin tingled against him as he held it, his hearts pounding, and he wanted to close his eyes to immerse himself in the memory, but more than that he wanted to stare up at Jay in these last moments of seeing the dhole's precious muzzle and russet fur. Jay's expression was as ecstatic as Nesbit felt, with unfocused eyes and a silly grin.

I did that, Nesbit thought. *I made him this happy.* He pressed the coin tightly against his scales.

Jay's hips slid up and down, slowly at first and then gaining momentum. He was stroking his own cock with his slick paw, so Nesbit pushed his hips up against Jay's softness and was rewarded with a gasp and a smile down at him.

"You can," Jay said softly, "ah, you can get a little bigger. Um. If you want."

"Okay. Get off for a moment?"

When the dhole lifted his hips, Nesbit grew just three centimeters taller. Jay didn't seem to notice, so he added another six, and a smile spread over the dhole's muzzle. He reached back to feel Nesbit's slick cock and said, "Mmm! Let's try this."

The fit was definitely tighter this time, and Nesbit could feel every ripple of Jay's muscles as the dhole clenched around him, soft-furred hips sat neatly on his own scaly ones. "Ah-huh," Jay breathed. "Ah, yeah."

Nesbit thrust up again, and Jay matched his rhythm, and soon the two of them moved together, so smoothly they might have been the same creature bound to an ancient rhythm. The dragon's tail smacked the ground as familiar sensations built in him, and above him Jay moaned, pushing his hips down harder, burying Nesbit's member under his tail over and over again.

Jay's eyes stayed locked on Nesbit's, his smile wide, and Nesbit felt his climax building. Jay had done this for him, too, had lit this fire in him that he'd nearly forgotten about, that his own fingers could only approximate even when he paired them with a coin-memory. This was different, this was something they were sharing—

A glitter of gold distracted him. Jay had tossed his coin aside.

Nesbit couldn't stop his body, nor Jay's. "Your coin!" he gasped out through his panting.

"I know," Jay said, and pressed his paw to the center of Nesbit's chest, covering Nesbit's coin and fingers.

"You—ah—you can't—that's—" Nesbit wriggled, but his body's course was well set now.

Jay pumped himself, his hips moving faster. "I, I felt its

magic," he said, "but I don't want my own—I want to share yours."

"It won't—" Nesbit's words were lost in a keen of pleasure, and those were the last words either of them spoke before their shared pleasure crested.

Nesbit was dimly aware of a spatter of warmth on his chest scales and Jay's harsh panting moans, but overwhelming all of that was the bright warmth that exploded through his body. He gripped Jay's leg and thrust up into the dhole, his member pulsing as he emptied himself, and on his chest the coin pulsed with a life of its own. *This feeling*, Nesbit thought, *this joy, this physical joy and spiritual joy, this, save this, remember this, hold on to this, this thisthisthis...*

"Ah-huh. Ah-huh. Ah." His own panting rasped in his ears, and above him, Jay was panting too.

The dhole's eyes met Nesbit's. "Did it—" he asked, and before he could get the last word of his question out, his body stiffened. "Oh. Oh! Ahh!" Again he shook, and his cock spattered a few more drops onto Nesbit's chest, as the paw covering the coin shimmered as though Nesbit were seeing it through waves of heat. Russet and white fur melted into rust-colored scales, shimmering with an opalescent sheen, and now Jay's whole arm was scales, and then his heaving chest's white fur hardened into cream-colored scales. His muzzle became a scaly snout, his ears hard ridges, his headfur a line of stubby spikes that ran from the top of his head down his back. A pair of wings rattled loose from just below his shoulders, making Jay turn and look at them in delight. His tail was hidden, but Nesbit felt the soft fur against his legs become hard and scaly. The fur under his fingers vanished, replaced by smooth scales, all the same rust color with pearl highlights. And Jay's cock changed from pink skin to cream-colored skin, matching the scales around it.

Nesbit remembered his own transformation. It had seemed to be over in a second, but it took Jay nearly half a minute to change, the magic working its way leisurely over his body. He looked at himself in fascination, his smile and his eyes the only things not changed.

No, that was not quite true; his eyes, when they met Nesbit's again, glittered with golden flecks. Jay the dragon ran his slickened fingers over his body. "It worked," he breathed.

As his physical pleasure faded, Nesbit's dread resurfaced. "How do you feel?" he asked.

"I feel wonderful! I feel so much more...connected. I don't know how to describe it." He dropped his chest to Nesbit's and flung his arms around the dragon. "Thank you, Nes," he said. "Thank you so much. This is incredible. It's so incredible."

The movement lifted Jay's hips enough that Nesbit slid out of them, and the red dragon giggled. "Oops," he said, his nose to Nesbit's. "That's okay, though. I'm excited to try that again, but..." He rubbed his red scales against the blue ones below them. "As a dragon."

The coin pulsed with warmth between them. If Nesbit focused on it, he could feel that happy moment they'd shared, preserved forever. It still felt like his memory. "Uh-huh," he said, knowing that the next time might not be for months. Or years.

"It's funny," Jay said. "I can still feel echoes of it. I've had sex before, but never like that. Of course, I never got turned into a dragon before. Ha ha!" His laugh was deeper now, truer, relieved of the apprehension.

"That's the coin," Nesbit said.

Jay went still and then sat up. "What?"

"The coin. Dragons store memories in their coins. In their hoard. The coin I gave you was supposed to hold that first memory, but instead your memory went into this one." He held up the coin. "So this is yours, I guess, and I'll find some other things to give you when you're ready. Go on," he said, when Jay hesitated. "Take it."

"It's supposed to be ours," Jay said.

"Just take it. You'll see what I mean." Nesbit didn't want Jay to leave, but now he would have to, so there was no point in waiting until they started to fight, or whatever happened when dragons stayed together too long.

The red dragon reached out and took the gold coin in his fingers. "Oh!" His eyes unfocused. "I feel it. That's amazing. And all your things hold memories?"

"Not all of them. If someone only gave me one coin, I put the memory in that. If there were more, then only one of them. I can find the things that don't have memories to give you."

Jay laughed. "You don't need to give me anything. I'll work for my own hoard."

"It's custom," Nesbit said. "You get some things from me and…that's your hoard. I owe you because I changed you."

For the first time, Jay's smile faltered. "And then what?" he asked.

"Then you're going to want to go away," Nesbit said. "Your hoard is yours, and mine is mine, and it feels…weird for them to be together."

"Oh." Jay turned the coin over in his fingers. "I do feel possessive of this coin. But it doesn't feel weird. When do I want to go? When I have enough things?"

"Um." Nesbit looked up. "Doesn't it feel bad for you to be here now? Or unpleasant?"

"No." Jay's smile returned. He climbed off of Nesbit and lay down next to him on his side, resting the coin on Nesbit's chest. "I like being here with you."

Nesbit flinched when the coin touched him, but there was no shock of *not-mine*, no urge to push it away. The memory of their sex burned in it strongly, and next to him, Jay-dragon stared dreamily back at him, content, although he was touching the coin as well. And Nesbit realized that even when he'd thrust the coin at Jay, it hadn't felt *not-his*.

"Wait." Nesbit touched a finger to the coin and kept his eyes locked on Jay's. "Does this feel like yours?"

"Uh-huh."

"And it doesn't bother you to have me touch it?"

"No." Jay stretched out a wing, which distracted him for a moment. He watched it reach its full length. "Should it?"

"It feels like mine too," Nesbit said. His hearts jumped. "It can't be both of ours, can it?"

Jay's gold-flecked eyes met his. "Why not? We were both touching it."

"But then...but then..." Nesbit jumped up. Wings out, he ran in a circle and came back to Jay, his body buzzing with excitement. "But then you can stay!"

Jay grinned as though he'd known it all along. "I told you I would," he said.

Nesbit fell to his knees and wrapped his arms around Jay, sending the gold coin rolling across the floor. The other dragon hugged him back and laughed softly. "Did you not believe me?"

If he'd thought the physical pleasure of a few minutes ago was incredible, this was beyond even that. Words wouldn't pass through his throat. All he could do was hug Jay tighter, wanting to wrap himself all the way around his friend. Scales felt different from fur, but that didn't matter because underneath them was still Jay, and they were together.

"Shh," Jay said. "Shh, it's okay, Nes. I'm not going anywhere. I'm home. We're home."

PALADIN'S FALL

AJAX B. CORIANDER

I gripped the hilt of my sword and I focused on my breath to stay calm as we ventured deeper into the cave before us. I moved silently as the magic from our cleric, Sven, muffled the clink of my heavy plate armor. Myself and the other paladin of Niamh's holy order of light, Kira, scanned our surroundings as we moved. The female gnoll was steadfast in her movements, tall and powerful, just like all the women of her kind. She wouldn't have been nearly as tall as the wolfen creatures that made up part of my ancestry. The elves, as most called them now, once ruled the forests, seeming to be able to blend in with their surroundings and take down any prey. Sadly, the badger-folk half of my ancestry had stunted my height, and now half-elves like myself only came up to her shoulders. Poor Sven only came up to her chest, which always made things so awkward for the young, horny, chastised cleric.

I realized my mind had started to wonder, and I forced myself to come back to the moment in front of me. My keen pointed ears could hear things skittering in the darkness and water dripping from stalactites above us and onto the gray stone floor below. As we sank deeper, I could smell the scent of the creature's musk: a mix between charcoal and a stallion's jockstrap.

Up ahead we could see a space brightened from mage lights set into recessed alcoves carved into the stone. The magic cast everything in a rich warm light, making it seem comforting and inviting. Like a warm inn on a cold winter's night. Further into the cave there were rows of bookshelves, each titled and categorized, and tenderly cared for. The inviting aura was in stark contrast to the nature of the threat we faced.

The creature of legend.

Longreader.

My breath caught in my throat when he stepped out from behind one of the shelves. The dragon's bronze scales glimmered as he moved through the stacks, the mage lights catching off them, and causing them to reflect in dazzling ways. They were hard to miss, given that Longreader was naked except for a round pair of golden glasses perched at the end of his snout. The one adornment had a chain that came off the spectacles and connected to one of the ash-colored horns. The chubby bronze would have looked almost jovial, if not for the fact he would have towered two or three feet over me.

I steadied myself. Here he was. The scaled trickster who had stolen a sacred text from Saint Rince himself. The head priest at the temple of Niamh had tasked us with retrieving it. I'd seen the copies, but this was the original copy of the Book of Sacred Tomes. In days past, an army might have been gathered to go after the dragon, but too many rumors of the book had been chased without success. Because of this, the priests could only send a small strike team to gather the book, if the rumor even turned out to be true. The priests enchanted our armor and Sven's robes to withstand any hellish retribution the dragon might unleash. His claws and flame stood not chance against our faith. My companions and I shared a look, making sure we were ready for what we were about to do. Sven gave a silent prayer, gesturing with the sign of Saint Rince's horns, and adding his blessing to our strength. We turned back to our target, and then charged into the light.

The dragon's head snapped towards us, a look of alarm melting into confusion as he saw us.

"Can I help..." His words were cut off as he was forced to leap back as Kira slashed at him with her broadsword.

"We're not here to talk foul lizard," I bellowed. "We're here to right the wrongs done to our temple by your wicked deeds." I jumped forward, and took a slash at him with my sword, it glowed with the holy white light from Niamh's blessing, before it met his scaled arm and left a cut along it. He bellowed out in pain and clasped a scaly hand to the wound.

"What wrongs? The hells are you talking about?" Longreader hissed, "Why are the paladins of Niamh in my home?"

"Don't play dumb scaled serpent!" The cleric growled, "Three hundred years ago you tricked high priest Rince out of his sacred tome! We've found you at last and we've come to get it."

The dragon only seemed to grow more confused.

"I have no idea who that is."

"I wouldn't expect such falsehoods from a bronze dragon like yourself. I was told your kind are honorable. I figured you would remain so until the end," I growled. "But I guess those tales must have been taller than you. Just like the lies you told Saint Rince."

"Wait," the dragon said as he paused to think as he took a step back. "Rince the Minotaur? Red fur, gold capped horns, and bad taste in cheap wine?" His back was against one of the stacks now, his wings pressed into it. His eyes narrowed, "I didn't steal any damn tome. He gave it to me, so I'd pay off his tab to the barkeep. It cost me a fair sum of silver at that."

"Don't you dare try and defile Saint Rince's holy name," the gnoll growled. "We know the truth lizard, and we'll have his book back, no?"

The dragon growled, "It's mine. I own it. It is part of my hoard. Don't you dare touch even the R section of my books or you'll regret it."

"No, it belongs to our order, our temple, our church, and our goddess herself," I snapped back.

"I have it!" Our cleric shouted, and I saw him do just as we planned, running as fast as his legs would take him out of the cave. The minotaur sized book easily a third his size clutched tightly to his chest. The dragon's head snapped to the sight, and he blinked. His eyes went from round blue irises to yellow with drank black slits in the center.

"No!" Longreader hissed. I could see his throat twitch and his lips parted to show his tooth filled muzzle. I could see his hot breath bring a haze to the air as rage boiled inside of him and he got ready to flame. I might have died there, if not for his eyes that darted to the books all around him. The dry, dusty, easy to burn books. His muzzle instantly slammed shut, and he looked pained as smoke poured from his nostrils. Changing tactics quickly with a grimace, he lunged forward, and Kira quickly punched him right in the nose. His round glasses flew from his face, the chain connecting them to his horns snapping in two, and he fell back into the stacks.

We were a strike force, not a kill team. We just needed to get in, get the book, and get out. Our job nearly done, we both turned, and ran after our cleric. Our long strides caught up to the encumbered Sven in no time, and I took the heavy book from him as we ran. With a burst of speed, the unburdened badger pulled ahead of us. We laughed as he neared the mouth of the cave. The exhilaration of besting a dragon and stealing his treasure coursed through us. We might even become saints ourselves after this.

However, that joyous feeling was cut short as a loud roar echoed through the cave. The sound was like the death throes of a man who had seen his whole family die before him. It shook the rock beneath our feet and rattled our very bones. Fear gripped us like a tangible force clasping around our bodies. In Sven's unfortunate case, he tripped, and caused all of us to stop. We turned our heads and watched as the bronze dragon darted towards us. Fire licked at the corners of Longreader's muzzle, and his muscles twitched under his skin. He let out a puff of which formed into a large ball of fire, and he leapt up into it. The fire surrounded his form, heat and magic blasted from the sphere he road within. His bones snapped and popped, sending more terrifying echoes through the cave, and his form grew larger inside the fire, before his mighty wings unfurled with a flourish that banished the last of the flame, and the jovial man I saw before was gone, leaving only a monster behind.

The creature's four legs hit the ground and began to run without missing a beat. His scales gleamed brighter, his muzzle and neck elongated, and more spikes had grown across his chin and back. The short horns on his head had grown larger and sharper looking, and his tail now sported deadly spiked thagomizer that would have put any morning star to shame. The fire burned away what he was and transformed him into something else. The feral dragon's wings flapped as sharp claws dug into the stone below them. The fairy tales of what a monster dragons could become were true. The old stories he'd heard said those who tried to steal or harm a dragon's horde would cause it to change into a ferocious beast. The monster's legs worked with its wings as it hopped, leapt, and pushed itself forward in large bounds. Even with its still impressive gut, it was fast, too fast for any of us. Kira lifted her sword uselessly as claws racked across her chest— tearing through her armor like paper. She slammed into the wall of the cave in a bloody heap.

"Kira!" I shouted. I went to drop the book, but a massive, clawed hand came down and slammed me into the rock floor.

Sven, may Niamh bless him, turned and tried to save me with his magic, but he was no match for the dragon. Longreader inhaled deeply, his flabby chest expanding, before the muscles in his long neck twitched and he breathed out flame that washed over the badgerfolk cleric. The fire was hotter and brighter than anything I'd ever seen. I had to turn my face away or lose my sight. I didn't even hear him scream. I could only smell the scent of burning fur and feel the heat of the dragon's rage.

When I opened my eyes again, there was just a puddle of melted rock and scorched earth where Sven had once stood. It tinked and pinged as it slowly cooled, the red glow burned itself into the back of my eyes and I knew it was all that was left of my friend.

"You monster!" I shouted at the dragon. My arms were pinned against my chest, still clutching the book, and unable to move.

"Monster?!" It roared in a deeper growly voice than before. It looked down at me, rage bright in its eyes. "You broke into *my* home. You attacked *me*. You stole from *my* hoard. You damaged *my* books. And you call *me* a monster?" Longreader growled angrily, flames licking at his lips. I could feel that he wanted nothing more than to burn me to ash, but the book held in my grasp kept him from doing so. He turned his head towards the ceiling and let off a blast of fire. It flowed over the surface of the rock, dissipating among the stalactites and burning the moisture off of them.

The dragon growled at me, and he leaned his head down low. I could tell he was deciding what to do with me next. He shifted his claws, and I felt pressure on my throat. I gasped for breath, struggling under his massive strength. He locked his eyes with mine, watching as my eyelids drifted closed, and I passed out in his claws.

"Insolent hatchlings," Longreader muttered under his breath.

Pain pulsed inside my skull and I slowly opened my eyes. I turned my head towards the sound of the voice, and I saw the large feral dragon marching up and down the rows of bookshelves and piling things onto a large table just the right size for his form. The books in his claws were massive, bigger than the minotaur Saint's, and clearly made for dragons like himself.

"Coming into my home, trying to steal from *my* hoard," he grumbled. Smoke licked at his lips, and it was clear the only thing keeping him from flaming again were the dusty dry books around him. He muttered to himself about the damage done to his home, the expensive preservation runes we'd damaged, and the audacity we'd had to go after his hoard. I'd never doubted the wisdom of my church before, and it made me uncomfortable to do so, but with Kira likely dead and Sven just dust in the wind; I realized maybe the priests of my temple weren't as infallible as I thought.

Was this our fault somehow? Was it my fault for not trying to be sneakier about things? I felt like I'd failed my friends. I'd failed my church. I'd failed everyone. My chest tightened as guilt oozed over my heart. I let myself wallow in that feeling for just a moment before I pushed it aside.

No!

Niamh's chosen could do no wrong. I could not fail. The goddess and the temple had sent me on this quest. Surely, they knew I was supposed to succeed.

I tried to stand, but a weight kept me held down. I looked to my chest and saw that my broad sword had been bent like a piece of wire and used to pin me down to the ground. I struggled under it, trying to slip free, but it was wedged into the stone too tightly.

"Foul lizard!" I shouted, "What have you done with Kira?"

Longreader stopped and looked at me, rage in his eyes.

"I am a dragon, if you call me a *lizard* one more time, you will regret it," he growled. "As for your remaining companion, I used a healing potion, altered her memory, and sent her on her away with a copy of the original tome I got from Rince. Something I could have done if you'd only *asked*, and not just burst in and steal from *my* hoard before trying to kill me." He snapped as he marched over to loom above me.

"The priests in the temple will never fall for a fake! We need the real thing," I yelled back. "Others will come for me."

"They already think you're dead. Like I said, I altered her memory. In her head, I'm dead, and everyone else in your party died by my claws. Besides," the dragon grinned toothily, "considering how weak the enchantments on your armor were, I doubt any of your priests are strong enough to break past what I've done."

"They'll figure it out somehow! Priest Troth will see through your trickery and hunt you down in this cave!" I shouted and struggled.

"In that very unlikely event, it's a good thing we won't be here if they do," he snorted before turning away from me. His tail lashing out, and his thagomizer smashed the stone stalagmite next to me.

"What do you mean, *we?*"

"Well, I came up with a fitting punishment for you, welp," the dragon explained as he walked back over to the table, while his tail slashed back and forth while his heavy scaled testicles swung between his legs. "You compromised my home, and damaged not just one, but several, books when you and your companion knocked me back into the stacks. You're going to help me repair them and help me find a new home. I need someone to carry my extra bags of holding as we search," Longreader explained. He opened one of the books, and a claw started to trace along the lines. He flipped through the pages, before shaking his head and doing the same with another.

"As if I'd do that. I'm a noble paladin of this land, I won't debase myself as some dragon's squire. Just kill me now," I growled.

The dragon turned his head to me, and cocked an eyebrow, "Since when have half-elves been noble? I remember when the first of you were born between the elves, the wolfish creatures in the forests, and the badgers of the mountains. You're just the only race that's ever mingled identities, taking on features of both parents and becoming something new rather than splitting into one or the other."

"When did you last pay attention to the world? The elves died in the War of Light, when their home was burned by Krich."

"Krich, you say? The god of fear, nightmares, and paranoia?" The dragon mused as he sat on his haunches and thought for a moment. "A long time ago I had a merchant try and pawn a bunch of charred elfish scrolls on me. He said they were rare, but I'd assumed the ram was trying to fleece me. I guess maybe they were." Longreader shrugged, "oh well."

"You have to know I'll do everything to escape," I growled. "I'm not just going to let you order me around."

"That's the best part," the dragon said as he smirked back at me, "you'll want to help me. You'll *need* to help me, everything inside you will tell you to."

"Never," I growled.

"We'll see," the dragon said before turning back to his book, his tail thrashing behind him. "I've never been one to force someone to do something. But if they want to do something, that's hardly my fault now is it?"

"Ah, here we go!" The large bronze dragon lifted up a book and held it close to his face as he scanned the text. He leafed through a few pages, and then turned to walk over to me in an awkward three-legged gate as he held the book to his chest. He very carefully set the book down a little way away, and I could see a drawing of a creature being licked by a dragon with the Draconic language scrawled all around it. He turned back to me, and he reached down with one of his clawed fingers to the steel plates on my legs and he easily punctured it. His claw tip easily slid through the metal, the enchantments that were supposed to protect me, and the magic that sparked and hissed around his digit didn't even singe his thick bronze scales. When he reached my hip, he yanked the cut he'd made further open, and tore the armor off my leg. He repeated the process with the other leg, and my plated boots. I felt my blood run cold as I saw the claw go towards my crotch, and I whimpered like a pup.

"Wh... what are you doing! I won't let you sully my honor!"

Longreader cocked a scallie eyebrow at me.

"Oh relax, I have no plans on doing *that* to a half-elf. I prefer someone with more scales. The fur is just so... unsettling against my loins." The dragon shuddered in disgust at the thought. He carefully cracked open the metal codpiece over my crotch and threw it on the heap with the rest of my armor. He used one clawed hand to hold me down, before yanking my bent longsword from the stone, and then started to peel me out of the rest of my armor and under clothes. It must have looked like someone taking the wax paper off a dubious meat pie bought from someone on the street.

In a few moments I was bare furred under his claws, and I felt so small and helpless as he looked down at me. Defenseless without my armor or sword. Naked before the beast larger than my parent's barn. As I searched for some way to escape, my eyes happened between his legs, where I saw his massive swinging testicles again and the slit above them that hid his cock. I don't know why my eyes kept drawing themselves there. It was like they would bounce, and my attention would be grabbed by them. Like a flicker of something that couldn't be real. He flipped me onto my stomach with ease, and then he began to lick my back and shoulders, just like in the book.

Longreader's saliva didn't feel like scalding water—which I thought it would. Instead, it felt like icy slush into my fur and down to my skin. I began to shiver as that thick viscous substance clung to me, while the dragon's hot breath contrasted with the subzero cold of his spit. He slid down my body, the insides of my ears turning bright red as he began to lick over my rump and then under my tail.

"H-hey! Y-you said…" I trailed off as this massive beast who had so easily bested me growled deeply in the back of his throat.

"Just relax, young one. This is just part of the ritual. Think of this as no crasser than a healer's touch. I am a dragon of my word, even if you might not think so now."

"You're preforming a ritual?" I asked with a gasp of breath as a tingling ran up my spine from the cold and sensation of his touch.

The dragon paused and gave me the blankest look I had ever seen. He looked to the book, back to me, and then rubbed his forehead with one of his foreclaws. "I see paladins are just as thick now as they were in my time." He took a breath in and then slowly exhaled. "Let's just say this will alter your," the dragon paused as he grasped for the right word, "*memory* of events."

"Like you did with Kira?" I asked.

"Something like that, but with you it will be a little more intense. Now, shall I go on or would you like me to come up with something else?" The dragon asked this with a dangerous tone. I gulped, before nodding for him to continue. The dragon finished licking the backs of my legs, and the soles of my hindpaws.

I shuddered from the odd sensation, and then he flipped me over onto my back with a wet plap. He began to lick my front, starting with my legs, then to my head coating every inch of my face and head fur. Doing it twice just to be sure he was leaving an extra thick layer of that icy cold saliva behind. That slushy substance ran into my eyes from my brow, it stung a bit, but the fluid seemed to seep into them and do no more harm than opening my eyes under water would. I looked into his mouth at one point, and I could see a set of glands oozing a bluish fluid into his muzzle that combined with his spit and made it thicken to the viscus concoction coating my fur.

He moved over my chest, and I had to bite my tongue to hold back a moan as he played with my nipples, and my accursed sheath started to plump of its own will. He moved down over my muscular belly, and then finally to the cursed appendage. Longreader started to lap and lick at my sheath and fuzzy pouch. He made sure he got every inch, even sliding his tongue inside of the sheath the best he could, and coating my cock in that ice cold fluid when it poked out more from the touching. Though, my balls did their best to retreat into my body from the cold feeling.

The dragon met my eyes, and he cocked his head to the side. He lowered his massive head, and our lips met, my muzzle dwarfed by his as his tongue forced its way into my mouth. I tried to scream as I felt that viscus coolant run down his tongue and hit the back of my throat, seeming to freeze my vocal cords. His tongue probed me, and I whimpered silently as he kept me pinned below him. That thick invader moved in and out, forcing my jaw open until it was sore. The cooling fluid dripping into my muzzle kept me from gagging as it numbed my throat. I had never tried to drink a frozen lake before, but I wondered if that's what the sensation would be as the slushy substance poured down into my stomach and coated my insides. The cold made my brain fuzzy, and without realizing it, I began to suckle on his tongue. I felt the cold spreading through my chest and gut, making my blood run cold and I started to shudder as it desperately tried to stay warm.

"There," he said with a nod. "Just one last thing and I'm done."

I wanted to run to try and escape, but the chill that filled me made every movement sluggish. Only my eyes seemed to respond quickly to my will. He sat on his haunches so his front claws were free to use, and he made some gestures in the air that left trails of glowing fiery magic. He spoke something loud and clear in Draconic, before he leaned back down above me. He opened his muzzle, and my eyes went wide as I watched him breathe in deeply. I saw the flame ducts in the back of his throat open and the liquid burst into flames as the substance encountered the air.

He breathed out and I was baptized in fire.

When the dragon's fire hit me, I expected to die. I expected to be turned to ash just like Sven. Left just a molten puddle under the dragon, and to finally meet the goddess I'd fought my life for. But instead, the flame tickled my skin, and I could still breathe. The fire and super-heated air traveled down into my lungs, and I felt myself start to warm inside and out. The stone around me melted and cracked, but I felt fine. It was such a queer feeling, like falling into a campfire and absorbing the flame instead dying to it. Things grew uncomfortable as the sensation inside me grew to a point I could no longer take. The comfortable energizing heat turned to pain, and I heard whimpers escape my thawed throat, before I let out a cry like I hadn't since I was a pup.

Longreader let up for a moment. The chubby dragon was breathing heavily as he caught his breath and I caught mine. My muscles didn't feel as stiff as they had, and I managed to lift my head to look at my body. My fur was gone now, but a blue sapphire sheen covered my skin. I tried to ask what it was, but the words came out as gibberish. My tongue didn't seem to remember how to form the words anymore.

He gave me a few more licks, while my head spun with

confusion. I was about to try and speak again, but he bathed me in fire before I could get the chance. The flames licked at my ears, sounding like cracks and pops, but there was no pain. In fact, it was like I was drunk. Magic from the dragon's flame seemed to flow into my core. The heat increased, and a new sensation washed over me. My flesh rippled under the cleansing fire, and it tensed before it hardened into something like metal scale mail. I felt pain surge through me again, but this time it was from inside me and not the out.

I wanted to look, but the blinding light from the flames kept me from seeing anything. My ears ached as they moved lower on my head, and that was followed by something pushing its way through my scalp. I'd never had bones burst from my flesh, but this is what it must have felt like. I cried tears that evaporated in the heat as my snout and muzzle broke to shift into a new shape. My hard-earned muscles melted away and new areas of fat rippled across my body. My tail lashed out, pain surging through it as it lengthened and thickened. Bone ridges burst out of the top of it just like what had happened on my head. My knuckles cracked, and my paws shifted into something new. My nails became like pointed boney claws, and my paw pads melted into my palms and became soft scales.

The dragon's flame stopped, and he breathed heavily as he recovered from keeping his fiery breath going that long. I could hear the rock crack and pop around me, the heat having melted everything except for the patch of stone my body had protected. Longreader gingerly picked me up and laid me on a nest of soft furs and blankets. I was curled into a ball, and I wondered if I should open my eyes again or keep them shut forever and never have to see what the dragon had done to me.

A gentle claw slid across my head, and the large dragon's breathing eased. He leaned down and nuzzled me with his large snout, and I could hear a smile and gentleness I had never imagined in his voice as he spoke to me.

"It's time to come out, little one."

I heard him lay on the ground, and I could feel his presence close to me. I opened my eyes and there was a haze. I found it hard to move, and I had to struggle. Something covered me in a thin hard film, it was clear, and felt like an eggshell wrapping around me. I grunted and wiggled. I felt the barrier around my body start to crack, and a voice above me continued to speak.

"That's it, little kobold, you can do it." It said softly and reassuringly. I managed to sit up, and the opaque crystal-like substance fell from my body and turned to dust as it hit the ground. I went to rub my eye, and my hand froze as I saw the clawed digits now attached to me. I started to panic as I realized scales now rested where my grey and black striped fur had been. They had a yellow brass coloration, with a lighter patch that went over my stomach, and down to my new hindpaws... hindclaws?

"What did you..." I trailed off before my hand slapped to my new muzzle, and my eyes went wide with horror. "Is... is this really my voice? It sounds so tiny, and squeaky?" I asked. I looked up at the dragon next to me, and I realized he seemed bigger now. Even laying down he seemed to tower over me. I wasn't sure how much size I'd lost, but it had to be around three feet. My muscles were gone, and I seemed softer than I had been before.

"Silly hatchling, you've always sounded like that," the brass dragon above me said with an amused chuckle.

I felt a pain in my skull, and something clicked.

He was right, I had always sounded like that. It was my voice after all.

"Okay, but have I always been so... small? And soft?" I reached down and touched my round belly and poked it with one of my claws. I yelped as it poked under one of the scales, and I yanked it back.

"Of course, you're a kobold. All kobolds are soft and small. It makes it easier for them to take care of their dragon masters," Longreader explained with a soft smile. "And you are a kobold, aren't you, little one?"

"No, I'm a..." I trailed off and looked down at my body. I ran my claws over my soft yellow-brass scales, down my sides, and then along the thick base of my tail, and to the two little spines that poked up halfway along it. "I'm... I'm..." I felt tears start to well in my eyes. Had I ever cried like this? Had I ever been like this when I was a pup... no, hatchling? I was an adult; I shouldn't have been crying like that.

I backed away from the dragon before me. I tried to remember what I'd been like, but it hurt. Every time I grabbed something from my mind, it felt like something popped painfully inside of my head, before vanishing. I put my paws... no, claws... over my eyes, and I tried to block out anything that might cause me pain.

"I'm sure you're confused, little kobold." The dragon cooed to me. "The fight with those adventurers was a hard one. I'm not surprised your memory is a bit scrambled." I felt a set of claws gingerly wrap around me and pull me in close. Soon I was pressed against the dragon's chest, the side of my head to his scales, and the reassuring sound of that massive heart beating filling my ears. "What do you want to know?"

"I... I'm not sure, everything in my head hurts when I try to remember." I said truthfully.

"Then let's start at the beginning, shall we?" The brass dragon said. "You're from a nest of kobolds far in the north. Two decades ago, some adventurers took a bounty to clear out the dens your people made. Your people fought to the last, but they were all slaughtered by the so-called heroes one-by-one. I found you a few days later. Your egg had been wrapped up to keep you warm, and you'd been hidden by someone in your tribe. The rest of your brothers and sisters had either been smashed or taken to be hatched for slaves. I pulled you out, and you hatched right before my eyes."

I tried to remember, I would catch glimpses, but fire would wash over them and they'd morph under the gaze of my mind's eye. Memories of running through grassy fields were replaced by ones of me running across stony mountains or desert sands. The people I knew changed to dragons or kobolds when I tried to remember them. The days at the temple learning about Niamh's text, became me reading in Longreader's library. There was a sharp stabbing pain in my head, but it cleared as the new memories slid into place.

The dragon pulled me towards him a bit, and he urged my hands away from my face. A large claw came up, and he lifted my head to meet his gaze. Those slitted pupils in the yellow eyes stared at me, but when he blinked, his eyes became a bright green, and his pupils became round. It softened his face and made him look friendlier. He smiled down at me and bumped my snout with his much larger one.

"Do you remember now, little one?" He asked me.

"I do, sir," I said blinking. "But everything still feels fuzzy, like it's not really there."

"I think I know just how to fix that," he nuzzled me, nearly knocking me over, and I giggled. He then whispered softly, "you're a kobold. You just need to do what a kobold is meant to do, and I'm sure you'll feel a lot better."

"What's that?"

"Please their dragon, of course." Long reader said as he rolled onto his side and lifted his leg, exposing the massive balls that hung between his legs, which were now resting on his thigh. His cock was already starting to poke from its slit, and I felt a blush creep along my scales as I looked at it. "Of course, if you don't want to you don't have to. I won't force you."

I looked down at my own body. Between my legs I found my own slit, and a pair of balls that were two little bumps under it. I ran a finger over it, and carefully poked my claw tip into the slit curiously. My finger felt warm and wet and I could feel the head of my cock just below my digit. I looked back up, and back down. Memories of my past sexual exploits ran through my head and were bathed in the same fire as before. They changed to me worshiping the dragon before me like I was meant to. Like my kind was made to. My muzzle started to water, and I walked forward towards that massive creature's lower half.

"N-no, you're not forcing me. I want to make you happy, Longreader." I ran my hand along his soft underbelly as I walked. When he'd been standing, it'd sagged heavily, and up close it was just as impressive. He groaned with pleasure, and I saw his cock slip a little further from his slit.

Each one of his testicles was larger than my head, and I looked at them with awe. I reached out and began to carefully rub at that champagne-colored sac. The scales there were the softest I'd felt, yet they were tightly packed, small, and barely visible as my fingers slid across them. I couldn't help myself as I shoved my face to the spot above his sack where it dimpled in and then met his sheath, and I breathed in deep. The dragon's musk filled my nose, and it sent a chill through me. It started at the base of my new stubby horns and moved to the tip of my tail.

My muzzle watered, and I couldn't help but slide out my tongue and start to lick across the dragon's massive sac. I cupped his impressive pouch in my hands, and I carefully played with them as I coated those impressive orbs with my saliva. Longreader moaned and I could smell and taste as his musk got stronger as he grew more aroused.

"Yes, little kobold, that's just what you're supposed to do," the large dragon praised. I felt a heat rise next to my head as his cock began to slide further from his slit. I felt my own shaft peak out from my warm folds, and I let myself get lost in worshiping his sac. I breathed him in again and again, not wanting to come up for fresh air, but my body demanding it.

That's when I saw his cock standing in all its glory. It was a dark red, and it had ridges that went along it like plate armor, it ended in a rounded helmet shaped head with little fleshy bumps on the underside. It was taller than me. The mage lights above almost cast me in its shadow. I turned to it in admiration, my hands reached out, and I felt across its slimy flesh. Longreader's cock was so warm beneath my touch. Hotter than it should have. I heard the dragon moan as I ran my smooth scaled hands over his prized treasure and I couldn't help but wrap my arms around it, just to see if my limbs would be able to circle it.

When I did, Longreader grunted and rolled onto his back. I yipped as my hindclaws left the ground, and I hung in the air for a moment dangling from the massive shaft in my arms, before I came to rest on the dragon's fatpad. I sank into the softness around his slit, and I had to hoist myself up to meet the head of his cock as clear pre oozed from the tip. I moved so my chest was pressed into the top of his dragonhood, and my tail would rest on his belly. Without thinking I rubbed at his shaft, getting a pleasure-filled groan from the massive dragon below me. I held out my tongue and was rewarded with sweet pre that poured out for me to lap up greedily. The musky taste was pure ambrosia on my tongue. It truly felt like I was made just for this.

I began to rub my soft underbelly of scales against his pulsing shaft, there was too much precum to lick up by myself, and I knew then why most masters would have had several kobolds like me to service them. The sweet nectar began to spill out and over me. My chest grew slick, and I could now easily rub my soft underbelly and chest against that pillar of dragon muscle. I felt that shaft twitching against me, his heartbeat coming through it, and making me tingle in ways I could never have imagined. The dragon's lance would flex, and it was so strong that I would move with it every time. I would sneak peaks at his balls, and they'd be churning in their scaly sac.

My own shaft twitched against the dragon's massive one. I reached down and felt it to get a gauge of what it was like now. My smaller cock was nothing compared to the might of this larger being. I reached down and felt my hot short sword; it was a smaller more delicate mirror of the massive lance before me as it ground against the sensitive flesh. Mine lacked his powerful ridges and was smooth. But it shared the little bumps of flesh under the tip like his did. The heat coming off it was incredible compared to the weak candle that was mine. It felt like being naked under the sun, my scales absorbing the heat as I basked in that holy light.

Niamh's light.

I paused then and my head began to hurt.

"Oh, don't stop now little kobold," he moaned. He shifted, and I felt the heat of his breath against my back. I stopped fondling myself and wrapped my arms fully around the massive tower of dragon flesh before me. Longreader licked along my spine, and it made me shiver. His spit wasn't cold like I distantly remembered; this time it was as warm as the shaft I clung to. His nose moved my long tail up, and I shuddered as a tongue slid between my thighs and licked his shaft, mine, and the area my balls poked from my body.

He licked my body again and again as I rubbed myself around his shaft. My arms clung to his cock tight, wanting to please him. My biceps rubbed against the ridge between his tip and his shaft, which incited pleasure-filled growls from the dragon below me. I felt his tongue start to probe under my tail, and I felt the tip of his tongue press against my tailhole. I gasped as he slipped inside of me as I rode his shaft. My tail curled, and I whimpered as new feelings bloomed through me.

The tongue's warmth spread through me as I drank the fountain of pre that ran from his cocktip. Longreader's precum made me as slick as oil, and my entire body glided along his cock with ease. I felt his tongue prob in and out of me, pushing deeper with each advance, filling me and making me feel so right. He gingerly wrapped both his hands around me and his shaft. He began to pump me up and down as I held on, my legs rising to wrap around his member as well as I tried to hold my tail high for him.

I whimpered while my cock now firmly pressed against his shaft. My balls ground against that slick flesh as he used me like a toy to jack himself off. I panted for breath as that pre never seemed to end. My muzzle dipped into the opening near the tip when he lifted me higher, and I was able to lap right from the source. Before sliding back down along him.

His tongue pressed something inside of me, and I shuddered. That pleasure knot within me getting assaulted again and again as I rode him. My face scrunched up, and I gave a high-pitched yip as I felt my cock twitch and my small load burst onto his pulsing shaft. It made him stroke me quicker, my body thrashing as he rubbed my sensitive trapped dick against his warm scales. I wanted to beg for him to go faster, but when I'd open my muzzle more dragon nectar would just slide in. It coated me like I'd been pulled from a gelatinous cube. The precum oozed over me in thick rivulets. His tongue didn't stop his assault, and then I felt him peak.

His cock surged and he started to cum. The first shot blasted from his tip, I watched in awe as it almost smacked the ceiling of the cave, but instead Longreader's cum arched down and landed with a wet plop on his belly. His cock flexed again and again, the jets of cum starting to shoot straight up and splash over me and his lance as he stroked me faster against him. All I could do was hold on as he used me for his pleasure, and I was lost to his draconic desires. I was drunk on that dragon's musk and cum. My head spun, and I knew it was doing something to my brain. I instantly became hard again, and before I knew it, my small cock was adding to his massive load, mine getting drowned out by the gallons showering over me.

He pulled his tongue free from me with a warm wet pop, and he went limp below me, his cock twitching as he held me to it. Finally, he lifted me up, and brought me to his muzzle. He held me with two fingers, and I watched as his massive maw opened, and I saw the rows of sharp teeth. His tongue slid up and he started to lick his cum and pre off me. I giggled as he worked me over, getting me clean, and leaving me feeling warm. He leaned his large, long neck forward and I saw a muscle twitch in his throat as he licked at his cum and left thicker saliva there, he set me down next to the patch and I touched it. The viscus light blue coolant from the glands in his throat felt cold, so I moved up higher on his chest, and he gingerly stroked a claw down the back of my head.

"That felt amazing, little one."

I laid down and nuzzled at his long beefy neck the best I could as I hugged him. "I'm glad, Longreader. Thank you."

He smiled and gave me another lick on the cheek.

"I'm about to do something, but don't be afraid, my flame shouldn't hurt you. Your scales should still be embedded with my coolant for a few more days," he said before he leaned his head up, and blew out a cloud of fire that surrounded us. This wasn't white hot flame that could melt rock, it was like that of a campfire, and it tickled my scales and dried me off. I felt clean as it touched me, and I felt the body below me start to change. I felt it shrink, the limbs change as they rose up to hug me close, and then as the flame dispersed, I was laying on a naked anthropomorphic brass dragon. He was larger than me, about eight feet tall. My head fit comfortably in his soft chest, my crotch against his soft belly, and my tail able to lazily rub at his thick upper leg.

He looked down at me with kind eyes and leaned down to kiss between my horns. I smiled and my hands rubbed over his chest. Longreader yawned as he slowly stroked my back, and I closed my eyes. I was so sore, but it filled me with joy to see him so relaxed. I'd done my duty as a kobold. Something tugged at the edges of my mind, but it soon vanished and nothing but this moment and who I was now was left. I heard one last thing before I drifted asleep to the rhythm of his beating heart.

"Sleep well my kobold, because we have a long trip ahead of us tomorrow."

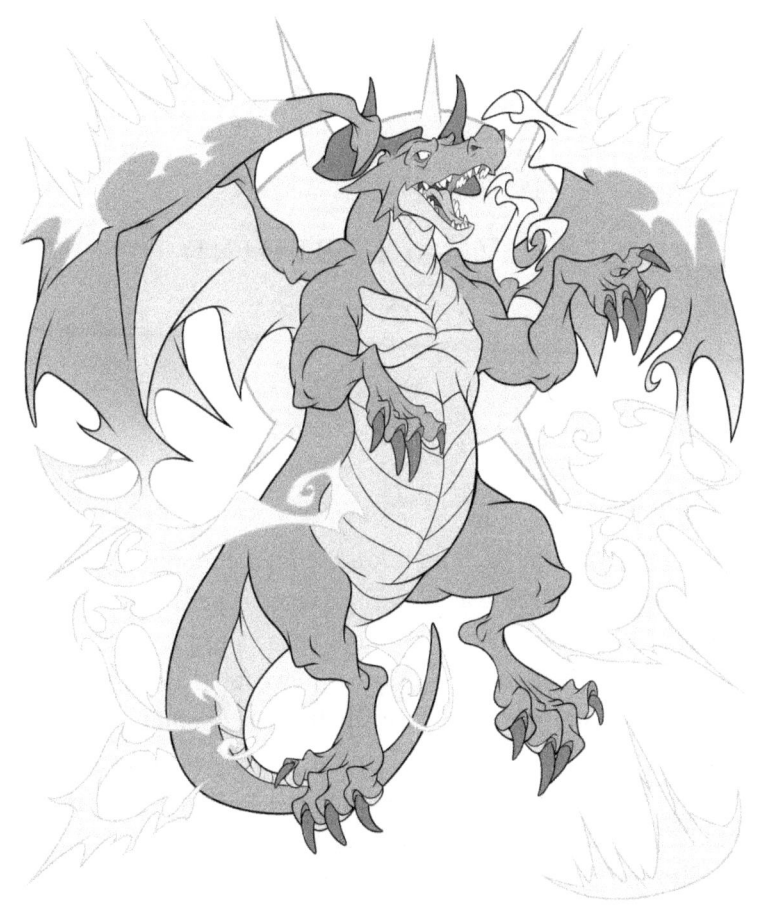

LEAVING IT BEHIND

ARIAN MABE

Cassian paused, the spell book on the kitchen table before him. The shirtless canine was a mix of breeds, his fur longer and rougher, not well-groomed, though it had been a golden shade at one point. Not for a long time, however. Not as the wind whistled through the small kitchen, the hearth empty. The table and chairs—along with his bed upstairs—were the only items of furniture left in the four-room cottage. The beams had cracked and the holes in the wall let in draughty, cold air.

That little cottage held so many memories for him as he stood there, poring over the book with his head lowered. Cassian's dark hair hung into his face, ragged and unkempt, though Cassian didn't notice it. He didn't have the luxury of bathing and his grubby appearance lacked importance. People of his commoner class—poorer than poor—didn't get even the basic needs of life met. And the country did not care for poor folk, no. The kingdom as a whole held nobles and the upper classes in high regard, as they were the ones who could exploit and utilize the wealth of the land.

Those who had not had to scrape a living did not know the wealth in a single drop of dew or even how the sun on a summer's day could make a heart beat a little more strongly. Nobles forgot about that, in their riches and finery, laughing in the palaces and the gardens where anthros like Cassian would never step.

Those with money...they had all the power. And he did not. Not even to keep himself well and not picking at the scraps others left behind. It led to a dangerous existence.

And that was why he had to move on. His shoulders shook, a single tear falling from his eye as he hunched over the book as if he was trying to protect it or himself.

Hold it together.

But Cassian had been doing that for so long already. He'd done his best—his very best—to hold together every thread in the family, even as it unraveled around him.

His mother, sick. Gone.

His little sister. Put to hard labor in the fields until the toll on her body had proven too great. He'd been the only one at her meagre burial.

His older brother, off to war. Unheard from.

He'd never known his father, so that made little difference to him. There was still a hole there, a pang of loss, but few in his village had all their parents with them, regardless. Not many commoners lived to a great age, whether accidents or sickness took them.

Cassian, however, was the only one left. He had done his best for his family and he still had an aunt a few villages away who was doing well for herself...but he no longer had any responsibilities where his home was. His aunt did not need him and she had not helped when his family had dropped away, one by one. Cassian didn't have anyone left to look after now, as much as that pained him.

"It's just me." He breathed, lifting his head, tears glistening on the fur of his cheeks. "Maybe now I have a chance."

He sobbed, a knot slipping free in his chest, fingers digging into the rough fur behind his ears and his claws—chipped as they were—scratched at his skin. He tipped forward, curling into himself, but Cassian had a life ahead of him if he chose to take hold of it.

He could shed tears for those who had gone, but that would neither bring them back nor him the release he so sorely sought. A release from the shackles and bonds of an anthro life, the exhaustion that brought a weary droop to his tail and the load of sustaining a family when those he loved slipped away, one by one. If he had been born a noble perhaps things would have been different, but Cassian was in no position to help others or, as he was, to continue along his own path in life.

The dog sagged, holding down the wracking sob that was bundled up in his chest, shaking behind the cage of his ribs. He couldn't let it out. He tried to inhale evenly, yet even his breath was ragged.

But Cassian could not cry anymore; he had something more important to do. Finally, one thing for himself, even though he was unsure if it would even work.

The spell, yes… All Cassian had to do was to look at the spell and use the skills he had been working on, however clumsily: for the next stage of his life was to begin.

Some in his position took drastic measures, ensuring their fate came to a close, so they did not have to suffer through further pain. Cassian understood that. And maybe he took an extreme risk in sneaking into the wizard's home to steal his belongings, hoping there was something in there that could give him passage to another life—a better life. He'd thought of taking something he could sell—but then the spell book caught his eye and he knew that was what he'd come for.

Cassian only needed a single spell, in the end. He'd looked through the book over and over again and practiced basic magic casting, drawing on his weak reserve of mana. It made his ribs show through his rough coat of fur with the sheer amount of energy it drained. Yet Cassian strained, forcing his body to expend energy, as casting a spell taken from the ancient tome was the only way he could see to change his life. There were too few options for those truly poor and he was willing to take the risk.

The tip of his broken claw traced the written spell on the page in the old language. It was a wonder he was even able to learn some of it, considering his start in life and the challenges Cassian had faced. If he'd been born of a higher class, he would have been considered a prodigy.

"From one form to another," Cassian read aloud. "From one life to another…"

He trailed off, mouthing the words as he translated what he could. The spell suggested enacting a change in the spellcaster's life, though he didn't have enough detail or understanding to decipher the full extent of it. The focus on "form" made him think he'd be put in a different body, which seemed like a fresh start, but no one would know or recognize him. He could begin anew and, perhaps, he could build a new future for himself. That chance alone was more than enough for Cassian.

He took a breath, blinking slowly. The cottage would be left behind; he could not bear to stay there any longer. He hoped the memories would take on a lighter glow in time, remembering the good and softening the bad so they no longer struck painful jabs into his heart and soul. Maybe someone would move in after he was gone, after he had stepped into a new life. Yet Cassian did not even know what form he was about to take on. It was the only transfiguration spell he felt he could perform— and there would be no going back from it. If he had more skills or greater natural mana, he would have been able to do more than recite from a sacred tome. He may have had other options if the book had not been focused on the singular topic of trans- figuration. Alas, Cassian neither had the time nor the training to study as he would have liked and investigate more intricate spells in the book. So, he dedicated his learning to, as far as he understood, his best option.

With limited resources, at least in his case, came decisive action. He had practiced it before, without the use of his mana, so he got the words correct. He had not practiced that exact spell before with mana, which he only drew on for smaller transfiguration spells. When practice drained him, he struggled to refuel through rest and good sustenance. So, Cassian was forced to practice cautiously and sparingly.

If only he had uncovered his mana before, the source of magic inside him, and his natural talent for drawing on it. Maybe it would have changed the fate of his close family, although he had only uncovered it through the act of taking the spell book.

Though it was not time for Cassian to hold on to the past, but to step forward into the future. To take on the life he could. There was nothing to hold him back and the ghosts of the cottage would not be released to the afterlife, their heaviness hanging around him, until he released himself too.

"Malae id inscribatur," he intoned, speaking aloud, not making a conscious decision to enact the spell. "Se diversitus rumpus phsyas." He called on the mana inside him, feeling like a dancing flicker of warmth and fire, as the incantation rolled from his lips.

Cassian grunted as his head spun, though he couldn't allow dizziness to get the best of him. A biting, metallic taste filled his mouth as heat swirled around him, as if warmer air from another land was being carried to his form.

He wanted to growl, to say something, though nothing would pass his lips as he swallowed them down, holding the spell. With his hands shaking, he steadied his position, afraid to move even a single inch for fear of disrupting the magic.

Whereas there was no visual evidence that the magic was being cast, Cassian sensed it acutely in his body. Growing tired as his mana drained, fear snatched at him, though he shoved it away. There was no time for fear, even if the spell itself may well kill him. His last chance was in his own hands, at the very least, and Cassian gave a strangled, croaking groan as spots appeared in front of his vision.

Yet, it held. Against all odds, against every risk: it held. He exhaled, swaying where he stood, leaning heavily on the table as he repeated the initiating words of the spell, bringing it from beginning to end.

"Malae id inscribatur," he said, voice wavering and eyes watering from not blinking when he should have. With his exhaustion, there were longer pauses between each word than before. "Se diversitus rumpus phsyas."

The spell concluded and he shivered, the words falling from his lips, the cottage oddly quiet around him with the old, cracked stone in the walls and the boarded-up window. The covering never helped all that much, but he wasn't shivering from the cold; it was from the energy it had taken to cast the spell. The mere act of casting it had set his hackles up and had his chest tight, as if iron had clamped around his lungs.

He sighed and hunched forward, waiting, his fingers tingling as something shifted within him, like a pull on his heart. His heartrate increased and the dog drummed his fingers on the worn smooth grain of the table. Chunks taken out of the edge had been from his brother, in better times, when he had got a little too happy with a kitchen knife.

Ah, yes. It was good to recall times when things had been simpler and he breathed more easily. That was better, now that he'd grounded himself again. Only a few moments had passed as the spell patiently bloomed like the first flower of spring unfurling its petals. Like so much in the world, one that big needed a moment in which to grow.

The spell gripped him slowly, like a giant paw closing around the anthro, and his stomach dropped, giving him the sense of something heavy settling there as his head fell back, his pulse leaping and bounding in his throat. Heat flooded his body, as if he was being filled, from the toes up, with steam—it had been so long since Cassian had felt the touch of hot water. He'd even had to sell the pot he'd used to boil it.

Yet it was time to leave it all behind. He might have been captured and thrown in the dungeons of the nearest city if anyone knew he had stolen the spell book, but they wouldn't even know who he was after he transformed, even if Cassian did not yet know how that transformation would come to be.

"Yes," he hissed out the word, relishing in how long and drawn out it was, as if he couldn't stop his tongue from flickering back and forth. With his flesh rumbling and bubbling softly, he tried to twist, though it abruptly took a great effort to even move at all, as if everything had been pinned in place, regardless of how he was posed.

His body swelled and the sensation of being too large for his skin pulled through him. Breath dragged through his windpipe as if it was catching on the tender flesh within. Cassian grunted, trying to swing his head back and forth, but he barely managed a twitch.

His spell, as fragile as it'd been, had been enough as the dog's fur flattened to his body, all the knots and tangles smoothing out as each individual hair, slowly, sank into his skin. His body itched furiously and the canine spread his legs apart slightly, though his movement was extremely limited. It was only an incremental shift and yet it made all the difference as his torn pants showed skin where, before, there had only have been fur.

His bare chest was narrow and appeared skinnier and weaker as his brown-grey fur flattened, showing every bit of definition. Cassian only had enough muscle so that he could go about his day, do his labor, pick up the odd jobs he could around the village and on the farms. Yet he had never been strong enough to do the work that sorely needed to be done, which would have—at the very least—put consistent food on the table. Grueling, low-paid farm work, day in and day out, would not have allowed him to fix up the little, run-down cottage. And even if he had been able to work more lucrative jobs, he still would not have been able to save the others.

He exhaled shakily, staring at his hand as his heart pounded a fervent beat against his eardrums. He didn't know what exactly was happening and how he was changing, only that he had to allow the spell to pull him along with it. His back strained as he braced himself. More muscle layered over his body, slowly bulking up his arms and his thighs, though it was a softer feeling, dragging at his lungs to incite him to take a short, sharp breath.

Muscle was...strange. His back ached but in a good way, not like when he labored heavily and had that soreness clawing at his body like a wild beast. He remembered when he'd been young, very young, and ran through the woods, splashing in the stream all day. Those days had been short, but the dog cherished the remains of the memories. It felt like back then, when his body was sore and aching but in a good way, in a way that told him he'd used his muscles—but not past the point of it being able to recover well.

He'd never been that muscular, of course, without good food to fuel him. He needed nutrition to build muscle, but his skin didn't seem to sit as it had before—straining and stretching a little through the transformation—as the last vestiges of fur and even the shaggier, longer hair on his head retracted. Cassian blinked down at his paw, wiggling his fingers where they rested on the table, still beside the spell book.

His claws were becoming longer, darker, chunkier; the chips in them smoothed out as they grew whole once more. Cassian took a shuddering breath, his brown-grey fur transforming, rippling as his skin prickled. He trembled, fighting the urge to shift his hips back and forth. His lower back twinged and he grunted softly. Yet even that sound was a little gentler coming from his lips.

Even as his skin transformed, showing not fur but scales, he peered down at his arms, absorbing every moment visually as well as by feel. Each scale rose in definition, tinted red and orange like the colors of fallen leaves in Autumn. There was no brown in there, just bright, crisp shades that settled into different nuances, as if they would change hue when viewed from different angles.

A soft gasp broke his lips and his face pressed forward, as if he was straining to reach something—only his head and neck were still in the same place. It was his skull and muzzle that were growing, Cassian struggled to keep pace with his transformation. Just what was he turning into? He'd thought he'd take on a new body with a fresh persona to fit, head off into another city, find a job somewhere else with a fit, healthy body. That would have given him the fresh start that he'd needed. Though the spell was not fixed; he had not known how to add a defining clause to it, which would have allowed him to choose his species.

As it was, Cassian only assumed he was going to transform into another anthro.

But that was his assumption and perhaps not an accurate one at all as his face reshaped itself, his skull crunching and crackling as his muzzle shifted. The flesh of his face bubbled as if it was as fluid as water, scales rippling over the top like a soft film on a pond when the algae was thick. Even the rippling tickled, like nails scratching him too lightly without a satisfying pressure. With a start, he realized it was partially from his ears sinking back into his skull. He twitched his tail, but…it didn't want to move anymore—not easily, at least.

One thing at a time...

He tried to breathe deeply, fully inflating his lungs with every breath, even if he was locked into place, still leaning over the table and the spell book. The old wood creaked under his weight, but it wasn't up to Cassian to draw back, to relieve it of any pressure. If it broke, it broke. So much there had been broken already.

"Ah... What is..." Cassian tried to talk, working things through out loud. Yet the changing shape of his jaw mumbled his words and he gave up. Hopefully, afterwards, he would still be able to talk; that was a possibly Cassian had not considered.

He grunted, trying to lick his lips, but saliva spilled lightly from his mouth instead—not much, just a trickle. His muzzle crunched and he groaned as it pulled at the corner of his mouth, though the outline of his lips seemed to remain somewhat in an elongated shape. That was something, at least; he would not have known what to do with a body so vastly different from what he was used to.

His eyes shifted, a little more forward facing than before. They strained and gave him the odd sensation that they were bulging as they moved. Thankfully, that was short-lived, but a deep, pounding ache set into his teeth—like a toothache but more biting, pushing up into his jaw. Cassian heaved and groaned, yet his teeth becoming sharp points resounded in his skull, willing himself through the strain.

The change in his muzzle brought to mind his stomach, gurgling as his guts adjusted their position within the growing barrel of his belly. Even with the changes, Cassian hoped the yawning ache of a frequently empty stomach would not be present in his new life. He'd just needed a life in which to find himself and carve out a path where he never had to go hungry or cold or push through exhaustion ever again. It wasn't an opportunity often afforded to poor folk but he wouldn't be poor for much longer, whatever happened.

One way or another.

Yet those thoughts were pushed from his mind as he was forced to focus on the uncomfortable pull of his transformation.

His tongue slipped forward against his teeth as it narrowed and elongated simultaneously. How was he ever supposed to keep a tongue like that in his mouth? It slid all over the place, like he couldn't control it. Cassian worked his jaw, drooling a little as those sharp lines filled out his muzzle, his slimmer tongue flickering around against them, even then trying to explore his mouth.

He shook his head lightly, shifting it barely an inch from one side to the other.

"Erf…" Still, no ability to speak, though Cassian tried instinctively. Words would return to him, he was sure, letting the notion settle inside him. He just had to be sure of himself, confident in who he was so he could take that part of himself forward into the new body.

For now, all he knew for certain was that he was scaled. His muzzle prickled as smaller, more delicate scales settled into place, though there was a sense of resilience too in how they nestled securely up against one another, as if they would not be cut too easily. A defensive body could be useful to him.

His top half seemed to fall heavier and heavier as he tipped forward, his fingers hooking over the top of the table. Before his eyes, the canine's claws grew longer and darker than they had so far in his transformation, biting into the wood as they sliced through the old, worn grain with little resistance. He'd always wondered just how long that table was going to last and now he knew.

It was more fitting that Cassian was the one to destroy it, than it fall down of its own accord as if it was a symbol of their suffering. Conversely, it became a symbol of his empowerment, in taking charge of his own destiny. His tail, stiffened hopefully by the spell, stretched back away from his body as it lengthened. Yet as the table crumbled and cracked under his weight, though it only felt natural for his shifting body to smash through it as his body dragged him into place.

His landing was far from gentle as he crunched down through the shattered table, his paws on the floor of the kitchen. However, they didn't look like paws anymore but…feet. Cassian shuddered. Was he turning into a quadruped? That would be different from his expectation, although it wasn't a bad thing. If he could fill his belly and live a simple life, he was sure he could manage a quadrupedal body.

But what creature was he transforming into with scales?

His mind rang through with the truth and Cassian's head shot up, his startlement striking in a burst of adrenaline that allowed a snap of movement, even though the rest of him remained dull and sluggish. His body had to give some energy still to the transformation, after all.

His shoulders felt thick, almost meaty in a way, and pushed back as his arms lengthened, becoming forelegs. It was easier to put things into place mentally now that he understood a little more.

He wasn't a dog anymore… Well, he wasn't anything, not when he was between two bodies, still shifting. But he was turning into a *dragon*, a beast of the wind and the sky.

He would have jumped for joy if he'd been able to, even as his shoulder blades grew hard and lumpy, new bone extending from them. Oh, wings? Yes, wings! They had to come in too and he focused on them as they drew out and out and out, like a spoke being drawn from its resting place. They belonged there on his back, despite their unfamiliarity, as his body rippled with warmth, flesh and muscle, growing all around.

Cassian did not focus on his size, even as the confines of the kitchen felt like they were closing in on him. It had never been the largest of kitchens, but his tail stretched out nearer the wall to his back as he grunted and worked his jaw, having gained a little more freedom in his physical form. Even then, he fought to get to grips with all the new sensations and uses of his muscles.

He tried to talk, opening and closing his jaw and clearing his throat.

"Mmm... Am... Ammm... Daagon."

He had some ability to talk, though his difficulty was in how to actually work his new jaws and lips and tongue to form intelligible words. He almost wouldn't have minded no longer being able to talk, not when he was transforming into something as big and as powerful as a dragon, but to have verbal capabilities —like the anthros he'd grown up with—was reassuring still.

Even if his body was different, he would still have the ability to say who he was. And being a *dragon* was going to be much greater than anything his old life could have led him to.

His wings pulled out and out and out, the spikes of them stretching down in a smooth arc, though he could not yet flap them, only quiver. The membrane came with an unusual tugging sensation—straining taut between every spoke—and he wanted to flex and twitch them, even if that was not yet possible. Cassian hoped they were the same rich autumnal colors as the scales he could see.

The walls of the kitchen closed in around him as he grew. His tail was forced to curl as it became long enough to push up against the wall, getting in the way of the hanging pots and pans. The clatter of them spilling to the old stone of the kitchen floor rang through his ears; Cassian only then realized his ears had become little indents in the side of his head as he could no longer swivel them to follow the sound. He could still hear, even though the tiny hole of ear canal was protected. On the contrary, the hole seemed to have a dip and a curve to it, so it could filter sound more directly.

Not that he knew all that much about dragon anatomy— they flew around from time to time and he had always been wary of them with their gaping maws and dagger-like claws. And now Cassian was going to get up close and personal with them in a way he could never have expected.

His wings filled out completely and he exhaled as he flapped them lightly, up and down. Yet his tail had to find some space to move into, long and reptilian, twisting back and forth—but not because it was him controlling its movements. His transformation was seeking space, muscle layering thickly down either side of the tail as more and more vertebrae added to the length.

Stretched from both ends, his neck extended as he sucked in a breath, blinking rapidly, his eyes wide. Yet the dragon wanted to close his eyes, panting heavily, relishing in the moment. It stripped everything away from him, every worry he'd had in the past, forcing him to focus on the moment.

No future. No past. Only the present. And that was a gift indeed.

"Oh," he moaned softly, warmth trickling through him, flowing under his skin. He hadn't felt comfortable like that in ages as the ravaging heat that had come with the initiation of the spell faded pleasantly. And now there was a lot more of him physically to fit in the cottage as his tail pressed into the wall behind him, a little crushed and cramped, even as his hindquarters filled out too.

Not his buttocks... Well, Cassian guessed he could call them his legs and thighs still. But his body was different, more settled on all fours than it had been before, his feet pressing down into the ground, taking solace from the solidity of the aged stone. The stories they told in their wear patterns would be something he took with him.

When he left.

The muscle bulking out on his hindquarters surprised him. He'd never been that muscular and the dragon tested out just how much was actually on his body, clenching and tensing them as he tried to understand where each one lay. A little more movement returned to Cassian as his neck stretched out, elongating with a little prickle and crack with every new vertebra until it was fully formed. Something slotted into place at the base of his skull, his head resetting itself in a more comfortable, forward-facing position—for a quadruped, at least. He no longer would carry his head on top of his body but extended out before it.

His claws scraped over the stone floor—but the kitchen was too small for him altogether as the point where his tail joined his body pressed to the rickety wall. Cassian grunted and tried to twist, but the old stone jostled against his hind end, threatening to tumble down even then. There were so many cracks in the walls, even where they had been filled in and boarded up, that he could not truly fear growing too large for his kitchen when it had already been in the process of falling down.

As he transformed, however, heat pooled in his crotch. His member had usually been softly contained within his sheath, except on those rare occasions when he was aroused, but something changed there. As the scales softened and grew smaller around his groin, his sheath flattened out to tuck his penis, inside his body along with his testes.

Cassian grunted and shuddered, his tongue spilling out over his sharp teeth and lips. The transforming dragon—not too far off being fully a drake—reeled with desire. Sensation clawed at him and he couldn't help shifting his weight, snaking his head faintly back and forth with need rising thick and fast inside.

His cock pushed out from his slit, as if it knew it was wanted —only, it was not the cock he remembered as he peered at it from an awkward angle. His shaft, before, had been smooth with a tapered tip and a knot that swelled at the point of orgasm, yet this cock was fatter and slicker as it produced its own lubrication, perhaps inside that new slit of his. The dragon's testes ached deeply and he panted, licking his lips, gaining a little more control over his body.

The kitchen, however, could only hold around him for so long. He bowed his head, trying to shove his muzzle into the space of the hearth, but really, he had to let the transformation come as it needed. As his flesh rippled and his tough scales pushed against the walls, his tail finally broke through a weaker point into the world outside. Even though Autumn was coming, it felt warm out there and he leaned into the tickle of fresh air on his scales through the hole, growling as he pulled his head up to break through the haphazard stones of the hearth.

He'd cooked so many meals there when food had been available. One thing he had always been able to find, however, had been firewood, and Cassian had spent many a night before the stone hearth, warming his bitterly cold fingers and toes. It had not been enough to fully chase the chill from his bones, but it had been enough.

"Mmmm…" He smiled faintly, parting his jaws as he released that memory. It longer deserved the space in the forefront of his mind or to weigh so heavily on him.

He chose lightness. He chose the open skies. He chose to be *free.*

The kitchen could not hold him as he drew his head up higher, cracking through the stones of the outside wall. His back humped against the roof of the kitchen but it didn't take much for him to break through the wood, making splinters cascade down around him as beams cracked and shattered.

His cock twitched under him, protected from the deluge of wreckage. Cassian had never focused on self-pleasure and arousal before; he'd been so overwhelmed with merely striving to live that it had never had much of an appeal. He'd been too wrapped up and worried about what the next day was going to bring. The mind was an important precursor to such pleasure, after all.

Cassian let out a shuddering grunt that had his flanks tensing as he broke through to the musty eaves of the cottage, fresh air filtering in through a break in the thatched roof. He'd meant to patch that up. Truthfully, Cassian had spent little time up there since he'd been left on his own.

Trying to avoid the eaves blocking in his head, the dragon sighed, the sound rolling in a heave from his lungs. There was no sense in them anymore. Not even as his body bulked out further, toppling walls and crushing the wooden frame underfoot. Even where the back door had been boarded up against the cold did not escape him, his right hip bashing brutally through both the rotting doorframe and the boards as his body made room.

The cottage was never meant to hold him. And that was fine. The spines of his back ripped through the eaves, digging into the wooden beams and tearing up the thatching.

As his spine arched into a hump-like shape and his tail curled down and around through the shattered wall of the cottage, jagged spines shot up from his back. It was a sharp burst that made him gasp, trembling as the roots of them settled into the vertebrae of his spine.

Horns too… Yes, he would need those. The crackle and crunch of his skull forming new matter had him blinking, eyes watering from discomfort, though he could neither stop them nor will them to transform more swiftly. His growing horns sent a resounding ache driving through his skull from the back of his head to the front as his head cracked through the weak thatching. They curved out, ridged and bumpy, angled forward at the very tip as if they could have been used for offensive or defensive maneuvers alike. Smaller, bony protrusions poked through his cheeks, framing them and the line of his jaw, while his nostrils pulled up into sharp curves on the upper side with a little ridge above them.

Cassian parted his lips as his body outgrew the cottage he'd spent his life in. The building was reduced to rubble. But maybe that was a fitting end for it too, even as his cock ached and throbbed. His claws dug into the ground floor of the cottage, tearing up the foundations.

The dragon let need flow through him, tail twisting free,

ripping out of the hole in the kitchen wall and into the open air with the weak sunshine streaming down over him. Yet it had never felt as good to Cassian as it did right there in that moment, tickling his scales with warmth.

"Mmmm… Yes. That feels…nice." Words came more easily to him as he gained further control over his jaws and the movement of his slippery tongue. The dragon could not resist a soft chortle. His tail flicked back and forth as he tried to control it and his clawed front feet dug down into the wreckage as he tried to dig his way free. Yet the cottage crumbled as the growing dragon clambered through the remains, crushing his old home that had not felt all that much like a home for a while.

What did that mean for him, now that there really was no home left? It was gone, crushed, trampled on. His new body smashed through the final wall that was partly standing as if in testament to his transformation, shaking a slice of the thatched roof aside, as he extended a pair of trembling wings out on either side of his body. He shifted his weight, crushing what had been a storeroom before, wood splintering under his foot. It hadn't held anything anymore. A swing of his tail took out the back wall of the property that had faced up the hill. The dragon barely felt the stones toppling away from him, though it had not taken much effort for the cottage to crumble as the elements had weakened the entire structure over time.

He grunted, shuddering softly. If he was leaving so much behind, what did that mean for what lay ahead of him?

Pleasure called to him. And was that a lure? Was that something he wasn't supposed to be paying attention to? Guilt pulled at his mind and was swiftly swept away. It didn't belong there, for there wasn't a place for guilt in the mind of a dragon. Even in the mind of an anthro, it came when there was knowledge of wrongdoing.

If he accepted pleasure and paid attention to his powerful, muscled body for once, Cassian could do no wrong.

He glanced down at the surrounding cottage and its resulting rubble, shuddering faintly. There was pain there…but it was not his pain to take to heart, not anymore. It didn't need to rest there. And he had been gripping it to him for far too long.

Cassian blinked from his new vantage point, looking down the valley from where the cottage was set in a windy spot on the hill near the village. The city gleamed and sparkled in the distance. There were so many shiny things there… Something in the dragon pulled towards them—but he had to hold back. A dragon's lust for hoarding, gold, all things that shimmered… Well, that was already legendary throughout the kingdom, but it wasn't the time for him to let his deeper draconic instincts get the better of him.

He'd contend with that later.

His shoulders rose above the cottage, several feet taller as he stood to his full height—yet Cassian would need somewhere else to live at his new height, seeking perhaps a caves or other settlement to make his home. For now, he settled at thirty feet tall at the shoulder; he was taller if he extended his neck all the way up, thick and round with muscle. Even when he swallowed, it took an inordinately long time for it to travel all the way down his throat, the reflex softening at the base.

Cassian took a breath as his transformation settled over him —yet it came with a lightness too. With the expansion of his lungs, inflating with much greater capacity than had been present before.

Just like he knew the transformation was complete when the weight of his body felt like it had all slotted into place, at ease in himself. Even if it was still a new body to him, the dragon shifting his weight through the wreckage, his heart pulling just a little for the home he had lived in, even if it had never been the home he'd wanted it to be.

Time to move on.

As he lifted a foot, the spell book came into view, the pages crumbled, the spine cracked. Really, it was a miracle it had survived so far, but the drake only grinned at it. His jaws parted, heat bundling in the back of his throat as he set a strike to the rising gas by clicking something at the back of his mouth, firing off a jet of flame directly at the spell book. It burned swiftly, pages blackening and curling, succumbing to ash. Not even magic, if it had even been imbued with any protective spells, could hold up to the incinerating force of dragon fire.

And the fire was cleansing, stripping it all down to the ground, the flames taking hold in the old beams. Even his flames found those damper parts of the cottage difficult, however, where rot had got into the wood of the house, though it was no longer any of Cassian's concern. All that was in the past.

And there it should stay.

His cock throbbed and, finally, the dragon could step free of the wreckage, turning around just to see what was under him. It was not what was expected now that he had a little more time to get a better view, ridged with the raised lines spiraling around his cock. They seemed to draw the eye, though the dragon was not all that interested in his shaft—not visually, at least. The lack of balls was intriguing, but he could still "feel" them inside him, for there was no sense of loss, just a warming pull deep within his hind abdomen.

"Mmmm." He rumbled a long, low growl, glancing down to the village where no one yet seemed to have uncovered him. They would soon, though he had a little time. His cock hung out and bounced lightly up against his belly as Cassian tensed the muscles of his abdomen, close to the point of his groin.

Cassian panted, licking his lips, the lingering, acrid bite of smoke on his tongue not bothering him in the slightest. It was all a part of being a dragon, after all.

The spines on his back rattled and bristled against one

another as he steadied himself, though the dragon would still have to come to grips with the smoldering remains of his cottage. Healing was to be done in time. What Cassian could do in the moment, however, was find that pleasure he had not allowed himself before—pleasure there had not been time to indulge in.

He could follow the lure of his thoughts instead of stopping himself and turning back to the act of survival. He has desired to for a long while, but only now could he do as he pleased. He flexed his abdomen, tensing his muscles to make his member slap up against the underside of his belly. If his new body was aroused, why shouldn't he chase after the urge inside him? He couldn't have ever imagined doing it before, his tail sweeping back and forth, but, as a dragon, it simply felt natural.

Easy? He scoffed, a puff of air rolling over his tongue as he tried to do so with a new muzzle. Oh, things had never been easy. Even the roll of his gait as he took a few more paces away from the cottage was simple, finding and steadying himself, even though walking on four legs and not two should have been disorientating for him. Cassian extended his head and neck out to steady himself, licking his lips, though he had to keep rocking his hips lightly, tensing his hind end to grind forward a little.

Yet it was contracting those muscles that proved the most useful to him. His cock jerking and splattering; it was crude and so lewd, something that would never have been a part of his life before. And he wanted that—oh, Cassian wanted it so terribly. He groaned long and low, deep in the back of his throat, the sound reverberating all the way down his neck into his gut.

The pulse of desire within him rose in a flutter into the pit of his belly and he ached, though the gnaw on his insides was not quite like hunger. It was so much *better* than hunger as it sank its claws into him and the dragon hissed through his teeth, snaking his head and neck back and forth. Following another course of instinct, knowing what to do without honestly knowing, he bent his legs, folding his much larger form to the ground. It felt like Cassian came down with a lot more weight than usual, a solid thump reverberating through the earth, but he settled there, pushed back so he was partly on his side, his cock exposed.

It was only natural to curl his tail around to tease his length, pressing the long appendage up against his shaft to grind it back temptingly against his own stomach. The tail and temptation might have been too rough for the dragon if not for the lubrication coating his cock; the perfect amount of slippery wetness.

"Ah... Heavens... Ahhhh." He moaned, tongue hanging out, sparks of magic flowing through him—at least, that was what it felt like to Cassian. His cock tensed, every fiber of his being tingling with need, his gut lurching softly, though the tingling pulses spreading out from his groin urged him on. His tail wanted to twist and thrash back and forth but he had to focus, had to keep it pressed up against his cock, rubbing along the ridged length. He masturbated in the only way a dragon could, considering he had four legs and no longer had the use of anthro paws.

"Mmmph... Oh," the dragon growled, his tongue swiping out to lash against the outside of his muzzle, though he was exactly where he needed to be in the moment. Heat warmed his scales, prickling as if that fire was, again, building in the back of his throat, but it was a different flame he coveted. It simmered and flickered, leaping hungrily to lick at the back of his mind, a new, throbbing glow swelling to encompass his body.

Dimly, Cassian wondered if he should exercise modesty and extend his wing to cover himself, but, really...was that going to change anything? No one would know the dragon was him and there was no one in sight anyway. He could be discovered and all he would have to do was fly away: an easy solution for once in his life.

There was no longer anything to fear, nothing to hide, not as

ARIAN MABE

Cassian's great flanks heaved with breath, letting his jaws hang open and releasing excess heat from his massive maw. His teeth parted impossibly wide and he let out a throaty chuckle as he curved his tail slightly to better grind and rub his cock up against his own underbelly.

"Mmmm." He'd never made a sound quite like that before—a growl tainted by fire and brimstone, the snarl and snap of a beast who did not follow anthro wiles and whims. It was much deeper than his canine growls, though Cassian had become far from a dog. No, Cassian was so much greater than that, struck by the urge to extend his wings, to take flight and soar. That would have to wait until another base need had been met—the deeply rooted lust seeping through him, curling within his gut.

The dragon grunted, closer and closer, even though he did not yet know and understand the nuances of how climax would come to him as a dragon rather than an anthro canine. Oh, that time and life seemed so far away already and he focused on the moment, curling the claws of his forepaws, digging them into the dirt. He'd leave it torn up in his wake but, there was no concern there.

Not as his cock throbbed, twitching as he masturbated himself closer to the edge, breath hitching in his chest. The tip of his tail twitched and wriggled back and forth and Cassian heaved for air, everything tighter and tensing, closing in around him. Yet it was not like the bounds of the cottage, which had caged him for so very long. It was a pressure he could lean into, soothing, rippling through him with the knowledge that a greater delight still was coming shortly.

"Oof... So...mmm...close." Cassian tried to talk, just to work words around his maw, to figure out how to say them again, even though his voice was rougher. He sounded older—but he had been in his twenties before, not a young lad by any means. Yet it ceased to matter as his pleasure shot up, eyes wide, jaws snapping, twisting his head back and forth in an attempt to secure his need, tension flooding him.

Yet only one thing could send that need softening once more and that was the bliss of orgasm as his cock erupted, long, hot spurts of dragon seed splattering the ground. It was thinner than he would have expected, soaking into the soil as he gave the offering of his semen back to the earth.

All the drake cared about, however, was bliss; letting the feeling of it thrum through him, though it was not predictable, tossing him first one way and then the other on ebbing and flowing peaks, like a sly wind. He moaned, ducking his head as he tucked his chest down, though all Cassian wanted was for climax to roll through him. Reveling in every drop of liquid joy, his entire body warmed through, fresh and renewed.

He'd never felt like that before. But, as a dragon, he could finally enjoy it, taking it for his own. Cassian's tail fell away from his body as he let every throb tremble through him, riding out his high to the very last spurts. His cock was left shiny with lingering lubrication from his slit and the final drips of semen too as it pulsed lightly. His seed soaked away into the earth and his scales were left pure and clean.

"Unff... Whoa..." He chuckled at his own reaction, shaking his head. Could pleasure really feel that good? Was it like that for those that didn't have troubles weighing them down? Well, that was something Cassian could dig into, uncovering bit by bit, but that would come in time. Finally, all he had was time. Though the dragon would have to learn to hunt too, sustaining himself in the dragon way.

Rising smoothly, barely making a sound bar a rustle of grass, he stood tall, resting his muscles. With his legs braced apart, he steadied himself, a lick of wind on his muzzle guiding him to look towards the sky, where the clouds had parted to allow a brighter shine of sunlight to the ground below.

Even the day appeared lighter as a dragon. It was enough.

He exhaled softly through his nostrils. It was time to let go. His family would never have wanted him to suffer. They would never have wanted him to fade away, to fall as they had.

In living his life, he would honor their memory. The dragon raised his head high, flaring his wings, eyes gleaming as he parted his jaws and bellowed a roar that trembled even through the cavern of his chest.

He would take every pleasure that came his way, so they would be proud of all he had done, how far he had come.

In leaving it all behind, Cassian emerged anew, reborn.

MATES OF DREAMS

JADEN DRACKUS

The sapphire dragon Ryninth wasn't wealthy judged against others of his kind. But he was still young—not even a century old. Though by the standards of the Small Folk, he could match the wealth of many of the largest, longest reigning monarchs. Such *accumulations* needed looking after and Lord Ryninth was wise enough to know that he needed assistance in the endeavor. And so, the young dragon had engaged the services of a clan of kobolds. The clan was about twenty members and lived in the series of caves that dragon had taken over near the town of Tradeway—unimaginatively named for the fact that it sat along a series of trade routes that had grown as more caravans moved to avoid The Troubles—a century long war between two ancient dragons and their allies. As the routes developed, the town had grown both in size and riches. Both of which turned the minds of the townsfolk to protection, and when a dragon showed up a decade ago, it seemed the problem was solved. Ryninth would take a small percentage of the town's income and would provide protection for the town. And for a decade, things proceeded until one early spring day, the Council of Tradeway unexpectedly requested an audience from their dragon protector. Ryninth winged off to see what the Small Folk wanted while the kobolds conducted the annual inventory of the blue dragon's growing hoard.

Magnis rummaged through a pile of gold coins that was almost as tall as he was. He winced and muttered as the metal disks scattered and rolled away from his claws. He would collect them later and hope he didn't mix denominations up. It was hard to keep track of when so many were the same size. And with all the regions they came from, the markings didn't always help. The kobold sighed.

But the coins weren't his concern right now. He was trying to locate a large ruby that had been misplaced somewhere in the hoard. The bronze scaled lizardfolk grumbled to himself at the need for the search for the gem—it wasn't even to his knowledge enchanted. Maybe it was magic in a way he didn't know how to detect? The ruby was shiny though, and maybe that was why the Clan Mother felt it was essential to locate. She'd been insistent about it, tasking Magnis specifically to find it without explanation.

The kobold could appreciate that, but he didn't share most of his kin's obsession with shiny things. While such things were nice, he'd learned to see that things had value beyond how that measure. Still, shininess was a good judgement of value in many things. But not all of them. And there were some things that couldn't be valued with coin. Things like spending time with Lord Ryninth, or Ryn as the dragon insisted Magnis called him.

He shook his head. He needed to find the ruby, and thinking about his dragon was a distraction. The inventory of the hoard was the most important matter at the moment—everything else could wait. Because while Lord Ryn was patient and understanding, the Small Folk of Tradeway were sending a party in a week to take an accounting, and they were very adamant about having an *exact* idea of what their protector was paid. Magnis wasn't looking forward to that. They would probably grumble the whole time about the expense—especially the fennec and the gnu. The kobold didn't understand it. It wasn't like Lord Ryn even set unreasonable prices or was strict in collecting his fees. Plus, it wasn't as if the entire hoard had come from the town—Lord Ryn had brought some of it when he'd come to the area. But the blue dragon insisted that the Small Folk be humored. And whatever Lord Ryn wanted, the kobold wanted too.

Finally, with a triumphant squeak, Magnis wrapped his claws around the ruby he'd been searching for. He held it over his head, allowing himself the fantasy of imaging Lord Ryn returning and praising him for his efforts. Rather effusively, in ways only a handsome male dragon like him could express his gratitude. For a fleeting moment, the fantasy was strong enough that he could almost smell the wonderful scent of his lord's sandy musk...

The image shattered as the loud scrapping of stone against stone signaled that the boulder door to the cave had slid opened. Magnis jumped at the noise, almost dropping the ruby he'd been searching for all morning. He bobbled the jewel before catching it in both claws. It wouldn't do to lose it after all that effort. Wouldn't do at all. Especially when that sound meant that Lord Ryn had returned. The kobold's tail thumped the ground in excitement as he shoved the gem into his pouch, retrieved his inventory log, straightened his tunic, and scampered to meet the returning dragon.

The cave entrance was large, as one would expect for a dragon, but was covered by a massive boulder carved to be flat that rolled back and forth to hide the den. It was an impressive feat, even for a magically inclined being like a dragon, Magnis thought. But Ryn seemed to think it was both simple—even though he was barely trained in magic—and necessary. The kobolds didn't mind, after all they wouldn't have to worry about random intrusions.

Lord Ryn was just turning around, his lean body shining in the sunlight as the kobold scampered into the entrance cavern. Karna'th, the Clan Mother, was already there and greeting the dragon. She was an older kobold, well into her sixth decade so Karna'th had served a few dragons in her time and didn't stand on formality with Lord Ryn.

"Wad'did they want?" she asked as Magnis arrived, apparently without preamble.

"It was bizarre," the dragon replied with a shake of his massive head and a thump of his tail. He looked around, his eyes landing on Magnis. He gave a happy snort before turning his attention back to Karna'th.

Magnis looked around and realized that the Clan Mother and he were the kobolds here to greet the dragon. From deeper in the caves, he could hear some of the other's voices as they worked on counting Lord Ryn's collection. He felt his scales warming with embarrassment and started to edge back towards the inner cavern he'd just come from. This conversation sounded like it was just between the two of them, and not meant for a lowly kobold like himself. But before he could bolt, Lord Ryn motioned for him to stay before the dragon launched into the strange demands of the townsfolk.

"I'd expect anything those idiots came up with to be," Karna'th grumped.

"Now, now. Anya is a lovely badger and has been a good mayor to Tradeway, and to us." Lord Ryn tutted. "And come to think of it, she seemed quite done with the whole affair before I even arrived."

"Fine, then who's brilliant idea required the summoning of the town guardian with no threat in sight?"

"The heads of the bank and the merchant's guild."

"That mean fennec and the grumpy gnu?" Magnis interjected before slapping both claws over his muzzle in embarrassment.

"Yes, those two," Lord Ryninth answered with a smile. "And they were quite insistent that I get 'married' of all things."

"What?" Magnis asked, his claws keeping his muzzle from dropping open in shock.

"I don't suppose you explained to them that dragons don't do that," Karna'th said dryly.

"I attempted to," the dragon rustled his wings—a gesture of frustration, Magnis had learned. "But it's what they want. And if I don't bring a mate to the Winter Festival, they plan to run us off. Or worse. They've already started to make contact with The Spears."

"The dragon hunters?" Magnis asked.

Lord Ryn nodded, and for a long moment silence descended on the chamber.

Karna'th shook her head and snorted. "Mammals are strange creatures. I don't suppose the asked any important questions, like what color scales you preferred?"

"Really, Karna'th?" Ryn said with an arched eyebrow. "Do not tell me you are taking this seriously?"

The Clan Mother cocked her head and thumped her tail. "Are you not?"

For the first time that Magnis could remember, the blue-scaled dragon looked genuinely concerned. Ryn blew out a deep breath in disgust. "I do not know. I cannot see how I *can* take it seriously. Anya sent them packing when all they wanted to do was hide what they wanted in fawning over me. That does not seem like something to be taken seriously."

The older kobold stared at the dragon incredulously, as if Lord Ryn hadn't seen something painfully obvious. Magnis' muzzle must have displayed a similarly puzzled expression to the dragon because he hadn't either. Both of them cocked their heads at her.

"So. Both of you missed the part where they threatened to at the very least drive us out, and likely try to kill us?"

The two males blinked hard. Apparently, they had. Magnis shifted back and forth on his claws. "But the townsfolk are always happy when Lord Ryn comes to the festivals. They even tolerate the clan's drunken antics."

Karna'th turned her gaze to the younger kobold. "The Spears rarely care if their prey is loved or not. They will kill Ryn if it comes to it. No questions asked. The merchants know that for sure."

Magnis blinked. "But why are they offering up two completely opposite solutions? Either more dragons or no dragons. It doesn't make sense!"

"If there's anything merchants want," Karna'th said resignedly. "It's more money. Make dragons look positively charitable. My guess, and our dear mayor's reaction makes me even more sure, is that they would prefer no dragon. But we have a contract, so to invalidate it without breaking it, they are asking for something they know is impossible. Especially when the dragon in question doesn't have his eyes on a female."

Ryn's scales seemed turn a deeper blue before he met the Clan Mother's knowing gaze. "But with The Troubles spreading, there's word that other towns have made contracts with multiple dragons," he said with a huff.

"True," Karna'th replied with a knowing smile. "But that only makes it plausible. Not preferred. Two dragons protecting Tradeway would be a selling point, likely bringing in more money. So would not having to give a dragon an increasing protection fee. Either way, they win."

Ryn blew out a snort. "Indeed. Well. We have half a year to think of something. I'm sure between all of us, we can come up with a plan. If it comes to it, even though she scared me by getting tough, Anya is probably on our side. I got the impression that she used to be an adventurer."

"Not that I want to do it," Magnis said suddenly. "But why

don't we just leave? There are other towns that would be just as happy to have a dragon."

"*This* town is also happy to have a dragon," Karna'th said. "Except for those that dream of being dragons themselves. Or rather, the ones who's dreams of being dragons only focus on the wealth..." Her eyes passed from Ryn to Magnis, and an indulgent smile flashed on her muzzle as her eyes settled on the kobold.

It was gone as soon as it came, but Magnis caught it. He fought the urge to squirm as the heat rose in his ears. He couldn't help but think for a moment that the Clan Mother was commenting on his private fantasies. It took him a moment to realize that Ryn too had pulled his wings in close and was staring at the ground—something he only did when he was embarrassed or admitting he was wrong... Though the one eye that Magnis could see was almost looking in his direction...

The dragon shook himself and met the Clan Mother's gaze again. "Besides, I like this town too. It's been good to me, and most of them are just fine with me being here."

"But then why don't you want to have another dragon around, my lord?" Magnis asked before he could stop himself. Lord Ryn had clearly ended the conversation, and it wasn't his place to extend it. He winced and looked for a way to retreat, but it was no use—both Lord Ryn and Karna'th were staring at him. Instead, he prepared himself for a tongue lashing. It wasn't forthcoming.

The dragon shook his head. "It's complicated, Magni. But at my age, most dragons are focused on making a name for themselves, making their way in the world. Most of them are standoffish at best and combative at worst. And with The Troubles going on for longer than I have been alive, most just assume combative. Very strongly."

Magnis nodded, feeling a slight swell of pride in having a nickname. While he knew he spent more time with Lord Ryn than most of the clan that served the dragon, he had no idea that Lord Ryn held any sort of affection for him above the other kobolds.

"I always wondered why you had such a meager hoard when you arrived," Karna'th snorted. "Now it makes sense. You got run out of your old territory."

Magnis' jaw dropped open in shock. He'd heard of kobolds being eaten by their dragon masters for suggesting weakness before. But Ryn just shook his large head ruefully.

"It was a long time ago. And it wasn't mine. It was all that was left of my parents' hoard."

The Clan Mother nodded. "I always thought you had more enchanted items then could be expected of from a dragon your age."

"Well," the dragon said with a sigh. "Maybe there's one of them that can help us out. Magnis, how is the inventory going?"

"It's been going well," the younger kobold replied, pulling his notebook and swelling with pride at being asked. "Currently we have started with the coins and gems…"

Spring turned to summer, and while the kobolds and the dragon pondered a solution, they couldn't find one. Ryn and Magnis began spending more time together discussing the problem.

That evening had started like most of the others, with Ryn inviting Magnis to spend it with him.

"What should we do tonight?" the kobold asked as he plopped down next to the dragon. "Games? Reading? Just talk?"

"I don't know," Ryn chuckled as he adjusted himself so Magnis could lean against him. "We've talked a lot."

That was true, they had talked a great deal. Ryn insisted on conversing with the kobold. The dragon had opened up more to Magnis during these nights, speaking more about his feelings and thoughts than he had before. He also told Magnis about his experience in The Troubles and how he fled to Tradeway as little more than a wyrmling with nothing but what treasure he could carry and a dragon led army on his tail. Ryn told of the decades he'd spent hiding until he'd become aware of the town when a caravan—guided by Anya of all people—had sheltered in his cave from a storm.

"We have," Magnis replied. "I feel like I know you better than any of the other kobolds, except maybe Karna'th."

"You probably do," Ryn agreed as he casually rubbed the kobold's belly.

Magnis squeaked happily, letting the dragon's big digit wander over his body. The attention felt so good. His mind wandered into more…forbidden thoughts. Well, not really, it was a drinking time joke that all kobolds wanted to be fucked by the dragons they served—but it wouldn't do to give in to those thoughts here in front of his dragon. Fortunately, Ryn's voice gave him something to focus on.

"I still haven't figured out a solution to the damn town problem. Truth be told, I've been ignoring it and acting like nothing happened. Though I haven't given the Council the time of day, greedy bastards."

"But the townsfolk still seem happy," the kobold put in, shifting a little as the claw drifted lower. He didn't try and get away, but he was a touch nervous about what the wandering digit would find.

"That they do. But still, I wish we could figure out an answer. It would be so much easier if we could have a solution between us."

Magnis nodded, wondering if Ryn meant more than he was saying with that comment. The dragon's tone had sounded even more affectionate than usual. "It would be nice…"

"I think Karna'th is working on something. She might be

close to an idea. I've seen her around a lot more, especially since we have been spending more time together."

"She hasn't said anything to me…" Magnis said. The only thing Karna'th had mentioned to him that felt outside the norm was she had insisted that he keep that ruby he'd collected on the day all this started but didn't say why.

"Nor I, really," Ryn said with a sigh. "Only something asking if I was enjoying our nights together."

"Are you, Lord Ryn?"

"Ryn in private Magni. How many times do we have to go over this?" the dragon chuckled.

"Sorry."

"Don't be. But yes, I have been enjoying our nights together. It's been good to feel like I have a confidant again. I haven't had one since I was a wyrmling…"

They talked and eventually read together for several hours. Magnis would read aloud from any codex that was too small for dragons to use. Lord Ryn still expressed embarrassment that he'd never learned to change his form, but Magnis didn't mind —especially as Ryn kept caressing him the whole time. But eventually, both the dragon and the kobold grew sleepy, and they parted for the night.

Magnis could barely contain himself as he trotted down the corridor. Behind him, he could hear Lord Ryn rumble and let out a contented sigh, followed by scales rubbing against each other as he settled down. The kobold shuddered as he walked— it was so easy to imagine those sounds as the dragon taking care of the *issue* that Magnis himself needed to deal with as soon as he got to his chambers. It was a pleasant thought, but the horny kobold shook his head. He was probably just projecting. But he couldn't help but imagine Lord Ryn rolling on his back, displaying himself, and requesting Magnis to stroke a cock that was probably half as big as the kobold.

The fantasy became so vivid that his paw began to wander

down towards his rapidly plumping sheath. He was just about to slide it under the waistband of his kilt when he realized he wasn't alone in the corridor.

Karna'th stood just coming out of the doorway of the main library chamber, watching him with a knowing and indulgent smile.

Magnis felt the heat rise in his scales. The Clan Mother had made it clear to each of her charges as they came of age—sexual behavior was supposed to be kept to appropriate venues. Groping himself in a public corridor was definitely *not* one of those. He dropped his paw back to his side and slowed his pace to a respectable walk.

She continued to watch him silently as he approached, saying nothing. Magnis thought she looked tired, but the smile on her face looked almost proud. Of him. He racked his brain trying to think of something he'd done that she would be proud of him for, but his mind was locked on the fact that he'd almost fondled himself in front of her. He looked down at the stone floor as he walked. It was only when he passed her that she spoke.

"It is good that you spend time with our dragon. But I think you have missed the point of these meetings."

"I'm not sure what you mean Clan Mother. I thought he just liked me because I am more interested in books and history than the rest of the clan."

"I thought not," Karna'th said with a sigh. She drew herself up to her full height. "You know, young one, that Lord Ryn prefers male partners."

Magnis hesitated, but when he turned to look, Karna'th was gone.

Wheels began to turn in the younger kobold's mind. Was the Clan Mother suggesting that *he* might be a good match for Lord Ryn? How could that be? No answer came, and Magnis realized he might look silly staring at the wall of the corridor. He checked to see he was alone before setting off to his chamber at an undignified run.

Of course, every kobold dreamed of becoming a dragon and the comment from Karna'th pushed the idea even more into Magnis' mind to be that partner for Lord Ryn. It was a nice dream, but it wasn't something that usually happened in the real world. But the Clan Mother was suggesting that it was possible, wasn't she? He stewed over it in his mind, thinking about all the possibilities and he kept coming back to the same two questions —why had she made such a comment? And why had she made it to him?

For weeks, he rolled the questions around in his mind, so much so that Ryn seemed to notice. The dragon made a few disappointed comments that perhaps they should halt their nightly meetings so that the kobold would not be distracted from whatever he was working on. That comment finally made Magnis realize just how much he was focusing on the mystery of why the Clan Mother had spoken to him. He needed to find out.

———

It was a quiet afternoon in the autumn, and the caves were all but empty. With the leaves mostly fallen, the trails and roads were covered, and Lord Ryn felt it important for the kobolds to assist the Small Folk in clearing them. Once again, the dragon and the kobolds pointedly ignored the Council—minus the mayor—and interacted only with the townsfolk, who were still grateful for their dragon protector. With most of the clan, and— unusually—even Lord Ryn himself out clearing the trails there was time for private conversations, and Magnis took the opportunity.

He trotted down the corridor, sticking his head into the various side rooms. It took roughly an hour to find what, or rather who, he was looking for. Karna'th sat at a desk in a small library with some books and parchments spread before her. Surprisingly, she wasn't studying them, instead her gaze was on the door, watching the younger kobold approach.

"Took you long enough youngster," she said with a snort. "I expected you weeks ago."

"You didn't make it very clear Clan Mother."

"I suppose not," she returned as she stood and stretched. "But then, that was also the point. And drop the formality."

"The point, Cla... err, ma'am?"

"Close enough," Karna'th sighed and shook her head. "Of course! If we are to proceed, an inquisitive mind is required. Now we can keep going."

Magnis blinked and padded into the room, his tail twitching nervously behind him.

He was a head taller than the green scaled matron of his clan, but he still felt like a cub that barely came to her waist. Her stance, her steely gaze, her silence, all made it clear she was testing him—but why? And why had she made that remark that Lord Ryn preferred male partners. The thought made him pause and hesitate.

For a moment, he pondered turning back. Something about this whole thing felt... off to him. Magnis let out a quiet hiss as he thought it over. That was when it dawned on him that he was scared. Scared! Why? There was nothing in any of this that should be frightening. And yet, there was something—something that made him so nervous about the whole thing.

He shook his head. If he was right about this was about, the Clan Mother had a damn good reason to be testing him. And Karna'th prided herself on being both fair and reasonable with her charges. If she thought that *he* was the best for this... *whatever*, then that had to be the truth. She challenged him, and it was up to him to rise to it. He took one final look at the door and rejected it.

Magnis focused on the Clan Mother and bounced towards her.

———

Magnis couldn't believe what he'd been told. But at the same time, he knew it was true. The Clan Mother would *never* lie about something this serious. The solution to all their problems, and his own dreams and fantasies—and he'd held it in his claws the whole time!

An hour after his conference with Karna'th, he checked to see if any of the clan had returned. None were about except for one helping the Clan Mother return the materials from her conference with Magnis to their places. He waited outside the door for a bit.

"Thank you," heard Karna'th tell the other kobold. "Once you're done putting them away, we'll head out to see how Ryninth and the rest of the clan are getting along."

Good. That meant for at least another hour, Magnis would have privacy. He retreated into one of the deeper chambers in the cave system. The cavern he'd chosen was also one of the largest, easily able to accommodate several fully grown dragons. The kobolds had mined and worked the stone to create several areas that were comfortable for those theoretical dragons to sprawl and sleep on.

He stood at the edge of the chamber wearing only a loin-cloth, staring at his reflection in the large pool on that side. He'd never thought much about how he looked before, so it was a strange feeling to be studying himself. Magnis had a slender build, slight enough that his tail seemed thick on him. His small bronze scales glinted in the warm glow of the magic lanterns spread around the chamber, though enough were unlit that his horns were almost invisible. Golden eyes that blended into his scales stared back at him. He was there for a long time before it occurred to him that he was being silly. He shook himself and moved to the center of the warm chamber holding on tightly to the item he'd brought with him.

When the kobold reached the middle of the chamber, he opened his claw and stared at what he held—the ruby he'd been searching for when the trouble with Tradeway's bizarre desire for a mated pair of dragons had taken over their lives—so much so that the merchants hadn't even shown up for the audit. Ironic that it could be the solution to all their problems. And yet, according to Karna'th, it was exactly that. He set it on the warm cavern floor, stepped back, and took a deep breath.

A dream stone, the Clan Mother had called the gem. One of the few items Ryn managed to grab from his parents' hoard when he'd had to flee. An ancient magic locked in various gems that could grant the dreams of those that possessed them—within reason. Karna'th had explained that a dream stone couldn't grant things like making a pile of coins appear right in front of you, but it could possibly shift a valuable mineral vein to where it could be easily found. Or business deals could suddenly come up and go in your favor. That was what most of them did. Some could do more than just alter random chance, and if the Clan Mother was correct, this was one. Of course, there was only one way to find out.

Magnis didn't hesitate. He'd been back and forth over every excuse, every fear, every concern in the past hour. He knew what he had to do, and what could happen far outweighed those fears and concerns. He dropped to his knees, slapped his claw over the crimson gemstone, and focused his thoughts on his goal. That was what Karna'th had said to do—even a creature with limited magic like a kobold could work them.

For a moment, nothing happened. It stretched just long enough that the whisper of doubt returned to the kobold's mind. But even before the doubt fully formed, suddenly something changed.

A warm sensation grew in the claw pressed into the dream stone. Slowly, the feeling spread up his arm, across his shoulders, and down his spine. Magnis hissed to himself as the tingling warmth ran across his face and down to the tip of his snout. His tail flicked instinctively as the sensation spread down it. As the feeling passed through his entire body, it left behind a comfortable numbness. Magnis shuddered, the last doubts vanishing as his body relaxed. The heat pulsed through him in waves, and each time he felt more and more like he was floating in a sea of comforting clouds.

The kobold let out a deep sigh as his breathing slowed. His mind became sluggish as well, and he found himself feeling the most relaxed he could ever remember. It was all he could do to keep himself upright and not flop on the warm ground. Right before he surrendered to the urge to relax completely, he focused his thoughts one more time on the gem, feeding his desire into it. The ruby pulsed under his palm and sent out another burst of heat throughout his body, almost as if he had caught fire. He squeezed his eyes shut and let himself fall into the warmth.

Instantly he felt himself *stretch*. His entire body went taught before instantly relaxing again. Another pulse from the gem, and he felt as if his claw filled like one of the balloons that Tradeway decorated the market with in the spring and summer festivals. The sensation moved up his arm, and Magnis gasped at the feeling of it inflating. The swelling slowly moved all the way up his body, taking the same path as the warmth. It never became painful, and had he not been so numb it likely would have been unsettling. Instead, it felt almost erotic.

All over his limbs swelled and stretched. His fangs grew heavy. He was panting with the sensation, a surge of energy shooting up his spine. He swore he could even feel his horns lengthen. Then, without warning, the gem pulsed again, and again, and again. Magnis threw his head back and moaned as a sense of power filled him from nose to tail. He was sure now that he was growing by the moment, his body swelling into a new form.

His bones began to shift, popping and taking on new shapes. Despite all the noise, none of it hurt and mostly felt like cracking the joints in his fingers. The kobold felt his stance change as his legs and hips reshaped themselves, and for the first time he knew for sure that the means to fulfil his dream was in his claws. If only Ryn's parents had lived long enough to tell their child what the ruby actually was, this could have happened much sooner.

The sound of fabric tearing echoed through the chamber as his loincloth shredded, allowing his bits to flop free. Magnis barely noticed, he was too focused on the sense of joy that filled him as his spine realigned into a quadruped stance. His rib cage expanded, and a gasp forced him to fill his newly massive lungs. That was when the sensation of strength, of being powerful truly hit him. His muscles surged and bulged, pressing against his skin until that too stretched with the pressure. It all felt so wonderful.

So wonderful in fact that he could feel a tingling in his loins. Like all male kobolds, Magnis' bits had been described by the Small Folk as if a canine had scales—his balls were out and a sheath. As befitting the small stature of a kobold, they weren't overly large, but his slender build had given them the illusion of being generously sized. Now he swore he could feel them drooping with new weight. He moaned as they tingled, pushing him close to full blown arousal. The feeling grew until it bordered on painful. Magnis sighed in relief as he felt his shaft slip free of his sheath. Like his balls, it felt massive and weighty —made for a frame that his expanding body hadn't caught up to yet. His eyes stayed shut, but from the feeling, he would have sworn that the mighty shaft between his legs reached his chest. He giggled—sounding even to himself that he'd spent an hour or two in Lord Ryn's stock of fine whiskies—at thought of such a huge, dripping cock on his kobold body. He had just started to wonder if he could suck himself without moving more than his neck when the sensation changed again. The best he could describe it to himself was as if a massive paw grabbed his cock and balls and then gently but forcefully shoved them back into his crotch. They didn't shrink, but were definitely pushed inside his body.

One final physical change set in, as he felt new muscles and bones forming and stretching from his shoulders. But he was distracted from the sensations by the flood of mental changes that poured into him. Magnis squeezed his eyes shut even harder as images, scents, instincts, and memories of how to use his new anatomy flashed before him. Nothing was pushed out—he still remembered his life as a kobold and everything that had happened to him—just more information that would allow him to be able to use his altered body right away without struggle.

Eventually the sensation of growing faded, the numbness wore off, and the flood of information in his mind slowed to the collection of sounds and scents that he was used to. Though they were much sharper, and his brain was still getting used to processing them. The stone under him was warm, and the ruby that had filled his claw when he'd started was now a tiny pressure against his palm. Finally, he opened his eyes.

The first thing he noticed was that his low light vision, which had been good to begin with, was much improved as the chamber seemed much brighter. He refused to look down, instead focusing on the pool at the back of the cave. He took a wobbly step and almost fell. He blinked and realized how numb his body felt, as if it had been standing in place for hours. How long had that taken? He shook himself several times to get his muscles warmed up and then tried again. It took longer than he wanted, but he made it and stared into the water.

A large bronze dragon met his gaze.

Magnis blinked, and the reflection's golden eyes widened and its muzzle split in amazement. His head swung back and forth, taking in his new form. He was a dragon. He was really a dragon! He spun in a circle as he examined himself. His scales were the same shade as they had been, but his body was powerful and heavily muscled with a massive tail and huge wings. He guessed he was almost as large as Lord Ryn, though perhaps a bit bulkier than the sapphire dragon. But the thing that captured his attention the most was the black mark on the tip of his muzzle around his nostrils—in the shape of a kobold's nose. He pondered it for a moment and came to the conclusion that it must have been part of his desire to remember what he used to be.

Magnis stretched his new frame, reveling in the knowledge that the scheme had worked—right until his wing tips slammed into the roof of the cave. He swore, more startled than hurt, and glared up at the offending stone.

"It takes a lot of getting used to, Magni. Even when you've had them your whole life."

Magnis jumped and spun to face the chamber entrance. "Lord... Lord Ryn!" He shuddered and bowed as best he could.

The sapphire dragon stood framed in the archway, studying the former kobold with an amused smile on his muzzle. When Magnis relaxed, Ryn padded into the chamber until he was only a few paces from the other dragon. Magnis could see he'd been right—the bronze dragon was slightly smaller than the blue, but had the advantage of muscle. Not that he'd need it. Ryn chuckled.

"I think we're past such titles. Unless you wish to be 'Lord' Magnis..." He trailed off and stared at something at his feet.

"How long have you been there?" Magnis stammered.

"Oh, since about the time your loincloth gave out," Ryn replied as he picked something off the floor in his talons. As he brought it to up to study, Magnis realized it was the ruby.

"Amazing that I owned this for so long… and never sensed what it was. But it does indeed seem to have granted a dream. For both of us."

"Uh, I can explain…"

"There's no need, handsome." Ryn set the gem down and pressed in closer. "Karna'th told me everything. Why do you think I left today? I probably would have been here sooner to try and help you through the whole thing, but we thought you needed privacy. I admit it was a shock, though a pleasant one, to learn you felt the same way about me." He paced around Magnis, his eyes taking in the new dragon. "She guessed right. Being a dragon suits you."

Magnis felt heat rising into his face at the combination of being called "handsome" and Ryn's scent—a heady combination of warm sand and some sort of exotic spice—filling his nostrils. He swallowed and managed to meet the other dragon's eyes.

"You. You like me like this? You're not mad?"

"No. Why would I be? You did not make your feelings very clear, but I could guess. And Karna'th was sure about them. That is why I've wanted to spend so much time with you as of late. I admit, I was nervous to make my intentions known, since fully acting on it would be a, well, challenge to say the least. And you did tend to get a little spooked when I was rubbing too low on your belly…"

"I. Uh. I thought you'd think I was strange…"

"Shhh…" Ryn pressed in close, their scales touching now, and whispered in Magnis' ear. "It's not a problem anymore, is it? If you want it, I want it too. I think I know the answer. But I won't assume. This is your dream, Magnis. What do you want it to be?"

Magnis closed his eyes and took a deep breath. He didn't really need to think about it. How long had he fantasized about this very thing? But he wanted to make sure Ryn knew he was being serious about it. And like Ryn himself had said, the worry that this was all just a dream and he would wake up soon was very much present. He didn't care. He knew what to do. If it was a dream, well, he was going to enjoy the hell out of it.

"I want to be yours, for as long as you'll have me."

Ryn pressed close and rubbed against Magnis, letting out a growl that sounded like a cat's purr. The bronze dragon pressed back, imitating the sound that the sapphire made. Heat rushed through Magnis, gathering in his loins as the other dragon's scent took on a spicier note. He huffed, pulling more of Ryn's arousal into his nostrils. His body relaxed, and he could feel his new slit beginning to spread. Ryn chuckled and reached a claw down to rub between Magnis' rear legs. The bronze dragon moaned and spread his legs to give his lover better access. The blue kept rubbing, cooing as Magnis' shaft began to make its appearance.

"So," Ryn said. "As I'm sure you've never done this before, would you like to top?"

Magnis hesitated a moment, stunned by the thought that *he* should assume such a role over a superior. But as he looked into Ryn's eyes, he realized that the older dragon was asking honestly. With that realization, Magnis shook his head.

"No. Like you said, this is my dream come true. And this body is exactly what I wanted," he pointed to his nose as he spoke. "If this body is perfect enough to have this, then it definitely should be perfect enough to let me take you."

Ryn thought for a moment, then nodded. "Well. As long as it's what you dreamed of. Over here."

With that, the blue dragon moved to one of the raised platforms at the edge of the chamber. Magnis knew they'd been covered in straw and pine needles for comfort, and that they were—more than once he'd walked in on Lord Ryn rolling on his back in here. And if they were that comfortable... Magnis grinned broadly and followed with a bounce in his step. Ryn pointed to the bed with a smile.

"On your back and see if it's good," the blue said. "If it's not, that's perfectly acceptable. You need to be relaxed for this. I want you to enjoy it."

"You liked the beds," Magnis quipped as he clambered onto the platform and flopped over. It took him a minute to arrange his wings, but he quickly found a good spot with his tail hanging over the edge into the main part of the chamber. "This is actually nice."

"This view is rather nice as well," Ryn returned as he placed his head on the base of Magnis' tail, provoking squirms of delight as his warm breath passed over the bronze's hole and slit. "Now, let's get you ready."

Without another word, he ran his tongue up the smaller dragon's tail. Magnis moaned as the warm slick weight passed over and around his hole. Ryn worked quickly, running his tongue over his lover's entrance. Then he pushed into Magnis' hole, drawing a gasp from the new dragon. He huffed and squirmed as the warm wetness stretched him. He'd been right, the feeling was so good, so filling, but it wasn't painful like he'd heard first time experiences could be. Instead, it was all pleasure making him moan and gasp as Ryn's tongue found an especially sensitive spot. As the blue dragon pushed deeper, Magnis' shaft slipped free of his slit and flopped against his belly as it continued to harden.

Ryn noticed his mate's arousal and withdrew his muzzle. He stepped back so that Magnis could see his own erection. Magnis licked his muzzle and growled in appreciation. The blue stepped up and pressed his chest to the bronze's stomach and rubbed his dripping shaft against the underside of Magnis' tail. The bronze huffed and squirmed as his lover got into position.

Ryn paused, with his tip resting right against Magnis' ring. He met the smaller dragon's golden eyes. "You ready, lover? Gods it feels so right to call you that."

Magnis tried to form words, his muzzle opening and closing

soundlessly as he failed to find what to say. The heat of pride at being thought of being the worthy mate of the dragon he had almost worshipped for years and his arousal filled him. Eventually, he just nodded enthusiastically. Ryn returned the nod and leaned down to give the bronze dragon a lick.

Then, smoothly but gently, Ryn pushed his tip of his shaft into Magnis' ring, drawing a massive gasp from the bronze. Magnis thought he'd been prepared, that it would just like the tongue. But this was so much more intense. Ryn's shaft was so much thicker and Magnis now realized it had ridges that stimulated his insides as the blue dragon pushed deeper. Ryn moved slowly, letting the bronze adjust to the thick shaft opening his insides. Then, he braced himself and went to work—pulling almost fully out of Magnis before rocking his hips.

The bronze let out a gasp that quickly became a moan as Ryn thumped his hips against his rear. The actual experience was far beyond anything the former kobold had ever imagined. His hole grew warm as it stretched with Ryn's thrusts, the ridges massaging areas his fingers could never have reached. Even as Ryn picked up his pace, he was still gentle and keenly aware of each twitch and sound from his lover. The blue never pulled out, but he did slow and catch Magnis' eye to make sure everything was fine before resuming his increasing pace. The new dragon could only moan in pleasure, but he was sure his erection bouncing back and forth between their stomachs properly expressed his enjoyment. Hells, as it throbbed in time with Ryn's thrusts, it was spurting pre all over both their scales, drawing giggles from both of them.

Magnis' head flopped against the straw floor, held higher than he was used to by his longer horns. His tongue lolled out of his muzzle, an act that vastly increased the intensity of scents he was receiving. Now he could smell his own arousal mixed with Ryn's, a warm metallic aroma blending with the sun-drenched sand of the blue's scent. His eyes closed as he lost himself in the rhythm of his mate rutting him, surrendering completely to his wildest dream being fulfilled. He barely noticed the pressure beginning to build in his loins, or that his breathing was changing to panting.

"Getting. Close."

The hissed words snapped Magnis back and out of his haze. Ryn's eyes were closed, his muzzle scrunched up in concentration and pleasure, and he was panting hard as well. The blue was slamming his hips against the bronze's rear. Magnis pushed his own hips up a little, suddenly aware of just how close he was as well. He hoped the action carried that message to his lover.

Ryn grunted and shoved hard, pinning Magnis to the ground. The blue's panting became a long, drawn-out moan and his whole body shuddered in ecstasy. Magnis swore he felt his insides swell as his mate's shaft throbbed and spurted. Ryn held him tight as he rode out his climax. The bronze whimpered at the joy of being filled, but the added pressure pushed him to the edge of orgasm and left him hovering there.

His mate didn't ignore him. A sapphire claw enveloped his reddish gold shaft. A few quick strokes were all it took to push Magnis over the edge. His whole body shook and tensed with the force of his first climax as a dragon. His shaft throbbed and exploded with seed, spraying both of them as he released again and again. Finally, he dropped back to the floor, utterly spent. He grunted in surprise as Ryn flopped on top of him.

They lay there for a long time, panting and giggling. Then Ryn began licking Magnis' face.

"That was wonderful Magni," the blue finally said. "I haven't done that in ages. This was only my second time. Thank you..."

"I'm the one who should be thanking you," Magnis replied. "For taking this so well. And for having that ruby. If this is a dream, I never want to wake up."

Anya, Mayor of Tradeway, looked out over the town. Even though the official opening of the Harvest Festival was still an hour or so away at full dusk, the party was already in full swing. The market was decorated, lights ablaze. Music and the scents of dozens of different cuisines drifted in the air, filling the wolverine's ears and snout as she inspected the crest of Wrym Hill. It was named that of course, because it was the closest hill that Ryninth could sit on with the full council. It was actually much larger, and Anya was sure it could hold up to four fully grown dragons, the council and a feast if needed.

Currently the shelf was occupied by herself, Ragavan, Council member and the head of the bank, and a massive pile of wood and debris that very soon would be a massive bonfire. Ryninth was likely on his way to light the pile and open the festival. The wolverine sat down to wait, while the fennec continued to pace.

"He won't do it," Ragavan said with a chuckle. "Almost halfway to the deadline and not a peep out of him on the subject. He won't do it."

Anya sighed. "It almost sounds like you would like to be rid of him. Need I remind you that it was the merchants guilds that came up with this arrangement in the first place?"

"Well. Yes, we did. We needed it ten years ago. Now? It's less necessary. But it doesn't matter either way. Either we get two dragons to guard us and will be protected against the Troubles, or a one-time payment to the Spears solves the issue. Who knows what he has in that cave of his and what it's worth?"

The fennec paced and rambled on, but Anya tuned him out. She'd long suspected that this whole thing was just an excuse to try and alter the deal the town had with Ryn, and the merchants thought they were being clever by offering him a way out. She found herself hoping that the dragon could find a way to fool them.

Her thoughts were interrupted by a high-pitched roar. She

looked up, knowing that the sound signaled Ryninth's arrival. The dragon had worked hard to come up with a roar that sounded non-threatening and was proud of himself for somewhat managing. From the eastern horizon, she saw the large form of the blue dragon rising into the sky and making his way towards Tradeway. Then her muzzle dropped open before stretching into a broad smile. Behind the blue dragon, another dragon flew. The second dragon was smaller than Ryninth, but the outline seemed more powerful than the blue. It reminded Anya of her build compared to a lioness. But it was another dragon. She turned to Ragavan.

"Well. It looks like your dream has come true..."

The fennec didn't answer. He just stared at the sky with his muzzle hanging open in shock.

NIGHT AT THE EASTENDER

TJ MINDE

The Eastender was noisy. But most clubs are to me. Loud music thumped from the speakers with a heavy beat. People filled the room from wall to wall; some dancing, some talking around the bar. The smell of sweat and alcohol was strong in the air, and it was warm—almost uncomfortable. I sat at the bar people-watching as I nursed my drink.

The almost non-existent lighting made it tough to see clearly. A coyote danced nearby in a gray crop top under a rope harness and blue jeans with a handkerchief in his back left pocket. I couldn't tell exactly, but it looked to be some shade of orange. *What did that one mean?* I thought.

I knew some of the more general ones—red, yellow, brown—but I wasn't familiar with orange. I pulled my phone from my pocket and searched for the hanky code. *Orange, orange...* I thumbed along the screen until I found the section. Glancing up to see the handkerchief again, I was disappointed to find the coyote was gone. *Not sure what shade it was exactly. Maybe "looking to lead" or a guy who wants his toes sucked.* I shrugged. *Different strokes for different folx.*

I stared into the crowd again. Most of the other patrons

dancing to the music were in leather. Some had collars and there were a few pet masks here and there. *What does it matter if I know what they're into? I've had too many bad experiences with folx in school to have the balls to approach anyone here.* I didn't feel I belonged. With a sigh, I finished my whiskey sour and turned back around to the bar, eyes downcast.

I was a thick ram and my wool stretched my shirt taut. In the middle of my belly and chest was a light blue oval with an image of an inflation tube. The short sleeves were dark blue and I knew the back said "Pool Toy" at the top like a sports jersey in the same color lettering. Below the title were two handles. While most of the print was darker shades of blue and matched with my white pants, the base color was a softer blue, almost white. But in the dark club…

I look like a blueberry. This was embarrassing.

From the corner of my eye, I saw a vinyl beach ball bouncing around the sea of bodies and rubbed a horn nervously. *Man, how nice it would be to… well, be like that ball. Full of air, with no care in the world. I could just charge at this crowd and get pushed above it all. No need to worry about my weight or horns or hands, cause pool toys are light, and just have pawbs, bapping people here and there as I was effortlessly pushed around the crowd….*

Yeah right. That could never happen.

I looked up, checking for the bartender when a lizard with spines along his chin squeezed in beside me. This bearded dragon was taller than me and seemed older, with longer spines and darker tan scales. Brown ones could be seen along his muscular arms and hid further under the gray t-shirt stretched across his chest, barely contained in the open leather vest. A leather flat cap sat atop his head and what looked to be leather pants hugged his hips. This man was attractive, but something felt… off. In the light of the club, it was almost like his color wasn't… right. Or his spines were too uniform. But neither was actually true.

"I like the handles on your shirt," he said. His voice was deep and carried a pleasant rumble with it. "They're cute."

I looked up from his hips and saw his eyes locked on me. "Shit, sorry. Didn't mean to stare."

The bearded dragon let out a deep chuckle that I felt over the music. "I wouldn't dress like this if I didn't want some attention." He winked. "What about you? Are you here by yourself?"

"P-probably?" I stuttered. "People from my school's GSA pressured me into coming out tonight. Not sure where any of them are, though." I crunched an ice cube from my glass and threw a look over my shoulder. "Could be out in the crowd or have moved on to another bar for all I know."

"I'm sorry to hear that." The elder lizard raised a hand and the bartender walked over. "Evening, Robert," he said.

"Evening, DT. What can I get you?" a fox not much older than me asked.

DT smiled. "Whiskey, neat. You know the one."

Robert nodded. "Certainly, sir."

"Thank you," he said, sliding a twenty from his pocket to the bartender. The fox took the bill and walked off. Meanwhile, the lizard leaned closer to me. "You seem a little out of your element. Is this not your scene?" he asked me, nodding to the crowd behind us.

Wait, is this hot guy still talking to me? Okay, keep your cool, Matt. I cleared my throat. "Uh, noisy crowds aren't really my thing. But people-watching can be interesting." My eyes wandered up and down the bearded dragon's body. "I mean, I enjoy the theme of the night. But this is, like, the only stuff I had that was on brand." I tugged lightly at my tee.

"Oh?" DT asked. "Not into leather, eh?"

I shook my head. "I didn't say that," I answered, fiddling with the collar of my shirt. "More it's out of my budget right now."

"Ah, I see." The lizard leaned closer still. "So do you just want to *be* a pool toy, or be *used* like one?" he asked with a sensual growl.

Heat rushed to my ears and I coughed. "Umm, I don't think feel comfortable answering that. I mean, I barely know you."

DT smiled as he stood up taller. "That's fair. If you'd like, I have a private room with a well-stocked bar, and you'd be more than welcome to get to know me there. We could just talk and people-watch from above." He nodded towards tall, dark windows that looked over the dance floor. "Maybe play some cards. Just find something more your speed."

"I dunno." I gave the older man a side long glance and paused. He *was* really attractive… "Can I think about it some, first?"

DT nodded. "Of course." Just then, the fox returned with a rocks glass filled with deep-amber liquid. "Thank you, Robert. And get this man one more on the house. If he asks, point him to my office." He looked from the bartender, back at me. "No strings or pressure. Your desire is paramount." He squeezed my shoulder.

"You got it, DT," Robert answered. As I met the bartender's gaze, I felt the hand slide from my shoulder, along my back, and the presence beside me disappeared. I looked off in the direction he moved, and I briefly saw a handkerchief in his back left pocket. The edges shined, but I couldn't see the fabric clearly. Maybe a lighter shade of pink with some similar stripes? But between the low lights and mass of people, I couldn't tell.

"What would you like?" the bartender asked.

I looked back at the fox. "Uh, another whiskey sour?"

He nodded. "Do you enjoy dry drinks?" Robert asked with a smile.

"Yeah," I replied. "But I don't usually have the money for the nice stuff or the stomach for rot gut."

The fox laughed. "I like you. Let me make you something

else since it's on DT's dime. If you don't like it, I'll make you the sour. Deal?"

I shrugged. "I'm certainly not turning down the free drink."

"You got it." With a tap of the bar and a nod, Robert walked away.

I looked off in the direction DT disappeared again. *Why'd he talk to me? He was so attractive. And confident...* My mind wandered back to his body, curious about things I couldn't see. *No, I just met the guy—no horny thoughts. But what did that hanky mean?*

I pulled out my phone and opened the webpage I was on before and scrolled back through the list. The four that seemed closest were shades of pink—dildos, nipple play, arm pits or belly button. *Maybe the last one was because of my size? No, that's apricot. And still, all those are solid colors. His... sparkled.*

Before I could search further, the bartender returned with a clear high ball glass filled with bubbles. "Give that a try," he said.

I sniffed and was hit with smokey notes that reminded me of an Islay scotch. "Oh, that seems strong."

"It's more on the nose, trust me," he said, tapping the side of his muzzle and watching me.

I pressed the drink to my lips. While the peaty scent was still very there, it didn't carry over to the taste. Behind that was the milder flavor of whiskey with even less burn than the sour I was drinking. "Oh, that's... surprising," I said, smacking my lips. "I was expecting that to just punch me in the face."

Robert smiled. "So, I take it the scotch and soda is a keeper?" he asked.

"That's just a scotch and soda?" I looked from the fox to the drink and back. "I thought they tasted like an ashtray?"

The fox crossed his arms with a grin. "Special scotch from DT's collection and a house-made soda. Both have notes that usually make it one of our more expensive drinks, if you know it exists. And since DT said the house was buying, it sounded like you deserved the treat."

I set the highball down and stared at the bubbling concoction. "So, uh… who is DT anyway?"

Robert set his paws on the bar and tilted his head. "He's the owner. Nice boss. Felt it was important to have a welcoming place for everyone in the community. He actually owns a few bars around the Curry District here in The City, and most of them have at least one special event a week, if not more," he said. "Tonight happens to be kink night."

I nodded. "Sounds like you only have nice things to say."

The fox shrugged his shoulders. "it's hard not to say good things about him. It seems to me he's rather altruistic. Likes to helps others out, no strings attached."

I nodded again and took a sip of my drink, letting the earthy flavor wash over me.

"If you wanna find out yourself, his office is over there." He pointed to a heavy looking oaken door with a sign that said "By Invitation Only" on a gold plaque.

I looked at my drink and tapped the side of the glass, causing an eruption of tiny bubbles to race to the top. *Well, I mean, he seemed nice.*

"Sorry to do this, but I need to help other guests." The fox gave a broad smile. "I'm happy to chat while I'm free, but work calls." He locked eyes with a patron on the far end of the bar. "What can I get you?" Robert called as he made his way over to his guest.

As the fox walked off, I stared more at my drink. *What else was I going to do? Keep scrolling my phone, maybe text someone, go back to my room and jack off alone? At least I could thank him for the cocktail.*

Picking up my glass, I took another sip, letting the bubbles and delicate smoke flavor dance over my tongue. *Yeah, that's all I'll do, just thank him for the drink. Maybe ask what he was flagging.*

I looked over at the fox, still busy at the far end of the bar. *I hope he doesn't think I ditched him or something. But he directed me to his office. And I'll just poke my head in, say thanks, and then get a ride share home. Besides, he's been the only person to talk to me all night.*

I got up from my seat, cocktail in hand, and headed for the oak door about a dozen steps away. Gripping the knob, I felt a coolness I didn't expect, and with barely any pressure, it swung open, revealing stairs heading up to the left. After I crossed the threshold and set a hoof to the first step, the door closed, silencing most of the noise from the club behind me. No music could be heard, no people. Just quiet. I stole another sip from the drink and took a breath to steady myself.

"It's okay, I don't bite," DT called from beyond the stairs. "Well, not without your consent first, at least."

My mouth felt dry and I swallowed hard. I didn't know what to expect as I slowly made my way up the stairs. A full-on dungeon? The lizard looking out the big glass window at the scene below? I took another sip before clearing the steps.

"Ah, I'm glad you made it, cutie. Here for the view, or care to take up my offer on a card game?" The bearded dragon stood at a large rectangular desk in the center of the room. He still had the open leather vest on, but he had since removed his shirt. The brown along his arms draped over his shoulders and up his neck. And the cap he had now sat on the table, waiting.

As I finished climbing the stairs, I took in the sight of the room. On top of the desk in front of DT were cards laid out in the middle of a game of Solitaire. Across from him on my side of the desk sat a full, empty chair. Above his desk hung the only light, a soft lampshade that illuminated his game well, but did little to light up the rest of the room. And along the walls were a number of artworks of various models in different positions of dress and... compromise, some even bound and waiting. Off in the far corner sat a plush-looking leather couch facing the wall behind the bearded dragon and a mirror across from it. And beside the couch, closer to the stairs, was the promised bar cart with about a dozen or more unlabeled bottles, and a few hand towels on the shelf below.

"Never been to a club office?" DT asked.

My attention snapped to him. "Sorry. Didn't mean to ignore you. Please, finish what you're doing first," I waved my glass in the direction of the desk. "And, to answer your question, no, it's my first time being in *any* room this fancy." I stopped between the stairs and his desk. "I actually came up here to thank you for the drink," I said, raising the glass.

"What did Robert make you?" he asked, looking down to my drink and back before flipping over three more cards from the top of the deck and scanning the state of play.

Raising the glass, I looked at the last two inches of cocktail. "Um, he said it was a special scotch and soda?"

The bearded dragon grinned and nodded. "And what did you think?"

I chuckled. "Best drink ever."

DT's hands moved a stack of cards about and played a few more from the deck. "Well, you seem to be getting low." He looked to the drink again. Would you like another? I have the same ingredients up here." He nodded to the bar cart behind me.

I looked from the remains of my drink to DT. "Oh, I dunno if I should. I need to pace myself and I don't wanna impose on your hospitality," I said.

The bearded dragon nodded. "I hear your uncertainly and will read it as 'no.' And I appreciate the concern, but I wouldn't have offered if it were any issue. I certainly won't push it on you but let me know if you'd like another." He gave me a warm smile before picking up what looked to be the same rocks glass from the bar downstairs and sipped at the amber liquid.

I mean, he's still drinking...

"H-how about I meet you halfway: when you make another drink for yourself, I'll have one as well."

DT smiled wider. "Sounds fair," he said before looking back at his state of play.

I watched the lizard move cards around. And he was still sexy—even without trying to be. *I can do this... It's a simple question.* I took another sip of my drink before I continued. "So, uh, I wondered if I could ask you something, too?"

"Of course. I'm almost done with my game here, too," the bearded dragon said, scanning the cards before waving his glass to the plush chair across his desk with his drink. "Take a seat and tell me your name, kid."

As I sank into the soft chair, his gaze returned to the cards in front of him. "My name's Matt. And I heard you go by DT, right?"

"Mhmm," he nodded. "Short for 'David Tyler,' my first and middle name. But everyone calls me DT," the bearded dragon said, eyes still on the table.

For a moment, I just watched him move cards about as I finished my drink and enjoyed the quiet. It was nothing like the main floor downstairs; the only noise was the flick of the cards; the main scent in the air was of leather, but there was also... something else. Not quite sweat or cologne, but something masculine.

He flipped over the last card from a stack, leaving the rest face up in various piles. "Everything from here is just moving cards about. I'll call that a win." He finished the last of the liquid in his glass before moving around the desk and grabbing mine as well. "So, you had a question for me?"

"Yeah, uh..." I started as he moved towards the bar cart. DT was now wearing tight fitting chaps and a gray fabric hugged his lovely package. As he passed me with a grin, my gaze followed to his exposed rear; His long brown tail was tucked under the waist of the chaps and his cheeks were firm. Black straps of a jock were barely noticeable along his hips.

Finish your thought, dummy. I coughed and looked back at his desk. "Umm, downstairs, I saw you were flagging something, but I couldn't see it clearly. It looked pink-ish, with stripes? And it seemed to shine? But maybe I was seeing things as you, uh," I coughed again, "don't have it now."

Liquid gently filled a glass as a soft chuckle rumbled deep in DT's chest. "Yeah, heat rises and this building is older, so I do what I can to keep cool in here. And I wanted to stay within the club's dress code in case you showed up." Ice clinked in a second glass as he made my drink. "I can put the leather pants back on if it makes you uncomfortable."

And hide the show? "Oh, no. Don't change on my account. It's your office." He walked back and handed me the glass. With him came a soft chill, like a breeze. "But also, sorry for, like... staring." I quickly took another sip, letting the smokey flavor hide my shame.

"Don't worry. As I said downstairs, I wouldn't dress like this if I didn't want the attention," he said, still grinning, as he gathered up the cards.

As the bearded dragon worked, I focused on his muzzle. And it almost seemed like spines on his neck lined up with others and shrunk, looking slightly smoother. *That can't be right.* "So, uh. The hanky?"

DT stacked the deck beside his cap and opened a drawer beside the desk. He ruffled through it and removed a square piece of fabric. "Was this the one?" he asked as he unfolded it and laid it flat. The fabric was mainly a pastel pink with thinner silver stripes and shiny silver thread.

I stared at it for a short moment before I pulled out my phone and looked at the chart again. "Yeah, all the pink hues here are solid colors. Is this a sub-kink of those?"

The bearded dragon sat back in his chair with a chuckle and shook his head. "No, this is a very obscure one: 'dream maker.' I really enjoy helping folx reach their goals." DT raised his glass to the pictures around the room. "Each portrait is a reminder of someone I helped. Like, one guy had a weight goal, another wanted a leather title. Some are more sexual than others, but I only help when asked."

"That's interesting. So is your kink, like, altruism?"

DT laughed deep from within his belly. "That's an interesting way to put it. But not far from the mark." He picked up the cards and started to shuffle them. "You now know one of my kinks; since you're at kink night, you've got to have a few of your own. What things are you into?"

I paused. "I don't know, DT..." I stared at the other man. "I still don't think I'm ready to venture into that territory yet. Maybe once I know you a little better."

"Hey, that's a safe practice," he said, nodding. "Well, you already know my name. And if you didn't ask Robert about me, I own a few bars in town. I'm usually only here for the summer or so; I trust my managers and work remotely from up in the mountains." DT bridged the cards as he talked. "I like being outdoors, so hiking is a big plus for me. But I also like some nerdier things like LARPing and friendly gambling."

I held back a spit take. "Wait, LARPing? Like, D&D but in the woods?"

"You know of it. You ever been to one?" the bearded dragon asked.

I shook my head. "My roleplay has only been in video games or online," I replied.

"Oh? What kind of scenes do you play online?"

I rubbed at my horn with one hand and gave an embarrassed grin. "Oh, this and that."

DT chuckled. "Ah, one of those subjects you don't want to talk about yet?"

I held the glass closer to my body and looked away. "I mean, maybe..."

The bearded dragon let out a thoughtful rumble from deep

within. "I see. Well, I have an idea, then. Have you played any videogames set in a casino. Or with casino areas?"

I scratched at my chin in thought, stealing a glance back at him. "I mean, I think so. I know poker exists. And roulette. And I understand the basics of blackjack, but I don't remember everything about doubling and splitting."

Smiling wider, DT pulled out two more decks of cards, all with the same red-bordered back. "Well, doubling and splitting matters more when money is on the line. But how about this." His eyes were on the table, focusing the cards. "Why don't we play some basic blackjack. No splitting, no doubling. Just trying to hit twenty-one."

I gave the older man a sidelong glance. "Maybe. What were you thinking of betting then, if not money?"

"Something maybe a little flirty and fun. How about the winner of the hand gets to give a 'Truth or Dare' to the other. And I'll only give you Truths—though you have the option to not answer, because this is supposed to be fun."

I thought about it. "Well, I think I can tell the kinds of questions you wanna ask me. But you sound like an open book."

DT nodded. "I'd tell you just about anything you'd want to know." He winked.

"And," I continued, "I can see the direction you're trying to take this and I don't know how ready I am for… Dares."

"And I won't push you out of your comfort zone. Things only happen with your clear, enthusiastic consent." DT looked up as his hands continued to move, mixing, cutting and shuffling the cards. "How about this: I'll start a special tab for you. Every hand you win gets you any free drink on the house? On top of the choice to ask me a Truth or Dare."

My brows furrowed. "Are you sure that's a good idea?"

The bearded dragon smiled wide. "Of course. I know what the club brings in. Even if it ends up costing me a few hundred dollars, it'll just be like losing it at a casino."

I was still unsure. "And if you lose a few hundred dollars, what do you get out of this?"

DT smiled wider. "I get to keep talking with a cute ram and help ensure he has a good time. Though if you'd rather head back downstairs, you are more than welcome. You can leave at any time."

I set my glass on the table and thought about his offer. *He seems nice enough, and he's very easy on the eyes. I kinda wanna keep talking with him...*

"If you'd rather just sit and chat," he added, "I can tell you about the LARP I'm going to in a few weeks?" He set the cards off to the side.

"Actually, I think blackjack sounds interesting." I scratched the back of my head and looked away from the taller lizard. "Rules sound good to me."

DT nodded. "Sounds like a plan," he said extending his hand to me. "Do you want to shake on it?"

I started the offered palm before slowly reaching out. And when my digits wrapped around him he gave me a light squeeze. The skin on his palm was warm to the touch—warmer than it had any right to be. Instantly, I felt calmer, safer, in DT's presence. And after a quick up and down, he slid the deck to me. "Care to cut? I won't count the cards during play either, for the record."

I reached out and lifted about half the deck and set it next to the other half, before stacking the original bottom of the deck on top. "Ready?" DT asked before sipping his scotch again. Without a word, I nodded.

He dealt out a card to each of us face up, a six of hearts for me and a nine of diamonds for him, then a second to me—a ten of spades—and one final card face down to himself. "We can take turns dealing, so we each have the chance to have the mystery hand. Oh, and to keep it fair, twenty-one isn't an instant win; worst case we push and no one loses."

"What's 'push' mean in this context?" I asked.

He nodded. "Good question. It basically means we tie. At a casino, it would mean you wouldn't lose your money or gain any from the house. In this case, you don't get a drink added to your tab and I don't get a Truth. Make sense?"

"I think so." I nodded and looked at my cards. I had sixteen. "Then... hit."

He flipped over the top card and set it in front of me. "Five of clubs. That's twenty-one."

"I'll stay."

The bearded dragon across from me chuckled. "Good idea. Now let's see what I got." He flipped over his mystery card and revealed a jack of hearts. "You win. That's one future drink on the house." DT gathered the cards and started a discard pile. "Oh, and Matt, to clarify: I *do* mean any drink. From well vodka to the top shelf scotch. Cocktail or neat."

I nodded. "Thank you."

"You're welcome. Care to ask a Truth or Dare?"

I shook my head. "Still not ready yet." DT nodded, and I felt no judgment; he asked a question, and I answered it. "My turn to deal, then, right?"

Sitting back in his own chair, DT nodded. While I wasn't as smooth as he was, I mimicked his actions, dealing a king of hearts to him and an ace of diamonds to myself, then another ace of diamonds to him and a face down card to me.

"I stay," he said with a smile.

I nodded and flipped over the mystery card: an eight of clubs. "Well, either I bust or push, right?" DT nodded in reply. "Then let's see if I have the luck of it." I drew a card and revealed a three of hearts. "So close." I shook my head. "Let's see how red you get me with the first question."

"Hmm." The bearded dragon scratched his chin-spines for a moment before his eyes lit up. "Let's start off tamer: since you seem rather well versed in the Hanky Code, if you had to flag something, what would you flag?"

I cleared my throat. "Uh, give me a sec. I don't know all the colors super well." I pulled out my phone again and scrolled through the options. "If I had to pick one, probably white velvet worn on the left." I locked my device and put it away again.

"You'd want to watch others do things?" DT clarified before silence took us over again. It seemed his patience knew no bounds.

I coughed and took another sip of the scotch and soda before answering. "I'm not much of a top, but it would mean I don't have to do anything myself. I wouldn't need to worry about getting rejected for my looks," I explained.

DT nodded, collecting the dealt cards into the discard pile. "Is that something you have to deal with often?"

I opened my muzzle to answer but closed it with a smirk. "Hey, you already snuck one extra answer outta me. Think you'll get a second?"

The bearded dragon let out a deep chuckle before dealing out the next round. "I was going to let you talk as much as you were comfortable talking."

I looked at my seventeen—Jack/seven suited—versus his five of diamonds. "Stay."

He nodded and flipped over a nine of hearts. "I'll hit." DT showed an eight of clubs. "A second drink for you."

I stared at the cocktail and sipped it again. *I can do this.* "This should probably be my last for the night. But I got a Truth for you." The bearded dragon grinned, awaiting my question. "Well, what kinks push your buttons?"

He leaned back, lacing his digits behind his head and took a deep breath as a smile widened on his face. "Well, there's the standard stuff—leather gear, D/s play, impact." His gaze locked onto one of the portraits behind me. "But you aren't the only one with some... fantasies."

"Oh?" My eyes widened with curiosity.

DT smiled. "You want to ask me what they are?"

I finished my drink and thought for a moment before I nodded.

He slid the deck to me. "Then win the next hand," he said with a wink before reaching for his own whiskey.

Staring at the bearded dragon, the buzz of alcohol hit a little harder between my eyes. The room wasn't spinning, but I knew it would if I had another drink. I set a hand to my head and closed my eyes for a moment.

"You okay, Matt?"

I nodded. "Yeah. Just might be a smidge more inebriated that I thought."

"Oh?" He sat up, concern clear across his features. "Is there anything you need? Some fresh air? Water? We can stop; your safety comes first."

I shook my head again. "No, I'll be fine. I don't want the game to end yet. I might just be a little tired. But I think some water would be nice, too."

"Sure thing." DT rose from his seat and began to move across the room. "Anything else? A snack or something?"

I looked at the glass. "Well, I don't want you drinking alone. Is there something I can ask for like that scotch and soda without the alcohol?"

The scoop crunched into the ice and stopped as DT laughed again. "Yeah, we can definitely do something like that." I looked over my shoulder and my eyes danced along his body, focusing more on his exposed backside before slowly working its way down to his tail, skittering from side to side.

As I concentrated on the tip, something caught my eye. *We're those strands of hair at the end? Almost like a trimmed tuff of fur. Did I miss that before?*

"You keep surprising me, Matt," DT said as he mixed something up.

"How so," I asked.

"The fact you're so engaged in our game. I slightly worried I would have scared you off by getting you drunk."

I shook my head, then remembered he was behind me. "Nah. I already had a drink downstairs and consumed two very good ones rather quickly. Just prolly hit my limit and wanna be responsible." I chuckled at myself. "Besides, don't need to waste your good liquor on someone who can't fully appreciate it."

He returned, again with that cool breeze, and set two glasses beside me; one with water and the other almost looked like another scotch and soda. "That's a bitters and soda. Technically something like ninety proof, but there's only about half a teaspoon in that whole glass." He walked around the desk and sat back down. "Same soda though, so it's another high quality drink—just a mocktail instead of a cocktail."

I sniffed the drink and the nose was similar to the prior cocktail, but a hair more floral and less smoke. But the taste was even more surprising: there was a soft bitter bite at the front of the drink with an earthy follow through as the flavor developed. And no burn. "Oh, that's lovely, thank you."

"Glad you like it."

I picked up the water and sucked back about a third of the glass. "Sorry, guess I was thirstier than I realized." I looked from the cards to the bearded dragon across from me. "My deal, right?" Again, the lizard nodded and I dealt out the next hand, a two and nine to DT and a ten of hearts to myself.

"Hit." DT said, and I showed a three of clubs. "Hit." A six of diamonds. "Stay on twenty."

I flipped a nine of spades. "Damn. I'm not pulling an ace." I reached for the bitters and soda with a sigh. "Alright, what's the next Truth?"

"Well, I figured that leather is something you're interested in," he tugged on the edge of his vest to emphasize his point, "but what kink's do you roleplay online? Not asking for details, just tags."

I gathered the dealt cards into the discard pile with my other hand before sitting back in the chair and taking another sip of the drink. *Well, here we go...*

I looked away from the bearded dragon. "Mostly stuff that can't be done in real life. A few different kinds of transformation," I pinched my shirt, "like becoming a pool toy. Micro/macro play, like... with a fantasy-esque dragon." I blushed. "Goo or tentacles. Various forms of mind control. Being used by lots of guys at once... Not that I think it would ever happen."

"Oh hey, a number of our fantasies line up."

"Oh really?" I asked, leaning forward.

DT nodded, grabbing his drink again. "I'm happy to hear we share some interests." He raised his glass of scotch to me and finished the contents. "My turn." He set the glass down and pulled the deck towards himself. The lizard delt me a nineteen and a five to himself before looking at me expectantly.

"Stay," I said with a confident smile. *I gotta have my next question ready...*

DT flipped over a queen then a six of hearts. "Twenty one."

"Gah, so close." I pushed the cards to the discard pile with a playful frown.

"Do you find me attractive?"

I stopped. The bearded dragon leaned on his elbows with his digits steepled in front of his muzzle. *I bet he's hiding a grin.*

My nervousness quickly returned and I grabbed my glass to take another sip to delay the answer. *He's been nice so far. No reason to think he's trying to make fun of me.* "Umm, yeah. You're fit and tall and muscular. Not that, like, a twink is bad, but I've always liked guys that look like you and... the attitude of a person that can take care of me." I quickly raised my paws. "Not that I expect you to do so or think you will."

DT chuckled. "No worries, Matt. Questions and answers are not invitation." He sat back. "Though you are quite handsome and attractive yourself."

My eyes locked onto him. "Huh? What makes you say that?"

I smiled wider. "Well, the back of that shirt certainly let my mind wander." He gave me a wink and I felt my ears warm. "And while you aren't tall, you look nice and sturdy, like you can take a lot of... attention." He raised his eyebrows suggestively. "I don't know about you, but I'm feeling a little warm, still." The bearded dragon stood up and in a smooth motion, removed his vest and draped it over his chair. The brown scales on his back rained down to his tail. DT stretched his arms high as he turned around to face me, showing off his toned, muscular body and flat tan stomach and leaving his bulge on view. And I couldn't help but stare. With mocktail still in hand, I reached for the water and drank heavily again, finishing the glass.

With a contented sigh, he relaxed and sat back in the chair. "Okay, that feels better. Where were we?"

"Uh, it was your deal." I quickly sipped my mixed drink, realizing it was getting low.

With a nod, DT reached for the deck and dealt. I had a king/three to his ace. "Hit." Five of clubs. Eighteen. "Stay."

Again, DT nodded, and flipped over his hidden card. A nine of diamonds. "That's twenty and my hand. Your question is this: why do you think your dreams—your fantasies—can't come true?"

I cleared my throat, partly to delay answering and partly to clear my mind. "I mean, most of them aren't in the realm of reality," I said.

He was ready for me. "You could be used by a bunch of guys at once."

I nodded, then stared at my drink. "Well, I don't have much practice...back there. And what little I've tried hasn't been comfortable. Also, I have a real bad gag reflex. So the idea of a bunch of guys going at me doesn't sound... comfortable. Which I think is why I like the idea of the pool toy transformation so much: stretchy material doesn't care about the top's size." I peeked up at DT; he was still sitting there, arms laced behind his head.

I knocked back the last of the mocktail. "Um, would it be rude to ask for one more?" I set the glass on the desk. "If you have a less fancy soda water, that's fine too. No need to waste the good stuff."

The bearded dragon smiled. "Again, a gift is not a waste."

My eyes went right to his bulge as he rose and walked around the table, grabbed my glass, and walked back to the bar cart. I stared at his nice, firm ass. Both sides of DT were a sight to behold. I couldn't help but wonder just how *big* he was behind that jock. I melted into the chair as I gazed at his rear swishing from side to side while he took his time stirring the drink.

As my eyes wandered up and down his body, the longer I stared, the deeper his color looked. Almost as if it were changing before my eyes; his brown swaths of leathery skin looked more... blue in the darkness.

And a moment later, he turned back around with a grin that transformed into a worried gaze. "You okay, Matt?" DT asked, making his way over to me.

I closed my eyes and took a breath. *That part of the room is darker. I'm a little drunk. And my vision isn't the best under normal conditions, so...*

"Yeah," I said. "I might be a hair less sober than I thought, but I'm not driving anyway."

"Okay. Just let me know if I can get you anything else." DT stopped at my chair, dark brown scales more apparent in the light, bringing with him that soothing cool wave of air. And his bulge at eye level. "Here you are," he said, holding out the drink.

With his groin so close to me, it finally clicked as to what that masculine scent was: DT's musk. And with him in so little right in front of me, the scent was strong and alluring. I reached a hand out for the glass, but my eyes were on his package, gray fabric still surrounding tan skin with darker patches of brown. "Uh t-thank you." I finally had to look up to ensure my hand grabbed the drink without making a mess. *Fuck, he's so hot.* I coughed and sipped the drink as he sat back down. "Shall we continue with my deal?" Before he could respond, I started setting out cards.

"Someone's eager to play," DT said with a teasing tone. In front of him was a seven/four to my two. "Hit," he said. Eight of hearts; nineteen. "Hit." Jack of diamonds.

"Bust at twenty-five."

The bearded dragon raised his eyebrows. "Indeed. Another drink on the tab. And do you have a Truth or Dare?"

Why hit then? I asked myself. Looking from the cards to the lizard, I found him watching me with a sultry gaze. *Wait, did he throw that one?* I took a bigger sip of my drink and set it back on the table with a heavy clack. "Dare." I paused with a deep breath. *Keep going...* "C-can I see your dick?" I asked before I could stop myself.

DT's grin widened. "That sounded more like a Truth. Care to rephrase that?"

I swallowed hard. "S-show me your dick," I commanded, with a nervous breath.

Still smiling, the bearded dragon rose from his seat and slowly made his way around the table and walked over to my side. All the while, my eyes were again glued to his bulge filling his jockstrap. As he made it to my chair, he reached down and began to grope himself over the cloth. "So, you want to see what's hiding here?"

I nodded. "Yes please." I took a deep breath, softly getting the scents of leather, whiskey and oranges mixed in with DT's musk.

"So," the bearded dragon began with a teasing tone, "let me make sure I understand." He continued to grope himself, clearly filling the pouch out more and more. "You want to see," he paused, holding his digits just in front of my muzzle and I deeply breathed in the scent of his musk. "...where that smell is coming from?" DT finished.

With a needy whine, I nodded.

He removed his hand from my nose and slid the chair about forty-five degrees, setting it to face him directly and crouched down. "Then I need you to understand this first: I hear what you want and I want you to know I have your best interest in mind. And remember, you can stop anything going on whenever you like. Understand?"

I nodded again.

"I need words, Matt." He reached out and set his hand on my cheek. "Tell me you understand."

I closed my eyes and leaned into his touch; his musky scent was still clinging to his skin. "Yes, DT. I understand." I lazily opened my eyes and met his gaze.

He stood up with a smile, sliding his digits across my chin. "That's good to hear." DT set his palm over the center of the fabric and slowly gripped the side of the pouch before pulling it down and over, letting his balls and shaft hang free. DT still wasn't hard and his uncut cock was already a digit and a quarter longer than my middle digit.

My breath quivered. "May I... touch it?"

DT let out a soft chuckle. "You can do whatever you want."

Reaching out my left hand, I slowly wrapped it around his half-full shaft. It was warm and thick, and the skin easily slid back as I pushed, exposing all if his dark tip. A bead of pre formed from his slit, and I looked up at the bearded dragon; he stood there patiently with no expectation. I leaned forward, lifted his cock up and licked the drop away.

The bigger man twitched in my hand, still growing in length

and girth. Shifting my legs under me, I leaned in closer, angling his shaft higher and pressing my nose to his balls. The scent of his musk was strong and heady, and I wanted to remember it forever. My tongue washed over his sack, dancing with the orbs safe inside. *I want to suck it so bad. I want his seed in me.*

I dragged my tongue up his shaft as I reached my hand around his hip, gripping his ass-cheek tight, while the other steadied his girth. Opening my muzzle wide, I leaned forward, sliding my lips around his cock, filling my mouth with as much of him as I could take.

DT wrapped a hand around my horns and I moaned. "You like that?" he asked.

"Mhmm," I grunted around his member before eagerly holding my breath and sliding forward. But when he twitched against my tongue, I gagged and pulled off, coughing. His shaft covered in my drool.

"There's no need to rush, Matt."

I wiped my mouth with the back of my hand. "I know. But I want it."

DT let out a rumbling chuckle. "Well, we have plenty of time. Why not just focus on the tip." He pulled my horns up, lining my face with his shaft again.

I didn't need to be told a second time; I licked at his cock from balls to gland. And as he set a hand on the back of my head, I wrapped my lips around his tip. Again, I felt him twitch in my muzzle, but this time I didn't gag.

"Mmm. Just like that," DT said. I moaned in appreciation again before he grabbed both my horns, pulling me off his cock with an audible suck. My tongue lolled out, still trying to taste him.

"May I kiss you, Matt?"

I looked up to him and back down at his cock and I reached out a hand, keeping a gentle yet firm grip on it. "Only if I can keep holding on to this."

He grinned. "Sounds like a fair trade." He let go of my wool and moved his hand to my cheek again, guiding me to my feet. With my grip still firmly around his shaft, DT pressed his lips to mine. When he twitched in my hand, I felt my own need respond in kind. *I am kissing the sexiest man ever; fuck, that's hot.*

While my hand slid back and forth along his dick, my other moved to his cheek, matching his touch on mine. A new warmth slowly spread over my body. It started at my lips and spread over my head, down my neck, all the way through to my digits, chest, legs and toes. *It's the kiss making me feel so much hotter, right? Like embarrassment warms your ears, horny feelings warm the rest of a person...*

DT broke the kiss. "You feel a little hot, Matt. No pun intended. Why don't we move over to the couch; it's cooler over there," he said, nodding to the other side of the room.

While words escaped me, my head moved up and down in agreement. As DT began walking backwards, I let my hand fall to my side as I followed with a musk-drunk wobble in my step, one foot in front of the other and my hand on this highly attractive man's cock. *I was gonna get to keep kissing up on this attractive man! Heck, maybe more...*

As DT reached the long couch, he slowly lowered himself down and laid back with his head against the arm rest. In the dull light, his skin looked more blue than brown and again his beard spike seemed to disappear. But right now, I didn't care. I raised my knee to follow, but stopped. "Wait, I... weigh a lot. I don't want to crush you."

The taller man just laughed. "Don't worry about that; it won't be a problem for me."

Wait, he really doesn't care about my size. Can this man get more attractive? With a nod, I leaned forward, bracing my other hand beside his head. With my grip still between his legs, I kissed him again. DT placed his hand behind my head, and I closed my eyes. His tongue licked at me, asking for permission to enter and I slowly opened my muzzle. His soft fleshy muscle rushed in and danced with mine. I couldn't help but moan; with DT holding my head and him kissing me with both our mouths open, it got me so worked up.

When the lizard finally broke the kiss, I was panting. "Fuck... that was..." Words were tough.

A deep rumble emitted from DT's chest, and he smiled. "I know what you mean. Do you want to keep going?" he asked.

I wasn't quite sure what he meant, but I had hopes and nodded. "Yes please."

"Good. Just relax and enjoy the ride." He pulled me back down and pressed his tongue into my muzzle again.

As we made out, I started to feel... lighter. I shifted my elbows to either side of his head, bracing myself against the armrest. It was then I noticed my shirt felt... tighter. And finally, my hands started to cool. I broke the kiss, eyes still closed and ground my hips against his with a smile. And when I opened my eyes, that's when I saw the horns.

From the top of his blue forehead, curved horns stood about six inches long, gray at the base and ended in ice blue points. *What the...?*

As the coolness slowly moved down my forearms, I finally looked at my... pawbs. *Holy shit, pawbs?!* At the end at my arms were two fist-sized translucent blue vinyl... bappers. And where the coolness spread, so too did the vinyl. It crept along my fleece, leaving taut material stretched over my body. When the coolness began to spread over my chest and stomach, heat spiked in my back. It was both uncomfortable and so arousing, I let out a moan.

"Deep breaths, Matt. Don't worry, you're in good hands," DT said, his hands on my hips, holding my fleece as I changed.

I looked... through my chest, seeing the same pattern I had on my shirt now covering my vinyl skin, and noticed dark spots on my back where the handles were. *I... have handles now! Oh man, someone could really hold me in place while using me.*

As my neck and face cooled, another moan escaped me. This time, however, the noise was... squeakier. My throat felt tighter, and my tongue was stuck to the bottom of my mouth. *Almost like... it would be a great cock sleeve; tight enough to be used, and stretchy enough to fit any sized shaft.*

The coolness flowed down my legs, sending an extra spike of arousal over my bulge as the change took place. Then, like my back, two spots on either side of my hips warmed and I assumed handled formed there, too. I had to see it; I looked down to where my tent was and, again, saw vinyl. And, through my thighs, I could see two more hand holds on either side of me. With my groin gently rested against DT's still-erect shaft, I ground my hips forward. Somehow, it sent the biggest shiver of pleasure up my spine—*what spine?*—that I'd ever had. Almost like there were even more nerves than before. With another squeaky moan, I rested my head against DT's chest.

When my body temperature felt... stable?... DT set a digit on my chin and lifted me up to meet his gaze. "Don't you feel much more comfortable over here?" he asked. He looked from me, up towards the ceiling. "It's the air vent over here. Keeps this side of the room cooler."

I opened my muzzle to speak, and a squeak escaped my throat. This time, I wasn't really trying to, it just happened. *I... can't speak?* I took a deep breath in through my nose and felt my chest and back stretch and swell. And when I opened my mouth, the air escaped, but again no noise. *Maybe pool toys can't talk?*

"You ready to keep going, Matt?"

I looked up at DT. The man under me had no spines along his chin, and his scales—full layers of scales—along his neck were dark blue with a softer, lighter blue skin running down his neck. And again, the horns. *This man was no bearded dragon. No more than I'm a ram right now. DT is a* dragon... *And I can't physically say no.*

I blinked.

This is so fucking hot.

I leaned forward and eagerly pressed my lips to his as I ground my bulge against the shaft under me. With a soft rumble of appreciation, the dragon opened his muzzle and kissed me deeply again.

"Good boy," he said, when he finally broke the kiss. His hand traveled down between us and I lifted myself, but his hand stopped right at my crotch and his eye met mine, waiting for permission.

I nodded.

His hand groped the tent between my legs where my own need should have been. I felt the spike of arousal even stronger at another person's touch, but it was still different. There was no definition to the attention, no sensation of relief at my shaft being touched. But it turned me on nevertheless.

He slid his hand back up from between my legs and held my chin. "Let's get me ready for the main event, shall we?" His other hand grabbed my horn, which was surprisingly still firm, and pushed me down his body, while the other moved something below me. My legs compacted under me with a rubbery squeak as I was pushed. And when he stopped, I was face-to-face again with DT's cock.

This dragon was no Arthurian creature stories tall, but a real-life dragon. Of course his equipment was going to be different than what I might expect. His cock was still uncut with maybe a lighter blue skin. His balls, however, were covered in smaller protective scales. And along his length were ridges like I'd never seen. I positioned one of my pawbs between his legs and tucked it under his orbs, watching them slide along my vinyl surface.

With one hand still on my horn, DT reached down and

gripped his dick, gently tapping it against my muzzle. "Open up."

I moaned in submissive surprise and nervously complied. He positioned his tip between my lips and pressed down on my head. I could feel his cock in the same place as before, his thick shaft filling my mouth from the base to the roof. Moisture from our kiss—I assumed—coated his cock. While I couldn't move my tongue, I could still smell and taste him. His earthy musk carried his own note of dominance. And his tip gently leaked salty pre. I loved it. I wrapped my lips around him and swallowed as best as I could, feeling butterflies in my stomach(?) all the while. When he pressed my head down, I was nervous I'd gag again. With my other pawb on his hip, I took a breath and pushed with him, swallowing as hard as I could.

"Oh yeah, just like that Matt. You're almost there."

And a moment later, there was a low squeak from in my throat that I felt more than heard as he pushed past a barrier in me and slid in. I screwed my eyes shut, worried I was going to gag again, or worse. And I waited. And waited.

Is it not gonna happen? I opened my eyes and just saw DT looking down at me.

"There we go. Just like that," the dragon said, petting the side of my head. After a moment, he guided me with both hands on my horns up and down, allowing his dick to glide in and out of my throat. *Oh my god, this is going so damn well.* And knowing this sexy man with this amazing cock is pressing his pelvis to my nose made me moan again.

Somehow, I was still able to breathe normally. I could still feel my chest expand with each breath, but my throat kept a tight seal around his shaft. With each shove of my head, DT grew in length and girth, stretching my throat more. My lips and nose were dampened with saliva as I worked up and down his cock.

"Such a nice, tight hold you got there, Matt," DT purred. The dragon sat up and reached forward, grabbing one of my handles before sliding back to the armrest. "And while I really," he shoved me up and down on his cock, "love how you feel here," he thrust into me again, "I think we're both ready to move on." He pulled me off him with an audible pop. A strand of drool connected my chin to his cock but it finally broke when he moved to stand. I kept staring at his cock as long as I could. *I just can't believe I had all that in my muzzle.*

He walked around, dropped his jockstrap to the floor, and sat behind me as he rubbed my hips and stared at my rear. "You still good to keep going, Matt?" he asked? I could feel his warm breath on my hole. It was erotic in it's own right.

Without looking behind me, I nodded my head, setting my pawbs on the arm rest to brace myself.

"Good. Got to get you prepared for the biggest ride you've had." Another electric shudder ran down my body as he began to lick at the outside of my exposed hole, causing another moan to escape my muzzle. Quickly, I raised my pawbs trying to hide the noise.

"Oh no, don't worry about the sound. Just relax and enjoy. Be as noisy as you want," DT said, gripping my hip handles before pressing his tongue deeper into me.

A louder moan escaped as I lowered my arms to my chest. Nerves I didn't know I had sparked and tingled as his muscle explored my insides. I pressed one pawb to my groin and bapped at my bulge, shuddering as the pleasure grew with both ends being stimulated.

DT chuckled, sending wonderful new vibrations through my core. "There you go. Now you're getting into it. You like how that feels?"

"Mhmm," I moaned in affirmation.

The dragon sat up and leaned forward, clawing at my back, sending new waves of apprehension and excitement flying through me. I let out another whine of bliss. "Good. Then let's see how you enjoy the main attraction." As he positioned himself behind me and grabbed a hip handle, I looked to the mirror.

I was a fucking pool toy. There were white handles on my hips and back, and my horns shared the same color. And DT was there in his full glory: long tufted tail, horns, and smooth blue-scales shining in the soft yellow light. *I'm about to get fucked by a dragon!*

"You ready?" he asked.

In response, I pushed back, feeling the vinyl squeak as his tip pressed at my entrance.

"Eager, eh? Then let's get you bred." With one foot on the floor and a hand on my hip handle, he pushed and my hole continued to resist. "Take a deep breath for me, Matt."

I nodded and rested my head on the armrest as I filled my chest with air.

"Just like that. Now let it out, long and slow."

Through my nose, the breath escaped slowly and gradually. My body relaxed and my vinyl surface slacked ever so slightly.

Then he pushed. My entrance gave enough that his head got in, and I sucked in air in surprise. DT stretched my ring and filled my guts. I expected pain, but instead there was... pleasure at being used. And a stronger need to be filled.

I moaned in desire.

DT chuckled again. "Don't worry. You'll get all you want, and you're doing a great job, Matt." With both hands on my hip handles pulling back, he thrust forward into my spit-slickened hole. With each pump of his hips and tug of his hands, he slid further into me, stuffing me with all his length.

And it was heaven. The vinyl resisted, but there was no pain. Just a vacuum for DT's cock. I looked under me and watched as my core filled with his shaft like a condom wrapped around him. And I wanted to see him unload in me. With each thrust, he pushed deeper and my insides became more used to his size. When his hips met mine, I shuddered again in pleasure.

"Sounds like you're needy," DT said. He kept his right hand on my hip handle and moved his left to one on my back. And with a firm grip, he pulled half his shaft from me and slammed it all back in. He continued thrusting deep into me, with each tug of my handles pulling my whole body down harder on his shaft.

I whimpered in pleasure at each rough thrust. He pulled back and slammed his hips against mine with a vinyl squeak again and again. The dragon set an even pace, sliding out and back, just using my handles to keep me in place.

"Look at you, Matt. You're having no problem with all my cock." With each thrust, DT buried himself deeper into me and my pleasured moans kept pace with him. "I bet I could get some friends of mine to come over and use you without any problems."

I nodded. At this point, I wanted his seed so bad, I'd do just about anything for him.

"Oh, the little ram wants my load?"

My pawb slid under my forehead pressed against the armrest while my other massaged my bulge as I whined and nodded in agreement. I turned my head to the mirror, watching his cock fill my insides again and again. The sight mixed with the thoughts of others using me and my pawb massaging my crotch all mixed into ecstasy.

"Then let's get him what he wants." Without another word, DT slammed forward. Again and again, the dragon thrust his shaft into me. And it felt like he was getting thicker with each smack of his hips. "Not much longer now, Matt. Let me hear you beg for it."

My insides craved his seed, and I was right on the edge. I knew no matter how much I bapped at my bulge, I needed his help to cum. I moaned and whined in desire as loud as I could.

"Well, here," he continued to thrust, sliding out less of his cock, "you," he was only moving inches now and set both hands to my back. "Go!" He pulled me up as he buried his dick in me.

As he lifted me off the couch, my eyes went down to my stomach as he ground into my guts. With each press of his shaft, my vinyl inside squeaked and tightened around him. My pawb was moving as fast as it could as he swelled. And when the first white creamy shot began to fill me, my own wave of pleasure crashed. I kept staring at the dragon's cock filling me, focused on the feeling of his shaft pumping me full and a new, more familiar brand of warmth spread through my body, starting from my groin and spreading out, up my back and to my brain. After a moment, I closed my eyes as I rode out my own orgasm and long breaths escaped me in moans. Again and again.

And as DT's cock finally stopped twitching, I looked down. Inside me, his head and half his shaft was covered in white. Streaks painted my insides. *Fuck, that's hot.* I panted, slowly coming down from my own orgasm.

The dragon slowly laid me back down, and I rested my head against the armrest. "You did a great job, Matt. I knew you could do it." He placed his hands on my hip handles and slowly removed himself from me. "Let me get you a towel and help clean you up." DT stood naked watching me for a beat before making his way to the bar cart.

As the blue dragon walked away, I took another deep, contented breath, set my pawb on my belly full of seed, and closed my eyes.

The muscles in my neck began to protest against the position I had laid in with my head on the arm rest. I curled my legs up and laid my head flat against the couch, nose to the back cushion. *That was the best sex ever. Shit, my best orgasm ever. I really don't want to deal with the mess. Especially with white pants...*

I sighed and rolled over, pushing myself up. Reaching up to stretch, I was surprised to find a small brown sheet around me. When I pulled it off, I saw I was back—is that the right world?—in my white pants and pool toy shirt. I didn't feel sweaty, and my pants didn't seem to be soiled or drenched with cum. *What in the world happened?* Looking around the office, the light over the desk was still the only thing illuminating the room. The cards were no longer on the desk, but his flat cap was still there. I couldn't see any signs of DT. And without my host, it almost felt wrong to be in his office alone. I headed for the stairs, feeling mostly sober, but still... off. *Maybe I'll get some water from the bar before heading home.*

Using the handrail, I made my way back down. And pushing the door open, it almost felt heavier than when I first entered.

The club music was still going and the lights were still low. And Robert, the fox bartender, was still behind the bar. "Last call," he shouted to the crowd. A few people moved back to the bar, some with drinks still in paw.

I walked up as well, and that's when I saw him: tan scales with brown spots along the back of his arms disappearing under his leather vest and spines along his chin.

DT saw me, whispered something to Robert, then hurried over. "Hey, sorry to leave you alone. Bert was getting swamped and needed some help. Can I get you anything non-alcoholic? You cut yourself off already, remember?"

I nodded. "Umm, another bitters and soda?" I asked. "I need to settle my tab anyway."

The bearded dragon grinned. "Glad you enjoyed that. Coming right up." He scooped ice into a glass and began building the mocktail.

"Hey, uh, DT?" My voice was softer, but he raised an eyebrow in recognition. I looked around; most of the patrons were further down the bar. As he passed me the drink, I slid my debit card to him. "We had sex, right?"

The bearded dragon nodded as he processed my payment and slid me the receipt and pen before resting his elbows on the bar. "As I started to ask if you needed a hand to finish yourself off, I saw you fell asleep. So I cleaned you up and covered you with the sheet." I nodded. "Oh, and final total: you have three free drinks at any of my bars in the Curry District under the name 'Matt Ram,'" DT added. "Hope you don't mind the improvised last name."

I shook my head. "Not at all. That's perfect. And thanks." I looked at the mocktail for a moment. "I had a lot of fun tonight."

DT smiled. "That's good to hear. I did too. If you're interested and want to hang out again, there's a LARP going on in a few weeks out at another bar. Smaller crowd and it's just role play."

"Hey, boss," Robert called before I could answer. "Can I steal some more help from you?"

The bearded dragon stood up. "Be there in two shakes of a ram's tail," DT answered over his shoulder. He pulled a business card from the inside of his vest as he turned back to me. "If you're interested, shoot me a text. I can send you links and talk you through whatever you need. And if not, that's fine too. Hopefully I'll hear from you later."

Before I could respond, he walked away, leaving me to stare at the card. I looked up at the lizard as he started to make drinks. He was attentive and cared about what I wanted. *I took a lot of big steps today... what's one more in a few weeks?*

ONE DAY SHY OF FOREVER

SNEPITOME

Shadowed by the gleaming skyscrapers of Orison, and haloed in amber by the young light of dawn, Venn made ready to fly. The liger darted around his dragon with an efficiency born and bred of two decades spent on the wing, and the creeping spectre of Urseille climbing ever higher in the morning sky. He tugged on the lengths of leather that formed Kolvur's lightest flight harness, little more than a few bands wrapping around his chest just before the wingjoints, and lashed his tail as he considered everything he still had to do.

Kolvur shifted uneasily. They wouldn't have long before someone noticed their absence. "Eighteen hours until midnight," he said quietly. "Somehow I didn't think it would actually come."

Venn shot a glance up at Urseille as it marched slowly across the sky. The moon's oceans were a soft blue against the golden light of dawn. The lushness of its continents had to be taken on faith, as the two worlds' atmospheres conspired to tint them an aqueous seafoam. An entire world, inhabited entirely by dragons. "We've still got today."

"True," Kolvur replied, though Venn could tell by the gouges his claws were digging in the earth that his nerves weren't soothed. Venn didn't blame him; how could eighteen hours be enough, when twenty years hadn't been? In less than a day, Kolvur would be gone.

He tried to put it out of his mind. "One last day together," he reminded Kolvur as he tugged the last buckle into place, "let's make it count."

Kolvur gave him a long smile. If nothing else, he was going to try. Venn clambered adroitly up Kolvur's leg and into his customary riding position at the base of the dragon's neck. Out here, beyond the weather-controlling spells that kept Orison temperate, cool winds skimmed tall grass. Soon, the Winter chill would render the field barren, but for now the blades stood tall, unaware and uncaring that time was coming for them. Attached to Venn's belt were two straps ending in carabiners, which he clipped onto a pair of metal rings embedded in Kolvur's harness, before tugging his goggles down over his eyes. "Ready?" he asked.

"Ready," Kolvur replied. He crouched down and Venn followed suit, chest low against the dragon's neck. This close to his black scales, he could see the motes of red that shimmered within the glossy surface like embers sparking off a campfire. To either side, Kolvur's wings spread wide, their membranes rippling as they got a feel for the wind. Nearly prepared, Kolvur's expectant energy rippled up through his back and into his rider, who closed his eyes. In just a moment they'd be aloft, free both from Hyperia, and the expectations that came with it.

"Kolvur," came a voice from down below, breaking the focus of both dragon and rider. Venn's eyes flashed open, and he looked out over Kolvur's shoulder to where a fox wearing the long blue coat of an envoy was standing, wearing a large bag.

"Tyrin," Kolvur responded, disappointment obvious within his voice.

Venn winced, both at Kolvur's tone and at Tyrin's terrible

timing. One more minute—if that—and they would have been gone. "I was hoping to borrow Venn a minute," Tyrin said, still addressing Kolvur, "if you can spare him."

As desperate as Venn was to fly away from Orison, and the pyramid within, Tyrin was his mentor and the man responsible for him becoming a dragonrider in the first place. They owed him too much to say no. With one last look up at the moon hanging overhead, Venn unhooked his carabiners and dropped back down to the grass with a practiced feline grace.

Before Venn could even start in on an excuse, Tyrin gave him a swift look up and down. "Heading out?" he asked. Venn grimaced. While the Parting wasn't a strictly necessary part of a dragonrider's upbringing, being more ceremonial than anything else, he knew that Tyrin and the other envoys had worked hard to ensure it would be rich with all the bittersweet sanctity they could muster.

"I talked him into it," Kolvur said, beating Venn to the punch. "If today is going to be a tragedy, I at least want it to be a private one."

"Tragedy?" Tyrin laughed. "You're grieving, but this is natural. You might as well call growing up a tragedy."

Kolvur bobbed his serpentine neck in a draconic approximation of a shrug. "Maybe growing up is, if someone has decided that this is what it entails."

"Kolvur," Venn hissed. A rider wasn't responsible for their dragon, but both halves of the pair reflected on one another. A dragon who spoke out of turn was assumed to have an equally ill-mannered companion.

Kolvur snorted. Venn knew he was unhappy—and Kolvur had to know he was, too—but until now Kolvur had mostly kept his complaints private, beyond the occasional not-so-subtle question about any options that didn't involve him flying to Urseille alone. These were the sorts of conversations Venn was used to having behind closed doors, but he thought that Kolvur knew there was a time and a place for expressing feelings like that.

"It's alright," Tyrin said, putting a paw up to halt the conversation. "He's far from the first dragon to grow upset as the Bridge draws closer. I think it's the link to Urseille strengthening; it makes juvenile dragons emotional." Venn was glad that Tyrin didn't seem to be upset, but he knew from Kolvur's dour expression that the dragon didn't appreciate being condescended to. "I didn't track the two of you down to make you come to the Parting," Tyrin said, circling back around. "Truth be told, Firai and I skipped ours."

"You skipped yours?" Kolvur asked, clearly interested. Venn had to admit that it came as a surprise to him, too. The fox had never shown himself to be anything but an exemplary dragonrider.

"It was a tough choice to make," Tyrin said. The smile he gave the dragon was bittersweet. "I imagine the thoughts running through our heads then, are running through yours now." He turned back to the liger. "I came to give you something, Venn." He lifted the top of his satchel and drew out a long coat in the same vibrant blue as the ones he and all the other envoys wore. "Since you won't receive it at the ceremony."

Venn's eyes widened. For years, he had stared at the mark of the envoys, dragonriders who had parted from their original dragons and become emissaries to the species as a whole, and known that this was what he was being raised for. He had known, but that hadn't made the prospect of one day saying farewell to Kolvur any easier. Now that he was about to take up a mantle that signified his time with the dragon was over, he found that he wasn't ready. "I'm not an envoy," he protested, "I can't take it."

"You'll be an envoy tomorrow," Tyrin responded. "Yesterday you were a rider. Today, and today only, you are both." He held the coat up, a clear invitation. Venn looked to Kolvur, but his expression was flat and unreadable. Tyrin was still waiting. After a moment's hesitation, he took the coat. The thick wool felt heavy in his paws, and as he pulled it on, it settled tightly around his shoulders.

Tyrin beamed. "Just look at you," he said. "I had to fight to let you have a shot with one of the eggs. The other envoys were worried about taking a risk on a foundling. Thought you might not take to the life." He laughed, but Venn could tell that he was trying to cover up a well of emotion threatening to choke him up.

Venn rubbed at the coat's lapels nervously. Wearing the coat still felt premature, and unearned. How could he have any claim to it, when he hadn't yet said goodbye to Kolvur and proven that he was up to the task? "Won't people talk, when I'm not there?" He didn't care what they said about him, but this would reflect on Tyrin.

"Venn, even if they think you ran off to join Kolvur on Urseille," Tyrin laughed, leaving little doubt as to what he thought of that option, "come tomorrow they'll see that you did the responsible thing, the mature thing, and let him go." He smiled, and patted Venn on the shoulder again. I should get going. Last minute preparations. Just make the most of today. You'll have a long time to look back on it." He looked up at Kolvur. "That goes for both of you. You have a long and lonely flight ahead of you: better to begin it happy." With that, he turned and began the walk back to Orison.

Venn took a deep breath, the coat shifting as he pulled his shoulders back. Kolvur leaned down to nose at him, rubbing the fabric against the soft flesh at the end of his muzzle. "It's handsome," he admitted.

With Tyrin gone, Venn felt his posture soften. He couldn't find it in himself to be frustrated with how Kolvur had spoken to their mentor, not with the imminent threat of their separation making every moment loom larger than the last. He rubbed

Kolvur's muzzle and tried to force a smile. "We've waited long enough. Ready to go?" Kolvur nodded, and Venn was atop his shoulders a moment later. The coat felt strange, but he would just have to get used to riding Kolvur with it on. The thought came naturally but stung a moment later. Of course, he wouldn't have time to get used to it. He shook himself out. He could dwell on that later, when he was alone. For now, he had to make the most of the day.

Kolvur crouched, and it was just like before. Quivering energy as Kolvur primed himself, releasing in an explosion of energy. Venn clung tight to Kolvur's back as the ground fell away, shrinking moment after moment until the finer details resolved into the sum of the whole. Orison spread beneath them, draconic influence writ large across the surface of Hyperia. The glass-paneled buildings had been designed for a dragon's scale: those in the northern quarter could house a few dragons, the rest could house hundreds of anthros. Tamed canals ran through the city, carving out arcane glyphs beneath the streets that could only be read from on high, and a twinkling mist of arcane energy hung over the city, the inevitable byproduct of so many dragons living together. Venn watched it shrink as they flew over and away: he knew both that he would see it again, and that it would never feel the same as when he was with Kolvur.

Their destination was far to the south: the Rena Peninsula, where a series of colossal whirlpools spun eternally off the coast. Neither of them had ever been, and that was why Venn had advocated for it. If they only had one day left together, they owed it to one another to share in one last new experience.

Away from Orison, Kolvur sped up, putting distance between them and the city. The fierce winds caught in Venn's thin mane, and something caught in his chest. It hurt, thinking that anything they did together today might be their last. There would be a last time he took Kolvur's saddle off, a last time he brushed his snout, a last time they locked eyes and knew, without saying a word, precisely what the other was thinking. A snarl built in the back of his throat and erupted out as a roar, a challenge belted out into the oncoming wind. Kolvur's sides bowed out as he inhaled, before thrumming as he echoed Venn's cry. The feeling was mutual.

They passed over a village he recognized: Kolvur had once weaved water out of a nearby river to put out fires that they had noticed from overhead. They had stuck around afterwards to help with the rebuilding: older structures had been replaced with magically-assisted designs. The fields were irrigated by water that responded to magic's beck and call, and the forges and hearts were stoked to preternaturally hot and consistent temperatures by spells woven by resident dragons. Venn could see a couple, their thirty-foot lengths easy to make out even from above. They must have chosen to make a home there: it was easier for the older dragons, who didn't need to return to Urseille quite so often. They could afford to spend a few cycles on Hyperia, if they so choose.

He had thought he was prepared to spend much of his final day with Kolvur on the wing, but after less than an hour he was feeling antsy. "Kolvur," he said, interrupting the silence that had settled between them. The dragon hummed in response, and half-turned to look at him. "I don't want to go to Rena."

Kolvur squinted at him. "You're the one who argued for it," he reminded the liger. "Why the sudden change of heart?"

Venn shook his head. "I'll explain on the ground."

Kolvur nodded. "Where, then?"

"Why don't you decide?"

A smile spread along the dragon's muzzle, and he changed direction. Venn reclined until he was supine on the dragon's back, cradled by his wingjoints to either side. The firmament opened above him, with Urseille as the jewel in its crown. He studied it: what would life be like up there, if he were to throw it all away and join Kolvur on the moon?

His coat caught awkwardly in the wind. That wasn't how he should be thinking, this close to the culmination of his time as a dragonrider. He was supposed to be letting Kolvur go, as hard as it was. Apprentices learned their master's secrets, scholars finished school, and riders parted from their dragons. Nobody stayed paired with a dragon long into adulthood: the bond between a dragon and rider was too strong for it to ever be anything but someone's top priority. It would eclipse their ability to form a family, or to fulfill an envoy's role of being the bridge between anthros and dragons as a species, rather than an individual. Too much time had been given to him, to spend with Kolvur and learn to see dragons for all they were worth, for him to do anything but repay that debt to society. Venn wiped a paw across eyes that weren't quite as dry as he had hoped: he didn't want Kolvur to see him tearing up once they landed.

Venn took a deep breath: it tasted like salt. Between wing-beats, he could just make out the rhythmic lapping of waves down below. Rolling onto his stomach, he stared out over Kolvur's shoulder at a verdant cliffside collapsing away to the ivory sands of a beach far below. Perched on the edge of the coast, and tumbling down into the water, was the desolation of an ancient castle, salt-rimed and austere. Kolvur settled into a languid spiral that brought them down to shoreline and dug his claws through the soft sand. Venn had already unbuckled, and he leaped down to the ground, finding it warm on his pads. "Do you remember it?" Kolvur asked, looking out at the castle.

"Tideskeep," Venn answered, unable to keep a smile from spreading across his muzzle. The familiar sight of the castle hanging perilously over the water brought memories flooding back piecemeal, like the waves washing over the sand. "You brought me out here when we first realized that you would have to leave."

"You never told me I was wrong for running away," Kolvur said, "even when the envoys implied you were a bad influence on me."

"You were upset," Venn said. "Honestly, if you hadn't suggested we get away, I would have." He had only been seven, and Kolvur just two, when one of the envoys had made a callous remark about enjoying the time they had left together. Once they had wheedled the information out of him, they had been inconsolable, and fled the moment they could get away. It had taken all day for another dragon to find them, shielded as they were from the sky by the thick sea arch that supported the crumbling towers and collapsing walls up above.

Venn thought that Kolvur was going to say something else about that day, but instead he smiled, showing off the thick pillars of his teeth. "Want to go for a swim?" he asked as he lowered his chest close to the ground and kept his rear high in the air, tail swinging about playfully.

Venn knew that smile, and also knew enough to shield his face with his paws: Kolvur leaped high into the air, wings flapping down to give him extra height, and plunged down into the shallows of the bay. The earth shook, and Venn lost his purchase on the soft ground just before a wave of chilly water washed over him. Soaked through, he sputtered and stood back up. "Not funny!" he called, though he was grinning widely. Kolvur's barking laugh told Venn that he disagreed.

Hurriedly, and with no sense of modesty, Venn stripped naked, lay his clothes on an outcropping of rock far enough up the beach that they—hopefully—wouldn't get soaked by a dragon-sized splash again, and ran out into the water. Kolvur had waded out deep enough that he could no longer touch the bottom, making for a considerable swim for the liger. Venn caught up to him and playfully slugged him on the shoulder. Kolvur brought his head around to nuzzle at his side, making him bob in the water.

Venn swept his arm under the water and splashed his dragon's snout. "That's for earlier," he said in response to Kolvur's indignant glare.

Kolvur snorted and retaliated by swinging his tail around, sending up a frothing crest that crashed over the liger's head. Venn snarled and dove under the water, darting beneath Kolvur's stomach and between his legs to emerge on his other side and splash him again.

They settled into an easy rhythm, and for just a little while midnight didn't seem to be quite so soon. Kolvur had the undisputed size advantage, thirty feet from his muzzle to the tip of his tail, but dragons weren't known for being fantastic swimmers, and Venn was able to outmaneuver him with ease. Grinning to himself, he thought about the other reason he and Kolvur had wanted their final day together to be a private one. Doing his best to keep quiet, he crept around behind Kolvur and landed a slap to the dragon's soft flank.

"Hey!" Kolvur called back indignantly. He swiped his tail and caught Venn hard in the side and would have sent him tumbling through the water were the liger's reflexes not fast enough to grab hold and wrap the tapered length in a fiercely-tight, full-body, hug. It squirmed in his grasp, the black scales nice and warm to the touch.

"Gotcha," Venn had just enough time to tease, before the world flipped upside down.

Kolvur swung his tail up and to the side, dangling Venn out over the water. He waved it back and forth, making Venn cling ever tighter just to stay in place. "I don't know about that," Kolvur growled playfully, "From where I'm standing, it looks like I've got you."

The liger just growled back. He was holding on just fine—years of riding meant he could have kept a grip on Kolvur bareback through a hurricane—but there was another problem. The sun-warmed black scales of the dragon's tail felt a little too nice between his legs; every time he slipped and had to readjust, he thrust up against Kolvur's tail. His cock was already at half-mast, and only growing harder with each successive grind.

"Having fun back there?" Kolvur asked, as he roiled his tail, deliberately grinding the soft scales into Venn's groin.

"You tease," Venn gasped as his dick was pressed firmly against his stomach.

"Says the one humping my tail," Kolvur grinned. "But fine, I'll spare you." Before Venn could react, Kolvur shook his tail out so vigorously that there was no hope he could hold on. His grip failed and he dropped the scant few feet to the water with a splash. "Maybe that'll help you cool off."

Busy shaking water out of his face, it took Venn a few seconds to respond. "Right, and if I dove under the water right now, I wouldn't find your dick out?"

"No promises."

Venn licked his muzzle. "I can't exactly help you with that out here."

"No? I thought you'd be an expert at holding your breath by now."

As obvious as Kolvur's wink was, Venn's eyeroll was even more unmissable. "The sooner we're back on dry land, the sooner I can get you off."

"You make it sound like I'm the impatient one here," Kolvur said, though he lowered in the water all the same, to make it easier for Venn to climb atop his back.

The liger pulled himself up by the straps of Kolvur's harness and lay down, dick pressed into the dragon's back. If he noticed —and Venn suspected that he did—he didn't say anything as he made for the beach. Rather than setting down on the shore, he continued up to the base of the looming cliffside, where a strip of grass huddled in the shadow. Venn slid down and took a look between Kolvur's legs. Sure enough, his slit had parted to reveal the tip of his length. "Not so modest, yourself," he said, and took a step through the soft grass.

Kolvur pressed his head into Venn's chest, stopping him where he stood. He opened his eyes, staring Venn down with one of those giant rubies. "You first," he rumbled. "You look like you're about ready to blow, and I'm not letting you finish without getting a taste. He pushed at Venn's chest more insistently, poking him hard enough that he was forced to take one step backwards, and then another.

"Okay, okay," Venn surrendered, holding up both forepaws as he awkwardly backpedaled. There he crashed against a misshapen boulder that had to have fallen from higher up on the cliff and been weathered down to smoothness over an untold number of years. Before and above him, Kolvur loomed large, a shadow blocking out the sun. His heart thudded in his chest: he could never be afraid of Kolvur, but something so massive staring at you with an intensity that fiery couldn't help but be exhilarating. The dragon's muzzle slowly parted, and out came his tongue, long and serpentine. Venn shivered as its warm tip traced the insides of his thighs, ran up over his calves, his knees, his thighs, and stopped just before his balls. Even this tiny part of him was comparatively immense.

Rather than go straight for the prize, Kolvur turned his attention elsewhere, licking his way up Venn's middle and coiling his tongue around until it encircled the liger's torso. Venn tensed reflexively and shuddered in his grip, every breath drawn at the mercy of the tongue enveloping him in wet warmth. The dragon's breath misted over him, hot and humid and coming in quick, impassioned, bursts. He reached out to hold either side of Kolvur's head. Even just that much weighed more than him, drawing their differences into stark contrast. That he had not just managed to love, but be loved by, something so great was a miracle. The scales at the end of Kolvur's snout were soft to Venn's stroking touch. The dragon's nostrils flared in response, and his eyes half-lidded trustingly. Down below, Venn's cock throbbed. As happy as he would be to spend the rest of his life holding Kolvur like this, his body had needs. "Please," he begged.

Kolvur's grip around his middle loosened, and he backed off as Venn reclined. Venn looked up at the sky, half-hidden by the overhanging cliff, and shuddered as that familiar warmth smothered his cock. Kolvur pressed his tongue down and massaged every inch of the liger's length at once, pressing it down into his stomach and making him squirm against the rock.

The dragon licked, long and slow, dragging his tongue along the underside of Venn's dick. It just seemed to go on and on, an endless ribbon of soft, warm, enticing, flesh. He closed his eyes and rubbed against it, each thrust answered in kind by a hot press of Kolvur's tongue. When it had finally all passed, after what seemed at once like an eternity and no time at all, the tip of Kolvur's tongue was right there again, tracing the underside of his cock and licking indelicately at his tip. The treatment was rough, but you didn't start dating a dragon to be handled gently.

Venn squirmed on the boulder; his claws slid from the tips of his fingers and scrabbled on the hard rock, finding no purchase. Though he wanted the moment to last forever, his body had other plans, and he could feel himself growing closer to the edge by the second. A growl thrummed in his chest and fought its way upwards even as he struggled with everything he had to hold it down, at the same time as he fought to keep his climax from cresting. The two forces pressed in on him from both sides, until with a heave of his chest he collapsed against the rock, tossed his head back, and let loose. His roar, full-bodied and loud enough to make his ears ache, echoed out across the beach and cliffside, as he shot his load across Kolvur's tongue.

Warmth suffused Venn, even in the shade, and he could have

fallen asleep right then and there were it not for Kolvur, and a favor he had to repay. He groaned and forced himself to look at Kolvur, even if he couldn't quite bring himself to sit up.

"I like it when you roar," Kolvur said as his tongue flicked across his muzzle.

"Yeah?" Venn asked, still fighting through the hazy afterglow threatening to knock him out.

Kolvur grinned. "It means you let go." He stood up and strutted down the beach, swinging his rear more than he had any need to. Venn's cock throbbed. Leave it to a dragon to get him excited again so soon. The liger pushed off of the rock and suppressed a yawn. If this was going to be their last day together, there was no way he was going to pass out and lose what little time they had left. He hurried down the beach as Kolvur turned to face him. "Lie down," the dragon said.

"I was lying down back there," Venn said, "we didn't have to move for that."

"We did," Kolvur emphasized, "because I didn't want to break your spine on the rock."

Venn swallowed as Kolvur strolled over him, eclipsing the sun and driving home just how massive he was. Venn's eyes roamed over him: he was gorgeous, even among dragons, and he didn't care if any of that was bias. His chest was broad, and his sides tapered to the narrow width of his waist, drawing Venn's eyes downwards to the slit between his legs. It was deeper and more obvious than the clefts between his scale bands, and parted to reveal the crimson tip of his cock. Venn obediently lay down in the soft sand and Kolvur carefully lowered himself so that his slit was just above the liger's chest, framed on either side by a pair of supremely powerful legs. "Ready?" Kolvur asked, like they were about to fly.

"Ready," Venn answered quickly. He reached up and rubbed a paw over the tapered head. The world around him shivered as he dragged a finger up underneath the tip, and Kolvur shuddered in response. A long, viscous, thread of dragon pre stretched between him and Kolvur, glittering in the low light. He licked the mess off his paw. The taste was unearthly, alien, and spine-tingling. It was as though electricity had been bottled: an experience his tongue wasn't equipped for, but he couldn't get enough of. He reached up again, feeling braver this time, and slid his paw down Kolvur's cock to where it met the bulging lips of his slit. Clear dampness leaked out from the crack, and it was easy to slide his paw up and inside.

Kolvur groaned, a wet gurgling noise that reverberated down his throat. Venn paused, but Kolvur managed to choke out, "Keep going," a moment later. Venn did as he was told, sliding more of his arm up into the dragon's nook. Kolvur's semi-hard cock throbbed against his paw, desperate for his touch, and he was every bit as eager to give it. Once he had gone as far as he could reach and was sure he'd found the base of Kolvur's shaft, he spread his fingers, palming as much of the dragon's meat as he could. Kolvur's claws carved trenches into the ground as his paws curled, and more of his dick throbbed out from his slit. Venn slid his other arm up inside and mirrored his original motion, extending it until all ten fingers were stroking the monstrously-huge cock above him. His rubs were slow but thorough, massaging the titanic dick to full mast. As it grew, it forced his arms back out of the limited space available, coated in a thick layer of draconic slit-slime. He couldn't care less. Not if it was Kolvur.

Fully revealed, the dragon's anatomy was gorgeous. It was thickest and darkest at the base, a rich maroon that shaded brighter towards the tip. The underside was ribbed, almost gilled, and the upper curve was marked with equidistant bumps. After the initial narrowing just above the base, it flared back out in a long and shallow curve towards the head. The tip itself was angled, longest at the top and shortest on the underside. Most importantly, the crimson head was practically a fountain, gushing thick splashes of dragon precum aimed directly at Venn. It slicked his chest and dripped slowly to the sand. Every taste of it was as deliciously electrifying as the very first, back when they had stolen away to explore one another as teenagers. Venn wrapped his arms around Kolvur's cock and hugged it to his chest, making Kolvur squirm in his grasp. It was intoxicating, to have a behemoth like that shivering just at his touch. He breathed out over Kolvur's tip before taking the plunge, and lapping at the dragon's dick-slit.

Kolvur's moan echoed off the distant clifftop, frightening a flock of gulls high into the air. He pressed down, just shy of crushing Venn into the beach, and rutted, forcing the stiff, curved, length of his cock up against Venn. Venn held tight to it, wrapping it in a full-body hug just like with the dragon's tail before, leaving him slick with the dragon's natural lubricant. Beneath it all, his own cock was hard again, and throbbing in time to each of the dragon's slow, deliberate, thrusts.

Venn tossed his head back and cracked his eyes open: he could see Urseille, even though Kolvur was blocking out the sky, as though the moon were superimposed over his scales. It was hazy and indistinct, but as he stared the image sharpened until it was preternaturally clear, right there in front of him. He could make out the shape of its continents, the water crashing over its coasts, the vibrant cityscapes that coexisted with the natural landscape as though they had been cut from the same cloth. At the same time, a glowing warmth washed over him, growing brighter and hotter with every pass of Kolvur's massive cock. It called out to him like a home he had never been to.

The liger's chest heaved. The glow wasn't spreading any further, but he could feel it waiting expectantly. He knew what it was asking: whether he wanted this feeling to carry on, to be a part of him forever, binding him to Kolvur, to dragonkind, to Urseille above. He wanted to say yes, to give in, to let it wash over him and never let go, but he couldn't. He had responsibilities to his home down here, on Hyperia, and they were bigger than he was. He knew the answer he had to give, but he didn't have to give it just yet.

Venn panted and focused back on Kolvur. The image of Urseille faded, but refused to vanish entirely, ghosting over his scales like mist. It would have been easy, given the size of the dragon above him, to lie there and take it, but he wanted to do more than that. Lifting his head up off the sand, he waited until Kolvur pulled back, until he could see the dark slit of his tip, and stuffed his face forwards. He licked eagerly, tongue scoping out the inside of the dragon's length like he was in a desert, and this was the first oasis he'd seen for days. His tongue was swallowed completely as Kolvur's cock throbbed and gushed out another deluge that slicked Venn's mane back. "Venn," Kolvur groaned, voice tight with barely-restrained intensity. Venn did his best to answer, moaning wordlessly against the warm flesh of his dragon's cock. "Venn," he repeated urgently. His cock throbbed, forcing Venn's head back and pushing him further down the beach.

Kolvur pulled back, but not quickly enough to spare Venn from being hit in the face by a thick glob of dragon jizz. He sputtered and wiped a paw across his eyes, clearing enough of the vicious substance that he could see Kolvur jerking, crazed and feral. His hips thrust into empty air as his cock heaved, erupting a geyser of pearly dragon cum that arced, glittered in the sunlight, and crashed across the beach. That golden glow, the invitation, faded from Venn's awareness.

It took a long time for Kolvur to finish. The last waves of his orgasm came out sluggishly, and dripped across Venn's body. Thoroughly spent, Kolvur took a step to the side and collapsed to the sand, sides heaving. Venn stood and took stock. His whole body was slick, and every muscle ached, but he wouldn't have traded that soreness for anything. When he looked up at Urseille, the moon looked no different than it had that morning, blurred once more by both atmospheres. The only difference that it was higher: try as they might to make the most of the day, time insisted upon itself. There was an ache in his chest. He knew he had made the right choice, but that didn't make it any easier. He placed his forehead on Kolvur's side, and though the mystical glow he had been sharing with him just a minute ago was fading, the close intimacy was just as powerful a substitute.

A quick dip in the water helped Venn to clean up, and then he settled back on Kolvur's back to dry off. His black scales had grown warm in the sun and felt cozy after the cool water. He sighed and sprawled out, cradled on either side by the rises of Kolvur's wingjoints. Supine as he was, Venn couldn't help but look up at Urseille. It was high now, higher even than when he had been beneath the dragon. If there was any time to talk, it was now. "How much do you remember about Urseille?" he asked, his voice barely carrying. For all the time he had known Kolvur, he had barely dared to ask about his personal experiences with the moon, as though maybe if he didn't mention it, Kolvur would be able to stay. Kolvur hummed at him curiously, roused from watching the gulls twirl overhead. "You form your first memories in the egg, right?"

"They're more like impressions," Kolvur said after a moment. "Everything is indistinct. Ephemeral. I could try telling you about them, but I wouldn't be able to separate dream from reality, and they'd change each time I shared."

"That's pretty much how it is for us. Our really early memories, I mean." He took a deep breath. "I could barely tell you about the last time the Bridge formed. I might as well be seeing it for the first time tonight." A few months later, Kolvur had hatched, and everything from that point onward was sharper and clearer in his head, like returning to solid ground after days at sea.

Silence settled in again, and Venn suspected that Kolvur's thoughts were in much the same place as his. It might have been awkward with anyone else, but with Kolvur the pause was comfortable. "I remember the Bridge," Kolvur finally said, "it was like being carried through the sun. There was light all around, and then nothing." He paused. "I don't remember much about Urseille at all, just the feeling of energy everywhere. It's… quieter, here on Hyperia. I waited in the darkness until I felt your paw on my egg."

Venn slid his paw over Kolvur's scales, remembering how soft the dragon's black muzzle had felt when it breached the shell. "I wasn't the first one to touch your shell," he said. "They let three other kids try before me."

Kolvur shrugged. "So I've been told. Yours was still the only touch I felt."

Venn smiled at that, but it couldn't hold long in the face of Urseille above. "I don't want you to go." Kolvur shifted beneath him, and Venn regretted saying anything. "I know, you have to. I'm sorry."

"It's alright," Kolvur said, "I wish I didn't have to, either." Venn could feel him look upwards, both of them staring at the moon. "A lot of your people think that dragons just channel magic, but that's not quite it. We're made of it just as much as we are vessels for it. The entire moon, all of Urseille, is tied together. I can feel it up there. Getting stronger. Calling me back."

Venn ground the heels of his palms into his eyes. It didn't seem fair: if Kolvur had been born on Urseille, then he would have been exposed to enough magic to store more, and stay on Hyperia for multiple cycles, but then he wouldn't have hatched down here, and they wouldn't have shared their lives thus far together. "I shouldn't have said anything."

"I'm glad you did," Kolvur admitted. "It means you care."

The liger's heart ached. He rolled over and hugged Kolvur's back. "Of course I care," he murmured into his partner's warm scales. "I've always cared."

Kolvur rumbled happily beneath him and closed his eyes. Almost sleepily, he breathed, "You could come."

The offer hung in the air, heavy with implication. Not only would he be stuck there for twenty years until the Bridge formed again, but only dragons could survive the concentrations of raw, unfiltered, magic found on Urseille. There was, of course, the unspoken solution to that last problem that neither had voiced.

"Kolvur," Venn choked, not wanting to have to say it and shatter his hopes, "I can't become a dragon."

He had thought about it, of course he had thought about it, every night for the last year as he had tried and failed to think of a way not to give Kolvur up. But he couldn't go through with it: to become a dragon was to become a vessel for Urseille's magic, and the change was irreversible. He would be abandoning his home, and everything he had pledged himself to. Everything except for Kolvur. "I know," Kolvur said, his voice barely more than a whisper.

Frustration set in. Venn knew the question had to have been on Kolvur's mind all day, one last attempt to keep them together. Kolvur knew what being an envoy meant to him, how hard he had been forced to work, outdoing the other riders in training just to prove that they weren't better than him because their parents were envoys. He didn't want to be feeling like this, didn't want their last hours together to be tainted by this sense that Kolvur had just been waiting until they were both awash in a soothing afterglow to ask him to give it all up to transform into a dragon and fly to Urseille.

Sunset gave him a convenient excuse. "We should get back to Orison," he said, keeping his tone level. Kolvur nodded silently and waited while Venn retrieved his clothes. The liger watched Kolvur as he pulled his envoy's coat over his shoulders, and sure enough the dragon winced. He knew Kolvur was upset, but it was like Tyrin had said: today was supposed to be just as much about them growing up, as growing apart. Venn mounted and they were off just as quickly.

The return flight seemed to go even faster than the one out to the cove, try as Venn did to hold on to every passing second. The sun set as they flew, an ever-present reminder that there were only a few hours left until Kolvur returned up the Bridge. By the time they were over Orison, the city's arcane lanterns had taken over for the daylight, beaming technicolor radiance out across the glass skyscrapers. Kolvur made for the Draconic Quarter in the north, and the Lunar Square at its heart. The city's towers hadn't taken here, leaving bare an immense artificial basin surrounded on all sides by palatial glass edifices. At its heart was the Altar, a monumental square-based pyramid whose four sides were marked by dragon-sized steps. This was where the Bridge had last formed twenty years ago, and where it would form again in just a few hours. Kolvur set down in the square, where close to a hundred dragons were milling, accompanied by only a handful of anthros. The majority of them were young and were returning for the same reason Kolvur was: they had no other choice. Venn dismounted. A gulf seemed to separate him from that morning when he had left the city, and still had a full day left to spend with Kolvur. The arousal and excitement from earlier had inverted into a maudlin funk.

Kolvur took note of his mood almost immediately. "Are you alright?" he asked quietly, though his own voice was nearly choked. Venn shook his head. How could he be? Kolvur frowned. "I know you already said no," he whispered, "but there are other options."

Venn's eyes widened, and he studied his dragon closely. "What do you mean?"

Kolvur took a shuddering breath. "I don't have to go to Urseille," he said, "I could stay here, and—"

"Kolvur," Venn tried to interrupt, but the dragon spoke over him, tone urgent.

"I know, I would have to hibernate, but I have enough magic left that if I was only awake for a few days a year—"

"Kolvur," Venn interrupted again, harder this time. He hated speaking like that to him, but this option was even worse. "I'm not going to let you do that. You're not going to spend the better part of twenty years sleeping your life away just so that we can share the same space."

"Then we'll wait," Kolvur insisted, "I'll come back in twenty years: you know how long dragons live."

Venn did: he also knew that anthros lived, at most, one twentieth that long, and the disparity suddenly stung. If a full twenty-year gap wasn't meaningful to Kolvur, if it didn't seem like an insurmountably-long period of time, then what of the twenty years they had spent together? If one could mean so little, what about the other? He shook his head. "It's a long time," he said.

"You'll only be forty-five," Kolvur said, "and I'll still love you then." He smiled earnestly. Hopefully.

The liger could only shake his head. "I'm sorry. I can't wait that long." A dragon's face was so big, so expressive, that try as Kolvur might, he couldn't mask the hurt. "I've got a life to start."

"To start?" Kolvur snorted. His nostrils flared, and Venn realized he had said something wrong.

"I didn't mean—"

"You speak like you've been waiting for me to leave," he said, "when I'm not even sure why you want to stay."

"It's what's expected of me, just like returning to Urseille is expected of you. It isn't any different. You're set on living your life, and I'm set on mine." He didn't want to fight just as Kolvur was about to leave, but the worry of emotions going unexpressed was greater than the fear that they would ruin what little time they had left.

Kolvur tipped his head back and looked up at Urseille. "It's not the same at all; I have no choice, you're making one." He took a sharp breath and let it out as a defeated sigh. "But I understand."

The fire was gone, and Venn desperately wanted it to come back. Despite this being the end of their time together, he found that he wanted that passion, wanted that fight. It would be better than resigning themselves to this separation that he knew had to be final. He was only mortal: waiting twenty years would be throwing a huge part of his life away. "I have to know. Dragons bring their eggs down here, and you hatch on Hyperia. We bond with you, you keep us safe, you've changed our world. I know what we get out of it: but what about you?"

The dragon looked at him, starlight reflected in his eyes, and slowly smiled. "Venn," he said, his voice little more than a breathy exhalation, "isn't it enough just to love another?"

Venn's heart ached, and he felt pressure welling behind his eyes. He didn't want the last thing Kolvur remembered of him to be tears, so he took a step back. "I should go."

"Stay," Kolvur begged, "please."

Venn shook his head, his mane flowing around flattened ears. "I'm sorry," he said. "Don't wait for me up there. Find someone."

Kolvur's eyes widened, but Venn turned and left him at the Altar. He could feel Kolvur behind him, watching the whole while, but extended his claws into the soft flesh of his palms to keep himself from turning around as he crossed the square and made for one of the streets that yawned canyon-wide at its edge.

Venn found himself adrift in Orison's twisting streets and canals. Brightly-colored stalls were hawking commemorative wares celebrating the formation of the Bridge. He kept his eyes to the ground and moved on, not stopping to think about where he was going. He didn't want to return to his home in the Draconic Quarter, its high ceilings and courtyard-sized rooms now ostentatious without Kolvur to justify them. Without meaning to, he found himself outside a familiar apartment complex. With nowhere else to go, he let himself into the lobby and began the climb upwards.

Ten floors up, he made his way down a hall and knocked at a door. It opened just a moment later to reveal Tyrin, dressed in a casual button-down shirt and slacks. The fox took one look at him, and must have seen just how miserable he looked, because he smiled sadly. "Oh, Venn. Come on in." He stepped aside to usher Venn into his living room. It was expensive: a loveseat and armchair of black leather facing one another across a glass coffee table, and a large window with a view out over the city. Items from all around the world, cataloguing and commemorating his travels with dragons, lay piecemeal on shelves and side tables around the room. His coat, the twin to Venn's, hung on a rack by the door.

Venn hung his coat next to Tyrin's and seated himself in one corner of the loveseat, tail curled up in his lap, while Tyrin busied himself in the small kitchen. He came back out with a pair of glasses and a bottle of something sweet-smelling. He poured a little of the bright red liquid into each glass and handed one to Venn. The liger sniffed at it: cherry.

Tyrin sat down in the armchair. "I knew you would be strong enough to do it."

Venn nodded. That wasn't really what he wanted assurance about, but he chastised himself for the thought. He wasn't going to mature if he kept begging to be coddled, for wanting everyone to commiserate about how hard it was to part with your dragon. "Barely," he confessed, "I almost wasn't."

The fox sighed. "That's what we all think, but here we are. Every one of us who keeps our bodies, we proved that we could make that sacrifice, put the greater good ahead of ourselves. It's what makes us envoys."

The word, once sparkling, had lost some of its lustre. Venn

swirled his glass: he still hadn't drank so much as a sip. "I know. It's my duty."

"It's more than just that," Tyrin smiled. "Venn, tonight is hard, and you'll continue to think of Kolvur, but it will get easier. Your life isn't over now that he's gone: there's so much more to look forward to." Venn looked up at him, but stayed silent as Tyrin picked up a sphere of glass from his side table and passed it to Venn. It was roughly the size of his fist, a bright red shot throughout with fluorescent blue ribbons that twisted and writhed as he spun it.

"What is it?" he asked, not sure where Tyrin was going with this.

"Fifteen years ago, when you were just ten, I was part of a polar survey. We used orbs like those, crystallized magic, to keep warm as we approached the pole. Dragons can't fly in extreme cold like that for so long, so we had to go it alone." He spoke with a rich tenor, and his tail flicked quickly. "They helped us melt through the permafrost, and we found an island below, as well as evidence of previous draconic presence on Hyperia."

It was clear that he was excited, so Venn tried to force a smile, but it felt fake. "As an envoy, you'll learn so much about our world, and be instrumental in shaping it. We left most of the orbs up north, and they're still heating research settlements. There are even talks of expanding operations, creating entire new cities kept warm through our efforts."

Venn frowned at that. "But it's all thanks to dragons, right? It's not as if we can channel magic from Urseille ourselves."

"No, but that's what we're for. We are the go-betweens. We go where dragons can't and interact with the world on a more local level than they do." Venn had heard this all before; it was part of their symbiosis. It had made sense then, but as he tried to think of his place in it all, he couldn't help but pick at the dynamic. He and Kolvur had been in conversation with one another, sure, but he was sure that Kolvur could have made decisions on his own. Speaking with Venn about them was more out of consideration for the shared life they lived than because he wasn't capable.

Still, Venn nodded. Tyrin knew what he was talking about, and in any case the decision had been made. He had left Kolvur, and this was his life now. He was sure it would make more sense as he settled into it. His mind drifted to Kolvur down below, and Urseille up above. "Did you and Firai make plans to see one another?" he asked, thinking about Kolvur pledging to wait for him.

Tyrin turned away and looked out the window. "No," he said.

"I'm sure you'll be able to find her," Venn said optimistically. If there was hope for Tyrin and Firai, then there was hope for himself and Kolvur, even if that hope was two decades away.

Tyrin shook his head. "I won't hide from her, but I'm not going to seek her out."

Venn puzzled over the downcast look in the fox's eyes, and the way he wouldn't quite look up from the hardwood floor. "Why not?"

"We let our dragons go for a reason," Tyrin reiterated. "We can't build our lives around just one dragon, when we owe our world so much more. If I went back to her now, it would be no better than flying off with her in the first place, only she would resent me more."

Venn's heart was beating fast in his chest. He had told Kolvur not to wait, but the thought of not even seeing him when he returned hurt. He could stand them not being lovers, but as he imagined never having him in his life whatsoever, his stomach roiled and he set his wine down on the coffee table. "But Kolvur and I... I mean, we..." It was an open secret among riders and envoys that bonded pairs occasionally took one another as lovers, but that made it no less awkward to admit to a man who had helped to raise him.

Tyrin smiled. "It's okay. Firai and I weren't exactly chaste."

Venn just about choked on his tongue. "How did you know?"

"Venn, do you think I didn't notice the way the two of you looked at one another?" Tyrin laughed. "You made it just about as obvious as you could that you loved him." He coughed and muttered, "Plus, you always come back with your fur all messed up."

Loved. A love that he had, presumably, broken by leaving Kolvur. Venn arched forwards and held his muzzle in his paws, a queasy feeling roiling in his chest. "I need to go," he said.

Tyrin shook his head. "You need to *let* him go. I almost made the same mistake—I almost went with Firai."

"Why didn't you?"

"Because she had a home to build up there, and I had one to build down here." He sighed and tossed back another swallow of the cherry wine. "This life is a lot to ask of anyone, and I'm sorry, but this is just part of growing up. You and Kolvur shared a wonderful youth together, but eventually you've both got to grow up and think about the lives you're going to leave. You've got to settle down, find a home, and create a life for yourself."

Venn gripped his glass tightly enough that he was worried he might shatter it. Not wanting to get glass everywhere—concern for his paws was only secondary—he set it down on the table. "What if the life I want is with him?" he asked.

Tyrin stared him down. "You'd be giving up on your home," he said, "On Hyperia, on your life." Venn's expression didn't change. Transforming wasn't forbidden, but it was absolutely taboo: to transform was to fail as an envoy and abandon the decades of training and effort invested in you. A moment later Tyrin added, "Worse, you'd be doing him a disservice."

This gave Venn pause. He didn't want to sell Kolvur out, to imply that his dragon had been tempting him, but he could feel the weight of Urseille hanging overhead, and his tongue was loose. If there was anything left to say, now was the time. "He invited me to come with him."

The fox shook his head. "I thought he might. The bond is always strong, but you two were especially private. Maybe you spent too much time with one another." Venn grimaced; with only twenty years together, there was no way he would have opted to spend less of it with Kolvur. "Kolvur may have hatched here, but his homeworld is Urseille. If you're with him, he'll never grow into the dragon he could be. He'll always be distracted. Let him make a home for himself, just like you'll make one down here."

Venn couldn't take it. His breath had been quickening, and his heart felt as though it was going to crack his ribs clean open just to escape and be with Kolvur. He imagined waking up tomorrow, the iridescence of the Bridge long since washed out in the glaring light of day and knowing that he and Kolvur were in different worlds. How was he supposed to build a life, build a home, without Kolvur by his side? He stood up quickly, ready to make his apologies.

Tyrin was right there, grabbing his wrist. "Venn," he said firmly, "I know that this is hard, but I know you can do it."

"Just because I can doesn't mean I should," Venn said, "I left him down there. He said he'd give up twenty years just to spend a few days with me, and I—" His throat closed up, and he had to shake his head to dispel the thought. "I'm going." He pulled his paw from the fox's grip and made to leave, but Tyrin followed him to the door.

"You're going to regret this," he said. "There's no going back. You won't be able to change your mind once you get there and realize you made a mistake. You've worked to be an envoy, Venn, are you really just going to throw that all away?"

"Better that than throw Kolvur away," Venn said, and pulled the door open.

"Venn." Tyrin's voice was harder than Venn had heard it, and he froze in the doorway. "I know you're emotional, but don't be childish."

"It's not childish to fall in love!" Venn cried, not caring who heard. Tyrin squinted at him, unused to being spoken back to like this. "Do yourself a favor," Venn said, "and go find Firai. Apologize to her, and hope she forgives you." Tyrin froze, eyes wide, and the liger could see that he had struck a nerve. Behind the fox, the apartment's window glittered and shone. His heart throbbed. The Bridge. Without waiting to hear what Tyrin had to say, he spun on his heel and raced down the hall, leaving his coat hanging in the fox's apartment.

Venn had twenty years of dragonriding to thank for the miracle of not breaking his neck during his frenzied sprint down the stairs. He hit the lobby running and burst out onto the street, eyes turned skyward. Up above, Urseille was growing an ethereal green. A corona of light danced around its edges and as he watched, motes of neon stardust drifted across the gap between worlds.

The Bridge.

Venn darted around people staring up at the spectacle, little more than obstacles in his way, and vaulted over a market stall that had been set up in the middle of the thoroughfare. He raced to the Draconic Quarter, where the streets widened and dragons milled, and weaved desperately between their legs as they stumbled to keep from stepping on him. His chest burned by the time he made it to the Lunar Square, but he kept going, pushing himself farther than he had in ages. Up above, the glow was growing brighter by the second. Webs of light wove themselves into existence between anchoring wisps, forming a contiguous line between the two celestial bodies. Dark shapes flitted against it, coming down to and ascending up from Hyperia, the telltale silhouettes of draconic wings obvious to a rider.

At last he came to the Altar. It stood out stark against the flat plane, perfectly geometric save for the dragons climbing over it. He gasped out a breathless prayer that Kolvur hadn't already left as he closed the final gap between himself and the great stone construct, climbed awkwardly up steps that had never been meant for someone his size, and topped the mesa. There had to be a dozen dragons there, most wearing leather harnesses laden down with eggs. They had all come down from Urseille—none were making their first trip up. They looked at him with curious eyes, but even if he had possessed the breath to speak, he didn't want to get into it with them. There were dragons of all shades that existed in either world, but none were Kolvur's Stygian black. None were his. The heat of his run ebbed until Venn could feel the chill Autumn wind biting at his fur. Somewhere high above, Kolvur was flying to Urseille, and he might not ever return.

He just about collapsed then and there, but he still had just enough dignity to make his breakdown a private affair. He descended the steps slowly, dimly aware that he had nowhere else to go. It wasn't like he could go back to Tyrin and ask to stay the night, and he couldn't bring himself to return to an empty home.

"Venn!" cried a voice so loud and urgent that he thought his eardrums might burst. The ground thrummed with the successive impacts of a colossal sprint, and the liger whipped around to see thirty feet of dragon surging towards him, lit by the kaleidoscopic neon lightshow up above.

"Kolvur!" Venn yelled. It was pointless to run, his dragon could close the gap so much faster than he could, but he didn't care. Even if it only brought them together a second faster, that was one second less spent apart. They crashed together, Kolvur collapsing around Venn and cradling the liger in his paws as he rolled to the ground.

Venn was drowning in an ocean of scales, Kolvur had him pressed so tight to his chest. When Venn was finally able to squirm free and catch his breath, the first thing the dragon said to him was, "You came back."

"I had to," Venn said. "I couldn't leave you like that. I'm sorry."

"All that matters is that you're here," Kolvur said, and it was clear to Venn that he thought the same: every last second was precious, and it would be a terrible thing to spend what few of them they had left on apologies. "I know you told me to find someone, but I won't. I can't, knowing you're down here. Even if you've moved on, I'll wait. I'll come back, and if you don't want me anymore, then—"

Venn wrapped his arms tight around the dragon's head. "I want you," he said. "I don't care if this is escapism—if I'm supposed to be an envoy. I want you, and I'm tired of pretending I don't." The dragon beneath him thrummed happily, practically purring. He stroked Kolvur's head and Kolvur nuzzled back, his nose brushing between his legs. Even if the dragon wasn't aware of quite where he was rubbing, Venn couldn't help getting hard. He cleared his throat. "If you'll have me—"

"In a wingbeat."

"Then we'd better make sure I can survive on Urseille, huh?" Venn kept his tone light, but his heart was racing.

Kolvur stared at him. "You're sure?" he asked. Venn nodded. His muzzle was too dry to speak. Kolvur's muzzle slowly broke out into a sharp-toothed grin. "Then we'd better find some-where more private," he said, "unless this sudden change of heart means you're an exhibitionist now." Venn laughed, and Kolvur scooped him up in his forepaws, too impatient to raise him up to his back. They flew a short way, out over the city limits to a grassy hill topped by a lone tree.

Aware of the Bridge behind them, and the time limit of a few hours it imposed, Venn hurriedly undressed and asked Kolvur to lie down. The dragon rolled over, revealing that he was already hard. "Someone's eager," Venn laughed.

"You only get to transform your rider once," Kolvur grinned.

Venn smiled just as broadly back and approached the dragon's dick. The ribs on the underside pulsed. It was far different from his own cock, and even at full-mast, it had been softer too. That would come in handy. He straddled the dragon's tail and felt it twitch under him. He had never sat on it like this and was thrilled to find that there were still new ways of experiencing his dragon. Soon, they would have a whole host of new things to try.

Easing himself into position, Venn lined his sheath up against the underside of Kolvur's dick. Though he had teased him, he was every bit as hard as his dragon and more than ready for a third round.

Venn rubbed his dick against Kolvur's and found the flesh warm and yielding. His shaft slid easily along the slick underside, and for all the size difference between them, he could tell that Kolvur was enjoying it every bit as much as he was. His hindlegs were twitching; Venn could feel the dragon's tail struggling to stay in place. He closed his eyes, smiled, and wrapped one arm around Kolvur's colossal pillar of a dick to steady himself as he humped again, more confidently this time. It was soft enough to frot easily, but firm enough to give him something to press into.

Venn tilted his head back and cracked one eye open. Urseille was glowing overhead, lit by the Bridge between their worlds, and he swore he could feel it. A tether between them, wrapping around his heart and enveloping it in a warmth that felt strangely familiar. He ground himself against Kolvur's dick, faster now, as a fiery energy spread out through his veins with every pulse. It found its way into his thrusts, urging him to go faster, to press deeper, to stuff his face against Kolvur's dick, breathe in the dragon's enervating scent, and taste the thick layer of clear fluid that coated him.

He opened his eyes. Even in the alien glow, he could see the change running through the arm cradling Kolvur's meat. It was shimmering, obfuscated by a haze like that of the Bridge, through which he could see scales forming. Little patches at first, just small stony bumps, but they spread and grew, connecting to one another and extending along the full length of the limb until there was no trace of fur. The frenetic energy was only growing stronger, and as it tightened its grip on him he knew there was only so long he could keep going like this. His legs were growing, lengthening, but more than that they were shifting. Bones were disconnecting and twisting, melting into new positions that felt as natural as though this was their true form, and the last twenty-five years had been spent in waiting. He expected pain, but there was only the igneous glow of heat, and the warmth of the dragon beneath him.

A dragon who seemed smaller by the second, as his own point of view shifted. Venn looked down at himself: his pink cock was darkening, mostly towards the base, and shifting to look more like the one he was grinding against. He sped up, watching with lustful glee as each thrust closed the gap in their respective sizes. He was staring down at Kolvur and grinding two equally girthy dragon dicks against one another. He collapsed forwards, and to his instinctive surprise caught himself on paws that resembled Kolvur's more than the memory of his own.

It was becoming too hard to focus on fucking as the change overtook him. He found himself caught somewhere between liger and dragon: long and attenuated, far taller than he should have been, but not yet filled out. His neck slowly lengthened, losing its fur as it stretched, and he found he was able to look at himself from the side, from above, from below, as the newly-serpentine nature of his body let him wrap in on himself. He watched as his tail thickened, becoming fatter at the base and growing from there, tapering down to an end that was still several times thicker than his old tail had ever been, before flaring out right at the end into a pair of razor-like fins. His scales were coming in fully now, replacing the vestigial fur that still clung to a form it had no place on. To his immense satisfaction, he wasn't evenly-colored: bands of caramel scales stood out against his golden hide, echoes of his stripes.

He was massive. His paws dented the earth wherever he stood, with claws that could have sawed right through trees. He tested them, digging a score of trenches into the ground and shivering. Power, raw power, coursed down his spine and through a newly dexterous tail. He gave it a swish, finding that it sliced through the air with razor-like precision.

"Enjoying yourself?" Kolvur asked, his face wearing a smile every bit as broad and excited as the one that Venn knew had to be plastered across his brand-new draconic muzzle.

"Abso—" He choked and bobbed his head at the unfamiliar voice that came from his muzzle, before hissing out a laugh that echoed through the night. Of course his voice would sound different.

Kolvur laughed, and it was easy. "You still look like you have some unfinished business," he said, nodding his head towards the massive dick still throbbing between Venn's legs. "Now that you're bigger, maybe we could—"

Venn arrived at the idea before Kolvur. Using strength that he never would have dreamed he would possess, he grabbed the other dragon's shoulder and rolled him. Kolvur let out a startled cry before settling down, chest pressed against the ground, and swishing his tail to the side. The message was obvious: get in there.

Venn was only too happy to oblige. He stuffed himself up beneath Kolvur's tail without a second thought, pressing himself deeper in one fell swoop. Kolvur groaned around him, every muscle tensing around a dick that was going through its test drive. Venn found, to his moan-inducing surprise, that a dragon's cock had way more nerves than an anthro's.

Tons more.

An order of magnitude more, with some to spare.

Synapses he hadn't possessed just minutes prior flared into magically-enhanced overdrive, making his entire body twitch with a pleasure he could only describe as rapturous. The immense pair of wings he now sported shivered, and he had to flatten them down against his back to keep himself from impulsively flapping. Every thrust was pure electricity, unadulterated energy, rising through his cock and short-circuiting his brain. His neck curled and he tossed his head back with a roar, a wordless cry that shook the air around him. He pinned Kolvur to the ground with one immense paw placed on his shoulder and arched down low, muzzle against the back of the other dragon's neck. He pressed their heads together, the two of them in a perfect synchronous rhythm, and plunged deeper inside.

With all the new sensations running through him, it was no wonder he finished quickly. Jets of thick draconic cum blasted from the end of his dick, filling Kolvur's ass and spilling out around his shaft to land on the dirt in heavy globs. He kept pumping, kept pounding, riding his orgasm out for all it was worth before sliding out and gasping. He saw that the ground was wet with Kolvur's seed as well, the two pools mixing together in the trenches he had carved. The two dragons looked at one another, and then up at Urseille.

Venn felt a stirring in his stomach, like the one he had felt on the beach, when he had thought of Urseille as home. He knew now that that wasn't quite right: Urseille might have been his home, but not through some intrinsic allure to the moon. It was his home because that was where he and Kolvur would build a life together. Stretching his wings to their fullest, he cupped the air and let the cool winds of Hyperia wash over them. It was the last they would feel of this world for the next twenty years, and yet all his reluctance towards leaving had vanished. He looked over at Kolvur, who had picked himself up from the dirt. So long as they went together, he would be home.

A MATCHING REFLECTION

J.F.R. COATES

It was hard to believe a small pink pill could change so much.

Sam stared at the round tablet on her palm, fingertips quivering as she considered tilting her hand to drop it into the sink. Her mouth was dry. She had jumped through so many hoops to get here. So many grueling meetings and sessions. Her heart laid bare for countless psychologists.

Another hand closed around hers, steadying her wrist.

"I don't think I'm ready for this." Sam could barely speak, her voice little more than a cracked whisper, deeper than she intended. Hot tears burned at the corners of her eyes as she struggled not to weep.

The hand tightened around her wrist.

Slowly, but forcefully, Alex pulled Sam around, bare feet spinning easily on the tiled floor. Hands moved from wrist to elbow, and then to chin.

"You are ready. I know it."

Sam did her best to lower her eyes. "How do you know, though? How can I be sure of this?"

Alex sighed softly. He lifted Sam's free hand and lightly kissed it. "Because I've watched for three years while you've poured out your soul to dozens of shrinks all trying to expose any reason to deny you this. And what was the end result? You. Holding that pill. The first of thirty."

Sam felt a choking sob build in her throat. She tore her eyes away from her boyfriend's gaze and stared down at her trembling hand and the precious pink pill on her palm. "I know all of that. But what if I'm wrong? What if I do this and I'm not happy with how it turns out?"

"Are you happy with how you look now?"

Sam faced herself in the mirror, inspecting her nude figure. It wasn't that she looked bad. Pale skin, short black hair, hazel eyes with little flecks of green. A five o'clock shadow that never quite went away, no matter how closely she shaved. Sam knew most people considered her very attractive. For a man. But the reflection in the mirror never looked right, like it was a stranger that just happened to move as she did. Like she expected someone else to look back at her.

She clenched her hand tight around the pill that could change all of that. That could give her a reflection that matched her expectations.

"No."

"It's still your choice. But I think you know what you need to do."

Sam took a deep breath and held it. She nodded once, then before she could stop herself, put the pill into her mouth. Drinking from the glass she'd put beside the sink, she swallowed both cool water and pill. Her breath came out in a long, deep sigh.

Before Sam could say anything, her boyfriend pulled her into another tight embrace, arms squeezing around her torso. He tilted his head down to press his forehead against Sam's. She didn't know which of them started to laugh first, but in a few seconds they were both crying and laughing together, wrapped in each other's arms.

There was no going back now.

———————

For two days, there was nothing. No changes that Sam noticed, but for a slight heat in her sinuses and the constant, irritating urge that she was on the cusp of a sneeze. There were moments when she had forgotten all about the pill and the euphoria she had felt that evening, ground down by the monotony of the day job, laying down the foundations for the promised promotion that would come at the end of the year.

It wasn't until Wednesday morning, tired and barely awake when she trudged into the bathroom, that she noticed the first change. Staring out of the mirror were not the eyes she had grown used to over the years. They were yellow. Primal. The pupil a vertical slit running from top to bottom, no whites visible.

A shocked yelp escaped her mouth. Alex came running a moment later. He stopped, hands clapped to his face, as he joined Sam in staring at the reflection in the mirror.

Sam slowly reached up, fingers pulling at the skin just beneath her right eye. She tugged down enough to expose a little of the whites of her eye, her enlarged yellow iris contracting slightly.

"Look at that," she whispered, barely able to believe what she was seeing, her mind half convinced Alex must have slipped in some bestial contact lenses in her eyes during the night. No such thing had happened. "That's me. That's real."

Alex wrapped his arms around Sam from behind, his chin bumping against Sam's ear. One hand rested against Sam's belly, the other gently pressing against her sternum. "Are you going to be alright going into work today?"

Sam chewed on her lip as she continued to stare, unable to pull her eyes away from her reflection. So many thoughts whirled through her mind as her heart began to beat faster, apprehension building like bitter nausea in the back of his throat. She swallowed and grimaced. "Yes. I should go in. They're going to see it all soon anyway. No point hiding it."

Alex kissed his girlfriend on the cheek, then slowly slid his arms away to return to his morning routine. Sam remained in front of the mirror for a few minutes longer, turning her head back and forth to get every angle possible of her new eyes. A quick exploration revealed that nothing else had changed about her body. Though she was a little disappointed, she also knew that this would be a long process. Her heart pounded at the thought of what might change next.

The rest of her morning routine took place as normal, and within half an hour she stepped outside in her formal pants and shirt, nondescript tie around her neck. Presentably masculine to the world. Despite the overcast and dull day, she put on her dark sunglasses and made her way into work.

Sunday came around once more with no further changes, but with a growing anticipation in Sam's chest. All weekend she had been thinking about the packet of pills in the bathroom cupboard, with only the strong warnings of sticking to the schedule stopping her from taking the second dose early.

Dinner that evening was simple and casual, with idle chatter between Alex and Sam as they both tried not to think too hard about the work week to come. Neither mentioned the small pink pill next to Sam's plate, but Alex quietly smiled when Sam silently and quickly swallowed the pill with a mouthful of water after putting his cutlery down on the empty plate.

"Did I mention Jessica said she liked my eyes?" Sam said, breaking the companionable silence that had fallen after Sam finished her dinner, waiting for Alex to scrape away the last mouthfuls of his.

Alex smiled as he rose to his feet, holding out his hand to take Sam's plate. "I don't blame her. They're stunningly beautiful," he said, turning to take the dirty crockery to the dishwasher.

"I'm still getting used to them." Sam blushed as she touched the tips of her fingers just beneath her eye. She had noticed her vision was clearer than before, able to pick out small details easier. Conversely, staring at computer screens all day at work had caused a few more headaches than usual.

"You'll have all the time in the world to get used to them now," Alex said, running the tap to rinse off the plates before putting them into the dishwasher. "Soon, everything will be as beautiful as your eyes."

Sam's cheeks warmed as her blush deepened. She turned in her chair to face her boyfriend, who still had his back turned to the rest of the kitchen and dining area. "And it's all because of you. Without your support and encouragement, I'd never have had the confidence to do this."

Alex turned around, hands still dripping. He smiled widely. "And I will keep supporting you right until the end and beyond. I can't wait to see you for who you truly should be."

"Twenty-eight more pills and I'll be there."

"It will be here before you know it."

***

Sam's skin itched terribly in patches, most notably around her cheeks. Her nose twitched multiple times as she tried not to scratch while she cooked dinner. It had been three days since the second pill, and she had been disappointed not to notice any further changes that morning. Instead, she had to deal with this frustrating itching.

Whenever her hands weren't busy with the utensils, she kept them down by her side, fists clenched with fingernails digging into her palms just to stop herself from scratching. She closed her eyes for a moment, letting the smell of mince, sauce, and herbs wash over her face. The steam that billowed from the bolognaise soothed her irritated skin a little.

A sudden noise from the other side of the kitchen startled her. She opened her eyes and looked back, surprised to see Alex. She hadn't heard her boyfriend come home, late from work. He deposited his backpack on the dining table and slumped down on the nearest chair, a tired smile on his face as he looked up to Sam. His eyes slowly widened and his head tilted.

Sam furrowed her brow. "Do I have sauce on my face or something?"

"No, it's not that."

Sam's eyes flicked down. "Is it a rash? I've been really itchy all day and..."

"It's not that either."

"Then, what?"

Alex rose to his feet and slowly crossed the kitchen, pulling Sam away from the stove. He lifted his hand and lightly rubbed his thumb over Sam's cheekbone, right where the itch was strongest. Flakes of skin fell away with Alex's touch, bringing with it a blessed relief from the infuriating sensation.

Alex's smile brightened even more. "You should go and have a look in the mirror. I'll finish up with dinner."

Curious to know what had so intrigued her boyfriend, Sam handed off the wooden spoon, and hurried out of the kitchen. She didn't stop until she was stood in front of the bathroom mirror. Once more, her changed yellow eyes surprised her, but they didn't hold her attention for long.

Running in a line beneath her eye was a flash of pale blue. She held trembling fingers up to her cheekbone. Underneath her skin, now partially exposed, was a small group of blue scales. They were soft to the touch and, as Sam gently rubbed a little more, a few more were exposed with her skin flaking away. Before long, there was a patch on each cheek the width of three fingers of brilliant, glistening blue.

Tears dripped down onto those new scales. Tears of the purest joy.

With a great effort, Sam tore her eyes away from the mirror and made her way back to the kitchen, where her boyfriend waited patiently. She made no attempt to hide the tears that wetted her skin and new scales.

"What do you think?" Alex asked, not that he needed to question anything. He slowly stirred the bolognaise while he waited for the pasta to cook.

Sam smiled brightly, feeling those scales stretch and pull against her skin. "They're the perfect color. I know they said it would be like this, but I always worried it might not look good enough."

"You're going to look into the mirror and see the person you've always wanted to be."

Sam nodded vigorously. Fresh tears welled in the corners of her eyes. Feeling the bumpy roughness of scales where before had been smooth skin made everything feel so much more real. Much more so than her yellow, primal eyes. There really was no going back now. She would never be able to hide her scales, even if she wanted to.

Sam inspected her naked form in the mirror, teasing her hands down the small bands of scales that dappled her body in a chaotic pattern. Her thickened fingernails dimpled at soft skin, finding firmer resistance in those temporary stripes that wound across her.

In the three weeks since her scales had first started to

emerge, they had slowly spread across her body. The itchiness had faded somewhat, until now she barely noticed even as her skin slowly flaked away to reveal the aqua-colored beauty beneath.

Here and there were the small changes she had noticed in the past few weeks. Other than her scales, her fingernails had toughened into thick, sharp claws that still snagged in her jeans when she wasn't careful. Her ankles almost constantly ached as the joints shifted, and many of her teeth had developed notice-able points. But there was one possible change she couldn't be sure was her imagination, and one that thrilled her more than any of the others.

"Alex, do you mind helping me with something?" she called, hoping to get her boyfriend's attention in the bedroom.

Sure enough, it was only a moment before Alex poked his head around the door, a smile on his face the moment he saw Sam's nude body. "What do you need?"

Sam turned from the mirror and faced her boyfriend, naked and ready for bed. Stunningly handsome as always and so very human. It was only now that she was starting to lose those traits that Sam could really appreciate the soft perfection of the human form. She loved staring at Alex and admiring his body. It just wasn't something she wanted for herself.

Before she could get too lost in Alex's beauty, she pulled his boyfriend close, and lifted up on her toes to even their height. She then reached down to grasp both their cocks. Alex gasped and, eyes twinkling with lust, he leaned in for a kiss.

Sam tilted her head back, free hand rising to gently touch Alex on the lips to deny the kiss. "Not yet. I want to check something," she whispered. She slowly pumped her right hand up and down on their shafts, grinding them together to quickly stiffen them up.

Alex grinned. "Well, whatever you're checking, I think I like it."

Though Sam rolled her eyes, she didn't look up. Her attention was on the pair of cocks in her hand, teasing her thumb over the heads until she was sure they were both hard. She pushed her hips forward, pressing the bases of the shafts together. They were both almost the same length, Alex's cock a fraction longer and thicker.

Sam's heart pulsed as a blush darkened the skin around her blue scales. "I was right. It is different. It's smaller."

"I didn't think that would start happening so early," Alex said, dropping his hand down to enclose around Sam's.

"Nor did I." Sam's throat was dry, her cheeks and crotch hot. This really was everything she had ever wanted. Her body was changing into her perfect form. Her scales were the exact shade of blue she had hoped for, and now this. It was all happening so fast, and yet not fast enough. She flexed her hand, human but for the claws, and pressed it against the back of Alex's head. She pulled her boyfriend in close and gave him that kiss earlier denied.

"Shall we make use of it while we can?" Alex whispered.

Sam groaned, lust overtaking her. "While we can," she repeated. "Fuck, I love the sound of that." She let Alex pull her to the bed.

Sam struggled to keep her focus on the computer screen. Her leg twitched idly as she kept her hands on the desk, eyes out of focus as she stared in the vague direction of her workstation. She knew the threads in her pants leg strained and tore, almost to breaking point. Any attempt to fix the problem would draw attention to it, and she didn't have time to hurry to the washrooms to sew fresh patches on to cover the damage.

The clock ticked to eleven. Right on schedule, the door to the office at the far end of the room opened. A raised hand was all it took to summon Sam. It should have excited her almost as much as the little pink pills, eight of which were already gone. Instead, she felt only confusion and a nauseating sense of foreboding.

Sam winced as fabric tore more as she stood up, her pants pinched tight around her waist. She no longer bothered with a belt or a tie, especially as she could no longer do up the top button of her shirt. Her physique had been changing so much in the last month especially, she hadn't bought any new clothes yet until she was sure everything had settled. It meant she looked scruffy and awkward for now, but soon she knew she would look her dazzling best.

John held open the door for Sam, before shutting it behind them, closing away the sounds of the office. The managing director gestured to the chair in front of his desk, before settling down himself. The grey-haired man steepled his fingers in front of his lined face, a ballpoint pen pressed between his palms.

"I'm sure you've heard around the office already that the business expansion has been approved," John said, lowering his hands and tapping the pen against the multiple booklets scattered over his desk. "We've been looking into who will be fronting this new team."

Sam felt her worst fears forming. She tried to keep her eyes high, meeting the eyes of her boss, but the nausea in her gut was unsettling. The cloying scent of John's cologne filled her nose, barely masking the acrid smell of his natural body odor.

She swallowed around the discomfort and forced her mouth open. "Already? I thought the new project wasn't starting for another six months."

John had the decency to look awkward, if even for a moment. He then shrugged. "Things changed. We needed to bring things forward."

Sam nodded rather than address the lie. She kept his hands

on her lap in an attempt to quell the nervous bounce of her legs. Her nose itched, while a dull ache persisted in the sides of her jaw. She knew about everything about the expansion. A new project with a team developing software for an exciting international partner. The vice-president had assured her of the promotion months ago. She had timed everything around her transition to fit in with that schedule.

"We've chosen Angie to lead it, and we'd like you to help train her so she's ready for the launch in two months," John said, his smile wide and friendly.

Sam's vision narrowed. Her heart pounded, the thumping beat all she could hear for a few long seconds. She didn't understand. Her eyes flicked up to John. The managing director still smiled as though he had given Sam a great opportunity. She opened her mouth. Closed it. Licked her lips and tried again.

"You want me to train the person who is being promoted ahead of me?"

John spread his arms, letting the pen clatter to the desk. "Well, I wouldn't put it that way. We're expanding the company, and you'll play an integral role in ensuring that is a success."

Sam licked her lips again. The tip of her forked tongue flicked against her sharp teeth as she twisted her hands into a tight knot beneath the desk. It was everything she could do not to growl or raise her voice. "I was given assurances…"

"Oh, nothing has changed about our confidence and trust in your skill," John said, speaking quickly and cutting Sam off. His smile became weak, and he looked anywhere else in the small office. His odor became stronger, breaking through the mask of his cologne. "It's just that some of our priorities for the direction we need to take changed. We didn't think those goals were suitable for you at this time. Especially not with all of… this." He gestured a hand towards her.

"I see." Sam dropped her head and clenched her hands so tight that her claws drew tiny pricks of blood. She understood perfectly. Nothing had changed about the project. She had. "Was there anything else?"

John let out a little sigh, as though in relief. He relaxed in his chair as his wandering hand found his pen again. "Good man. I knew you'd be on board. There's nothing more for now. We'll send you everything you need to help get Angie set up in her new role."

Sam didn't trust herself to say anything. She simply nodded and rose from the chair, hoping the rips down her pants leg wasn't too obvious. She hurried from the manager's office without a word and fled directly to the washrooms. The tears were too strong to hold back.

Sam hugged her arms around her legs as she leaned back on the sofa, wiggling her toes to try and ease some of the tension in her feet. A half-eaten tub of ice cream wobbled precariously between her thigh and belly. She barely paid attention to the television, playing some documentary about an archaeological dig, while she lazily scrolled through social media on her phone. She tried to ignore the hysteria about politicians making up lies about bestials, instead choosing to focus on the daily life of those she admired.

A few messages buzzed in, some of her bestial friends passing on messages of sympathy and understanding. Some of those friends were mundane animals, otters, and tigers, or wolves. But others were mythological. She knew two gryphons and even a chimera. But none were like her.

She longed to speak her friends in person, to exchange words face to face. But she had yet to come across anyone local. She was an ocean away from those who knew what she was going through, and that isolation hurt.

She looked up when the front door opened. Alex was finally home from work.

"Back early again?" Alex asked, poking his head around the doorframe as he kicked off his shoes.

Sam merely nodded, mute and emotionless.

Alex sighed. He came across to slump on the couch by Sam's side, taking away the tub of ice cream and putting it on the floor between them. "Is this still about your boss?"

"No, it wasn't John this time. He hasn't said anything since that meeting last week. He certainly didn't apologize. It's…" Sam trailed off into silence, leaning away from Alex and staring at the television without taking in any information about the documentary on screen. She hoped Alex would say something to fill the gap, but her boyfriend stayed quiet, waiting for Sam to continue. She slumped her shoulders and picked at one of her claw tips. "It's not just the misgendering—which still hasn't stopped. I've noticed they're treating me different. Not talking to me as much. Avoiding me. Little comments when they don't think I can hear them."

"You know what I have to say about them. Fuck them. You can get a new job if you have to. We never needed that promotion financially. You only wanted it because you were passionate about the job." Alex's hand hovered close to Sam's shoulder, before falling to the couch cushions between them.

Sam swallowed, trying to loosen the tightness in her throat. "What if they're right, though?"

"How do you mean?"

Sam extended her hand and slowly turned it one way and then the other. A hand that was no longer fully human, partially scaled with claw-tipped fingers. "They whisper that I'm disfiguring myself. I suppose they're right. I'm not human anymore. I'm this… beast. I don't blame them for being scared of what I've turned myself into."

Alex slipped onto the floor, on his knees in front of Sam so that he could take both hands into his own. "You are not 'some beast,'" he said, managing a growl as deep and ferocious as any bestial himself. "I won't accept that, and I won't let you think that either."

"But just look at me," Sam whispered, trying to pull her hands away from Alex. Her boyfriend didn't let her move away, even with claw tips pressing at his skin.

"I am looking at you. I can see what you are now and what you are becoming." His hands squeezed tighter around Sam's, and he stared directly into her watering yellow eyes. "You look in the mirror and see something that isn't human, but also isn't your desired body. You're seeing this amalgamation of both, with too much of the old human body you hated, and not enough of the new one. Of course you're going to see your reflection now and not like what you see. But you will. In just a few months you're going to be perfect in every way, and nothing anyone can say will change that."

Sam sniffed, tears springing to her eyes. "I know all that, but–"

"But nothing. If your colleagues think you're disfiguring yourself, then screw them. They're horrible people who don't deserve to know the true you that's emerging. We'll find you a better job, where people will respect you."

Sam said nothing. Her lower lip quivered. She could feel the hot tears trickling down her cheeks, but she made no movement to pull her hands free and wipe them away.

"You are beautiful, and I can't wait to see the true you on the outside reflecting what has always been within," Alex said firmly. "Now, will you say it?"

Sam whimpered. Her head hung low. Her voice was barely a whisper. "I'm beautiful."

"Louder for me."

Her head shaking, Sam slowly looked up. Alex was blurred through her tears, shining bright in the evening sunlight streaming in through the windows. "I'm beautiful," she said, stronger this time. "I will be perfect."

Finally, Alex released Sam's hands. "Doesn't that feel better?"

Though a choking sob overtook her, Sam slid off the sofa to kneel with Alex, pulling him into a hug. "Thank you."

"Anything for you, my love."

Sam screamed as she jerked awake, thrashing in bed as she sat bolt upright, pain coursing down her back. Her heart raced. A hand rested on her thigh as Alex sat upright in the darkness.

"Are you alright?" Alex asked, alert despite the slight sleepy slur to his voice.

Sam dug her hands into the mattress, pressing her claws in deep as she struggled to resist the urge to bite down on her tongue. She took in a deep breath and let it out again slowly. "Yeah," she gasped. "Just must have rolled onto my back."

The sheets rustled as Alex turned to face her, a black shadow in the darkness. "You'll get used to it soon."

Sam grunted. She leaned forward and held her head in her hand, back stretching a little. That position allowed her to better feel the pair of growths over her shoulder blades, the protruding nubs of new limbs that were causing her all sorts of pain. To her frustration, she could also feel a similar ache growing from the base of her spine as well. Her wings and tail were coming in all at once, making it almost impossible to get comfortable lying on her back anymore.

Lying on her belly wasn't much better. Her body was changing so much now, and she was still just halfway through the ordeal.

Sam took another deep breath as the shadows of pain receded further. The echoes of that agony had chased away all tiredness, though. A glance at the alarm clock warned her dawn was still several hours away. She rubbed his eyes and groaned. Likely another day she would need to take off work, if she wasn't able to get any more sleep.

"This is only going to get worse. I don't know how much longer I can put up with it," Sam grumbled. She shook her head and thumped her fist down onto the mattress.

"When it gets really bad like this, just focus on the good changes. What feels nice."

Sam looked across the bed. Her boyfriend was little more than a shadow in the darkness, a silhouette formed by the small gap in the curtains that let the streetlight in. "What do you mean?"

"I mean here." Alex's hand touched to Sam's chest, to the soft and sensitive buds of growth. The caress was gentle, but it sent a powerful tingle of pleasure through Sam's body. She could hear the smile in her boyfriend's voice. The hand teased lower, a pair of fingertips trailing a path over her scaled belly. It came to rest at her crotch, cupping over Sam's cock, less than a quarter of its original size. And the narrow groove that had started to form beneath it. "And here."

Sam's face warmed. Her whimpers of pain transformed into moans of lust, yet still denied by a feeling of being incomplete. The changes weren't done. She wasn't ready yet. "Fuck."

"Soon everywhere will feel this good," Alex whispered. His fingers prodded and teased at that forming groove.

Sam's toes curled. Her breath shuddered in her throat as she closed his eyes. It might have been her imagination, but she thought she felt a bit of aroused wetness between her legs.

Her pain might not be gone, but Sam was able to focus more on the pleasure as she leaned in to give Alex a relieved kiss.

Sam's eyes kept flicking up towards the cashier who lazily stood behind the counter and giving surreptitious glances to what had to be their mobile phone. She was sure the cashier was about to question her. To ask why she was browsing amongst the racks of women's clothing. But she didn't. She barely even paid her any attention, even given her ill-fitting clothes and blue scales that covered most of her body.

Her small wings, still not fully grown, poked through rips in her t-shirt, which also struggled to keep her budding breasts decent. Her tail likewise played havoc with her pants, and it had taken a lot of patching and resewing to preserve her modesty down there. There weren't many options for clothes for those with her body shape, but it was getting too difficult to keep her old wardrobe functional. The time had come to make a change, and it was a strange thrill to browse away from the men's sections, even if she was terrified someone would berate her for doing so.

No such confrontation came, leaving Sam free to find something to fit her form. Before long, she had a skirt that could accommodate her tail, a dress and several tops without backs, and a few bras. He had never had to buy any of them before, having never had the confidence to wear feminine clothing in public before. She glanced nervously to the empty changing rooms several times before committing herself. She took over armfuls of clothes to try on.

Once inside the changing room, she quickly stripped out of her ill-fitting clothes. Catching sight of herself in the wall-length mirror, she stifled a gasp of admiration. She was almost complete now, though her legs still needed to finish adjusting and her wings and tail weren't at their full size. Small patches of human skin lingered, but those were shrinking almost by the day. Her face and head were taking longer to change, her jaw gradually stretching into her new muzzle, as scales partially replaced hair.

And then there was her sex, hidden by a torn pair of boxers but still very present. Almost gone was any trace of her male genitalia, and it was all she could do not to reach down and stroke her new, sensitive vagina through her underwear. The same for her breasts, soft despite their scales, and so very fun to play with. They were even worth the usual snide remarks of a scaled creature with breasts. She didn't care about any of that. She simply loved how she looked, and that only drew further anticipation for the last few weeks to come of the transformation.

She tried the dress on first. She had guessed with the size, hoping that her measurements matched the bizarrely complicated measuring system of female clothing, and it fit perfectly. It hugged her curves delightfully, the jet-black color contrasting beautifully with her scales. Her wings had space to flutter, and there was enough room for her tail to drape down beside her leg, the tip poking out beneath the hem.

Staring in stunned amazement, Sam slowly ran her hands down her belly and hips. Her heart pounded a ferocious beat. A sob tore itself free as the tears began to flow. Was this what euphoria felt like? To look into the mirror and finally see perfection looking back? Even as that reflection blurred through the tears, Sam knew this was justification for the entire ordeal. This was worth it.

A gentle knock rapped at the door to the changing room.

"Are you alright in there, miss?"

"Yeah, fine," Sam replied, struggling to speak clearly through the tears and stuffy throat.

There were a few seconds of silence before the staff member spoke again. "If you're sure. Call me if you need me."

Smiling brightly, Sam looked into the mirror again. The reflection smiled back.

It finally matched.

Sam whimpered as she held her hands against the side of her head. Her skull felt like it threatened to rip itself in two. Blood trickled down her cheeks, her nostrils flaring at the coppery tang in the air.

"Is there anything I can get you?" Alex said softly. He moved carefully. Gently. As though his mere presence could cause more pain.

"Hammer," Sam grunted. "It will hurt less."

"Anything other than that?"

Sam groaned in mock dismay. Despite her pain, she still managed a smile. "You never get me anything I want."

"I'm sorry. How about I get you some painkillers instead?"

"Ugh, fine. I suppose that will do," Sam muttered. She closed her eyes as Alex left her side, hoping to take the edge of the agony boring through her skull. Her fingertips crept up to where the pain was strongest. Hot, sticky blood unnerved her, but then she found the source. The points of thick horns, slowly pushing out from her scales.

She was so nearly complete. There was just this one final hurdle to overcome. After the ordeal of her wings and tail, it was a pain she was familiar with.

Her headache got worse as her phone started to ring. Out of habit more than any desire speak to anyone, she reached out and grabbed her phone from the desk and answered the call. Too late did she recognize John's number on the caller ID.

She cringed. "Hello?"

"Where are you? We need you in," John said, with no preamble or greeting.

Sam dragged her claws against her muzzle. The tip of her tail twitched. "I told you I'd be out for a few days."

"Yeah, yeah. I get that. But Angie really needs you today. She can't do this all by herself." Sam easily heard the irritation in his voice, coming across like a growl.

Sam bit down on the immediate answer. Her skull pounded and throbbed with pain, but where she may once have responded with a frustrated outburst, she managed to hold her tongue. When she spoke, her voice was still even and controlled. "John, I'm quite literally growing in a pair of horns. I'm in too much pain, so I can't come in. You knew that this was going to happen. I went through this whole process with you and what it will mean."

"This is more important than that, Samuel," John snapped back. "If Angie doesn't get this right, then the whole expansion could be hobbled from the start."

"Why do you think I scheduled this to be finished before the expansion was meant to happen? We agreed on this schedule. This was all planned well in advance. It wasn't me who changed that," Sam spat out. Her frustration spilled out before she could contain it.

John spoke as though he hadn't heard her. "Angie can't do this without your support. I don't care what sort of inhuman creature you've turned yourself into. I need you in today, and for the rest of the week."

Sam rubbed her muzzle. Her thoughts seethed, quite aware of what John had just called her. Yes, she knew she wasn't human anymore. She knew that her days off had caused issues, but she had been upfront and honest with John from the beginning, making sure the changes fit into the expansion schedule. And then they had changed that on her and demanded she help out the person who had been promoted in her place.

John's growling command broke into her concentration. "I take it that your silence means that you'll be coming in?"

Every tiny slight came to the front of Sam's mind. All those quiet whispers when people didn't think she could hear. The passive aggressive comments when she definitely could. The misgendering and use of her deadname. The snide comments. The missed promotion. And then, finally, Alex's suggestion from all those months ago.

She made the decision in that moment.

"No, I don't think I will be," she said, allowing a touch of a growl to come to her voice. Whereas John had sounded out of control, almost animalistic, with his growl, hers was a deep baritone that deepened and emphasized each word. "I'll be drafting my resignation and submitting that within the hour. Goodbye, John."

She did not give her spluttering ex-boss the chance to formulate a response. She hung up and switched off her phone.

Only then did she realize she was not alone. She looked up and smiled bashfully at Alex, who stood in the doorway. When he knew Sam's attention was on her, he held out painkillers and a glass of water for her aching head.

Sam gratefully took the offered painkillers, tossing aside her phone to also take the glass of water. Since her muzzle had grown, simple matters like drinking water had gotten a little more difficult, though she rarely went to such extreme measures like a straw. Instead, she pursed her lips and carefully tilted the glass back, letting the water trickle to the back of her throat slowly.

The painkillers never helped the pain much, but Sam still took them when she could. It was a placebo more than anything, and for as long as she had to endure the horns bursting through her scales, it was one of the few things she could do to manage the pain.

"You finally did it?' Alex asked, once she had finished her drink.

Sam's eyes flicked to her phone. She was sure there were several missed calls already, but with it switched off, those calls were not received. She nodded once. "Yeah. I just need to send it in writing, and I'll be done with them."

"About time," Alex said. He took the glass from Sam's hand and put it aside on the desk, before pulling her into a gentle hug, taking care not to touch anywhere close to her horns. "They were never going to respect you."

"I don't think they ever did. Even before any of this. I was always just that weird guy to them. I never really fit in before I transitioned because I wasn't confident with myself. And then they couldn't ever understand me. And then with this? They couldn't know who I really was."

Alex smiled. "Their loss."

Before Sam could say anything, he leaned in to kiss her on the muzzle. Her hands moved up to cup the back of his head, but they didn't stay pressed together for long. With a gasp of pain, Sam leaned back as another twinge flashed down the side of her face. It quickly passed, but Alex didn't return to the kiss.

Her loyal and wonderful boyfriend simply gazed at her. "It's going to take some time to get used to your new mouth. I'm just going to have to kiss you as often as I can."

Sam stuck her tongue out, the forked tip flicking in the air. She could pick up his scent on the air, fresh and clean with more than a little lingering trace of his favorite shampoo. Her sense of taste and smell were still overwhelming at times, and she quickly pulled her tongue back in. She nudged his arm. "You're such a hopeless flirt."

"What can I say? I'm a lucky guy to have someone like you. And when you're ready, I'm going to show you off to everyone I can."

Sam's hands trembled as she reached up towards her horns again. "I'm nearly there."

"Soon, my dearest love. Very soon."

Sam tossed the empty pack into the bin, the final pill resting on her hand. The bright pink of the tablet was vibrant against the pale blue of her scales. Like she had for the very first, she hesitated with the last, her hand still trembling. Then, it had been fear that had caused her indecision. Now it was excitement. This was it. She was at the end of this journey of transformation. A new path stretched out before her clawed feet.

She popped the pill onto her forked tongue and chased it down with a mouthful of water, then stood to admire herself in the mirror. Even with the effects of the final pill to take place, there was no trace of the human she had once been in the reflection.

Blue scales covered her entire body. Her yellow eyes, the first thing to change, were now so familiar she was already beginning to forget their previous color. She ran her hands over her short muzzle, thumbs lifting her lips to brush over her sharp fangs and teeth. They were the jaws of a predator.

From her head, she slid her hands down her scaled throat and neck, towards her breasts. Despite the scales that covered them, they were still soft and sensitive, and delight for both her and Alex to play with. She shuddered and smiled as her hands passed over them, rubbing down to her belly and hips.

Her tail flicked out. The new limb still took some getting used to, especially when it came to closing doors. Long and sinuous, it was flexible enough to grasp hold of objects and manipulate them.

Using her tail, she stroked down her toned legs. She flexed her clawed toes, bouncing on her altered feet and feeling the strength the muscles of her legs contained, like she was always having to hold herself back from unleashing that raw power.

Then there were her wings. She flexed them and spread them wide, her span enough to brush the opposite walls. The taut membranes between her long wingfingers were partially translucent, light shining through them from the bedroom. She couldn't stop touching different parts of her body, whether with finger or tail. That was the best way to remind herself that this was all real.

A shadow moved across her wing membranes, caught in the reflection on the mirror. Sam quickly dropped her wings and turned, a blush heating her cheeks even if they didn't turn red anymore.

Alex leaned against the doorframe, smiling widely. He had already dressed, looking sharp and handsome in a smart casual shirt and jeans. "I always love it when I catch you admiring yourself."

Sam grinned bashfully, showing off her sharp teeth. "It all doesn't feel real a lot of the time."

"You'd better believe it," Alex replied. His eyes flicked up and down, taking in Sam's naked form. "But as much as I love seeing you like this, I think the restaurant might want you wearing something. Best get ready."

Sam stuck her tongue out, but she said nothing as she sought out her clothes.

There was a strange thrill in walking at her boyfriend's side, his arm resting around her waist, as they strolled to the restaurant in the center of town. Sam always drew the looks and stares. Once, they had embarrassed her, but now they fueled the warm fires in her belly. The attention felt good.

Sam wore her favorite black dress, the one she had picked out that first time shopping for her new body. Her wings fluttered free, and her tail could move without hindering her gait.

More than ever before, she felt like a powerful beast, something so much more and greater than human. Everything about her body was perfect, and she reveled in the attention that gave her. She couldn't help but smirk and flick her wings at those who stared the longest. She laughed every time someone looked away in embarrassment, Alex always joining with her.

That euphoria lasted the entire walk to the restaurant. Sam almost started salivating at the mere scents of food that drifted out, her stronger sense of smell picking up a myriad of delights from within. But before they could step inside, she felt a slight tug on her wing. She turned to see a young woman behind her, face ashen white.

"I'm so sorry, I shouldn't have..." the women said, starting to retreat.

"Wait," Sam said, lifting her hand. She gestured for Alex to go inside the restaurant, while she took a tentative step forward. "It's alright. Did you want to say something?"

The woman hung her head. Her chest heaved. "I just... yeah. I wanted to say you look amazing."

Sam couldn't help but beam. "Thank you."

The young woman chanced a quick glance up. "Have you... you know, been this way long?"

"No, actually. I've only just finished changing. We're going out to celebrate," Sam said, gesturing to the open doors of the restaurant. She partially unfurled her wings. "I'm still getting used to everything."

"Was it worth it?"

The young woman finally managed to meet Sam's gaze. Those dark brown eyes were a reflection of so much of Sam's old self, of the person she had once been. The stranger had spoken only four words, but that question was so much more than that. It was a plea. It was hope. It was as though she was asking for permission.

Sam crouched so that her head was at the same height of the young woman's. She took hold of her hands, feeling so soft and vulnerable against her scales and claws. "Yes, it was worth it. Listen to your heart and you'll know what's right for you as well."

"Thank you," the young woman whispered, before she pulled away. Tears in her eyes, she smiled and nodded once, before she fled.

Sam stayed where she was a few moments longer. She felt tears welling in her eyes as well. It didn't take long before the thought of food pulled at her mind, though. Taking care to duck her head, she slipped inside the restaurant and quickly found Alex at their table.

"Everything alright?" he asked as she approached.

Sam paused. She looked back out the door. She smiled. "Yeah. Just helping out another dragon."

ABOUT THE EDITOR

TJ is a rat that found the furry fandom after moving to Ohio over fifteen years ago. It is there he picked up the pen—or grabbed a keyboard, as it may be—and started creating characters and worlds. TJ has grown to become more passionate about the craft and enjoys telling tales and aiding others with stories of their own. He is currently editing his first novel.

Some of TJ's other stories may be found in issues of *FANG*, *Heat 15* and other anthologies both in and out of the fandom.

ABOUT THE PUBLISHER

FurPlanet productions is a small press publisher serving the niche market that is furry fiction. They sell furry-themed books and comics published by themselves and most major publishers in the community. If you can't get to a furry convention where they are selling in the dealers room, visit their online stores: FurPlanet.com for print books and BadDogBooks.com for eBooks.

facebook.com/furplanet

animal.business/@furplanet

bsky.app/profile/furplanet.com

www.ingramcontent.com/pod-product-compliance
Lightning Source LLC
Chambersburg PA
CBHW071201020726
47502CB00002B/500